WAY PAST DEAD

WAY PAST DEAD

Steven Womack

HEADLINE
FEATURE

First published in Great Britain in 1995
by HEADLINE BOOK PUBLISHING

A HEADLINE FEATURE hardback

10 9 8 7 6 5 4 3 2 1

British Library Cataloguing in Publication Data
Womack, Steven
Way Past Dead
I. Title
823 [F]
ISBN 0–7472–1425–5

Phototypeset by Intype, London
Printed and bound in Great Britain by
Mackays of Chatham PLC, Chatham, Kent

HEADLINE BOOK PUBLISHING
A division of Hodder Headline PLC
338 Euston Road
London NW1 3BH

Acknowledgements

I'm grateful to all the people who have helped me with this novel, both with research and with endlessly patient readings of the book in manuscript. As always, my wife Cathryn was chief among the patient readers. Dr James Veatch of Nashville State Technical Institute read the manuscript with an effective and sharp critical eye as well. Gratitude and affection go out to my friends and colleagues in the Nashville Writers Alliance who provided input and support: K. Cheatham, Martha Hickman, Nancy Hite, Amy Lynch, Madeena Nolan, Sallie Schloss, Michael Sims, Alana White, Jim Young, and Ronna Wineberg-Blazer.

I also want to thank Scott Faragher, not only for his face-to-face insights into the nature of the country music business, but for his wonderful book, *Music City Babylon*.

And to Nancy Yost and Joe Blades, my unending appreciation and affection.

Chapter 1

The night the fundamentalist redneck zealots assaulted the morgue, I was hauling butt down I-65 from Louisville back to Nashville after spending three days lying in the grass videotaping a disabled, wheelchair-bound bricklayer shooting hoops on his brother-in-law's patio.

It was my first big insurance-fraud case, and I was feeling pretty good. The object of my surveillance was a contract bricklayer who had taken my client for a bundle, claiming a hundred percent disability as a result of a fall off a scaffold. The fact that he drank a six-pack of tall boys at lunch didn't seem to matter. I borrowed a van and a video camera from my friend Lonnie, threw some clothes and my old Nikon into a duffel bag, and followed the guy and his wife all the way to Louisville.

For three days it rained like fury. I got soaked as I plopped down in a field overlooking the house and hid underneath a stand of peach trees maybe a hundred feet from the brother-in-law's back door. I slept in the van, lived off cold burgers and french fries slathered in congealed grease, and shivered under a poncho. On the fourth day, Saturday, the sun broke through, the temperature went up about twenty degrees, and a gorgeous spring day erupted out of nowhere. Other than the chiggers, surveillance was a delight. Even the boredom seemed tolerable on such a beautiful day.

It was too beautiful; the bricklayer couldn't take it anymore. He drove his electric wheelchair through the open sliding-glass door onto the patio and watched his brother-in-law and a teenage boy – his nephew, I guessed – sinking baskets in the sun. He sat on the edge of the patio, whooping as he watched the two run around each other, bare-chested and sweaty, in a vicious one-on-one. I pulled the camera up and stared through the viewfinder. I was so close I had to back off the zoom.

Suddenly the boy bounced the ball a few times and tossed it toward his uncle, who caught it in the wheelchair and cradled the ball longingly in his lap.

1

My hand automatically hit the red button. I felt the gears inside the camera engage. There was the whirring of a motor in my ear to match the buzz of mosquitoes.

I couldn't hear what they were saying, but I know body language when it jumps out at me. Even from this distance, I could see the boy and his father standing in front of the wheelchair making *Aw, c'mons . . .*

The camcorder whirred on.

The bricklayer bounced the ball a few times on the concrete patio. The snap of the basketball next to the right wheel of his chair was staccato and sharp. The guy must have been good. Back when he could walk, I mean.

Then I saw him look around nervously, palm the ball, and lay it back on his lap. His hand went to the toggle switch and he threw the wheelchair into reverse, skating smoothly off the concrete and onto the grass. He reached down in his lap, his back to me, and released the safety strap that kept his useless body from falling out of the chair. Then he shoved the ball toward the boy, put his hands on either side of the wheelchair, and leaped onto the patio.

The brother-in-law applauded and cheered. The bricklayer ran to one end of the patio, whipped around, and took two long strides just as the boy bounced the ball in front of him. He became airborne right in front of the goal, did a three-sixty in midair, then slam-dunked the ball with a rim-shaking clatter.

The camcorder whirred on.

'Praise Jesus,' I whispered. 'It's a miracle.'

So life was good and business was terrific that Saturday night on my way back to Nashville with a solid hour's worth of sports highlights featuring the miraculously cured bricklayer. Monday morning, I'd head over to the insurance company, give them the tape and my invoice, then settle back to await that nice fat paycheck – with bonus – I needed so badly.

Down around Bowling Green, I flicked on the radio in Lonnie's van and started searching for the Nashville radio stations. Voices from home and all that. I tuned to the AM band and searched for the all-news station, the one that plays the audio feed off Cable Headline News twenty-four hours a day. The signal was scratchy, full of static, and a bit irritating over the noise of the van. What the hell, I figured, a little aggravation might keep me pumped up for the last hour and a half down I-65 to the city. I needed something to keep me awake after the week I'd had.

'—in from Nashville,' the announcer said as I tuned the station in. I perked up, reached down, and cranked the volume even higher. 'According to a police spokesman, an obscure, offshoot sect of a fundamentalist religious group has surrounded the local morgue, demanding the release of their founder's wife's body.'

I stifled a laugh. Then it hit me. The morgue. Marsha. Holy cow. I lost it for a second; an orange tractor-trailer barreling down on me from the passing lane barely missed turning me into road paste. The semi's horn blared in my ear as it roared past, with me swivel-hipping all over the right lane trying to keep it between the lines.

'More from CNN's Brian Larkin,' the radio anchor said. Then a change of voice: 'Local police say this is one for the books. About five o'clock this afternoon, an unidentified man showed up at the T. E. Simpkins Forensic Science Center, which is the Nashville, Tennessee, morgue, and demanded that officials turn over to him the body of Evangeline Lee Hogg, who died under mysterious circumstances yesterday afternoon. Mrs Hogg is the wife of Woodrow Tyberious Hogg, who has been identified as the leader and founder of an offshoot branch of the fundamentalist Assemblies of God. The group, which calls itself the Pentecostal Evangelical Enochians, claims that on Judgment Day, only those whose bodies are buried whole will be resurrected. An autopsy, cult leaders claim, will deny Mrs Hogg resurrection.'

I didn't know whether to giggle or scream.

The reporter droned on. 'When morgue officials refused to release the body, police said, at least a dozen Winnebagos crashed through a chain-link fence onto the grounds of the morgue and surrounded the building. Electricity and telephone wires have been cut, and cult members claim to be heavily armed. Trapped inside the morgue are an unidentified group of staff members who have been cut off from all contact with the outside. Police have set up barricades outside the morgue grounds and hostage negotiators are on the scene. We'll have more to report as the story breaks.'

I lowered the volume and tried to focus on the white lines in front of me.

'Pentecostal Evangelical Enochians?' I said out loud. 'Who in *hell* are the Pentecostal Evangelical Enochians?'

And why are they holding my girlfriend hostage?

Chapter 2

I always knew that sooner or later I'd discover the downside of being in love with somebody who cuts up dead bodies for a living. I've got to admit, though, I never expected it to be this.

As for the question *why?*, the radio had pretty well answered that. Dr Marsha Helms, Assistant Medical Examiner for Metropolitan Nashville/Davidson County, was going to slice open Evangeline Lee Hogg like a field-dressed deer on its way to the check-in station.

'Yuck,' I said out loud. The thought was an unappealing one. But even more unappealing was the thought of Marsha – and all issues of possessiveness aside, I'd begun to think of her as *my* Marsha – being held hostage by a group of armed wackos who didn't want anyone mucking around in Mrs Hogg's insides.

I laid down hard on the accelerator pedal, feeling like I'd been thrown suddenly into the middle of a 1970s Burt Reynolds movie. All I needed was a CB radio and a Red Man Chewing Tobacco cap to complete the picture. I was still wearing the same filthy jeans and work shirt I'd had on in the peach orchard, and I hadn't shaved in four days. I'd planned to go straight to Marsha's apartment and settle into a hot bathtub, preferably not alone.

So much for communal bathing. I'd been away not quite a week, and Marsha's absence from my life was becoming more keenly noted by the minute. Our date last Saturday night had been canceled by the discovery of the body of a taxi driver who'd been executed by a couple of sixteen-year-olds he'd picked up at the Krystal Restaurant on Dickerson Pike after they'd robbed the place. A sack full of Belly Bombs, two large Cokes, and all your cash to go, please. Then they put one through the back of the driver's head so he couldn't identify them and took all of thirty-eight dollars off him. It never occurred to them, I guess, that all the people inside the Krystal would pick them out of a lineup the next day. You ask me, some of these demented kids are a couple of tacos short of a combination plate.

But then, nobody asked me. So Dr Marsha canceled our date and, instead, autopsied her third cabdriver of the month. I left town a couple of days later, fully expecting a passionate and heartfelt reunion on this very evening. An event that now, it seemed, was not going to take place.

I once heard someone define conflict as the gap between expectation and result. At that moment I was conflicted out the ya-ya.

I hit the Rivergate area in a panic just as the movie theatres were letting out. Rivergate Mall, an enormous, sprawling, congested shopping center in the northern part of the city, was a place I made every effort possible to avoid. Even though it was nearly eleven on Saturday night, the traffic was bumper-to-bumper on Two Mile Parkway in either direction as far as the eye could see. The spillover onto the freeway had slowed that traffic to a crawl as well, and all around us tractor-trailer drivers who'd just pulled fourteen-hour shifts at eighty miles an hour had to adjust to inner-city speeds. Brakes squealed, trailers went into graceful near jackknives, horns blared, bird fingers flew . . .

Welcome home.

After hiding in the grass for almost four days, being half eaten alive by chiggers, living off fast food, sleeping in the back of Lonnie's twelve-year-old Ford Econoline van, and then finding out my girlfriend was in the middle of a full-blown hostage situation, I only had one nerve left. And these people were getting on it.

Maybe she wasn't there. Maybe she'd taken a night off. Maybe she was okay.

Hell, I knew better. Marsha was professional to the point of compulsive. As assistant medical examiner, rather than chief, she would have been the one called in on a Saturday night. I shot straight down I-65 all the way to Shelby Avenue, then whipped off the freeway, nearly wiping out a Chevy full of beer-drinking rednecks. I bounced across the Shelby Street Bridge, over the river into downtown. I ran two stop signs on my way over to First Avenue, then cut right and headed up the hill toward the morgue.

I didn't get very far.

A line of Metro squad cars, their blue-and-white beacons cutting through the sulfurous streetlight glow like artillery bursts, had stopped traffic in front of the Thermal Plant. A single patrol officer in an orange safety vest swung a flashlight back and forth in a wide arc, detouring cars onto a side street away from the action. The car in front of me turned right off First Avenue, as the officer instructed. I slid the van to a stop in front of him, slammed it into park, and jumped out.

'C'mon, buddy,' the cop yelled. 'Keep it moving.'

'Wait,' I yelled, palms out in front of me. I realized that I looked like a crazy man who just came into town from up the holler a ways. 'I've got to get to the morgue.'

I stopped in front of the officer, who took two quick steps toward me. He was young, thin, blond crew-cut, determined.

'I'm sorry, sir,' he yelled over the noise of sirens and engines racing. 'No one gets past this point.' Above us, the whopping of distant helicopter blades grew louder by the moment.

'But I've got to!' The chaotic flashes of light bouncing off my face must have looked like a shot from a Fellini movie.

'No, sir,' the officer boomed over the roar of a chopper as it appeared just above the rooftops behind us.

The driver behind the van sat on his horn and stuck his head out the window. I turned; he yelled at me and spit flew out of his mouth. I couldn't understand him, but I gathered his remarks weren't polite.

'But my girlfriend's up there . . .' I said, my voice plaintive. The cop probably couldn't even hear me.

'Move it, mister,' the cop instructed. His left hand moved ever so subtly to the baton that dangled from his utility belt.

Message sent and received. Defeated, I opened the van door and climbed back in. I made the turn, not even knowing which side street I was on, and tried to figure out what to do next. Then it hit me.

Lonnie.

I cut back across the river and maneuvered my way to the Ellington Parkway, then headed toward my East Nashville neighborhood. Traffic on the EP had thinned out; the only motorists I'd encounter this time of night were the freelance carjackers and the usual crowd of tire-squealing rednecks.

I kept the radio on, but there were no more updates on the hostage situation at the morgue. I ran up and down the FM stations as well, but all I got was music and commercials. I cut over to Gallatin Road off the EP and headed into Inglewood.

It was after eleven by now, but I figured Lonnie'd still be up. He kept pretty strange hours. The only way I'd miss him was if he'd gone on a repo run – either that or out working his latest line of business: bounty hunting. Lonnie'd gotten bored with repossessing cars the last few months and decided to expand his area of operations into snagging bail jumpers. When things got bad, money-wise, I'd made repo runs with him to pick up extra cash. So far, though, I'd resisted the temptation to join him in this new venture. After all, a Mercedes won't pull a .357 on you when you try to take it back.

The side street off Gallatin Road that led to Lonnie's place was crypt-black, cemetery-silent. What few streetlights there were had long since been shot out by the Death Rangers, the local East Nashville motorcycle gang. They sounded and looked ominous, but truth was they were largely just a bunch of ageing, beer-drinking unemployables. Mostly harmless – as long as you didn't mess with them – Jerry Garcia look-alikes . . . Their clubhouse was locked up tight, its windows cinder-blocked solid.

I pulled to a stop in front of the chain-link fence gate that was right on the street and maybe fifty feet from a pale green mobile home with rust streaks down the side. I hit the horn once, then climbed out of the van and rattled the gate. There were lights on inside the trailer, but the rest of the landscape was illuminated only by ambient light. The wrecked automobile hulks that filled Lonnie's junkyard jutted into the night sky at twisted, bizarre angles.

I stood at the gate waiting for Shadow, Lonnie's timber shepherd, who was absolute queen of everything inside that chain-link fence. I knew better than to go through the unlocked gate without getting her permission first.

No Shadow, though. Where was she? I rattled the chain-link fence again and whistled, then backed away and looked up. I knew there were security cameras mounted on the utility poles, some with night-vision capability. Lonnie was a freak on security. Nobody got near him without him knowing it first. I shook the gate again, the metallic noise abrupt and jarring in the night.

C'mon, damn it, Lonnie, where the hell are you?

The door to the mobile home opened. A lanky form in jeans and a white T-shirt stood in the doorway, shrouded by the blue, flickering light of a television. An arm raised, motioning me in.

I slid the gate aside, then hopped back in the van and pulled it inside. I shut the gate back and stepped through the door just in time to catch a bright silver can of beer that came sailing through the air toward me. I grabbed it quickly, smoothly.

Lonnie pushed the Frigidaire door shut and grinned. 'You're getting better.'

'Hell, I've had to. One of these days, you're going to take my head off.' I looked around. 'I need your phone, man. Quick . . .'

He tossed me a portable telephone. I pulled out the antenna

and switched it on. 'Where's Shadow?' I said absentmindedly.

He didn't answer. I looked up. Lonnie's face darkened. 'Vet's.'

'Oh,' I said. 'Bad?'

'Maybe. Won't know till Monday.'

'Damn, man. I'm sorry,' I said, punching in the numbers.

He turned the beer up, his Adam's apple bobbing in time to his swallowing. Then he uncocked his arm and stared at me a moment. 'Yeah, I know. Me, too.'

'C'mon, babe,' I whispered into the phone. 'Answer. Be home. Tell me you took a night off for once.' The phone rang four times, then the answering machine picked up.

'Aw, hell,' I muttered. When the message played through and the beep came, I said: 'Marsha? You there? C'mon, lady. Pick up if you're there.'

Nothing. I punched the hang-up button.

'How'd it go in Louisville?' Lonnie asked.

'Great,' I said. 'Probably win a freaking Oscar or something. Got film of the guy slam-dunking a basketball about thirty times in an hour.'

'Jesus. What a moron. Hey, dude.' Lonnie sniffed. 'You're getting kind of gamy, you know that?'

'Why don't you install a shower in that damn van of yours?'

'Well, pardon me, Sam Spade. . . .'

'I didn't expect to find you here, anyway,' I said. 'I figured you'd either be on a run or back at the apartment.'

'Just got in about an hour ago,' he answered. He raised the can to his lips and drained about half of it. 'Pulled down a new Lincoln Town Car. Guy followed me in his pickup truck. Getting smart with me, I guess. I decided to stick around in case he tried to get it back.'

I popped the top on the beer can and downed a healthy third of it, then set it down next to a filthy, oil-covered gear of some kind that occupied a corner of Lonnie's scarred coffee table. I don't know why I even noticed it; the trailer was littered with loose auto parts, electronic components, tools. Lonnie saw me staring at the gear.

'CV joint off an '85 Accord,' he said. 'Ellis's wife blew one out the other day.' Ellis was one of Lonnie's freelance repo men: big guy, tobacco chewer, half a dozen teeth left if he's lucky. Laughs a lot, gets on my nerves.

'What in the hell is going on down at the morgue?' I asked, aware of how irritable I must have sounded. 'Has this whole damn city gone crazy?'

'What do you mean *gone*?' he asked. 'Try *already there*.' Lonnie reached for the television clicker and started rotating through the channels. He stopped on the local NBC outlet.

'Look,' I said, 'they've pre-empted *Saturday Night Live*.'

'Must be some real shit going down,' Lonnie commented, his voice a monotone.

The picture was mostly flashing lights: blues and reds and yellows and whites like I'd seen at the foot of the First Avenue hill. I recognized the curve in front of General Hospital where First Avenue becomes Hermitage Avenue. Police barricades were everywhere. Fire engines sat hunkered down on the sidewalk, their engines racing. The orange-and-white paramedic vans lined up one after the other all the way down the hill.

'As you can see,' an announcer's voice narrated off-screen, 'police have cordoned off the area and no one is getting through. We're waiting for a police briefing, which is scheduled to begin momentarily.'

I sat down on the couch, then shifted around trying to get comfortable. I pulled my right hip up off the torn vinyl. My wallet, packed to the flaps with cards, licenses, and scraps of paper, was giving me a cramp in my butt. I pulled it out, then it hit me like the memory of a forgotten appointment. Tucked in a corner, scribbled on a cocktail napkin, was a telephone number that only a couple of people possessed.

I grabbed the phone off the coffee table and punched the numbers in, not knowing what to expect. I'd never used the number before. Never had to.

Marsha picked up on the first ring. 'Yeah.'

'You okay?'

She let out a sigh that was as deep as it was long. 'Yeah, I'm okay. Where are you?'

'Lonnie's,' I said, trying to keep the alarm in my voice to a minimum. 'I just got back in town tonight. What the hell's going on down there.'

'You tell me,' she said. 'All I know is one minute I'm checking in a fat dead lady, the next Kay's in here screaming about a bunch of people with guns yelling about Jesus and Judgment Day and all kinds of crap.'

Kay Delacorte was the head administrator at the morgue, a real take-charge cowgirl. If Kay went into the cooler and yelled, 'Jump,' you'd half expect the stiffs to say: 'How high?'

'Are you okay? Is anybody hurt?'

'Oh, no,' she said. 'They'll never get in here. Plus we've got a generator that'll give us limited backup power, as well as this cellular phone. But the cops won't tell us much besides lay low and stay away from the windows.'

'I don't know what they're worried about,' I said. 'The windows are all bulletproof.' The Nashville morgue had thick Plexiglas windows and doors like a bunker. Whoever designed the facility had a feeling that someday, somebody might want a body back bad enough to kill for it.

'Yeah, but nobody knows whether these guys are bluffing or not. They claim to have LAW 80s.'

'What'n the hell's a LAW 80?' I asked.

'Light antitank weapon,' Marsha answered. 'Sort of a mini-bazooka.'

'*Mini-bazookas?*' I said, aghast. 'These people are supposed to be *religious*, for Chrissakes.'

'Oh, that's not all. They say they've got H and K MP5s, whatever they are. And MI6s – I know what they are – and something called a . . .'

Her voice faded away, and I heard her in the background. 'What was it, Kay?'

Another mumbled voice, then Marsha was back. '—ARMSEL Strikers. Whatever they are.'

I looked at Lonnie. 'What's an ARMSEL Striker?'

He pointed the clicker at me. 'Something you don't want to fuck with . . .'

'Aw, c'mon, man. What is it?'

'Riot control. Looks like a big damn Thompson sub-machine gun, only it fires shotgun shells instead of bullets. Empties a twelve-round magazine in about three seconds. South African police call it a Streetsweeper.'

I held the phone back to my ear. 'What is it?' she asked.

'Something you don't want to fuck with . . .'

'That bad, huh?'

'Yeah.'

'I guess that explains why the Metros haven't just blasted their way in here and hauled 'em all off to jail.'

'They're outgunned, aren't they?' I commented. It was a question that didn't require an answer.

'Welcome to America in the Nineties,' she said. 'Have you paid your NRA dues yet?'

'This is crazy. Freaking Looney Tunes.'

'You ought to see it from my end,' Marsha said wearily. 'Another cabdriver got popped yesterday. Fourth one this month.

Guy had a two-month-old baby. His first.'

'Jesus, I'm tearing up my hack license.'

'I didn't know you had one.'

'I got it a few months ago, just in case times ever got real bad.'

'Hey, baby,' she said. 'Things ever get that bad, you move in with me. I'll feed you before I let you drive one of those puppies.'

'I'll remember that,' I said. I felt my mouth go dry and my throat tighten. 'I tried to get down there. Couldn't talk my way past the barricades.'

'No point in trying, babe. But don't worry, we're—'

Pop. Static. Crackle. *Damn cell phone.*

'Marsha!' I yelled.

'—sorry, the phone's fritzing out on me. Listen, I gotta go. I don't know how long the batteries are going to last.'

'Have you got a recharger?'

'Yeah,' she said through the ever-rising hiss. 'Only we're not sure if it works.'

'Marsh,' I said, almost desperately. Damn, I didn't want her to go. 'I'll call you tomorrow morning. You got food, water, the essentials?'

She laughed. 'Enough for a couple of days. We get real hungry, we'll pop Evangeline in the microwave.'

'Well,' I said, 'at least you've retained your sense of humor.'

'Who's laughing?'

'Listen, babe. Keep your head down.'

'In your dreams, smart guy. And that's *Doctor* Babe to you.'

'Okay, Dr Babe. Listen, I – I—' I got stuck, couldn't get the words out.

'Harry,' she said, 'don't get mushy on me. This isn't a private line.'

'Yeah. So take care, will ya?'

'Yeah. See you soon.' She hung up.

I laid the phone down next to the CV joint, wondering for the first time if I'd ever see her again.

Chapter 3

Lonnie pointed the remote control at the television and we got sound again. The station had cut away from the morgue to a conference room at the main police station downtown. I stared dumbly at the screen, exhausted, drained. As cameras flashed and reporters jostled for position, Chief of Police Harold Gleaves walked into the room and marched stiffly to a podium set up on a folding table.

'I've got a prepared statement for you,' he announced. Lonnie and I leaned forward in our chairs as he described for everyone what we'd all just seen and heard. After the short statement, hands flew up.

'Has the FBI been brought in?' one reporter yelled.

'No,' Chief Gleaves said firmly. 'At this point in time, we're considering this a local matter. The local FBI office has been notified, but for the time being, we have our own hostage negotiators on scene.'

'That won't last long,' I said.

'Yeah,' Lonnie agreed. 'The Fumbling Bunch of Idiots isn't going to let this party go by without crashing it.'

I smiled. 'Maybe they'll bring in thuh Bew-row of Al-key-hol, Tabacky, and Far-arms. . . .'

'Yeah.' He grinned. 'Bring in the *BatFucks*. That'll do it. Then we can all kiss our asses goodbye.'

'God, you're tacky,' I said.

'What about federal weapons charges?' a voice yelled. 'And kidnapping charges?'

'As I said,' Chief Gleaves shot back, 'as of this point in time—'

'Why do politicians always talk in clichés?' Lonnie interrupted. '*As of this point in time . . .*'

'Ssshh,' I hissed.

'—we have no proof other than the claims of the people involved that there are any illegal weapons on the scene.'

'But they admitted it!' another reporter yelled back.

13

'If you'll let me finish,' Gleaves instructed. I had to hand it to him; Chief Gleaves was cool. He was the first Nashville police chief to come to the job with academic credentials and a little professionalism, rather than just a hundred years on the beat and a lot of good ol' boys on the council as pals.

'There have been no charges filed against these people yet. The last thing we are going to do is go in there and provoke a confrontation. I'm not going to have another Waco here.'

'That's a switch,' Lonnie said. 'Old Baltimore Sims would've welcomed the chance to go in there shooting.'

Baltimore Sims was a North Nashville boy who'd come up out of the old city sheriff's department in the days before city consolidation. He had only a tenth-grade education, but he'd served as Nashville police chief for over a decade before being forced to retire for having his picture taken with guys in black suits at Churchill Downs one too many times.

I leaned back in the chair, exhausted. We listened to the press conference rattle on for another minute or so, and when everybody started repeating themselves, Lonnie hit the mute button.

'Want another one?' Lonnie held up his empty beer can.

'No. Too tired. I've still got to drive home. Guess I ought to stop at Marsha's first and make sure her place is okay.'

Lonnie got up and walked over to the refrigerator and swung the door open. The inside light chiseled ridges on his face while the blue flickering from the television danced on his back.

'You ever get the feeling the world's going to hell?' I asked. My eyes burned and my mind became a muddled blur. I thought of Marsha, murdered cabdrivers, slaughtered convenience-store clerks. All innocent people just trying to eke out a living.

'It's like a disease. Random chaos, violence. Where'd it come from?'

Lonnie smiled and shook his head, like *boy, are you dense . . .* He walked over past me and picked up the television remote control, then pressed a couple of buttons and the picture changed to an old black-and-white film of GIs spraying napalm out of a flamethrower into a cave. A second or so later, some poor soul comes sprinting out, a ball of flame doing the hundred-yard dash to death, then collapses in a burning heap.

'Channel Twenty-six,' Lonnie said. 'The War Channel, twenty-four hours a day, seven days a week. All you can stand.'

I stared at him for a moment. 'There has to be a point here somewhere.'

Lonnie dropped the remote control on the top of the television, then flopped down in his chair. 'You think we win wars because we're *good*, man? You think we whip ass everywhere because freaking God's on *our* side, and not on the other guy's? That somehow we're *righteous* . . .'

He threw a leg over the side of the chair and took a long swallow of the beer. 'Hell, no. We won the war because we are the single most meanest motherthumpers in the world. We even beat the snot out of the Japanese and the Germans, who up until they pissed us off were themselves the meanest motherthumpers in the world. I mean, these people gave us the Rape of Nanking and the Holocaust, for God's sake, and we pummeled them into slop. You think we did that 'cause we're the nice guys?'

'That's different, man. It's not the same.'

'Isn't it?' He leaned back, the can of beer cradled in his hands. 'Violence is America, man. Just ask the Indians. See what they think of us. It's genetic, encoded in the DNA. It's where we're from. It's who we are.'

'I don't believe that,' I said. 'That's lunacy.'

'So who's arguing? Of course it's lunacy. It's also reality . . .' His voice trailed off.

I stood up, suddenly very tired of Lonnie. I didn't know whether it was his preaching, or the message he was delivering. Either way, I needed some air. 'It's late. I've got to go.'

'Yeah,' he said, staring ahead at the television.

'Thanks for the loan of the van.'

'No charge.'

'I filled up the tank.'

'Thanks.'

I stood there a second, then stepped over and opened the door. 'Lonnie,' I said, turning back to him, 'I'm really worried about her.'

'I know you are, man. Just hang in there. She'll be okay. She's a tough lady.'

'Thanks, buddy. Get some sleep. See you.'

'Yeah, you, too,' Lonnie said without getting up. 'Watch yourself.'

As I stepped out into the darkness Lonnie turned the sound up on the television. I walked across the parking lot to my car, accompanied by the whistle of bombs dropping fifty years ago.

Chapter 4

So who needs sleep, right? I took a long shower, slid under the covers, and tried to fade out. Every time I thought I was going to drop off, road rushed at me again, as if the vision of white-lined asphalt rolling by had been tattooed on my retinas.

This day had started out so well. The badly needed cash the videotape would score took second place to my perseverance. I'd hung in there and beaten the guy! He'd rolled that damn wheelchair around for weeks with me watching him. He figured nobody'd be crazy enough to follow him all the way to Louisville, Kentucky.

Well, damn it, he figured wrong. I was that crazy.

But it was all meaningless. I couldn't stop thinking about her. On the way home from Lonnie's the night before, I'd driven once again past the barricades. The traffic was so bad it took nearly an hour to get in and out. Blue lights sabered the night, and off in the distance sirens meowed faintly and helicopter blades chopped. But, thank God, no gunshots. Spectators, drunks, street people, concerned family members, and rowdy teenagers all mixed into a potpourri of chaos; that uniquely American method of dealing with tragedy by transforming it into street theatre. I tried to figure out some way to get past the police lines and up the hill, but there was no way.

I finally drifted off. Around four in the morning, I woke up with a jolt and couldn't fall back off. I channel-surfed for a while, unsuccessfully searching for news bulletins, then popped the videotape of the bricklayer in the VCR. My landlady, Mrs Hawkins, was asleep downstairs, but I wasn't worried about waking her up. She's as deaf as a rock wall, can barely hear with both hearing aids turned up to max. So I cranked up the sound and listened to the laughing and the bouncing of the basketball on concrete, the birds chirping and shrieking in trees, the roar of a truck going by somewhere behind the house.

I made a cup of hot chocolate and watched the tape again. I

17

was preoccupied, drifting in and out. The tape took on a surreal quality, as if the TV screen were a window into another world, a world of much brighter colors and more acute lines than the fuzzy set of gray scales and soft lines that made up my world in the middle of the night.

I finally went under again, then woke up about daybreak with the bright silver flashing of the television dancing off the dirty cup in my lap. For a moment I couldn't remember where I was. Then it came back to me. I grabbed the clicker and ran frantically through the local stations, then CNN.

Nothing.

I fought the urge to call her, not wanting to wake her if she'd had as bad a night as I had. I showered again, this time to wake up, and made a cup of coffee. The carton of milk in my refrigerator had gone solid on me; I choked the coffee down black. The day outside was dreary, with the threat of spring thunderstorms in the air. I threw on a robe and walked down the driveway to retrieve my Sunday-morning paper.

STATE OF SIEGE the newspaper headline blared in seventy-two-point bold block type. I laughed when I saw the headline, but then remembered how I used to feel when something like this went down in my old newspaper days.

I'd have handled the story the same way. The newspeople had to milk the story for all it was worth. If this kept up, half the city would be talking to Ted Koppel by Monday night. I unfolded the paper and spread it out on the kitchen table. Most of the front page was taken up by the story. And there, down in the far right-hand corner, was Marsha's picture. Below the picture, a caption read: *Dr Marsha Helms, Assistant Medical Examiner* and another line below that: *Now held captive by cult members.*

Held captive. I read the words over and over. I'd never known anyone who was held captive, at least not outside the normal channels of incarceration.

Held captive.

I rubbed my forehead and poured another cup of coffee, trying without much luck to shake off the cobwebs. I lay back down, somehow managed to drift off again, then woke up an hour later. I called Marsha on the cellular phone, but got busy signals for nearly a half hour. It occurred to me that with the regular telephone lines cut, the cellular would be her only connection to the police outside.

I spent the rest of the morning trying to find out anything I could. Events were occurring so fast that everybody was playing catch-up. I called the city room at the newspaper where I used to work. I got some new guy who'd never heard of me – and who didn't want to talk anyway. Then I called another reporter I'd worked with, but he didn't know anything either. I phoned the police-department media liaison, but she wouldn't talk to me. I called Lieutenant Howard Spellman, my old buddy who was in charge of the Homicide Squad, but was told simply that he was unavailable.

I sat at my kitchen table, perplexed and frustrated. One more try for Marsha, one more busy signal. Then it hit me that I was ravenously hungry. I hadn't eaten since the burger and fries the night before on the outskirts of Louisville.

May as well get dressed and get out, I thought, given that there was nothing to eat in my apartment and the walls were closing in fast. Most of the time I enjoyed being a bachelor, especially when I remembered the last few months of my failed marriage. Occasionally, though, Sundays spent alone got to me. I had the feeling this was going to be one of them.

I threw on a pair of jeans and a frayed oxford-cloth shirt, then walked down the rickety backstairs of my attic apartment to the driveway. Mrs Hawkins stood at the window of her kitchen, washing a load of dishes and humming loudly off-key. She looked up as I crossed in front of her window, then cranked off the water and hurried to her back door.

'Hello, Harry,' she called through the screen. I turned and smiled at her.

'Hi, Mrs Hawkins,' I said loudly. 'How are you?'

'Just fine. I put your mail on your kitchen table while you were gone.'

'I got it. Thanks.'

'Did everything go as expected in Louisville?' she asked.

'Better than I expected.'

'Then you nailed the SOB!'

I smiled and raised a thumb at her.

'Good,' she called. 'It's bad to defraud the insurance companies. It just makes it harder on the rest of us. The insurance companies are only trying to protect us.'

Right, Mrs Hawkins, I thought to myself. And Santa Claus wiggles his fat ass down your chimney every December the twenty-fifth, too.

I'd replaced my eight-year-old Ford Escort – which had been incinerated along with Mrs Hawkins's garage in an unfortunate accident a few months earlier – with a sixteen-year-old Mazda

Cosmo that Lonnie had repo'd. The finance company didn't want the car. What are they going to do with a rotary-engine-powered rustbucket? So I got the car for five hundred. Lonnie tuned it up for me and now it ran like a top, despite the spreading bubble rust on its cream-colored skin and the quart of oil it burned with every tankful. It had electric windows that still worked and, more importantly with summer approaching, an air conditioner that pumped out cold air by the boxcar load. So what if nobody ever heard of a Mazda Cosmo? I considered it a future collectible.

I pulled the choke out, fired up the Wankel engine, and headed over to Shelby Street. Rather than take the freeway, I crossed into town on the bridge and maneuvered my way back to First Avenue. Midmorning Sunday had brought a quieter crowd to the barricades, but people were still milling about so thickly you couldn't get a car within half a block. Things looked quiet enough, though, and as long as I didn't hear any gunfire or explosions, I allowed myself to feel relieved.

A couple of minutes later I pulled off Demonbreun Street and into the parking lot of the Music Row Shoney's. The Shoney's breakfast bar is an institution in this city – one of those all-you-can-eat deals that runs until the middle of the afternoon on weekends. Eggs, bacon, sausage, grits swimming in butter, biscuits covered in gravy, coffee strong enough to make your nipples erect; my stomach growled and my arteries started clogging up with the anticipation alone.

The parking lot was packed with the usual conglomeration of tourists, Music Row hustlers, songwriters, good ol' boys, musicians, drifters, and cowboys, urban and otherwise. I took a number, sat down to wait for a seat, and flapped open the Sunday paper. I had my head buried in a sidebar on the Pentecostal Enochians when I heard my name called from across the room, above the din of voices and the clattering of dishes, pots, and pans.

'Harry!' a voice yelled. 'Yo, Harry! Ovah heah, boy!'

I looked up, stretching my neck in the direction of the noise. Sitting in a booth, halfway down the smoking side, were Ray and Slim, the two songwriters who were my next-door neighbors in our run-down Seventh Avenue office building.

The grin on my face hid the fact that I was gritting my teeth. I really didn't need this, but I didn't want them to think I was as snotty as I was feeling at that moment. I waved back and nodded my head.

'C'mon, Harry,' Ray yelled. 'Come join us, man!'

Ray was yelling loud enough for the whole restaurant to hear, and heads were beginning to turn in my direction. Slim, on the other side of the booth with his back to me, turned around and stared. He motioned silently – his usual style – for me to join them, so I figured what the hell, it beats waiting another twenty minutes for a table.

I threaded my way through the crowd over to their booth. Ray scooted over and slapped me on the back as I slid in next to him.

'Where you been, fella? We ain't seen you around here in a week or so.'

'I was up in Louisville, working a case,' I said, reaching across the table and shaking Slim's hand. The remnants of a record-breaking chowdown lay scattered and messy across the table. I'd seen Ray and Slim eat and drink before, and neither one of them ever put on an ounce. It made me want to slap them.

'How'd it go there, Perry Mason?' Ray asked jovially.

'Perry Mason was the attorney, doofus,' Slim said seriously, his soft voice barely cutting through the restaurant racket. 'Paul Drake was the detective.'

Ray stared back at him a moment. 'Kinda anal this morning, ain't we, Slim?'

'Everything went fine,' I said. 'Glad to be back home. I was just reading about the morgue. Sounds like a real standoff down there.' Ray and Slim didn't know I was dating one of the participants, so I chose to feign only casual interest.

'Yeah,' Ray said, picking his teeth with a ragged, well-chewed toothpick. 'You know who them people are, don't you?'

I shook my head. 'No, who?'

Ray turned around and pointed out the plate-glass front window of the restaurant toward the hill up Demonbreun Street. 'Up there, the other side of Mickey Gilley's place. The clothes store.'

The hill up Demonbreun across from Barbara Mandrell Country and just down the street from the Country Music Hall of Fame was a strip of tourist hang-outs, tacky souvenir shops, and cold-beer-and-hot-dog joints. At the top of the hill, a multi-storied gray building housing a saloon had Mickey Gilley's name out front in lights. I'd never been in there, but it was popular. There was always a line of cars in front slowing up traffic.

'You mean Jericho's, that place that sells the two-thousand-dollar rhinestone denim jackets with the air-brush paintings on the back?' I asked.

'You got it,' Ray said. 'They own it. Not too many people know it, either. If they knew their money was going to a bunch of religious cuckoos, they might not be so willing to spend it in such great quantities.'

Jericho's was as famous among country-music fans and stars as the Ryman Auditorium. For the past twenty years, the gaudiest, the brightest, the shiniest, the tawdriest of the tawdry, had been for sale at Jericho's. A matador could outfit himself in the hillbilly equivalent of a suit of lights from Jericho's, and all it would take is a fistful of cash. It was considered the height of country chic to show up at a place like the Stockyard Restaurant on a Friday night wearing one of their creations; the more sparkles, the better.

'Well, that certainly explains where they got the money to buy all those exotic weapons,' I said.

'Yeah, I hear they got some strange shit down there,' Ray said. 'Hear the Metros are afraid to take 'em on.'

'They ain't careful,' Slim, the master of understatement, said, 'somebody down there's gonna get hurt.'

The waitress stepped over, pad in hand. I ordered coffee and motioned for the breakfast bar.

'You guys going to stick around?' I asked.

'Sure,' Ray said. 'We ain't going nowhere.'

'Seems that way sometimes, don't it?' I cracked. 'Let me go load up.'

A couple of minutes later I was back at the booth with enough fat grams and serum cholesterol to send Richard Simmons into apoplexy.

'What're you guys up to these days?' I asked. 'That deal with Randy Travis ever work out?' The last time I talked to Ray, he was whooping that Randy Travis was going to run one of their songs on his next A-side.

Slim shook his head slowly side to side. Ray looked down at his coffee cup. 'No,' he said. 'We ain't got much going on in that area these days. That's all kind of fizzled out.'

'We're writing a few songs,' Slim added. 'But not much is happening.'

'Times are kind of hard everywhere, aren't they?' I said, with a mouth full of pancake.

'Hey, why don't you come out tonight and hear us at the Bluebird?' Ray asked. 'We're roundtabling with two other singers.'

The last thing in the world I felt like doing was fighting for a seat at the Bluebird Café on a Sunday night. With Marsha in trouble, I wasn't going to enjoy much anyway. But sitting around pulling my hair out wasn't going to accomplish anything either.

'What the hell . . .' I said. 'Maybe. Let me see what else is happening. What time you playing?'

'We start at nine,' Ray said. 'Oughta last a couple of hours.'

'Can the Bluebird pull a crowd like that so late on a Sunday?'

Ray laughed. 'When's the last time you went there?'

I settled back, swallowed a mouthful of wonderfully greasy bacon. 'Hell, Ray, I haven't been to the Bluebird since I moved out of Green Hills. That part of town's not my usual haunt anymore. Guess it's been a couple of years.'

Slim spoke over the rim of his coffee cup. 'Get there early if you want a parking space.'

Right, I thought, my girlfriend's hunkered down in a concrete blockhouse with bulletproof windows surrounded by religious wackos with bazookas in Winnebagos.... And I'm going to go listen to country music.

You ask me, the world has become completely deranged.

Chapter 5

'Oh, great,' Marsha spewed, her voice coming through the cellular ether crackling and strained. 'I'm locked up here eating canned ham and crackers, drinking *Nashville* water, for God's sake, and you're going off to the Bluebird with your songwriting buddies.'

'I didn't say I was going.'

Through the static, her laugh sounded like a titter. 'I'm just kidding, Harry. Go ahead. Go to the Bluebird. There's no reason not to.'

'You're not taking this very seriously.'

'Oh, I'm not?' she said. 'I'm the one who got to sleep on the couch in my office last night and has had the same underwear on for two days. How seriously do you want me to take it?'

I leaned back in my office chair and put my feet up on the desk. The effort stretched the tangled cord, dragging the phone across my desk. 'Would you feel better if I kept the same underwear on until this was over?'

'Oh, gross. Besides, that doesn't bother men.'

'Now wait a minute,' I protested. 'That's the kind of sexual stereotyping you'd bust my chops fo—'

'Don't get torqued on me,' she interrupted with a laugh. 'I was only kidding.'

'Not funny. You've got a shower in the building, right?'

'If you like cold water. Which is not bad, given how hot it is in here. There's no ventilation and the air conditioner's off.'

'I thought there was a generator.'

'There is, but it's not big enough to cool the whole building. It only drives the unit on the cooler. We take turns going into the cold room and sitting with Evangeline.'

'I hear she's not much of a talker.'

Marsha laughed again. Yeah, I thought, she's doing fine.

'No, the conversation tends to be a little one-sided. It wouldn't bother me so much, but there are three others in there right now that haven't even been cleaned up yet. Dr Henry phoned in and said to stop all work. He didn't want us in the middle of an autopsy if the shooting started.'

'So everything's on hold.'

'Yeah, big guy, including my heart. And a couple other parts of me.'

'I thought you said this wasn't a private line,' I said, contemplating all my parts that were on hold for the time being.

'It's not,' she said, her voice starting to break up. 'Listen, babe, I'm losing you. This phone's about dead. I'll have to plug in the charger for a bit. Guess I'd better go.'

'I read the stuff in the paper about these idiots,' I said, not wanting her to go. 'I think they're just bluffing. I'm reading the newspaper and watching television, but they don't really say much about what's going on.'

'We don't know either,' she said. 'We're staying in touch with the negotiators. We talk to them every hour. But there's not much to deal with here. They want Evangeline back and we're not going to let them have her.'

'So what the hell are they going to do?' I asked, an edge in my voice.

'There's not much anybody can do. We'll just have to wait it out. Nobody wants to see any shooting.'

'Ye—' The phone momentarily popped out, then came back on. 'Hope you're right. Listen, love—'

Snap, crackle, cellular pop . . .

'—later.'

Dial tone.

'Yeah, love,' I said to nobody. 'Later.'

Exasperated, I went by Marsha's apartment, watered the plants, and checked the locks. Bored with puttering around at her house, I spent the rest of Sunday afternoon restlessly puttering around my office.

There was mail to open, but no answering-machine messages to return on Monday. Business had picked up over the past few months, but then recently dropped off again. On a few rare days, it looked like I might even sort of kind of maybe might be able to make a living at this. Other days, the outlook wasn't so bright.

Funny, I'd taken on this new profession almost on a lark. After losing my job at the newspaper – and being pretty well burned-out on the daily grind anyway – I thought being a private detective would be kind of a hoot. I envisioned trench coats and late nights parked in front of sleazy motels waiting to take pictures of bank presidents sneaking out with the bimbo du jour. But bank presidents are smarter than that these days, and the people who sneak out of sleazy, twenty-dollars-for-three-hours motels are people I wouldn't want brushing up against me in a crowd. Might catch something a good shower couldn't wash off.

I'd been at this game almost two years now, and truthfully I'd begun to miss the paper. It's not that I haven't had my good moments; it's more that after a while the insecurity and unpredictability begin to wear on you. I can't remember when I didn't have what I diplomatically refer to as a 'slight cash-flow problem.' In other words, I'm always tapped out. Thank God Tennessee doesn't require liability insurance (technically, they do, but nobody enforces it). After the car fire, I couldn't afford the rate hikes. And as for health insurance – hell, the only way I'll ever get health insurance again is when Ed McMahon pulls up in front of my apartment with that ten-million-dollar Publishers Clearing House check he's been promising me every month for the past decade.

I know – bitch, bitch, bitch. Nobody has any sympathy for middle-aged white guys. Besides, I really can't complain. I answer to nobody, work my own hours, live my own life. And even though I knew her as a source back when I was a reporter, if I hadn't become a private investigator, I'd have never gotten to know Marsha.

Of course, I could always go back to repoing cars with Lonnie, although even that had lost its appeal. He mostly needed me in the middle of the night, and usually to run to someplace like northern Alabama or somewhere up in Kentucky. Lots of driving, tedium, lack of sleep, punctuated by moments of extreme terror.

The gig with the insurance company represented my best prospect. I'd been hustling them for a couple of months now, hoping to pick up just about anything. Their in-house investigators had given up after a couple of months of watching the bricklayer. He'd had all kinds of tests run: MRIs, CAT scans, the whole program. The doctors couldn't find anything wrong with him, but there was the incontrovertible evidence of the wheelchair. The guy never got out of it. He never slipped. He played his part perfectly. But so had I.

I'd taken the job on a contingency basis, which a half-dozen people had told me never to do. I only got paid if I came up with proof that the guy was defrauding them. If I hadn't gotten the videotape, it would have been wasted time. It was a gamble, and it had paid off. With a little luck, I'd be an insider now with the insurance company.

I reread the paper, with its sidebars on the Pentecostal

Evangelical Enochians and Brother Woodrow Tyberious Hogg. Brother Hogg, it seemed, had done a little time down in Texas for credit-card fraud and paper hanging back in the mid-Seventies. He'd undergone a jailhouse conversion and had come out a Bible-thumping sidewalk preacher in a polyester leisure suit with a head full of Scripture and Brylcreem. In the mid-Eighties he came to Nashville and took his shot at becoming a country-gospel cross-over star, a shot that thankfully missed the target by a Texas mile. He brought Sister Evangeline and a few other people, mostly runaway kids, with him, and they rented one of those decaying, once-grand houses on Belmont Avenue. They passed out religious tracts, leaflets, and pamphlets blasting the communist and/or Catholic conspiracy to pollute our spiritual purity, or some such crap. Standard paranoid religious deviant stuff. They had a thing for the Masons, too. They were passing out anti-Masonry tracts long before the Southern Baptists got their panties in a wad over them. Ahead of their time, I guess.

Somewhere along the line, the group-slash-cult started making clothes. At first, they'd buy stuff from Goodwill and the Salvation Army, then spray-paint pictures of Jesus and outline them in rhinestones. People, especially music types, started paying money for these faded denim jackets and torn blue jeans that had under-gone the Enochian metamorphosis. After a while the group didn't have to buy used clothing anymore. They rented an old building over on Charlotte Avenue. Then they bought the building. Then they took in more and more runaways, who worked cheap and hard and loved Jesus and didn't ask a lot of questions. Pretty soon the Pentecostal Evangelical Enochians didn't have to survive on handouts anymore. Now they owned several buildings, including a three-million-dollar, ten-acre estate on Hillsboro Road near the county line. Three million may not be much in New York or L.A., but down here it'll still buy you something that'll make reporters use the word *estate*. A high brick-and-stucco wall surrounded the ten acres, and the place was as secure as a fortress.

The main newspaper story outlined how it had all hit the fan Friday when somebody from inside the compound dialed 911 and reported Sister Evangeline Hogg had been found unconscious in her bedroom. Several bottles of pills and an empty quart bottle of Smirnoff were found by the bed. The paramedics arrived with a Metro squad car in tow, which was standard operating procedure.

The Enochians went ballistic. They didn't want any part of the Metro Nashville Police Department on their property. The cops didn't have a search warrant or anything, and there wasn't enough probable cause for them to think a crime had been committed, so they very politely waited outside the compound. They followed the orange-and-white ambulance to General Hospital. When Sister Evangeline was pronounced DOA and a probable suicide, the officers simply escorted the ambulance next door to the morgue before Brother Woodrow had a chance to claim the body, which he wouldn't have been allowed to do anyway. In this state, the law requires an investigation into possible suicides – including an autopsy.

As I sat in my office overlooking Seventh Avenue near Broadway, I could hear in the distance more whopping of helicopter blades and the occasional bursts of siren. The whole drama was *unfolding*, as the television news reporters would say, scarcely ten or twelve blocks away. I felt a curious detachment from it all, as if this was all happening in a different place or time than the one Marsha and I occupied. Maybe it was just that there was nothing I could do about it.

Part of it was shock. As a rule, people in Nashville just don't hold each other hostage. Nashville has more churches per capita than any other city in the country. Despite that, there's remarkably little religious tension. Everybody behaves and leaves everybody else alone. Until now, that is. Now we were just another Waco, Guyana, or Beirut: a place with innocent people held hostage by other people who were convinced they had a direct line to God.

Chapter 6

By that evening, after spending the rest of the afternoon in my office, I was too tired to do much of anything. Unable to resist temptation, I tried calling Marsha one more time. The phone rang once, twice, then about five more times before a computer voice came on and said: 'I'm sorry, the cellular mobility customer you are calling is unavailable.'

Click. Dial tone.

I made my umpteenth pass by the still-silent barricades, then crossed the river back into East Nashville and headed for the supermarket. I thought briefly of just grabbing a quick dinner at Mrs Lee's, the best Szechuan restaurant in a five-county area, and heading home. There was too much other stuff I needed, though. I even had a toilet-paper emergency, and once you're in the grip of a full-blown toilet-paper emergency, your options drop fast. You've *got* to go to the store, no matter how much of a bother.

So I restocked the thirty-five-year-old Kelvinator and the bathroom closet, then made a cheeseburger and a pan of home fries while I watched *Sixty Minutes*. Ed Bradley even alluded to the siege of the Nashville morgue in introducing a segment on a guy who debrainwashed cult victims. Jeez, we were hitting the big time now.

I sat around after dinner, grazing through the cable channels, then halfheartedly reading a paperback history of jazz in America. I was tired but too wired to sleep. Finally I decided Ray and Slim were expecting me at the Bluebird, and if I wasn't going to sleep, I may as well go have a beer and listen to some music.

The Mazda came to life with a pull of the choke and a twist of the key. A small puff of blue-black smoke appeared in the rear-view mirror, then drifted away across the neighbor's front yard.

Sunday evening is possibly the only time of the entire week when this city isn't plagued by a swarm of traffic. I cut over to I-65 by way of the Ellington Parkway and took the north loop across the river to the Four-Forty Parkway. In twenty minutes, I was driving down a winding four-lane road toward Green Hills, the upper-middle-class-to-snazzy part of town I used to live in, back when I still had my job at the newspaper and was married to the executive Vice-President of the advertising agency.

The Bluebird Café is located in a strip mall, hidden in among retail stores, past a nursery, down the road from the mall at Green Hills. It looked ordinary from the front, like maybe a small diner. Inside though, it was – as we say down south – ate completely up with atmosphere. Dark, smoky, with framed eight-by-ten glossies of all the famous people who'd played there tacked up all over the place, the Bluebird was a small room with a bar on one side and tables everywhere else. Somewhere back in the corner, a kitchen sat hidden and out of the way. Pipes in the ceiling had been painted and left exposed.

Truth is, the Bluebird Café isn't a hell of a lot to look at. But it is one of the most sought-after venues in the city. If you were an insider in the music business, showcasing at the Bluebird meant you'd arrived. I read in the paper a while back that somebody'd even written a play about it.

I parked three or four stores down and walked across the asphalt parking lot to the line at the front door. All the tables were occupied by people who'd been smart enough to make reservations. I paid my eight bucks cover and wound up in a gallery of folding chairs next to the bar, over in the corner out of everybody's way. After grabbing a beer, I climbed over three people to get back to my chair. I settled back to wait for the music to start.

In the center of the room, the tables had been pushed back to form a loose circle. Inside the circle, four metal folding chairs sat next to guitars in stands beside several amplifiers. Ray and Slim already occupied two of the chairs and were leaning over their Martins, tuning them up and talking real low. Slim wore a khaki bush shirt, with epaulets on the shoulders, and jeans. Ray wore a pearl-buttoned blue-and-red cowboy shirt and a broad-brimmed ten-gallon hat. I'd never seen Ray decked out like that. He looked kind of goofy, I thought.

Ray's back was to me, and Slim was to his left. Then another fellow, a tall, skinny guy with prominent cheekbones and sunken eyes, wearing jeans and a checked flannel shirt, made his way through the tables and sat down across from Ray. Ray said something, and all three broke out laughing as the tall one picked up a glossy, jet-black guitar and cradled it in his lap.

I looked down at my watch. They were ten minutes late getting started already. Gigs like this never start on time anyway, but if they didn't make music soon, I was going to pack it in.

There was an empty chair across from Slim, and it appeared that nothing much was going to happen until that chair was filled. I checked my watch again, then sipped on the beer and did a little people watching. The place was packed, the audience jammed in shoulder to shoulder at tables, waitresses twisting and turning, their trays held high overhead as they delivered drinks. A clamor of chaotic voices filled the room.

I thought of Marsha and wished she were here. Thick crowds in small rooms have never been my style. I'm not sure I like people well enough to be this close to so many of them. I'd come purely as a favor to Slim and Ray. But as long as I had to be here, I'd much rather have had Marsha with me.

Finally, after I'd run out of both beer and mental monologues to replay in my head, I was about to see if I could slip out of the place unnoticed. Just as I rose to leave there was a shift in the tone of the audience murmur and heads started turning toward the front door. I sat back down just as a high voice that bordered on shrill yelled from around the corner: 'Oh, good heavens, I'm so sorry, I'm late, oh, good heavens—'

Slim put his head down on his guitar and rolled it from side to side, like he'd been through this routine before. Two women sitting next to me put their heads together, and I heard one of them whisper: 'Oh, she always does this. She's always late. I think it's just to get attention.'

And then the other one whispered back: 'Yeah, either that or she just likes to piss Slim off.'

'What do you expect from an ex-wife?' The first one giggled.

'Oh, I think it's just an act. . . .'

Ex-wife? Slim had never mentioned an ex-wife. Why would Slim be sitting in a crowded club on a Sunday night singing songs with his ex-wife? My ex and I avoided each other unless it was absolutely unavoidable.

Music people are strange.

The woman walked into our view from the right, around the corner, her long thin arms waving at the crowd, hands splayed out chaotically, fingers pointing everywhere at once. A fat guy with a long, scraggly beard and thick glasses sat in front of me. I shifted in my seat to look around him and stared.

She was tall; nearly as tall, I figured, as Marsha's six-one, six-two. Her hair was straight, the color of dark ash, and hung down her back below her waist Crystal Gayle-style. She wore a pair of jeans that must have been painted on and a crocheted white sweater that was nearly see-through. Her face was thin, her features fine: pointed nose, sculpted cheekbones.

She made me ache.

'Becca,' Slim said into the microphone, his voice scolding her.

'Oh, hush,' she said in a voice loud enough and penetrating enough not to need amplification. 'Don't start on me, Slim.'

The audience howled. The two women next to me shook with laughter, as if they'd seen this before and were expecting it. The fourth singer, the one across from Ray, hit a loud E chord on his guitar.

'I'm Slim Gibson,' Slim announced to the audience, his voice its usual low and slow. 'And this ravishing beauty here is the late Rebecca Gibson, my lovely ex-wife and talented ex-songwriting partner.'

The audience laughter swelled. Evidently, I was the only one who hadn't seen this dog-and-pony show before. I found it hard to laugh; there was a sharper edge to all this than I liked.

Rebecca Gibson slid her long body between the tables, through the crowd, and onto the empty chair across from Slim. She sat down, crossed her legs, and pulled the microphone on its horizontal stand to her lips.

'I may not be on time,' she said brashly, 'but there's no call for you to refer to me as the late Rebecca Gibson.'

The audience roared.

'The romance may be gone, but the royalties remain, right, baby?' she said.

More roaring. She was animated, cheeky, seemingly in constant motion. In a different time, she might have been labeled brazen. She was as extroverted as Slim was introverted. The difference in the two must have made for interesting marriage, which as far as I'm concerned is only a slight variation on the ancient Chinese curse: *May you live in interesting times.*

I sort of knew what to expect next. At a songwriters' round-table, four singer-songwriters sit in a circle and take turns, each singing one of his or her own songs. The other three could jump in and provide a little background or harmony, but basically each one had the stage to himself. I also knew from the couple of other times I'd been to the Bluebird that Slim was in the starting position. In just a second or two, as Rebecca adjusted her mike and settled in, Slim ran his pick down the six-string one last time to get everybody's attention.

'This is one that Becca and I wrote a long time ago,' he said. 'Hope you like it.'

Then Slim played a three-chord progression that was elegant in its simplicity. Ray and the other songwriter, whose name I never did get, slid into accompaniment, the strings of their guitars filling the spaces in Slim's lead. Then Slim began singing, his voice plaintive and sweet, right on key, exactly where it needed to be. I recognized the song, 'All My Empty Heart Wants Is You,' as one that had been recorded a few years back by some minor up-and-comer who rapidly came and went.

Like most country songs, it hit somewhere real deep, on a fundamental, almost profound human level. Most country's like that – songs about loneliness and despair and struggling to find love in a cold world. Sometimes it could go over the top; 'crying in your beer' jokes about country music had become clichés. I wasn't much of a country fan, but only because I hadn't taken the time to learn it, study it. Maybe, I thought, I ought to give it a chance.

When Slim finished the first verse and transitioned into the chorus, Rebecca's voice melded with his in a harmony that made the hair on the back of my neck stand up. I realized at that moment why people who love this stuff get so damned crazy about it. When she talked, her voice was almost a yell. But singing there with Slim, their voices filling the room, the audience quiet enough to hear heartbeats . . . there was something about it that ran deep and strong and powerful.

After a few moments I got lost in it, my conscious mind on hold and something inside me just following their voices, not even aware of the words as words. The words and the music floated and bore me and everyone else in the room along. There was magic there, mystery and focus and intensity. Slim, who rarely said more than ten words to anybody, was liberated by the act of singing and playing. Something inside him soared. And Rebecca, who was loud and irritating and hyperactive outside the song, became calm and pure and sweet when lost inside the music. Each was yin to the other's yang; their opposites matched perfectly, their sameness blending into one. The marriage of these two gifted people had to be both fiercely passionate and powerfully doomed.

Nobody can sing all the time.

Slim hit the last word in the song and let his own voice fade away as he completed the last run on the chord progression. Ray and the other picker pulled back just at the end, leaving Slim's final notes echoing in the room to dead silence.

Then I was on my feet, clapping until my hands burned and my arms ached. My voice grew hoarse from cheering along with the rest of the room. They'd made the audience wait and fidget and grow impatient, and then just at the right instant, they'd knocked us flat on our butts.

'Whew,' Rebecca spewed, fanning herself with her right hand, 'if we'd been able to do that all the time, we'd still be married. Right, baby?'

Slim stared at her silently, his brown eyes boring a hole through her, almost oblivious to the crowd around them. It seemed as if the temperature in the room had gone up about fifty degrees. My chigger bites from Louisville – and I'll let you guess where most of them were – started itching again like crazy.

Ray hit a chord, then pulled his microphone closer. 'That's gonna be a tough one to follow. Why don't we shift gears jest a little?'

Ray exaggerated his Southern drawl to the point of nausea. I wondered how many people in the audience knew he was born just a block from the last stop on the double-L train in Canarsie, and still rode the subway to his job in Brooklyn up until maybe twelve years ago.

'Y'all sing along with me on this one, you've got a mind to. . . .' And then Ray went into this hilarious song about a revival preacher caught with his pants down in the Widow Walker's living room.

Then it was Rebecca's turn. She adjusted the microphone and fidgeted in her chair, as if it were physically impossible for her to sit in one position for longer than a moment or two.

'Well, as most of y'all know,' she began, 'I've just finished recording what I hope is going to be my break-out album.'

Somebody behind me cheered. Rebecca turned her head in our direction. 'You tell 'em, baby! 'Bout damn time, ain't it?'

More clapping.

'What I'd like to do for you tonight is the title song off the new CD. It's called "Way Past Dead". I hope you like it.'

She cleared her throat and nodded to Slim. Slim played an intro, then Rebecca began singing. As she did, Ray and the other fellow joined in, strumming with Slim and doing a real low backup harmony on her. The song was a mournful tune, part classic folk, part Patsy Cline, about a man trying to hold on to his love, and the woman in his life trying to tell him it was over and not knowing how. It was bittersweet from the get-go, and if I'd been a little more stressed-out or had a few more beers in me, I'd have probably choked up myself.

She sang each verse of the song brilliantly, followed by the chorus that tied it all together:

You ask me now
If our live still breathes . . .
If our love still grows,
Like the springtime leaves.
But my heart
Is filled with dread.
My love for you
Is way past dead. . . .
My love for you, darling,
Is way past dead. . . .

As the last notes of her voice and Slim's guitar faded away, there were about two heartbeats of the deepest silence I'd ever seen in a crowded room. Then the whole place exploded once again in standing ovation. Rebecca Gibson sat motionless, her head down, as the cheering continued. Then, as the applause ebbed, she raised her head, and I could see that her eyes were wet. She stared straight at Slim, and as the yelling faded out she whispered into the microphone: 'I'm sorry, baby. I really am.'

Slim's eyes were dark, intense, his jaw locked so hard the outline cast a shadow on his cheek. Whatever had happened to them, I thought, had resulted in more pain than anyone should have to bear, and was now irrevocable.

Then the other guy did a song, and I caught his name: Dwight Parmenter. Then Slim again, then Ray, and round and round and round, until the next thing I knew, it was two in the morning and I was driving up Hillsboro Road to the freeway on my way back to East Nashville. At the last second, I turned and headed out to the other side of town. The key to Marsha's apartment sat in my pocket like a chunk of lead. If I couldn't have her next to me, then maybe by sleeping in her bed, I could feel her next to me.

It was nearly nine when I came to, my head groggy and heavy. I had to get home fast, change clothes, then get out to my office, grab that videotape, and head to the insurance company. Somehow, though, the energy just wasn't there. I dawdled in the shower, made a cup of coffee, made up the bed, straightened up a little, brushed my teeth – the usual. I tried my luck at cellular-phone roulette, with the same frustrating results as before. I felt like a puppy who'd been yanked from his momma.

Marsha doesn't subscribe to the morning newspaper – she's usually at work before it arrives – so I sat at her kitchen table with a towel wrapped around me and coffee in front of me, then flicked on the television. The last segment of *Today* was just wrapping up, and then a local newsperson came on with a quick roundup of Nashville news, headlined, of course, by the hostage situation at the morgue.

It was right after that when I learned that the sweet-voiced, high-cheeked, long and lanky ex-Mrs Slim Gibson had been found murdered early that morning, beaten to death in the bedroom of her apartment. After last night's appearance at the Bluebird, she really had become the late Rebecca Gibson.

Chapter 7

Even though I'd never met Rebecca Gibson, certainly didn't know her, and her death had not touched me personally, I found myself shocked at her murder. Maybe it was her being Slim's ex-wife. Maybe it was that I'd seen her perform and had heard that sweet voice, now silenced for good.

The morning rush hour had ended by the time I got moving, and there was still another hour or so before the lunchtime rush hour began its slow segue into the evening rush hour. You want to get anywhere in this city, you've got about a forty-five-minute window three times a day to go for it. Then you're screwed. The Big Apple's got nothing on Music City, gridlock-wise.

For once, my parking fees were paid up, so I was able to slide into a space in the lot across Seventh Avenue from my office. I didn't know how long I was going to be able to keep the place; cranky old Mr Morris had raised my rent seventy-five a month after the fire in my office last year. Hell, it wasn't my fault some joker burned my car and my office in the same day, but try telling that to Morris. Rat bastard...

At least he'd let me stay, though. At first he wasn't even going to do that. Just to be on the safe side, I avoided him as much as possible. So when I took the steps up to the front door two at a time, I peered through the dirty glass first to make sure he wasn't there.

In a few seconds, I'm bouncing up the two flights of stairs to my office, trying to stay focused on what comes first. I wanted to try Marsha first, but I needed to call Phil Anderson over at the insurance company to make arrangements to deliver the videotape. I ought to stop by Slim and Ray's office down the hall as well, just to offer my condolences and make sure they were okay.

Then the thought struck me: does one offer condolences upon the death of an ex-spouse? Life is so complicated these days. I decided that, uncomfortable or not, I'd offer my sympathies. So

I turned right at the top of the flight of stairs, away from my office, and walked down to Slim and Ray's office. The door was locked and there was no reply to my knock.

In my office, there was still a stack of mail on my desk unopened from yesterday. None were checks, though; I could tell that, and I couldn't bear to open the rest. I'd spent the last month or so, including my expenses on the trip to Louisville, living off the plastic shark. A couple of windowed envelopes in the pile meant the shark had come for his vigorish, and I didn't have the juice to pay him.

Christ Almighty, I thought, I'm starting to sound like a dick. And I don't mean private eye. . . .

I thumbed through my Rolodex, located Phil Anderson's number, then dialed it on the speakerphone.

'Tennessee Workmen's Protective Association,' a young woman's voice answered.

Yeah, right, I thought. Protection, my keister.

'Phil Anderson,' I said.

'Please hold.'

This is why I finally bought a cheap speakerphone. Being on hold gives me a cramp in the neck, among other places.

'Fraud services,' another telephone voice answered.

'Phil Anderson, please. Harry Denton calling.'

Another round of hold, then Phil's deep voice laced with southern Mississippi twang answered. I didn't know much about Phil, beyond the fact that he grew up in the Delta, went to Ole Miss, got into the insurance business, moved to Nashville, and hates the Vanderbilt Commodores with a passion bordering on the pathological.

'Hey, bo-wee,' he practically yelled into the phone. 'Jew have any luck?'

Jew, I thought? What Jew? Then I realized that in the two weeks since I'd last spoken with Phil, I'd forgotten how to listen to him. It is, after all, an acquired skill.

'Yeah,' I said. 'I think you're going to be real pleased. I've got a little movie to show you.'

'Hot day-um,' he said, then: 'Hey, where you at, boy? You sound like you at the bottom of a fish tayunk!'

I picked up the handset and held it to my ear. 'Cheap speaker-phone,' I explained.

'Well, hail-far, I believe I'd take 'at sucker back and get me the next model up.'

'You pay this invoice,' I said, 'I just might do that. When can we get together?'

I heard a flipping of pages as Phil consulted his calendar.

'How about four this afternoon?'

'Works for me,' I said. 'Your office at four.'

'You got it, boy. Later.'

I hung up the phone, wondering how old a Southern male had to be before people stopped calling him boy.

I set the phone down inside its cradle and stared at it a moment or two. Should I? I wanted to hear her voice. I had begun, in fact, to ache for it. But could I get through? Would Marsha be able to talk to me? Would she want to?

Oh, hell, this is crazy. I reached over and grabbed the phone and punched in the number to Marsha's cellular phone, which I'd now committed to memory. Once again, that damn computer monotone told me where to get off.

I stared out the window five more minutes before giving up. There was no way I could sit still or concentrate on anything. So I trotted back down the stairs, outside into what was becoming a gorgeous spring day, and pumped thirty-five cents into a newspaper machine and pulled out the early edition of the afternoon paper. I wondered if Rebecca's murder had made the paper yet.

SIEGE CONTINUES the headline read. And below that: HOSTAGE DRAMA IN DAY THREE.

It was nearly eleven and I was getting peckish, so I bought a hot dog and a large Coke off a vendor's wagon on Church Street, then parked myself on a bench in the little pedestrian mall across from the Church Street Center. The government employees, who were about all that was left in a central downtown that everyone else had fled for the 'burbs, filed out of buildings and headed off for their own lunches in a flurry of suits and dresses.

I scarfed down the dog and flapped open the newspaper. It was hard to imagine that the words blared across the front page had their origin barely a mile from where I sat. First Avenue was still closed from the Thermal Plant on up to where the road curved around and changed names. As I sat there reading I could hear the dim buzzing of the helicopters circling the area. General Hospital, I read, had been evacuated of all but the most seriously ill patients; the rest were sent to Meharry Medical Center, Vanderbilt, and Baptist Hospital. The obligatory urgent call for blood donations had been made. The mayor announced that for the time being, he was not going to ask the governor to activate the National guard.

On page two of the first section, a long profile of Brother Woodrow Tyberious Hogg occupied all the space above the fold. I felt like I'd seen his picture a thousand times: the earnest eyes with droopy eyelids above a thickening set of cheeks and jowls, the head atop a thickening neck in white shirt and polyester tie. It was the same face that had been on the hundreds of religious stations that the cable companies were now required to carry – the tacky, sleazy appeals for money in God's name pouring forth from mouths that blended together and all started to look alike after you'd surfed around the channels long enough on a sleepless night.

And in a box on the front page, near the bottom, with a jump to the last page, were the details of Rebecca Gibson's murder. Police reported that neighbors heard the sound of a fight around four a.m., glass breaking, screams, the thud of bodies slamming, or being slammed, against walls. Someone had phoned 911, and when police got there, Rebecca was already dead. She'd been beaten brutally, the kind of brutal that only a closed casket can hide.

Witnesses reported seeing a white, mid-Seventies Chevrolet four-door speeding away from the house.

I leaned back on the concrete-and-wood bench and let the sun beat down on my face. The noon whistle from the tobacco factory behind the State Capitol blared. Behind me, on Church Street, a bearded driver in a yellow taxi slammed on his brakes and laid on the horn to keep from hitting a street person who'd stepped off the sidewalk in a daze.

A white, four-door, fifteen-year-old-or-so Chevy, I thought. A white Chevy. I'd seen one before. Then it hit me.

Slim Gibson had a white Chevy.

Chapter 8

I'd seen Slim Gibson's white Chevy parked, double-parked, and triple-parked on Seventh Avenue in front of our offices so many times it was like a landmark. Once, I'd even given Slim a ride over to the Metro tow-in lot across the river to retrieve it after it'd been hooked. I never knew why Slim didn't buy himself a slot in a parking lot somewhere.

One thing was for sure: the Chevy wasn't parked out front today.

I entered the building this time without even bothering to check for Morris. I scooted up the stairs, turned left at the top of the landing, and fumbled for my key as I approached my office. The jangling of the keys must have been like an alarm. As soon as I closed the door behind me, I heard footsteps.

Just as I was bending over to check the answering machine, the pounding on the door started.

'Hold on,' I said loudly. 'Just a sec.'

Truth was, I didn't have to yell. My office is only one room, L-shaped, with just enough square footage in the small part of the L for the door to open without hitting my visitor's chair.

I opened the door to find Ray standing there, without Slim, lines creased on his face deeper than I'd ever seen before. His eyes were bloodshot, and he looked like he hadn't slept for a week.

'Ray, c'mon in, man.'

Ray stepped in behind me as I shut the door. 'I guess you heard,' he said.

'Yeah, it was on TV this morning. And in the paper.'

I passed around him and slid into my seat, motioning for him to grab the other chair. Ray flopped into it, his butt barely on the edge of the chair, his elbows close into his sides, his hands pointing out toward me.

'Shit, I ain't never seen nothing like this.'

'What's going on? Where's Slim? The newspaper said witnesses saw a car like his pulling away from Rebecca's place last night.'

Ray brought his hands up and rubbed his forehead. 'Harry, there's a lot you don't know about Slim. He looks real quiet and laid-back most of the time—'

'Yeah?'

'But sometimes, you push the wrong buttons, ol' Slim'll get kind of wild.'

I leaned back in the chair and thought for a second. Marsha trapped inside a morgue, surrounded by armed Winnebagos, me with a stack of bills to pay, and God knows how long the insurance company's going to take to pay that invoice. Now this. So life's never dull.

Please God, I thought, give me a little dull.

'Where is he, Ray?'

'That's kind of hard to say.'

I crossed my feet and put them up on my desk, wrapped my hands around my head, and leaned back in my creaky office chair. Trying my best to look like a country lawyer, I guess. Maybe Gregory Peck in *To Kill a Mockingbird*.

'He didn't decide to jackrabbit now, did he?'

Ray looked me in the eye and I saw his lips start to move.

''Cause if he did, Ray, he's mega-screwed. Can't nobody help him now.'

Ray fidgeted a moment longer, then: 'Well, he ain't exactly run off. He's just staying low to try to figure out the lay of the land. I got a friend over at the courthouse who called me about a half hour ago, said the police were looking for him as a material witness.'

'You know how to get in touch with him?' I asked.

'Maybe.'

'I'm no lawyer, buddy, but I do know nothing good ever comes from running. If he's rabbitted out of here, they'll find him. If I was you, I'd get ahold of him, tell him to get a lawyer, and come on in. If he's innocent, then sooner or later they'll figure that out.'

I knew I was lying. Not about the police catching him, of course. If Slim's run off, they'll find him. I was lying about the if-he's-innocent-he'll-get-off stuff. Anybody who's hung around court-rooms and jailhouses as much as I did in my years as a reporter knows that once you enter the judicial system and the system thinks you're guilty, then nothing else matters. You can pretty well kiss your ass goodbye. But there's no good in trying to acquaint people with the truth when they don't have the basis upon which to accept it.

'You think so?' Ray asked.

'Absolutely,' I said. 'Tell him to c'mon in and clear himself.' Then I hesitated just a moment. 'He didn't do it, did he?'

Ray's mouth curled up. 'Hell, no, Harry. He didn't do it. That ain't Slim's style. You ought to know that.'

I didn't know *why* I ought to have known that, but I let the comment slide for the sake of propriety.

'I didn't mean anything,' I said apologetically. 'I just had to ask.'

'Well, he didn't do it,' Ray insisted. 'But appearances are going to hurt him. You got to understand, Slim and Rebecca fought like hell the whole time they were married. Most of the time, it wasn't any kind of big deal. Some people are just like that. It's the way they express affection. But if you don't know that to begin with, then . . . well, it could look pretty bad sometimes.'

I shifted in my seat and plopped my feet to the floor. Ray fidgeted uncomfortably. 'Harry, if this gets nasty, you'll help him, won't you?'

I felt a cramp in my chest. Oh, hell, I thought, here it comes. This was not something I had any interest in getting involved in; besides, even as cheap as I am, Slim couldn't afford me.

'I got an awful lot on my plate right now,' I said, with more than a hint of reluctance in my voice.

'Aw, c'mon, Harry, he's a buddy. You can't let a buddy down now, can you?'

I put my hands out in front of me. 'Now wait a minute. There's no indication whatsoever that Slim's going to need any help. You just get in touch with him and tell him what I told you.'

Ray stood up. 'I don't know, man. I got a bad feeling about this.'

I rose and stood next to him. 'Somebody you know got murdered, Ray. You're supposed to feel bad.'

He nodded. 'Yeah, I guess so.'

The phone rang as I was easing him out the door. My head was starting to hurt and I was about to let the machine take the call. On the third ring, though, I decided to pick it up.

'Denton Agency, may I help you?'

'Yeah, I'd like to phone in a pizza order, please. Can you deliver in thirty minutes or less?'

I sucked in a gulp of air. 'Hell, yes, just get me through that long blue line of cop cars.'

'How are you, babe?'

'I'm fine. More importantly, how are you?'

45

'Gamier by the minute. But other than that, surviving.'

I sat down in my chair and mashed the phone into my ear, as if that would make her closer.

'Are you all right? Really? Have you got enough to eat?'

'Enough for now. And the plumbing still works, so we've got water and a place to wee-wee. Other than being bored and stressed-out, we're all pretty much okay. The only place we've still got electricity is the cooler, so we ran an extension cord into the offices. At least we can run the microwave and keep the cellulars charged.'

'I tried to call you about a half hour ago.'

'We've only got one battery pack, and it's old as Moses,' she said. 'When it's charging, we're cut off. And it'll only hold a charge a few minutes.'

'This is so frustrating,' I said after a moment. 'I feel completely helpless.'

'Me, too,' she said. 'But it's okay, really. We're all fine, and it's just a matter of time until this gets settled. I'll tell you one damn thing, though.'

'Yeah?'

'Metro's going to owe me some comp time when this is over, and by God, I'm going to take it.'

I grinned. 'Maybe we'll get that vacation we've been talking about.'

'You're on.'

'Listen, Marsha, I just—'

'Ruh, roh, you're about to get mushy on me. Don't, Harry. Like I said, this isn't a private line. Besides, I've got to call Spellman before the cell phone dies again.'

'Spellman's down there?' I asked. 'Why homicide?'

'He's also head of MUST.'

MUST is the Metro Unusual Situations Team, the local equivalent of SWAT.

'Listen, babe,' she continued. 'I've got to go. I'll try you later if I can. You be at home?'

'Yeah,' I answered. 'Call me later. And please be careful.'

She hung up, leaving me once again with that hollow, damned electronic silence.

So my old buddy Lieutenant Howard Spellman was manning the barricades. Maybe there were some possibilities here, after all.

Chapter 9

I thumbed through the Rolodex again until I came up with Howard Spellman's office number. Howard and I went back a long way, back to the days when I had the police beat for the newspaper. Jeez, that was over ten years ago. I think I was still young then, although I can no longer remember that far back.

Our relationship hadn't always been an easy one. Cops by nature are leery of and fascinated by reporters at the same time. Most will cuss out reporters given half the chance, but then scramble all over each other to get their names in the paper. Better yet, get an interview with one of the TV-station pretty boys who pass for journalists these days. That was a coup.

After leaving the newspaper business, I expected that, if anything, private investigators would be held in even less esteem than reporters. I soon learned, though, that if you earned a cop's respect, he'd treat you accordingly. I'd tried over the past two years with Spellman, with mixed success.

Spellman's phone rang about ten times before I gave up. You'd think that the Homicide Squad would keep their phones manned during business hours, but Spellman was the only one with a secretary. If she was out of the office and nobody else was around, then it just rang off the hook.

Glad I wasn't trying to report a murder.

I had another two hours, maybe a little more, before I had to meet Phil Anderson over at the insurance company. I figured a long walk might do me good. It's quite a trek from my office down Broadway to the Riverfront, but there wouldn't be anyplace to park down there, what with all the squad cars and news vans.

So I took a stroll, and within a few minutes found myself maneuvering past the Al Menah Shriners' temple on my way down the long hill toward the Cumberland River. The day had really blossomed, with only a few thick gray-and-white clouds drifting lazily over the city. The lunch-hour pedestrian crowds hadn't let up yet either; I could see how somebody would hate to get back to the office on a day like today.

It had been a long winter, one of dark days that ended early. Headlights on by four and all that. I was glad to see it over.

Down by Second Avenue, I had to cross Broadway to the south side of the street to avoid the construction traffic. Nashville's been in a boom the last year or so, having itself come out of a long, dark economic wintertime. The company that owns Opryland had bought up a huge chunk of Second Avenue and was remaking it in its own image. At the foot of Second Avenue, right on Broadway, a Hard Rock Café had moved in last year.

Ah, I thought, we've arrived.

Only problem was that all the people who'd run restaurants and storefront operations that dated all the way back to the late nineteenth century were now being booted out. Some of the residents had to go as well. Too bad; progress in, people out. More tourists pumping their hard-earned dollars into the local economy. You know what they say: every Yankee tourist is worth a bale of cotton, and he's a helluva lot easier to pick.

Down by the Acme Feed Store, which thankfully hadn't been bought and gentrified, I rounded the corner and started toward General Hospital and the morgue. Up the sloping hill, a line of Metro squad cars, engines idling in the heat, blue strobes flashing, diverted traffic blocks before you could get anywhere near the action.

A few news vans, with their satellite towers cranked up, were parked half on the sidewalk. But the crowd of newspeople had thinned. Maybe the novelty was beginning to wear off.

It took less than five minutes to get up the line. A young uniformed officer, arms crossed, leaning against the front fender of his car, was the only one around. As cars approached he motioned them to turn right, away from the river, and head off in the other direction. There wasn't much traffic, though. Word had gotten out.

'Hey, officer,' I called as I crossed the street and approached him. 'How's it going?'

He gave me that cool, professional dealing-with-civilians look, the one they teach you at the Academy.

'Quiet today,' he answered.

I came to within a couple of feet and leaned against the back quarter panel. I crossed my arms like he did and stared down the hill.

'Had a little free time after lunch,' I said. 'Decided to take a walk in the sunshine, see what's going on. This beats being cooped up in an office, don't it?'

'Yessir.' He reached for his whistle as a car approached a little too quickly, blew it shrilly, and motioned firmly to the driver. The guy slowed, gave us both a dirty look, then turned onto the side street and sped away.

'How much longer you think this is going to go on?' I asked, trying to keep that casual, just-jawing tone in my voice.

'No idea, sir.'

I backed away from the blue-and-white Chevy and turned toward the cop. 'Say, you don't know if Howard Spellman's up there right now, do you?'

The officer turned and squinted at me in his best Clint Eastwood style. All he needed was a pair of mirrored aviator shades to complete the picture.

'You a reporter?' he asked after a second or so.

'One of them sleazeballs?' I laughed. 'Not me. I'm just a friend of his. Been kind of curious. Haven't been able to get him in his office the past couple of days.'

'He's been sort of busy.' The arms folded back across the uniformed and badged chest.

'Officer' – I squinted theatrically at his badge – 'Roberts, I don't suppose I could walk up the hill and say hi to him, could I?'

Officer Roberts shook his head. 'No unauthorized personnel past this point.'

I'd expected that. 'Say, could you call him on the radio and see if he'll let me come up. If he said it was okay, that'd be all right, wouldn't it?'

Behind us, from somewhere up the hill, we heard the whine of a helicopter engine coming alive. As the engine noise increased, the slow whop-whop-whop of the blades grew as well.

'What do you think?' I asked.

Th cop pulled his handi-talkie out of a leather holster on his belt. He held it to his mouth and pushed a button. 'Henry Seven to Henry One.'

'Go ahead,' came the disembodied voice through the static.

'Lieutenant Spellman up there?'

'Yeah, hold on.'

The helicopter noise grew louder. I looked behind us just as the olive-drab military chopper rose quickly, then darted off away from the General Hospital complex and the morgue towards the downtown area. A wind blew in from across the river, up near the northern loop of I-65, bringing with it the faint fragrance of the rendering plant, mixed in with the usual car exhaust and the odor of burning garbage from the Thermal Plant. My nose curled involuntarily.

Spellman must have answered, because the young cop put the handi-talkie back to his face. 'Lieutenant, I've got a man down here says he's a friend of yours. Wants to cross the lines and come up there.'

'Who is he?' Spellman's crackly voice answered.

'My name's Denton,' I said. 'Harry Denton.'

'Harry Denton,' the cop repeated.

Silence. I figured Spellman was trying to figure out exactly the right string of obscenities to put together to express just how pleased he was to hear from me.

More silence. The cop adjusted the gain on his radio, then held it closer to his ear.

'Tell him to wait right there.'

Ten minutes later a white sedan that had unmarked cop car written all over it rolled down the hill and pulled to a stop behind the line of squad cars. Spellman got out, alone, and motioned to me to join him over on the sidewalk.

I stepped between the squad cars, crossing the line between authorized and unauthorized personnel. Spellman was only glaring at me about half as irascibly as I expected, so maybe this wasn't going to be too excruciating. It could have been fatigue, though. Spellman looked about as whipped as I'd ever seen a man who was still on two feet.

'You want to tell me what you're doing here, Harry?'

'Howard, you look beat.' We were huddled under a streetlight, far enough away so that the uniform couldn't hear us.

'I haven't been home since Saturday morning,' he said, rubbing his face with both hands, the skin like putty beneath his fingers. 'Thank God for electric razors that plug into cigarette lighters.'

'Jesus, man, how long they expect you to keep this up?'

'Until it's over, I guess. C'mon, Harry, I don't have time for this happy horseshit. What's on your mind?'

How much could I tell him? I stood there for a moment, tongue-tied, clumsy.

'I've got a real good friend who's in the morgue right now, and I'm worried about her, man. I want to know if there's anything I can do to help, if there's—'

'For starters, get the hell out of here. Doc Helms is doing fine. Everything's under control.'

My head must have twitched at his mention of Marsha's name.

He grinned wearily at me, one of the few times I'd ever seen him smile.

'You know?' I asked, momentarily slack-jawed.

'Good God, Harry, what do you take me for? The whole damn department knows. It's the biggest unkept secret in the city.'

I had to laugh myself. 'Hell, Howard, we've been so careful, so discreet.'

'It's Kay Delacorte. She suspected something was going on and confronted Doc about it a few weeks ago. Doc Helms swore her to secrecy.'

'Which meant Katie bar the door, right?' I said, then laughed at the whole damn situation.

'Right, if you want something to spread through the latrine-o-gram network like wildfire, make Kay Delacorte swear to keep her mouth shut.'

'Oh, hell,' I said. 'I'm embarrassed. But now you understand why I'm so—'

'Of course. But there ain't a thing you can do.'

I felt my jaw tighten and my back molars scrape together. 'I know. That's what's driving me nuts. I hate this.'

'It's no picnic for us. This is a weird one. Most hostage situations I've ever been involved in, you've got a disorganized, usually panicked psycho holding a gun to somebody's head. This time, you've got a group of highly organized fanatics with enough fire-power to make a real fight of it, but your hostages are basically safe – as long as they don't starve.'

It was as if Howard was thinking out loud more than talking to me. 'So what can you do?' I asked.

'The mayor says he does not, emphasize *not*, want another Waco, Texas, here. He doesn't care what happens to anybody, as long as this city's image isn't damaged. It's all politics, Harry. The new arena, the Second Avenue renovation . . . they're thinking about expanding the Convention Center.'

'So whatever happens, just clean it up neatly, right?'

'You got it, cowboy.'

'I don't envy you,' I said, suddenly weary myself.

'You don't have to.'

I looked off to our left, up First Avenue. At the crest of the hill, there was a line of squad cars parked around a large box van, which served as the police command post.

'Howard,' I asked. 'Can I go up there? I want to see it.'

Spellman stuck his hands in his pockets. 'Damn it, Harry.'

51

'I've never asked you anything as a friend before. I'm asking now.'

He took a couple of steps toward the unmarked car. 'What the hell, I'll run you up there real quick. But you can only go to the second line, not the first.'

I followed him to the car. 'Second line?'

The air-conditioning inside the car was set on MEAT LOCKER. Spellman dropped the car into gear and we sped up the hill.

'We've set up three lines. The first is across the parking lot from their line of Winnebagos. The second is farther back, at the hill where you can just look down on the morgue. The outside perimeter is the command post on Hermitage Avenue.'

'The newspapers said the vans broke through a chain-link fence,' I said as he braked to a stop behind the command post.

He jerked the driver's side door open and hauled himself out. 'As usual, they got it wrong.'

I followed him as we stepped over to the van. Uniformed officers in blue Kevlar vests and helmets with face shields milled around, casually toting their assault rifles. Large block white letters – M-U-S-T – covered the backs of the vests. We walked around them and entered the van. Inside the cramped space, three men manned a bank of radios, with a detailed map of the area spread out on a small desk jammed into one end of the van.

'Any word?' Howard asked.

One of the men looked up from a row of blue digital lights. 'Nothing, Lieutenant. Been quiet for the last hour.'

'They actually came in through the General Hospital parking lot,' Spellman said, turning to me. 'The back of the hospital lot joins the morgue's parking lot right in front of a warehouse building. They drove the Winnebagos in a straight line down to the warehouse, then around the morgue right in front of it.'

Spellman pointed to the map. 'Right here, see?'

'Yeah.'

'I'll take you up there for just a minute, with a couple of ground rules.'

'Shoot.'

He lowered his voice. 'First, we haven't even let the family members get this close. So you haven't been here, right?'

'Right.'

'Second, we ain't even let the news media up here. So if word leaks about the physical setup, I'll know where it came from.'

'Wait, I can't—'

'And that will make me very unhappy,' he interrupted.

I stared at him a second. 'This is all off the record, Lieutenant. You have my word.'

'Let's go.'

We stepped out of the van into what seemed like an almost eerie silence. I expected helicopters buzzing overhead, the diesel roar of armored assault vehicles revving engines, the racking of shotguns.

But this was just plain quiet. No traffic, even. It gave me the creeps.

'Sergeant,' Howard said to one of the MUST members. 'We're going up the hill for a couple of minutes. We'll be right back.'

'Right, sir.'

We stepped off the asphalt at a military pace, with me a step or two behind Spellman, through the stone pillars on either side of the road, then into the morgue parking lot. There were dozens of century-old trees in the area, their arching canopies shielding us from the sun and casting long, deep shadows over the area. From where we were, you couldn't see much of anything. But then, as we approached the slight ridge in front of the morgue, where a line of Metro squad cars was parked, we could see the top of the building. Then a long row of RVs came into view. Howard motioned me to stop. I came up next to him. Ahead of us, maybe fifty officers lay hunkered down in flak jackets, helmets, assault rifles.

Fifty feet or so farther down, another line of squad cars faced off against the RVs not more than twenty yards distant.

'My God,' I said. 'They're right on top of each other.'

The line of Winnebagos was bumper-to-bumper in a half circle around the front of the morgue building from left to right, no more, I guessed, than twenty feet from the front door. The morgue sits on a bluff, with the Cumberland River acting as a barrier on the back. The Enochians, I realized, had taken up a virtually perfect and impregnable defensive line.

'It's going to be tough to get them out of there. That's why we keep talking.'

I looked at him. 'How long can it go on?'

Howard shrugged. 'Who the hell knows? They're not going anywhere. We're not going anywhere. It could last for months.'

'They'll starve!'

He shook his head. 'We're negotiating now to get supplies into the building. The Enochians will need food and water, too, you know.'

'You're not going to give it to them, are you?'

53

'If that's what it takes to keep them talking, we will. Hell, we'll have pizza delivered if it keeps the lines open.'

'I don't see anybody,' I said.

'They're all inside the RVs. Notice those little panels on the sides of the vehicles.'

I squinted and stared. 'Yeah, I can see them.'

'Far as we can tell, they're gun ports.'

'And it looks like they've sandbagged the tops of the RVs.'

'Right, and there're people lying down behind those bags with automatic weapons. Every once in a while one of them sticks a head up, or climbs down in a shift change. They've got the advantage on us, that's for sure. If we try a direct frontal assault, we'll get mowed down.'

'So get a freaking tank up here.'

'That's just what we're trying to avoid, Harry. But I will tell you this. If it comes down to blowing them out of there, we're prepared to do it.'

There was a military coldness and precision in his voice that I'd never heard before. What a hell of a lousy position to be in, though.

'Howard,' I said. 'This sucks.'

'I've got to get you back down the hill. They said they were sending out a negotiator at three. We're going to talk face-to-face for the first time. You mind walking down?'

'Of course not. So you're meeting the Reverend Woodrow Tyberious Hogg?'

'Hogg?' Howard asked. 'Hell, he ain't up there.'

'I thought—'

'These are his people. They're from his group, but he claims he hasn't got any control over 'em, and he certainly ain't up on the firing line himself. Hell, he's probably sitting in his mansion on Hillsboro Road in the Jacuzzi, watching all this on television just like everybody else.'

We walked back to the communications van and Howard radioed the officer at the roadblock that I'd be walking down alone. I didn't know if that was to protect me, or to make sure I didn't try to hang around.

'Hey, Lieutenant,' I called as I walked away. He turned in my direction.

'What'd you think about that country-music singer that got waxed last night?'

He waved his hand wearily. 'I haven't even had time to think about it. I gave that one to Fouch.'

So Reverend Woody had decided to skip the fireworks his own people had started. And Detective E. D. Fouch would be investigating the murder of Rebecca Gibson.

I had the sense life was going to get real interesting over the next few days.

Chapter 10

I threw my jacket over my shoulder and loosened my tie, then started up Broadway, in shock from what I'd seen. The walk back to my office seemed much shorter, as if I were unaware of what was going on around me or of time passing.

God, how weird.

I stayed in the office just long enough to throw the bricklayer's file, with an invoice and a copy of the videotape, into a briefcase and to verify that my answering machine was empty. Then it was back to the car and into the traffic.

There was a wreck on Broadway on the bridge over I-40 that was just being cleared away, so I missed the worst of the jam. Some poor sucker in an old Plymouth had turned left to get on the freeway, and what looked like a brand-new Toyota pickup – temporary tag still taped in the back window – had T-boned him on the passenger's side. Somebody's day was shot all to blazes.

Getting past that sucked up about ten minutes, so by the time I found a parking space on a side street off Demonbreun Street at the top of the hill next to Tourist Trap Row, my heart was beating pretty fast. I had less than an hour now before my appointment with Phil Anderson at the insurance company, the appointment that I hoped would bail me out financially.

So why was I running around working up a sweat on something I couldn't do anything about? I couldn't come up with an answer, so I just kept plowing ahead.

Jericho's was inside an old, renovated house that perched on the slight rise overlooking Broadway, next door to Gilley's. The building was two stories high, painted gray, with tasteful maroon shutters on tall, double-hung windows. The name was emblazoned across the front in bright pink neon, with red crucifixes blazing steadily on either side of the crackling light. In two display windows on either side of the door, mannequins dressed in the custom-made clothes stood on mute display.

It struck me as odd that there weren't a passel of news vans and cop cars outside here as well as down at the morgue. But then the Pentecostal Enochians had always been fairly discreet about owning the place. Unlike some other religious cults who'd opened up storefront retail operations in order to convert the infidels, the PEs had been content to make a fortune quietly.

I opened the door and stepped inside. The air was cool, dry, and scented with that stuffy textile odor I always associate with clothes stores or new carpet. An electronic bell chimed as I closed the door behind me.

The large front room was crowded with clothes racks, with shelves against the walls rising all the way to the top of what must have been at least a twelve-foot ceiling. Jackets, denim or leather mostly, hung on the clothes racks, while the shelves were piled with folded jeans.

And, God Almighty, clothes like I'd never seen before in my life. Pain quite literally came to my eyes and I found myself squinting to cut off some of the sensation. I pulled a stonewashed denim jacket off the rack and examined it.

Every seam had been studded with rhinestones, red and gold and blue and yellow and green. Light twinkled off chrome buttons. The damn thing had to weigh at least ten pounds. And on the back, an airbrushed painting of Christ on a Harley-Davidson, and the words BIKING FOR JESUS! airbrushed with a flourish across the shoulder panels. Jesus was outlined in sequins, and the tires of the bike were gold leaf, either fake or real; I couldn't tell which.

Then I saw the price tag: $1,200. Damn, I thought, better be real.

The rest of the stuff was in the same vein: airbrushed apostles at a long table staring beatifically at Christ as he spread his arms out to either side ($750); a sequined Virgin Mary staring up at a rhinestoned Christ on the cross ($900); and, of course, Christ in the clouds with his arms around *Ail-vis* as the two stare down at a miniature stylized rendition of mourners filing past the grave at Graceland ($1,400). The painted title above that one read THE KING MEETS THE KING.

You know, one of these days, a few centuries down the road, archaeologists will excavate the ruins of Nashville, Tennessee, and they'll come across this place. And they're going to think we were *all* like this.

I shook my head in wonder. As far as I was concerned, the success of this venture only validated my long-held belief that there is a significant portion of the populace whose wallets are bigger than their brains.

Other racks had clothes decorated in a more secular fashion. If I wanted, for instance, a six-hundred-dollar jacket with an airbrushed George Jones or a Hank Williams, Jr, or a Tammy Wynette, this was the place to get it.

A young woman with flowing black hair, wearing a floor-length paisley granny dress and sandals, stepped out from behind a curtained door at the other end of the room next to the counter and cash register. She looked to be early twenties at the most, with the glazed look that marks Nashville's considerable population of hippie wannabes.

'Can I help you?'

'Yeah,' I said. 'I'd like to see one of these jackets with Garth Brooks on it.'

'Oh,' she said, then let loose with a long sigh. 'We had one with Garth on it, but his people got a court order and made us quit selling them. Said the image of his face was his property and we couldn't use it. He's the only one who's ever complained. Most stars are proud to be on a Jericho's jacket.'

'Maybe you should have offered him a royalty,' I suggested.

'Naw, not worth it.'

I wandered between a couple of racks casually, fingering the clothes as the young woman watched me. We were the only two in the store, as far as I could tell. Of course, at these prices you didn't need a high customer volume.

'This stuff is really nice,' I said, hoping God wouldn't strike me down for bearing false witness. 'Who does it? The custom artwork, I mean.'

'Oh, we have a number of artists who create for us.'

'Hmm, they don't sign their work, though.'

'Most of them figure it's their way of doing God's work. They don't want any recognition. It's all His glory anyway, right?'

'Yeah,' I agreed. 'I've always been curious about this place, but never stopped in before. How long's it been around?'

She turned a blank look on me. 'I've been here almost two years. I don't know how long it was here before that.'

This young woman struck me as the kind of person a cult recruiter would look at and the words *Dead Meat* would come to mind.

I noticed a small, white plastic bin on the counter next to the cash register. Tucked inside the bin was a stack of leaflets. I walked over and picked one up, then unfolded it. It was an eight-and-a-half-by-eleven-inch sheet, tri-folded, printed in red ink. The headline across the top read ARE MASONS THE TOOL OF THE DEVIL?

59

The rest of the pamphlet was filled with a diatribe about how every evil in the world was perpetrated by the Masonic conspiracy in conjunction with the Illuminati and the Trilateral Commission, or some such nonsense.

I suppressed a chuckle. I always thought the Masons were those fat, middle-aged, balding guys who wore sequined fezzes and clown suits and rode miniature motorcycles in the Christmas parade and collected money for underprivileged kids. Or were those the Shriners? Hell, I always mix them up. In any case, it's hard for me to imagine either of them being a tool of the Antichrist.

When I turned back after scanning the paper, she was staring at me intently.

'What's your name?' I asked.

'Charlotte.'

'Hi, Charlotte. I'm Harry. You believe all this?'

She nodded her head. 'You should, too.'

'Tell me, Charlotte, who owns this place?'

Her expression shifted instantly to one of distrust, maybe mixed in with a healthy dose of pissed off.

'Who are you?' she said, sharp now.

'I'm nobody. Just curious, that's all. Where can I find Brother Hogg?'

Boy, that did it. Her eyes darkened; that deer-in-the-headlights look was gone, replaced by that of a dedicated soldier of the cross.

'You're a reporter, aren't you?'

'Everybody keeps accusing me of being a reporter today,' I said. 'No, Charlotte. I'm not a reporter. I just want to talk to Hogg.'

'I'm going to have to ask you to leave.'

'Oh, c'mon, Charlotte, lighten up. I might buy something.'

'I said *leave*,' she repeated, this time her voice about twenty percent louder than before. I saw a shuffle in the curtain, and two guys stepped out from the same room where Charlotte had been. They wore white T-shirts that let me know in no uncertain terms how much they could bench-press. One had hair the color and length of a lion's mane, with a short, well-trimmed reddish beard. The other was just plain dark and looked about as mean as a snake.

'Gee, I'm sorry if I upset you.'

'Goodbye, sir,' she said, one last time.

I stepped to the door and opened it, then turned back to her for a moment. She really was quite lovely; what a waste.

'See you guys around,' I said.

So *discreet* was apparently an understatement. The Pentecostal Enochians were not only disinclined to advertise their ownership of Jericho's, they were liable to pummel you to goo if you asked too many questions.

I cut over to Church Street, crossed the Viaduct just before you get to the Downtown YMCA building, then left again and found a parking space a couple of blocks down on the street in front of the Tennessee Workmen's Protective Association Building.

Phil Anderson's office was on the fourth floor, with a window that looked out over Capitol Hill and toward North Nashville. The blazing red Bruton Snuff sign over the U.S. Tobacco Company glowed like a landmark in the deepening afternoon shadows. Farther north, the traffic was just beginning to back up in the northbound lanes of I-65.

I sat in the reception area outside a bank of offices for about ten minutes. Once Phil saw the videotape of the Shaquille O'Neal of the bricklaying set, I was going to be an insider here. I could feel it. I'd do a written report once Phil told me what he wanted to see in it, and I'd be available for court testimony if civil suit or prosecution arose; at my customary fee, of course.

All in all, not a bad gig. I felt pretty good.

A long line of beige-colored metal doors ran down the hall to my right, past the middle-aged secretary whose fingers buzzed away on a word processor. One of the doors flew open and an imposing Phil Anderson stepped out. I'm about six feet tall and have a tough time maintaining one sixty. Phil's got at least four inches and a hundred pounds on me, and he moves like a hyperactive kid who forgot his Ritalin.

'Harry, you rascal, how are you?' he demanded in his booming voice. The secretary'd heard it before. She never broke rhythm on the keys.

'Fine, Phil, good to see you.' I stuck out my hand and he jerked it like a pump handle. A long lock of shiny brown hair drooped down over his forehead, and great bags hung under his eyes. I realized then where I'd seen him before; he's what Thomas Wolfe would have looked like if he'd lived into his late forties and spent too much time on the couch with a six-pack and a case of potato chips.

'C'mon down here. We've got a VCR and a monitor in the conference room. A couple of the other guys want to see this

61

tape, too.' He turned to the secretary. 'Jane Ellen, call Rick and Steve and tell 'em Harry's here.'

The secretary's left hand picked up the telephone handset while – I swear it's true – her right hand kept typing, covering both sides of the keyboard with one hand. Never missed a beat. Talk about a focused woman.

We walked down the carpeted hall into a large conference room with a rectangular table that would have seated about twenty people. At the other end, a big JVC monitor and tape player sat on a portable gray metal wheeled rack.

I sat my briefcase down on the table and opened it. 'I went ahead and got an invoice ready, Phil. I ran into some pretty sizeable expenses, equipment rental, mileage. No hotel bill, though. I slept in a van.'

'No problemo, amigo,' he said from the other end of the room as he turned on the monitor. 'We'll take care of it right after the meeting.'

I took out the videotape and slid it down the length of polished tabletop. The door opened behind me and two other guys stepped in, both in suits, striped power ties, the whole corporate costume.

'Harry, meet Rick Harvey and Steve White. They're the field investigators who were assigned to this case.'

Great, I thought, so they already hate me. I went out and did their job after they screwed up. May as well make the best of it.

'Hi, Harry James Denton,' I said cordially, hand extended. 'Glad to meet you.'

We did the corporate introduction ritual and immediately afterward I forgot which was which. They were both midtwenties, clean, well-groomed, polished. Probably applied to the FBI Academy and didn't get in.

'How much did you say you got, Harry?'

I settled into a seat and tried to relax. 'Little over an hour's worth of him actually out of the chair. I spent a week up there staking the guy out. It took a change in the weather to get him on his feet.'

'Oh,' one of the investigator clones said, 'so that explains why it was so easy.'

'It wasn't *that* easy,' I answered. 'I'm still scratching the chigger bites from laying in the grass for so long.'

'Yeah,' the other one said, his voice a caricature of a cop movie. 'Stakeout's a bitch, all right.'

Right, I thought. Barney Fife in a suit and tie. Guy probably carries a bullet in his shirt pocket.

Phil popped the tape in and started it. Immediately the back-yard in Louisville jumped on the screen, with the bricklayer in the wheelchair off to the side watching the action. The other adult male and the teenage boy passed the ball around, shot a few. Then the bricklayer held the ball.

I'd seen it all before, so watched the other three to check the look on their faces when the guy jumped out of the wheelchair. When it happened, the two young suits set their jaws and tucked their chins down toward their chests. This was, after all, the tape they were supposed to have produced.

Phil, however, howled like a true basketball fan, especially when the bricklayer did his three-sixty and slam-dunked the ball.

'Guy's good, ain't he, fellas?' Phil commented, looking around at his two investigators. ''At's a dang fine jump shot, too.' I turned back to the screen, trying hard to disappear.

We sat there for the better part of the next hour, until finally the bricklayer's wife came to the sliding-glass door, saw her husband bouncing around, and chewed his butt so hard the tiny video microphone caught parts of it. His shoulders slumped and all three men, caught and scolded, walked back inside. We saw the sliding-glass door slam shut and then the slide of drapes as the door was covered up.

'Holy cow, look!' Phil called. 'He left his durn wheelchair outside.'

I grinned. 'Yeah, just watch.'

In a moment the drapes were pulled again and the door slid open. The bricklayer ran back outside sheepishly, flopped down in the chair, then strapped himself in. As the wife stood there with her hands on her hips, locked and loaded in the pissed-off position, the poor guy drove his wheelchair back into the house.

Even the two suits behind me at the table were laughing now. Phil slapped the table hard and shook his head from side to side, his massive cheeks shaking with laughter.

'Oh, boy,' he sputtered. 'This is great. We not only got him, we've nailed his wife and the whole durn family for conspiracy to defraud. Harry, you deserve an Oscar for this one.'

'Glad you like it,' I said. 'I haven't prepared a written report, but will be glad to if you'll tell me what form you need it to take. I can also be available for affidavits or court testimony if needed.'

'You think legal'll turn this over to the DA?' one of the suits asked.

'Well, buddies, this is some pretty dang blatant fraud going on here,' Phil said. 'I ain't seen nothing like this in a long time.'

'It's a good one all right,' I said, pulling my invoice out of the briefcase. 'You got the guy dead to rights.'

'Heckfire, maybe the guy'll move to California and try out for the Lakers,' Phil said as I slid the invoice across the table.

He opened the envelope and unfolded my bill, then let out a long whistle. 'Dadgum, Harry, this is a pretty good hit here. *Five thousand for a week's work?*'

One of the young suits let out a disgusted snort, like the insurance company was some kind of benevolent organization that was always being taken advantage of.

'My deal with you was that if I didn't get the evidence, you paid nothing, and if I did, you paid double my normal rate as a bonus.'

'Well, what in the hell's your normal rate?'

'Four hundred a day plus expenses,' I said. 'On par with the rest of the industry. Five days, plus mileage, expenses, and the videotape charge. And you got a twenty-four-hour day out of me, rather than the standard ten.'

I fought my normal codependent urge to seek approval by lowering the bill.

'Phil, when you consider what I've saved you by not having to pay this joker disability for the rest of his life – not to mention scaring off other people who'd like to try the same thing – my fee's a pretty good deal.'

'Yeah, well, I just hope I can get this by accounting.' His voice had dropped, in tone and volume, and became filled with what he hoped I'd interpret as concern. Nice act.

'Why don't I touch base with you tomorrow and see how it's going,' I suggested, standing up. 'I can provide you with receipts and further documentation if you need it.'

Then I tightened my gut and let fly with the next one. 'How long do you think it'll take your accounting department to cut the check.'

'Oh,' he drawled. 'They're pretty quick. Generally takes about forty-five days, maybe sixty if they get backed up.'

I swallowed hard; sixty days, assuming they'd pay the bill at all. In sixty days, they'd have to send the check to me in care of the homeless shelter. There was no way I could float that long.

I got this real bad taste in the back of my mouth.

'I'm sorry, Phil, but I'm afraid I'm not comfortable with that. I'm a small, one-man operation. Sixty days is going to cause me some real cash-flow problems. I was thinking more along the lines of ten days.'

Phil shrugged his shoulders. 'Nothing I can do about it, buddy. Procedure . . . It takes as long as it takes.'

Out of the corner of my eye, I could see the two suits grinning. You little bastards, I thought, you'd probably scream like scalded dogs if your paycheck was an hour late.

What could I do? Powerless little man confronts faceless corporate bureaucracy. Powerless little man goes down the dumper. I could be a real jerk and demand the tape back, but then I'd lose the account forever.

Next thing I know, I'm on the elevator, jammed in next to a crowd of exiting employees at five-thirty, fuming, frustrated, hacked off once again. So much for this being a glamorous business. Wonder how Doghouse Riley did it all those years?

I stepped out onto the sidewalk, amid the throng of people heading back to the parking lots to begin the long commute home. I wondered where the hell next month's rent was coming from.

'Damn it,' I muttered. Then I saw it. A wire-mesh trash basket on the sidewalk about three feet high, one of those heavy-gauge metal city-owned types with a black-and-white sign on it that said PLEASE DON'T LITTER.

I reared back and kicked the shit out of it, yelped, then began the long limp back to my car.

Chapter 11

I was lower than whale effluent. I couldn't even bear to go back to the office. I cranked up the Mazda and made my by now ritual passage in front of the police barricades before heading over the river into East Nashville. Being preoccupied with money, among other things, I remembered that I was cashless. There was a drive-up ATM machine at the bank on the right, so I pulled in and withdrew a twenty; one of the last, few dwindling times I'd be able to, I feared.

Going home alone to my apartment was equally unappetizing as spending more time in my office. It was still early enough in the year for the sun to set early, but the darkness was no longer that oppressively heavy blanket that sends everyone to bed by ten. I needed to be around some people that I wasn't in conflict with, so just past the Earl Scheib Body Shop, I turned in to the parking lot of Mrs Lee's.

Ever since I moved to East Nashville, following the precipitous drop in lifestyle that accompanied my getting fired from the newspaper and subsequently divorced, Mrs Lee had become a kind of surrogate parent to me. My own parents retired to Hawaii a year or two before my divorce, and apart from occasional phone calls and the obligatory holiday visits, we don't see each other that much anymore. Mrs Lee's Hunan Chinese restaurant had become my refuge, despite the fact that Mrs Lee exhibited few nurturing instincts toward me. Hell, maybe it was just that she remembered my name, which in this day and age is nothing short of remarkable.

Excuse me. I guess I am feeling sorry for myself. On top of that, my toe still hurts where I kicked the wire trash barrel.

I parked next to an enormous GMC pickup truck with a rack of emergency lights on the top, recognized it, and smiled.

'Well, look who's here,' I said as the heavy glass doors of the restaurant hissed shut behind me. Lonnie looked up from his disposable plate – everything in Mrs Lee's was throwaway except the food – and shook his head.

'Look what the cat drug in.'

'Let me get a plate,' I said. 'I'll join you.'

I walked up to the counter just as Mrs Lee was turning around from the window into the kitchen with a scowl on her face.

'Gweat,' she said, pointing to Lonnie. 'Fust him, now you. You two give my prace a bad name. Too many car wepossess—' She stumbled. 'Car we—'

'Now why would car repossessors give your place a bad name?'

'This neighborhood,' she barked. 'People afraid to come heah. Think you pick they cars up.'

'Now, darling, that says more about the neighborhood than it does about us, doesn't it?'

She half smiled at me. 'Smaht-butt. What you want tonight? Let me guess. Szechuan chicken.'

'Unless you're sold out.'

'Hah!' She turned to the window and yelled something to her husband in rapid-fire Chinese. At least I think that's what it was; for all I knew, it could have been Venusian.

I laid my twenty on the counter and turned back to the tables. Lonnie had a folded afternoon newspaper held out in front of him as he ate absentmindedly. I stood there a moment, waiting. It'd been a roller-coaster ride of a day, and I was glad it was nearly over.

'Heah you go, mistah investigatah,' Mrs Lee said, sliding the white Styrofoam plate across the counter to me. She grabbed the twenty and returned sixteen bucks in change. One of the things I loved about Mrs Lee's was you got more food than anyone could possibly eat for four dollars.

'How's Mary?' I asked, gathering up little packs of soy sauce and a plastic fork.

'You doan worry about Mary,' she instructed. 'Mary not you problem.'

Mary was Mrs Lee's high-school-senior daughter; gorgeous, honor student, sweet, untouched. Hell, I'd keep her away from me, too. I'd tried over the last couple of years not to let my affection and admiration for her grow into anything more inappropriate than necessary.

'Tell her I said hi.'

I walked over to the table and slid down in front of Lonnie. He put down the newspaper and folded his arms across his chest. I raked up a forkful of rice, steaming vegetables, and chicken laced with red peppers and hot oil. As soon as it hit my mouth everything was right in the world, at least temporarily.

'So what's happening, dude?'

'Well,' I snarfled, mouth full of food, 'let's see. My girlfriend's a hostage, my bank account's empty, my clients won't pay me. On top of that, I don't know where the rent's coming from next month on either my apartment or my office. Otherwise, life's just a regular hoot and a holler.'

'You know, Harry,' Lonnie drawled, 'you're getting to have a regular attitude problem.'

'I really am worried about her,' I said, real serious and low. 'Kinda weird.'

'Talking about it all the time ain't going to do any good.'

'You remind me of when I was a kid and I'd fall down and bust a knee open or something and my father would say, "Don't cry." And I'd say, "But, Daddy, it hurts," and he'd say, "Well, just don't feel it, son." Just don't feel it.'

'Good advice, you ask me.'

A piece of a red chili pepper hit the back of my throat, a feeling I'd imagine was comparable only to accidentally swallowing a hot cigarette ash. I started choking and reached for the glass of ice water. Sweat broke out over my upper lip.

'Say,' I said when I'd recovered my composure, 'you haven't got a car or two I can pick up, have you? I could use the quick cash.'

'I lost the bank,' Lonnie said quietly.

I stared at him. 'What do you mean, you lost the bank? Who loses a bank?'

'Asshole, I didn't mean I *lost* it, lost it. I meant they're not my clients anymore.'

I set my fork down in my plate. The Nashville Merchants Bank had been Lonnie's main customer for years. He'd repossessed maybe three thousand cars for them.

'What happened?'

'They were bought by that bank in Virginia.'

'Oh yeah, I read about that.' Merchants was one of the last two locally owned banks in the city; the rest had been swallowed up in corporate takeovers. This just isn't a small town anymore.

'So they brought in new management.'

'Well, they still got to repossess cars, don't they?'

'Sure, they just aren't going to have me do it for them. You know how it is when new bosses come in. They got to change everything just to mark their territory. Sort of like a dog pissing on a bush.'

'Sounds like a done deal,' I said.

'It is. Nothing I can do about it.'

I crammed in another mouthful. 'You going to be okay?' A trickle of hot oil leaked out the side of my mouth. One of the niceties about my relationship with Lonnie was that table manners played absolutely no part in anything. One of those male-bonding concepts, I guess.

'Yeah,' he said wearily. 'Business had dried up over the past few months anyway. Times're getting better; people are making their car payments.'

'Times are getting better?' I asked, my mouth open. 'Damn, couldn't tell it by me.'

Lonnie grinned. 'Well, they are. Besides, I could use a little downtime. I got some money saved up. My other clients'll feed me a couple of cars a week, just to keep my hand in. Won't be nothing like the old days, though. Back when we were picking up two or three a night. Thought I was going to run my ass off back then.'

'Ah, the good old days of economic collapse.'

'Got that right. Besides, I'm working on a deal with a leasing company that may work out. Leased vehicles have to be repo'd, too, you know.' He unfolded the newspaper and held the front page toward me. 'See the latest?'

CULT LEADER NOT IN CONTROL the headline read.

'What the hell?' I reached over and took the newspaper out of his hand, then scanned the article. The Reverend Woodrow Tyberious Hogg was now claiming he was not in control of his followers, that in their zeal and religious fervor, they had surrounded the morgue on their own volition.

I looked up. 'You buy this shit?'

'That Hogg's not in control?'

'Yeah.'

Lonnie chuckled. 'Right, and the Pope don't wear a funny hat. The guy's just trying to keep his legal problems to a minimum. It's like if Koresh had been outside the compound in Waco going: "Hey, it's not *my* problem those people have locked themselves in there with all those guns." '

I read on. Hogg had held a press conference by phone from his walled estate just in time to make the afternoon paper deadline. His wife died of a stroke, he said, and this had been verified from the group's own doctor. Rumors of drug and alcohol abuse, and especially the vile rumors about suicide or even murder, were despicable and the work of the devil's own children seeking to stay the hand of God in the world.

'Guy's a paranoid psychotic,' I said offhandedly.

'Rooney tunes,' Lonnie said.

'I went down there today,' I said, distracted as I scanned the rest of the article. A sidebar related the history of hostage situations over the past decade or so. It was not an upbeat tale.

Lonnie cocked an eyebrow. 'Yeah,' I said. 'Talked to Howard Spellman. He's in charge of the hostage negotiations.'

'We're screwed now,' Lonnie said. 'Hang it up.'

I glared over the top of the paper. 'That was uncalled for. Spellman's not so bad, once one gets used to him,' I said, forcing a stiffness into my voice.

'A horsewhipping's not so bad, once one gets used to it,' he answered, mimicking my formality and raising his paper cup in a mock toast.

I looked down at the paper, below the fold to the second lead story. 'You see this?' I asked. 'They're looking for Slim Gibson in the Rebecca Gibson murder.'

'Yeah, I saw.'

'Police are searching,' I read aloud, 'for Randall J. (Slim) Gibson, thirty-seven, for questioning in the bludgeoning death of country-music singer Rebecca Gibson. Gibson, thirty-five, was found beaten to death in the bedroom of her Bellevue home at approximately four-twenty Monday morning. A police spokesman said the star returned from playing a concert with her ex-husband and two other musicians at approximately two-thirty a.m.'

'Nasty business,' Lonnie said. 'You ever seen anybody beaten to death?'

I shook my head.

'It's not pretty,' he continued. 'I hear it's a helluva lot of work, too. It ain't easy to beat a full-grown human being to death. They don't take kindly to it.'

I folded the paper in front of me. 'I sure as hell wouldn't.' I scraped up the last of my Szechuan chicken into a scrambled puddle of goop and swallowed it whole.

'Slim's partner, Ray, came over to my office today. Said Slim's running kind of scared. I advised him to check in. The cops have to come after him, it's going to look real bad.'

'If that article's true, he's in deep sewage now. You know as well as I do that when the police say they want you just for questioning, that means your ass is rolled, floured, and deep-fat-fried.'

'Ray wanted me to help him, but I'm damned if I know what to do,' I said.

'Ain't nothing you can do,' Lonnie agreed.

'Besides that,' I added, 'they can't afford me anyway.'

'Jeez, and all this time I thought you were a cheap date.'

Mrs Hawkins, my seventy-something, hard-of-hearing little old landlady, was already locked in her bottom half of the house by the time I got home. It was dark, but still refreshingly warm after the long winter. I parked in the back, beside the rickety black metal staircase that led up to my attic apartment, then trudged upstairs to settle in for the night.

The necktie had already been loosened after my disastrous meeting at the insurance company, but now it was off and flung onto the bed before I even got my jacket off. I changed into a pair of jeans and an old flannel shirt, then flipped through the television listings to see if there was anything worth watching.

I realized, as I stood there desperately scanning the cable listings, how empty my evenings were without her. Before Marsha, my evenings were equally empty, but they didn't feel that way.

I settled back in the chair next to my bed and pointed the clicker at the TV. I surfed around the early-evening stuff, pausing to watch a new Mary Chapin Carpenter video on Country Music Television, then jumping over to Comedy Central.

'Make me laugh, damn you,' I muttered to the stand-up comic who appeared onscreen.

When the hell is she going to call? I wondered. On the local stations, there was nothing but a brief recap of the morgue situation, then the regular evening stuff. For Marsha, it would be just another quiet evening down in the bunker.

I turned to the phone on my nightstand by the bed. 'Ring, damn you,' I demanded. That's when I noticed the blinking red light on the answering machine. I pushed the mute button on the remote control.

'Aw, hell,' I exclaimed, figuring I'd probably missed her call.

I pushed the button on the machine. The computer voice came on: 'Hello, you have *one* message. . . .'

Then a short beat, followed by Ray O'Dell's frantic voice: 'Harry! Where you at, Harry? They done arrested Slim, man! They done charged him with killing that bitch! Can you believe that shit? Call me, man, just as quick as you get home!'

There was a breathless pause for a second, followed by Ray's voice again leaving me a number to call.

I mumbled another obscenity, pointed the clicker at the TV, and unmuted it. Hysterical laughter erupted from the set.

72

Presumably the comedian had just told the funniest damn joke of the entire damn century.

And I'd missed the punch line again.

Chapter 12

I slipped the car into a space on Seventh Avenue just across
Church Street from my office. I walked back across Church, down
the hill toward Broadway, and stepped up into the alcove that led
up to the front door of my office building. It was eight-thirty at
night, and there was already a bundled-up wino cradling a bottle
of Wild Irish Rose sleeping next to the door. He stirred uneasily,
caressing his bottle, as I hit the step in front of him.

'Just going into my office,' I said soothingly. 'You go back to
sleep.'

He mumbled something and rolled over as I struggled in the
dim light to get the key in the lock.

The hall lights were off, the hallway illuminated only by the
glowing red Exit sign at the other end. The stairway to my left
had a silver cast to it from the streetlights outside shining through
a dirty window at the landing. I hit the stairs two at a time, got
to the landing, then turned back to my left and hopped up the
last half of the flight.

'That you, Harry?' a voice boomed from my right, down the
hall from my office.

'Yeah, Ray,' I called. 'On my way.'

Ray and Slim's office door was open, with the muted light from
a shaded lamp barely illuminating the end of the hallway. I
stopped at the door and looked in. Their office was bigger than
mine, but still consisted of only one room jammed with file cabinets and desks. Ray sat at one of the desks, his feet up, a large
acoustic guitar on his lap. His right arm draped loosely over the
body of the guitar, his left hand dangling off the side of the chair.

'You okay?' I asked, wondering if he was drunk, stoned,
shocked, or all of the above.

'Yeah, I guess,' he said.

I sat on the edge of one of the desks. 'When did they arrest
him?'

'About six.'

'They chase him down?'

'No.' The chair creaked loudly as Ray shifted his weight. 'I got hold of him and told him what you said. He called the detective in charge and went on down there. He said they just asked him a few questions, then Miranda'd him, then booked him.'

'What did Slim do?'

'Well, it appears he had the good sense to shut his mouth at that point. They let him call me so I'd know what was going on.'

'What are they holding him on?'

'Murder, but I don't know what degree. Arraignment's at nine in the morning.'

'No,' I said. 'Not arraignment. They'll have to have a preliminary hearing and a bond hearing first. That's when you get the first indication of how strong the DA's case is.'

Ray stared at me over the honey-colored wood of his guitar. 'Well,' I asked, 'how strong is it?'

'I don't know.'

I figured if his closest buddy and business partner wasn't jumping up to defend his honor, that was a real bad sign. 'Okay, next step is to find him a lawyer. Preferably an experienced one.'

'Yeah.' Ray seemed almost dazed.

'You guys got any money?'

Ray stood up and leaned the guitar against the wall, its neck balanced precariously on the shiny paint. He paced back and forth in the limited space between the desk and a window overlooking Seventh Avenue.

'Not much.'

'That's bad. Justice costs money.'

'We've got Roger Vaden. He handles all our contracts and does our books, what books we have.'

I'd heard of Roger Vaden. He was an entertainment attorney, a reputable one, but he wasn't the guy to get you off a murder charge.

'That'll do for tomorrow,' I said. 'But you'll need a criminal attorney on this one, Ray.'

Ray stared out of the window, his head leaning against the dirty glass. 'Slim's got his faults, Harry. I don't think he killed Becca.'

He turned and looked at me. 'But he sure as hell had reason to. That woman was a snake, Harry.'

I took that to mean that when the divorce came down, Ray'd been on Slim's side. I'd learned from painful experience that everyone feels compelled to take sides in a divorce. There were people I'd considered good friends, only to learn they wouldn't take my calls after Elaine and I split.

'Tell me about her,' I said.

'Rebecca Gibson was a Thoroughbred. Frisky, fast, creative. Could put a song together better than anybody I ever knew, me and Slim included. But she was unpredictable. You never knew what was going through her. All you could count on was that sooner or later she was going to explode.'

'She was the volatile one and Slim was the steady, patient type?'

'Most of the time,' he said, crossing the office and stuffing his hands in his back pockets. 'But she liked to pick at him, and it got her goat when she'd go to work on him and he wouldn't fight back. She'd nag and pick at him until he just couldn't take it anymore. Then ol' Slim'd pop his cork. Next thing you know, you got a domestic-disturbance call in the middle of the night.'

Damn, I thought, and the DA would be glad to mention each and every one of them to a jury, as long as the judge would let him.

'He ever hit her?'

Ray hung his head. 'Time or two. Hell, she hit back, though.'

'How long were they married?'

'Almost nine years. The last straw came when she booked a tour without him. Didn't even tell him about it. They were trying to make it as singing partners, working the nightclubs and the honky-tonks for a grand or two a night. She did a three-day gig down in San Antonio without even letting him know where she'd be. When she got back, Slim was gone. Just packed his shit and left.'

'Who filed for the divorce?'

Ray shook his head. 'I don't know. It just happened. I think she did, but I'm not sure.'

'What happened to all the songs they wrote together?'

'Most of 'em were sold to different publishers. This was back before me and Slim formed CKM.'

'CKM?'

'Cockroach Killer Music,' Ray said, grinning. His right index finger motioned towards the floor as his other hand pulled his left trouser leg up a couple of inches. He wore a pair of shiny gray snakeskin boots that had the sharpest pair of pointed toes I'd ever seen on human footwear.

'They get in the corners real good,' he added. 'Decided to name our publishing company after them.'

I smiled back at him. 'Okay, CKM it is. Does Rebecca own any part of CKM?'

'No, but we've published a lot of her songs. Even had a couple of them recorded. But the truth is, Harry, me and Slim have been struggling for a long time. On the other hand, Rebecca's career was about to take off. She was going to be up there with Reba and Dolly, Tricia, and Kathy and the rest.'

'Professional jealousy, then, right?'

'Yeah, that's what them bozos down at the courthouse are figuring. I know it. But you see, it don't make any sense. We've published enough of her songs that when she hits big, we're going to ride along with her at least a little ways, and so is everybody else who's ever worked with her. It's a gravy train, man. That's the music business. Most of the time, fame's a short ride. But when you're on it, it's a holler a minute.'

I pushed one of the chairs out from under a desk with my foot and plopped down on it. I interlaced my fingers behind my head and leaned way back, staring at the dirty acoustic ceiling tiles.

'So then the question remains – if Slim didn't kill his ex-wife, who did?'

'That's why I called you, Harry.'

My feet dropped to the floor, and I shot up in the chair. 'Oh, no, Ray, I—'

'Aw, c'mon, Harry, he needs your help.'

'I'm booked up right now,' I said. I thought of Marsha again and forced myself to bring her face into focus. Funny how when people are gone, it's not very long before you have to struggle to remember what they look like.

What am I talking about, I yelled inside my head, *she's not dead*!

'I know it's a lot to ask,' Ray pleaded. 'If it's the money you're worried about, we can pay you over time.'

'It's not the—' I stopped. Wait a minute, what was I saying? I didn't come into this office every day just because I thought it was a neat place to be. Of course it's the money. At least, part of it is. And I knew that if I took the job, it would be forever before they paid me, if they ever did. That was time and energy that could best be put to hustling clients with ready cash.

On the other hand, it's Slim. And right now he's sitting in a cell.

'I've just got too much going on right now.'

Ray resorted to the last refuge of the desperate. He rolled his lower lip out and scrunched his eyes together.

'Aw, c'mon, Harry,' he drawled. 'Please . . .'

It was another thirty minutes before I managed to talk myself free of Ray O'Dell's clutches. I anguished for them both. Obviously Ray was in acute distress over his partner and friend's fate. And I liked Slim enough, even though I didn't know him all that well.

Mainly, I just couldn't handle it. I was already going at life like killing rats. I had no reserves left, nothing to draw on.

No blinking red light on my answering machine, so if Marsha tried to call, she'd hung up. One of these days, I'm going to get an answering machine with built-in caller ID so I can know who the hang-ups are. Imagine the look on some poor sucker's face when I call him back and demand to know why the hell he hung up on me.

Some days you eat the bear; other days the bear eats you. This was one of those few rare days when I felt like I'd managed to fight the bear to a begrudging draw. I took a quick shower, dried my hair, and had just settled into bed with my history-of-jazz paperback when the phone rang.

'Yeah?' I said into the phone, fumbling with the mute button.

'You're home,' she said.

'Damn it,' I said, then let out a long sigh. 'I missed you earlier, didn't I?'

''S okay. Gave me a chance to wait until I could get back here alone.'

'How are you, lady? This's your third night.'

'Don't remind me. I'm okay, but we're all getting on each other's nerves a bit. The food's running low, too. We're all tired of eating out of cans anyway.'

I sat up in bed. 'Wait a minute. You telling me you haven't got enough food down there?'

'We're okay for another day or so. We've let the hostage negotiators know. They're working out the details to have provisions passed through the lines.'

'I know.'

'You know? How do you know that?'

I bit my lower lip. 'I was down there today. Howard let me through the lines.'

'Harry, what the hell did you think you were doing? I assume you had to tell Spellman what vested interest you had in visiting the trenches.'

'Marsha,' I said, hesitating for a moment. 'They all knew anyway.'

There was a long, static-filled silence over the cellular phone. 'Oh,' she said.

'Who cares? We're both single. Nothing to be ashamed of, right?

It's not like we're running around on our spouses or anything. I don't have anything to be ashamed of. Do you?'

'Of course not,' she snapped. 'It's just that ... Well, I've just never, well, not never, but it's been a long time since I've been involved with anyone so, so *publicly.*'

'Hey, screw 'em if they can't take a joke, right?'

She sighed. 'I guess so.'

'So what's the latest? There hasn't been much new on the news programs.'

'The PEs have modified their position. They're willing to let us take X-rays, do a visual and cavity examination, and take tissue and fluid samples for analysis. But they still don't want us cutting her open.'

'So, can you guys live with that?'

'Law's pretty clear. In all cases of suspicious death, you have to do an autopsy. But,' she added, 'Spellman's taking it to the state Attorney General's Office tomorrow morning for an opinion. The Pentecostal Enochians want to bargain for amnesty as well.'

'And in the meantime you all just sit there.'

'That's about it. We found one of those little battery-powered pocket TVs in Dr Henry's office. We charged it up in the cooler, so at least we can watch the news.'

I laughed. 'I can just imagine five people huddled around a three-inch pocket TV.'

Marsha laughed quietly. 'I've seen so many episodes of *Cheers*, I've got the hots for Norm Peterson. C'mon, babe, I'm tired of talking about me. What's going on in your life?'

'I met with Phil Anderson today over at the insurance company.'

'Yeah? What happened?'

I recounted the whole, frustrating story, then segued into Slim's arrest.

'You going to get involved?' she asked.

'No. I'm too preoccupied. With you, with my cash situation. It's just not a good time.'

'Can I give a little advice, darling?'

'Sure, of course.'

'You're not going to do anything but drive yourself and me nuts, not to mention hacking off the entire Metro Nashville Police Department, if you persist in trying to figure out some way to be a hero in all this.'

'That's not what I'm—'

'I know. I didn't mean it like that. But there is *really* nothing you can do, Harry. We just have to sit tight. And there's probably nothing you can do about the insurance money as well. So for the sake of your blood pressure and my nerves, why don't you find something to take your mind off all this?'

There was a ripple of an audio static wave in the phone, and I knew her batteries were on the way out.

'I'll give it some thought,' I said.

'You do that. In the meantime I'm going to make my last cup of herbal tea and stretch out on my office couch. If nothing else, the last few days have sure given me a chance to catch up on my paperwork.'

There was a pop in the phone, and the signal dropped out for just a second, then came back. 'Hey, listen,' I yelled into the phone, like that would do some good. 'Call me tomorrow.'

'Goo—' Hiss, pop. Dial tone.

I hung up the phone and leaned back into the pillow. On the muted television, a silent anchorman's image was replaced by footage taken at the police station earlier this evening. On the tape, Slim Gibson was standing before a magistrate, hands cuffed, head down, bathed in a corona of television lights.

What the hell, I thought. Maybe she's right. I reached over and grabbed a notepad out of my shirt pocket and flipped to the last page, then dialed the number written on it.

'Ray?' I asked, when a voice answered. 'What time did you say that hearing was?'

Chapter 13

High-profile murders always seem to draw high-profile crowds. The highest-rated TV reporter in the city was jammed into the cramped hallway in front of the courtroom in the Criminal Justice Center as fans, hangers-on, spectators, musicians, cops, lawyers, and about fifty other people jostled for a spot.

Over the background din, I could hear her delivering her live remote from the courthouse for the morning news:

'Yes, Bob,' she said brightly, 'the courthouse hallways are indeed packed as country-music fans, friends, family members, and onlookers struggle to get into the courtroom to see the man accused of murdering one of country music's fastest-rising stars. The ex-husband of Rebecca Gibson, Randall J. Gibson, known as Slim, will stand before Judge Rosenthal and hear the preliminary case against him. The District Attorney's Office has refused to comment on whether or not they will seek the death penalty against Rebecca Gibson's ex, but we do expect them to seek to have him held without bond.'

At the words *death penalty*, all the hairs on the back of my neck got together, stood up, and did the Wave. Christ, I thought, I didn't have any idea it was this grim. But then I settled down. The death penalty in this state is most often used as a weapon by prosecutors to scare the stew out of the accused, rendering him or her much more willing to negotiate when plea-bargaining time rolls around. Besides, Tennessee is historically reluctant to actually execute people. We hand out the death penalty like traffic tickets, but when it comes to yanking that switch, we really aren't like Texas or Florida, where they'll fry your ass for spitting on the sidewalk. We take almost a perverse pride in having a huge death-row population, but no executions in over thirty years.

I worked my way through the hallway past the television cameras toward the general-sessions courtroom where preliminary hearings are held. I'd spent many a morning in this building as a newspaper reporter; sometimes it was packed, other times I was the only one in the spectators' gallery.

This time, they were jammed in like a 1930s revival meeting. Inside the small courtroom, the benches held row upon row of human in every imaginable combination. Some wore suits, but most were dressed casually, many with the affectations of musicians. The walls were even lined with standing men and women. I looked around the courtroom, searching the faces for one I knew. To my left, eight or ten down, stood an exhausted-looking Ray.

'Excuse me, excuse me, oops, excuse me—' I muttered to dirty looks as I wove my way around the bodies and edged in next to him.

'You made it,' he said, relieved. Ray pulled at the skin on his face like a rubber mask.

'Parking's hell out there,' I said. 'I drove around for ten minutes looking for a meter, then gave up and went into the garage behind the Ben West Building. Hell, took me five minutes to find a slot in there.'

'This one's going to be pretty popular.'

'Yeah. You get any sleep last night?'

'Not much.'

'Who's going to be representing him?' I asked.

'We called Roger. There wasn't much else to do,' Ray said. He hung his head like it was a heavy burden. 'Jesus, Harry, this is bad. News said this morning they might be going after the death penalty.'

'Don't panic, guy. There's quite a walk between going after it and getting it.'

On benches in a special gallery to the judge's right, a row of suited lawyers sat talking and fumbling through papers. I recognized three of them from the Public Defender's Office. They were huddled over the rail, making deals with the assistant DAs, shuffling through a huge caseload as quickly as possible.

'Where's Vaden?' I asked.

'Second row, over there.' Ray pointed. 'Just sitting off by himself.'

Roger Vaden, I thought, had probably not seen the inside of a criminal courtroom since field trips in law school. He looked completely forlorn, lost, befuddled.

'This is *not* an encouraging sign,' I whispered.

'No shit.'

'This is just the preliminary hearing,' I said. 'It's boilerplate for now. F. Lee Bailey probably couldn't get him off at this point.'

The door to the judge's chambers bounced open and a flurry

of black robe entered the room and took the stairs up to the judge's bench two at a time. The court officer jumped out of his chair.

'All rise,' he shouted. There was a commotion of noise and movement as everybody stood up. 'Hear ye, hear ye, all persons having business before this honorable court are instructed...' Blah blah blah. '...Judge Alvin Rosenthal presiding.' The court officer finished his spiel and sat down.

God, I thought, remembering my days in Boston as an undergraduate, only in the South would a good Jewish couple name their son Alvin.

Judge Rosenthal banged his gavel. 'Before we get started, I want to address the spectators here. Now y'all listen. This is a courtroom, and the bench is going to conduct business with decorum and dignity. I want no outbursts, no talking aloud, no interference with the business of this court in any fashion.

'And, sir—' Judge Rosenthal pointed to a man in the front row of the spectator's gallery and lowered his voice half an octave. 'If you don't get that Co-cola out of my courtroom in about ten seconds, you're going to spend the next two days as my guest in the county jail. Understood?'

Some poor sucker in a denim sport coat, hair draped across his shoulders, two earrings in his left ear, hopped up and scampered through the crowd with his hand wrapped tightly around a can of diet Coke. A young woman quickly slid into the seat he vacated.

'Now we've got a lot of business to conduct this morning, and we're going to go through this docket quickly and in the order in which the cases are listed. Is the District Attorney's Office ready?'

Two fresh young law-school graduates – one male, one female, both in pinstripes – stood up at the table to the judge's left.

'We are, Your Honor,' the male half of the team announced.

'The officer will read the docket,' Judge Rosenthal ordered.

A suited, dark-eyed woman at a table next to the court reporter stood up from behind two stacks of file folders, each about two feet high. 'Case number 02–4597–346J,' she rattled off. 'Willie J. Smith, Willful Destruction of Private Property, Public Intoxication, Carrying a Weapon for the Purpose of Going Armed.'

'Who's for the defendant?' the judge asked.

Another suit stood up from the gallery on the side. 'Scott Webster, Your Honor, Public Defender's Office.'

I turned to Ray. 'This could go on for hours.'

'You mean they're going to work all those folders in this morning?' he asked.

'Yep,' I answered.

'He ain't going to do Slim first?'

'The last time I saw a high-profile murder like this, the judge wouldn't do the big case first because he didn't want the news media to think they could push him around. Figured he'd make them wait all day. After about an hour, though, he got tired of the crowd and bumped the big case up to get rid of everybody.'

'Send in the defendant,' Judge Rosenthal said.

Two marshals, a couple of beefy black guys in cheap suits with badges hanging out of their front coat pockets, left the courtroom by way of a door next to the one leading into the judge's chambers. A moment later they stepped back in with a rail-thin black teenager between them. He wore the orange jumpsuit provided him by the Davidson County Sheriff's Department. His head was shaved, and he looked completely in awe of the crowd and the commotion.

'Read the charges again,' the judge said.

The woman with the file folders spoke up and read the numbers and charges one more time in her machine-gun voice. The judge turned back to the assistant DAs, and their voices soon melded into an audio blur as I thought first of Marsha, then of Slim in jail, and finally of Rebecca Gibson's sweet voice and how I'd never hear her sing again.

Up front, the judge was moving them through one after the other. A string of orange-suited prisoners – mostly black, mostly young, mostly up on petty charges, all defended by the PD – filed before the justice system to begin the process. I wondered if the judge or the prosecutor or, for that matter, the defense attorneys ever remembered one face or one name from another.

A couple of times, the background din from the spectator gallery drew a gavel bang from the bench, and yet another warning to clear the courtroom if things didn't quiet down. Tension seemed to rise one small notch at a time as the long line of orange proceeded through the room. The observers sat, or in my case stood, for over an hour. My legs were tired. My back hurt. And I was sleepy from the stuffy air and the heat of a room packed with bodies.

'How much longer?' Ray whispered.

'Beats me. As long as it takes.'

There was another murmur as someone in the crowd grew impatient and shuffled loudly out of the room. The judge watched the scene with an irritated look etched on his face as the woman assistant DA argued a case in front of him.

The attorneys sat down as the latest defendant was led out of the courtroom.

'Attorneys, approach the bench,' the judge ordered.

The DAs stood up, along with a few of the PDs, and walked up to the bench. Judge Rosenthal leaned over and whispered something to the gathered suits. One of the PDs shrugged, shook his head, then pointed to Roger Vaden, who still sat quietly on a bench in the corner.

'Sir.' Judge Rosenthal's voice rose. 'Who are you here to represent?'

'This is it,' I whispered. 'The judge just got enough.'

Ray stiffened next to me. 'You think so?'

'Just watch.'

Roger stood up, his six-feet-two, skinny frame clutching his briefcase nervously. 'Defendant Randall Gibson, Your Honor.'

'Approach the bench, please, sir.'

Roger stepped around the railing and made his way through the maze of desks. Whispered consultations followed, then the judge rapped his gavel.

'Five-minute recess,' he announced as he stepped off the bench in a billow of black cloth.

'What's going on?' Ray asked.

'Slim's downstairs in a holding cell. They've gone to get him.'

The noise level rose in the courtroom as Roger Vaden moved behind the defense table and people picked up on what was happening. People jockeyed for position while others skipped out for smoke or bathroom breaks. Some even took the opportunity to do a little schmoozing and backslapping.

Since no judge in the entire history of jurisprudence has ever kept a five-minute recess to five minutes, we stood there another quarter hour. Finally, as my thighs were about to go completely numb, the judge entered the courtroom and gaveled everything to order. A couple of minutes of preliminary tap dancing went on, and then the marshals escorted Slim into the courtroom.

My psyche took a header right into the toilet. Jeez, I felt miserable for the guy. The orange jumpsuit was about two sizes too large, which gave him the appearance of having shrunk since I'd last seen him. His cheeks were hollow, and great purplish bags hung under his eyes. I doubted he'd slept much; anyone who's ever been on the inside of a jail knows they're not conducive to a good night's sleep. I imagine the chow didn't set too well with him either. But mostly he had that thousand-yard stare that most people get when they encounter the criminal justice system for the first time. There's nothing that can prepare a person for the experience of incarceration. No other human experience is like it, at least not the first time.

I'd never experienced it directly, but I'd met enough people who had. And I knew enough about prison to know it was no place for a sensitive-songwriter type, especially when he was good-looking and well built.

Slim and Roger stood before the judge as the charges were read one last time.

'I want you to understand, sir, that this is not a trial,' the judge intoned for the television reporters. He hadn't done this for the other prisoners, but for this case, he was – well, I think the word is *posturing*.

'This is only a preliminary hearing. We are not trying this case right now. The purpose of this hearing is to determine whether there is enough evidence to bind this case over to the grand jury for indictment. The prosecution will not even make a complete case against you, and you are in no way required to defend yourself unless you so choose. Now, are you the attorney of record, Mr Vaden?'

'No, Your Honor, I'm not,' Roger said, with just a tremor of fear in his voice. 'I am here as attorney solely for these proceedings, with the court's permission. Mr Gibson has not had time to engage criminal counsel.'

'Any objections from the state?'

'None, Your Honor,' the woman assistant DA stood and said.

'Very well, then, let's get on with it. Call your first witness.'

'The state calls E. D. Fouch of the Metro Nashville Police Department,' she said.

Fouch entered the courtroom from the far right while a court officer held the door for him. I'd run into Fouch quite a few times over the years; he had about twenty-two in and was eligible for retirement. Like a lot of people these days, though, he and his wife were raising their own grandkids and couldn't afford to quit working. He was a steady, plodding kind of cop. Not brilliant, but a guy who'd stay on your ass until hell froze over if he thought you were guilty. Knowing Fouch had been assigned the case made me even less inclined to envy Slim.

He rolled himself into the witness chair and brushed his thinning silver hair back across his scalp. My guess is he needed to lose about forty pounds and give up smoking. And even from where Ray and I stood in the back of the courtroom, the veins in his nose gave him away as one who looks forward to the sun being over the yardarm.

The court officer swore Fouch in and the woman DA approached.

'State your name and occupation, please,' she instructed.

'Sergeant E. D. Fouch, Metro Nashville Police Department,' he grunted back. He shifted in the seat and tugged at his pants. A thin sheen of sweat formed on his forehead. He'd been down the court testimony path plenty of times in his career, but Fouch always looked like he couldn't get used to it.

'Sergeant Fouch, you're presently assigned to the Homicide Division as an investigator, correct?'

'That's right, ma'am. I've been on homicide nearly nine years.'

'And on last Sunday night – early Monday morning, really – were you called to the scene of an accident that occurred at 530 Brooksfield Terrace in Nashville?'

'That's right. I was.'

'Can you relate to us the details of that call?'

Fouch shifted once again in his chair, trying to get comfortable. 'I was awakened at approximately five a.m. and instructed to proceed to 530 Brooksfield Terrace, where the on-scene police officers had reported a deceased woman and circumstances indicated foul play might be involved.'

'Would it be normal procedure for you to be awakened at that hour?'

'No, ma'am, it would not. But because of some other things going on right now, we've been shorthanded.'

Yeah, I thought, everybody's waiting for World War III at the morgue.

'Okay. Go on, Sergeant Fouch.'

'I drove to the scene and there found an apparently deceased, approximately early-thirties Caucasian woman. There was evidence of a terrific struggle in the bedroom of the house. Quite a lot of damage, actually. An investigator from the medical examiner's office arrived about five minutes after I did and pronounced the woman dead.'

'Were you able to establish the woman's identity?'

'Yes, we established the victim as being Rebecca Provost Gibson, who lived at the address.'

'What did you do then?'

'We initiated an investigation of the scene. I called in a homicide team, two other investigators, the on-scene crime lab, our fingerprint expert. We began canvassing the neighborhood.'

'Were you able to find anyone who had witnessed any part of the incident?'

'Yes, we found several witnesses who'd been awakened by loud

screaming and sounds of a violent struggle. The address in question is a condominium and the units are quite close to each
other. We found four witnesses who said they saw a white, early-
Seventies Chevy sedan leaving the scene very quickly. Burning
rubber, in fact. Two wrote down the license number.'

'Were you able to establish ownership of the vehicle through
the Department of Motor Vehicles?'

'We were.'

'And who was the owner of the car?'

Fouch pointed at the table. 'The defendant.'

'Let the record reflect that Sergeant Fouch has identified
defendant Randall J. Gibson as owner of the car seen speeding
away from the house at 530 Brooksfield Terrace.'

'So ordered,' Judge Rosenthal said.

'Was there any other physical evidence at the scene which might
establish the defendant's presence at the house that night?'

'There was.'

'Describe it for me, please, sir.'

'We lifted several sets of the defendant's fingerprints off items
in the house: a chrome-and-glass coffee table, a doorknob, and
on the bloodstained debris of a shattered lamp.'

'Holy shit,' I whispered to Ray. 'She was beaten to death with
a *lamp*?'

'There was also mud tracked through the house which was later
identified as being similar to that found on a pair of the defendant's boots. Blood was found on the boots as well.'

'How did you obtain these boots?'

'Under a search warrant executed after the defendant's arrest.'

'Was there any other evidence obtained under the search
warrant?'

'Yes, there was. A bloodstained, khaki-colored, bush-type shirt.'

'Where were these items found, Sergeant?'

'The boots and the shirt were found taped up in a cardboard
box and buried in a closet under a pile of clothes.'

'As if they'd been hidden, correct?'

'Objection, Your Honor!' Vaden jumped to his feet. 'Calls for
a conclusion.'

'Relax, counselor,' the judge ordered. 'This is a preliminary
hearing, not a jury trial. Objection overruled.'

Vaden sat back down, deflated.

'Were you able to establish the source of the blood on the
defendant's boots and shirt?'

'Yes, we were. We ran the standard battery of preliminary lab tests. The blood type on the boots and the shirts was an identical match to the victim's blood. The full battery of analysis and DNA tests, of course, will take several weeks.'

'Now, Sergeant Fouch,' the assistant DA continued, 'we'll have other witnesses to establish the exact cause of death later, but in your opinion as an experienced homicide investigator, was this a particularly brutal crime, say on a scale of one to ten?'

I saw Roger Vaden jerk like he was going to his feet again. Then he paused and settled back down. What was the point? I thought. No way was the judge not going to bind this one over.

'I've seen hundreds of bodies in my years as a police officer,' Fouch said. 'And investigated dozens, maybe hundreds, as a homicide investigator. And this woman was beaten to death about as bad as anyone I've ever seen. She was way past dead by the time we got there.'

I shook my head from side to side, suddenly overwhelmed with weariness. Like the woman's love in the song she'd written, Rebecca Gibson was way past dead.

And something told me Slim Gibson was way past screwed.

Chapter 14

Dr Henry Krohlmeyer, Marsha's boss and the chief medical examiner for Metropolitan Nashville and Davidson County, was the next witness. Dr Henry, as he was called by virtually everyone, described in his usual gory detail the procedures by which he'd determined the cause of death in the case of Rebecca Gibson. He also explained that he'd had to perform the autopsy at the Vanderbilt Medical Center hospital, what with his own morgue presently indisposed.

As a journalist, I'd seen a couple of autopsies before. Truth is, they're not as awful as one might think, as long as you have a decent idea of what to expect and the body hasn't been left out for so long it's turned fragrant. You detach yourself from it all. Dead bodies – to me, anyway – don't really look like people anymore. One of my first really bad car-wreck assignments as a young reporter was when a carload of drunks in a convertible took a curve at eighty miles an hour, then flipped. I got there just after the cops had set up the yellow tape and got past with my press pass. Five adults, two teenagers, thrown all over hell's half acre, killed instantly, splayed out in the most damnably bizarre angles I'd ever seen a human body assume.

But they didn't look like people anymore. They were like store mannequins that fell off the back of a runaway semi. I never blinked an eye. Completely professional, all the way.

This was different. I'd seen Rebecca Gibson when she was alive, had heard her sing, heard her laugh, felt her spark. I don't mean to go on about it. After all, I didn't know her. But I was attracted to her despite myself. So was everyone else in the room that last night of her life. Listening to Dr Henry talk about the results of her autopsy, and imagining her on a stainless-steel table with the awful Y-cut from her shoulders to the middle of her breasts, then down to her crotch; hell, I don't know. It made me cold everywhere. My feet felt like blocks of ice and I realized I was covered in a thin, frigid sweat.

'You okay?' Ray whispered, jabbing me in the left arm with his right elbow. 'You look pale as death.'

Interesting simile. 'I'm okay,' I whispered back.

Dr Henry finished his testimony. Rebecca Gibson had suffered over a dozen fractures to her cheekbones, skull, one arm, a collarbone, three ribs, with the accompanying cuts, bruises, abrasions. She'd suffered acute abdominal trauma; her gut was full of blood and fluid that shouldn't have been there. One eye had been crushed in its socket, her nose shattered. Cause of death was a toss-up: accumulated acute head trauma from a multitude of severe blows led to extensive damage to the lining of the brain, subdural hematoma, and fatal swelling of the brain. However, her throat had been ripped open as well – presumably by one of the shards from the shattered lamp – tearing the carotid artery and leading to a Class-IV hemorrhage.

I squirmed against the wall. Someone had beaten Rebecca Gibson to a textbook bloody pulp, and had done it with great zest as well. It was not simply a case of passion overriding one's best judgment and things getting out of hand. Someone with great physical strength had given themselves quite a workout. I stared at Slim as he sat at the defense table in his orange jumpsuit. The one-piece jumpsuit was short-sleeved, and Slim's thick arms were the only thing stretching the oversized garment. Slim was young. He was well built, kept himself in shape, looked, in fact, like an iron-pumper. He didn't smoke, had good wind.

I remembered one other thing Ray told me Slim had: a bad temper, accompanied by a history of domestic-disturbance calls.

I suddenly needed some air.

The sun on the plaza in front of the Criminal Justice Center brought me back to some level of stability. I sat on a concrete bench, the pedestrians passing by in a swirl of movement and color. The traffic stopped-and-started down the James Robertson Parkway in the long shadows cast by the courthouse across the street.

I took a few deep breaths and brought my hands to my face and rubbed hard, then leaned back and stretched, letting the bright sunlight warm my face. There were footsteps behind me, then Ray's voice again.

'Harry?'

'Yeah?' I said without looking at him.

'They ain't going to let him go,' he said in a monotone. He sounded as if he were in shock.

I lifted my head and gazed off down the parkway, toward the ageing Municipal Auditorium. 'Denied bond, huh?' That was bad. About the only time bond is ever flat out denied in this state is when they're going for capital murder.

'No, but they set it at three hundred and fifty thousand dollars.'

I chuckled. 'Hey, things ain't so bad. All you got to do is come up with thirty-five and he's outta there.'

'Thirty-five thousand dollars.' He sighed. 'May as well be fifty-five million. I never seen anything like it, Harry.'

I sat up straight. It was nearly lunchtime, and I hadn't had a bite since the night before. I needed to eat, get my blood sugar back to where it ought to be. Then I needed to think. This was a hell of a lousy mess.

'When can we see him?' I asked.

'I don't know. I think Roger Vaden's still with him.'

'I want to talk to him, Ray. I think you need to talk to him, too.'

I turned and stared at him. 'Why?' he asked.

'Ol' buddy,' I said, making a hammer out of my right fist and bouncing it once off his knee, 'I think we need to grok the possibility that our boy Slim just might have done it.'

Ray and I agreed to meet back at the office building on Seventh Avenue. I picked up a sack of burgers and a couple of orders of fries, then listened to my stomach growl as the food sat congealing next to me on the car seat while I searched for a parking space.

I fought off a sense of hopelessness, with mixed success. Rarely had I felt like life was completely beyond my control. Even during the worst period of my life, which I suppose was probably when I lost my marriage and my job all within a couple of months, I had never felt the sort of psychic impotence I was feeling at this moment. The marriage wasn't that great to begin with: there was more relief than anything else when it finally ended civilly and without drama. As for my career as a journalist, the truth was that I had become stale. After a while you feel like you've written every story in human history at least ten times. The challenge becomes to approach each assignment in search of the fresh insight, the new angle. After a certain number of years, the challenge becomes a tedious struggle, and then finally, not worth the effort.

So my transition from secure, staid journalist to freelance, on-the-edge investigator had been good for me in the long run. I hadn't had a dull day since. A woman who I was beginning to suspect was going to be a far bigger part of my future than I'd ever imagined was in danger of being snatched away from me at any given miscalculated moment. Another friend stood accused of murder. I was faced with loss on personal, business, and financial levels.

And to top it all off, I realized as I parked the car and dug into the sack of food, those rat bastards at the drive-in window put tomatoes on my burgers!

Damn. I hate tomatoes.

I suffered through the insult up in Ray's office as we snarfed down lunch and sipped slick, wet cans of Coke. Ray had put in a call to Roger Vaden's office, and there was little conversation as we sat chewing and waiting.

I'd checked my answering machine before stepping down to Ray's office. Nothing. No mail yet, either, which meant no incoming checks. But, I rationalized, that meant no bills either.

'When you reckon they'll let us see him?' Ray asked.

'Visiting hours are Wednesday nights and Sunday afternoons,' I answered, distracted. I was thinking about Marsha again in a generalized, unfocused way. I wondered when I'd hear from her, if they'd gotten food and supplies sent in. If she had what she needed.

'You mean we can't see him until then?'

'That's right. Lawyers can see prisoners almost anytime. But civilians are off-limits.'

Ray pulled the blinds back on the window and observed the traffic crawling by outside the window.

'I hate to think of him in there. You know, all my kids are up north. Since Amy and I divorced, well—'

He paused. I'd known Ray was divorced, but never knew his wife's name was Amy.

'Hell, I guess Slim's about all I've got.' Ray's head dropped and the skin under his chin sagged. He suddenly looked old.

It was a strange confession from a man who seemed in every other aspect of his life completely happy and carefree. I'd never known Ray and Slim to have anything but a good time. The music business is a tough row to hoe; the only way to make it through is to have a good attitude and a sense of humor the size of the Goodyear blimp. This was the first crack I'd ever seen.

And I thought again of Marsha and realized that, really, she was about all I had. Lots of friends, buddies, former colleagues, contacts, clients, but people who were my day-to-day, real family? Marsha was just about it.

I suddenly knew exactly how Ray felt. I put down my sandwich and scraped a rough paper napkin across my face.

'Ray, there's something I guess I ought to tell you. The real reason I've been sweating whether or not to get involved with all this.'

The phone rang, its electronic alarm bouncing off the plaster walls and abruptly jarring both of us out of our thoughts.

'Hold on, let me get this.' Ray stepped over to the desk closest to him and pressed a red button on the telephone. There was a cracking noise as a speakerphone popped.

'Yeah,' Ray called excitedly. Before the word could get out, though, a computer-generated voice spoke over his.

'Hello, you have a collect call from—' The voice paused.

'Slim!' we heard Slim say in the split second the computer gave him to talk.

'If you will accept the call, press one on your telephone keypad. If not, hang up. Thank you for using South Central Bell.'

Ray pressed the telephone keypad. 'Slim?' he yelled.

'Hey, Ray, how are you?' Slim sounded artificially cheerful.

'Fine, buddy. How the hell are you?'

'I'm hanging in there,' he said. There was the sound of metal clanging, loud voices, and a blaring television in the background. 'Listen, these phones are programmed to hang up after ten minutes. We ain't got much time.'

'Okay, Slim. By the way, Harry's in here with me. He's going to help us out.'

'Hey, Harry.'

'Hey, Slim,' I said.

'I'm glad you're going to try to give me some help. I could sure use it.'

'The best help I can give you is to try to get you out of there.'

'That ain't looking too good, man. No way I can come up with the bondsman's fee. But, Ray, there's a couple of things you could do for me.'

Between the tinny speaker in the phone and the background noise of the jail, Slim's voice sounded hollow, detached, like he was at the other end of a long metal drainpipe and we were yelling at each other.

'What can we do?' Ray asked.

'First, get the extra key to my house. It's the green key on the plastic ring in the center of my desk.'

Ray slid the desk drawer open. 'Got it.'

'Get on over to my house. Just let yourself in. It'll be okay. Back in the den, there's a small desk across from the TV. In the bottom drawer is a file folder. That's the paperwork on my house and the deed to my grandmother's house down in Winchester. That house is fully paid for. I can use it as a collateral on a loan or just sign it over to a lawyer if need be.'

'Okay. What do I do with it?' Ray asked.

'Just get it out of the house for now. That is, if the cops haven't already seized all my papers. I ain't got a lot, but if the law puts a clamp on it, then I'm really screwed.'

'Can they do that?' Ray asked me, lowering his voice.

'I don't know. Wouldn't be surprised,' I said, real low.

'While you're there, pick up the passbook to my savings account at the credit union. There ain't much in there, maybe two thousand tops, but it'll help. As soon as I get a lawyer, I'll sign a power of attorney over to you, Ray, so you can handle the money. If you could write the check for my house payment and my utilities, I'd appreciate it, too. That house and my grandma's place is about everything I own in the world.'

I didn't think it was a proper time to tell Slim that it was almost a certainty he could kiss all that stuff goodbye. If the law didn't confiscate it, the attorneys would get it in legal fees. The pursuit of justice had bankrupted lesser men.

'Slim, do you have any idea who you're going to hire as your lawyer?' I asked.

'No, not really. Roger Vaden says he can't do it. He knows a couple of guys he can call. I don't know, Harry, it looks to me like nobody wants to take the case.'

'Aw, hell, boy,' Ray boomed, 'don't you start talking like that. We'll get you out of there just as quick as possible.'

'They're saying it might be three months before my trial starts. If I can't find the money to make bond, there ain't no telling how long I'll be in here.' The first surge of panic flowed into his voice. Again, I didn't have the heart to tell him he might be in there a year before his case came to trial.

'Don't think about that right now, Slim,' I said. 'Take the Scarlett O'Hara approach; think about that tomorrow. For now, you can help us all by concentrating on anything that might send me off in the right direction.'

'Well, I—'

'But be careful,' I interrupted. 'Keep in mind these phones are probably connected to a tape recorder.'

Ray looked at me like, *aw, c'mon, they wouldn't do that, now, would they?* I shook my head like, *hell, yeah, they could. It's their jail.*

'So don't say anything you don't want them to hear.'

Slim was quiet for a moment, with only the metallic rattling in the background, punctuated rhythmically by bursts of distant yelling.

'I ain't got nothing to hide,' he said forcefully after a moment. 'I'll tell you what I told the police. We packed up our equipment after the Bluebird closed, and a few of us hung around after the doors were locked. Must have been getting on to about two-fifteen or so by then. Maybe a little later. I had a quick beer. Must have been maybe about eight of us total there. That's not counting the waitresses and the bartenders and stuff.

'Anyway,' he continued, 'Becca kind of pulled me off in a corner, away from everybody else. Said she had something important to tell me. It was going to make a big deal in her career.'

I looked at Ray. He nodded his head; he was there and that's the way it went down.

'Did she give you any idea what it was?' I asked.

'She never got the chance,' Slim said. 'Somebody else called me over, and I didn't pay a hell of a lot of attention to her. Becca was always passing shit around like it was some kind of big, important, earthshaking secret and I was her only confidant. Only problem was, she was feedin' the same shit to just about everybody she knew.'

He sighed heavily, as if he had a weight hanging from his neck. 'Becca liked her drama,' he said, sadness adding even more weight.

'What happened then, Slim? And cut to the chase. We haven't got much time left.' I didn't have time to worry about offending him.

'Anyway,' he said, clearing his throat. 'About twenty minutes later the party broke up. I didn't give Becca another thought. Just loaded my car and headed home. My house is over in Sylvan Park, but that time of night, the traffic wasn't bad, so I got home in about fifteen minutes. I'd just opened another beer – I don't sleep so well after a gig and usually have to wind down with a couple – when the phone started ringing. It was Becca.'

'Okay, what'd she want now?'

'She was – hell, Harry, I guess frantic's the word. Panicked. I've seen Becca get hysterical more times than I can count. This was different. She was scared. She said she needed me, couldn't talk over the phone. I've had my chain jerked by that woman so many times I figured once more wouldn't hurt. I'd had four or five beers by then. Maybe I wasn't thinking too clearly.'

'So you went to Rebecca's house not knowing what to expect.'

'Right. When I got there, the front door was unlocked and I walked in. I could tell something wasn't right, though. The living room was a mess, but that wasn't unusual. Becca never did get the hang of house-cleaning. But I kept calling her name and she didn't answer. I walked back through the hallway and her bedroom door was cracked open. Only the light was turned off. I pushed the door open and there was something against it. It wouldn't move. I pushed harder and whatever it was, it kept . . . kept . . .' His voice weakened.

'C'mon, Slim,' I said. 'We're running out of time here.'

I heard him take a deep breath and hold it for a moment. Then he let it loose.

'I finally laid a shoulder into the door and pushed it open about a foot, then wedged my way in. I stepped in something slippery, and my boot slid until it hit something that felt like a bag of dough or something. I looked down. There was a little bit of light from the hallway shining in now, and I saw the floor was all dark and wet. I fumbled for the switch.'

He paused again. I let him take another breath. 'That's when I saw her, man. She looked like she'd been run through a threshing machine. I never seen nothing like it in my life. I yelled something – don't remember what – then leaned down over her. There was broken glass and blood and pieces of, pieces of, Jesus, Harry, pieces of meat. Part of her face was ripped open and you could see her skull.'

Ray moaned and shook his head.

'I leaned down and put my fingers to the side of her throat that wasn't cut. Nothing. She was still warm, but she was gone, Harry. I picked up this piece of broken glass that was laying next to her and got blood all over myself. I got real sick at my stomach and thought I was going to heave. Then all I remember was thinking I had to get the hell out of there. I jumped up and backed out of the room real slow. Then I started running. Just running, man. I got back to my car, jumped in, and hauled ass.'

I rubbed my eyes wearily. This was incredibly bad. Goddamn it, boy, I wanted to ask him, didn't you ever watch *Perry Mason*? In my humble layman's opinion, Slim was looking at about twenty to life right now.

'Did you see anybody else there?' I asked. 'Any sign of anybody or anything?'

'Nothing, Harry. But it was late. Until I found Becca, I wasn't paying a lot of attention. After that, I don't know. It's all a blur.'

'Now this is real important,' I said. 'When—'

The computerized voice of the jailhouse phone interrupted me: 'This call will end in ten seconds.'

'When did you get there?' I demanded. 'Exactly what time was it?'

C'mon, blast you, I thought, answer me.

'I don't know, Harry. Maybe four-thirty in the morning. A few minutes before? Hell, I just don't know . . .'

'You sure, Slim? You damn sure about that?'

'As sure as I can be. I mean it was late and all—'

Then the computer cut us off.

Ray and I sat there staring at each other until another computer voice came on: 'If you'd like to make a call, please hang up and try again. If you need help, hang up and dial your operator.'

'Ray,' I said. 'We're going to need a hell of a lot more help than any operator can give us.'

Chapter 15

We sat there for a moment or two, struck dumber than bricks.

'Did you know any of this?' I asked. I don't think I meant to sound pissed off, but that's the way it came out.

Ray silently feigned innocence, and very badly, I might add.

'C'mon, Ray,' I said, 'don't give me that *who me?* shit.'

Then he sighed and his shoulders relaxed. 'He came pounding on my back door just before five o'clock. Woke my ass up out of a coma. He still had blood on his shirt where he'd wiped his hands.'

I felt my jaw slacken. 'Goddamn it, Ray, this could make you an accessory after the fact.'

'Hey, I'm the one told him to turn hisself in.'

'Yeah, twenty-four hours later. After he'd had time to hide his shirt and boots.'

Ray shook his head. 'I know. I can't believe he did that.'

'Me neither. What an effective way to make yourself look guilty as sin.'

'Hell,' he said, almost as an afterthought, 'I told him to burn 'em.'

I slapped my forehead. 'Thank you, Ray. Now that I know that, *I'm* an accessory after the fact. *Thanks* for sharing that with me.'

'You're not no damn access after the – whatever the hell you said.'

'Maybe not. I just happen to be aware of a failed attempt to suppress evidence in a murder case, that's all. You know something, Ray? Slim may not be guilty, but you two bozos are sure conspiring to make him look that way.'

Ray looked up at me, a pained look in his eyes. 'There's no need to start name-calling here.'

I jumped out of my seat and took a step toward him. He tensed. I must have looked as mad as I felt.

'Now, listen, bud, we're establishing some new rules around here, understand? If I'm supposed to help you, then you have to tell me everything. All of it. No more obfuscation.'

'No more what?' he asked.

'No more bullshit!' I yelled, then placed my hands palm down on the desk in front of him. 'If you agree to my terms, I'll go down to my office and get a notebook. I'll bring that notebook back here and start making notes, and maybe, just maybe, we'll figure out a way to keep Slim's permanent address from being in care of the Tennessee Department of Corrections. If you don't agree to my terms, then I'm not coming back.'

Ray gazed at me like he'd never seen me before.

'Deal?'

He nodded.

'Okay,' I said. 'Try to get that feeble brain of yours in gear. We'll never be able to prove Slim didn't do it; you guys have already taken care of that. The only way we'll get Slim off is to figure out who the hell did kill Rebecca Gibson and why.'

'Okay,' Ray agreed, his voice real low.

I walked over to the door and opened it, then paused. 'There's only one thing I can see that's obvious here,' I said.

Ray stood up. 'What?'

'Whoever killed Rebecca,' I said, 'was probably going out the back door at the same time Slim was coming in the front.'

I was talking to myself more than to Ray by then. I started down the hall, trying to figure out how the timing could have been as precise as it appeared. There couldn't have been more than a few moments' overlap. The neighbors heard two sets of noises: screams and fighting, then the squeal of tires burning rubber out of the parking lot. Slim caused the latter; he claims he had nothing to do with the former.

I heard a muffled phone ring somewhere ahead of me, but didn't realize it was mine until I was halfway down the hall and heard the relays in my answering machine clicking. I had the volume turned down low on the machine, so couldn't hear whose voice was leaving the message. I fumbled with the keys, then got the door open just in time to hear the machine cut off and begin recycling itself.

'Damn it,' I muttered. I waited for the machine to reset, then turned the volume up.

'Hello,' the familiar computerized voice said, 'you have one message.'

There were more clicks and the crackling of static as the heads in the machine hit the worn tape. The voice that came through was high-pitched male, deeply country, and mad as hell:

'Hey, you son of a bitch! I'm gonna git you, you got that, son? Yer ass is mine, and I mean it! You have a nice day, 'cause you ain't got many left!'

Click. Dial tone.

I sank slowly into my chair. What the hell? If I didn't know better, I'd say that was a threat.

I hit the button and played the message back. The accent was twangy and nasally, relatively common in these parts among the didn't-finish-high-school-and-pumping-gas-at-the-filling-station crowd. I tried to place it. East Tennessee, perhaps? I didn't think so. More like rural Mississippi or Alabama, maybe west Tennessee. There was no way to pinpoint it. The only thing I knew for sure was that there's only one region in the country where the phrase *son of a bitch* is reduced to a pair of slurred syllables.

I replayed the message, listening carefully for background noises, other voices, anything that might reveal the caller's identity. Nothing. I dug around inside my cluttered center desk drawer until I found a blank tape, then replaced the one in the answering machine. I tucked the tape with the message on it inside my jacket pocket, grabbed a spiral notebook, and locked my office door behind me as I headed back to Ray's.

Halfway down the hall, I stopped. I was alone, with only the cracked linoleum, green chipped plaster, and decades' worth of dust balls surrounding me. This wave of fatigue swept over me, and I found myself feeling almost dizzy.

'Okay,' I muttered, 'now you're getting death threats. Add that to the list . . .'

'I thought you'd changed your mind,' Ray said when I opened the door to his office. I took off my jacket and laid it across the back of the chair, then loosened my tie about down to the third button and rolled up my shirtsleeves. Then I sat down at the desk across from him, opened the notebook, and pulled the cap off a cheap pen.

'All right,' I said, 'let's get to work. First of all, let's consider all the alternatives. Could it have been just a random crime? Could Rebecca have walked in on a housebreaker?'

'Maybe.'

'Was anything stolen from her apartment? Money, jewelry, the television, a VCR?'

'No, definitely,' Ray said. He shook his head. 'Nothing was taken.'

'And nobody's ever made mention of her being raped or sexually assaulted, right?'

105

'Yeah.'

'So the police have eliminated the possibility of random crime, and so can we.'

'For the time being.'

I looked up at him after scribbling a note on the page. 'Yeah, for the time being. Now, what about lovers?'

He made a humming noise. 'I never thought of that.'

'With the severity of the beating she took, there had to be some degree of passion involved. Somebody had to loathe Rebecca Gibson to wear her out that bad. Whoever it was could have killed her a lot easier.'

The bags under Ray's eyes and the creases on his forehead lifted as he brightened. 'Yeah, I hadn't thought of that. The problem is, I don't know if she was seeing anybody. There were rumors, of course, about her and—'

He paused. 'Her and who?' I asked.

Ray settled back in his chair again. 'Naw, it couldn't be.'

I slapped my pen down on the paper. 'Don't do that to me. If we're going to help Slim, we've got to consider every possibility.'

'I don't see how Dwight could have—'

'Dwight who?' I demanded.

'Dwight Parmenter,' he answered. 'Dwight's the guy we were singing with Sunday night at the Bluebird.'

I pulled a picture of Dwight Parmenter out of memory and ran it past. Guy was tall, wiry. He was wearing a checked flannel shirt that night. During their performance, he seemed to be the quietest, the one with the least ego. He was also, musically, the least impressive.

'The guy on Rebecca's right?'

'Yeah.'

'So tell me about him,' I said. 'Did he and Rebecca have something going on?'

Ray plopped his elbows on the desk and leaned forward. 'Maybe. I know they'd been seen out a few times. I know Dwight was sweet on her.'

'I didn't notice any particular sparks flying Sunday night.'

'That's 'cause Slim was there. And partly because you have to get to know Dwight to see what he's really thinking.'

I paused for a moment. 'Let me get this straight. Rebecca was still singing and performing with her ex-husband, her ex-husband's partner, and the guy who may have been her lover – all at the same time.'

Ray grinned. 'Yeah, I guess that's about it.'

'Does any of this seem just the slightest bit strange to you?'

The grin widened into sheepishness. 'You got to understand, Harry. People in the music bidness do things a little bit different.'

'Apparently so. Okay, so we've got Dwight Parmenter. Maybe you're right and he wasn't involved. If he wasn't, he'll be easy enough to scratch off the list. What about other lovers?'

'How much time have you got?'

I drew a line beneath my notes on Dwight Parmenter. 'How much will I need?'

Ray straightened up. 'Harry, Rebecca was a grown woman, and she'd been around a while. And like I said, music-bidness types—'

'I know, I know. Operate under a different set of rules. Tell me this. Is there anybody out there who was involved with Rebecca and broke up with her under particularly bitter circumstances. More than just your usual soap opera.'

'The only one I know of is Slim,' Ray said. 'I mean, people come together, stay a while, and then drift back apart. Law of the jungle, man. I do known the only one she ever married was Slim, outside of some guy back in west Tennessee she married back when she was eighteen.'

'What about him?'

'Hell, I don't even know his name. But Rebecca used to joke about him. Said he was a tractor-trailer mechanic, chewed tobacco, and would rather hunt deer than have sex.'

'At least he had his priorities straight.'

'Maybe so. But they divorced with no big battles, and she came to Nashville to make it big as a country-music singer. That must have been twelve, thirteen years ago. As far as I know, she never saw him again.'

'So Slim was the only one where any . . . recriminations were involved.'

'Yeah, but even then, they still worked together. Their business interests were tied together real close. They co-owned songs, split royalty checks – the whole shooting match.'

'Only Slim was getting the fuzzy end of the lollipop on most of their deals, right? Otherwise, he wouldn't be so broke.'

'Not really,' Ray said after another moment's pause. 'Slim just ain't no good at handling money. That's why he never has any. It runs through his fingers like gas through a '66 Cadillac.'

'Well,' I said, encouraged, 'that may help. After all, if she wasn't screwing him, business-wise, there was no reason to kill her.'

'Yeah,' Ray mumbled. Then he looked away nervously.

'What?'

107

He looked back at me. 'I've seen their partnership agreements and all the contracts,' he said. 'Slim and Rebecca set up a weird arrangement.'

'What was the arrangement?'

Ray bit his lower lip. 'In the event that either of them died, the rights to the song catalog totally reverted to the other.'

'Oh, no,' I muttered. 'The rights don't revert to Rebecca's estate?'

'Nope,' Ray said. 'They go back to Slim.'

'And how much is that worth?'

'There's no way to answer that question. Right now the catalog brought in enough for both of them to live on, if they was careful. But if some major star was to pick up a song or two of theirs, say Garth or Wynonna or somebody like that, and make a number-one hit out of it – well, hell, the sky's the limit. Six figures easy. Maybe more. Could happen.'

Great, I thought as I finished scribbling down the note on what Ray'd just told me. One more reason for Slim to whack his ex-wife.

Just what we needed.

Chapter 16

I had about as much hope of pulling this off as a steerage passenger had of getting on one of the *Titanic*'s lifeboats. Every little piece of information I learned was one more revelation that could send Slim packing for the next couple of decades.

'One more bad piece of news. That's just what we need.'

'How is that bad?'

'What do you mean?' I almost shouted at him without meaning to. 'It's one more motive!'

'But the DA ain't going to find out about that,' Ray insisted.

'Ray, excuse me for allowing a little reality to intrude upon this discussion. But I think we'd both be better off if we assumed the District Attorney's Office and the police are going to know everything.'

I paused for a second. '*Everything!*'

He jumped back. 'Okay, okay!'

'Now let's move on,' I said. My stomach churned. 'Let's look at her other business arrangements. I don't know the music business very well. What other people did Rebecca work with?'

'Well, I guess the closest would be her personal manager, Mac Ford. Then there was her talent and booking agent, Faye Morgan over at CCA, the Concert Corporation of America. And then there was her accountant. What was his name? And the lawyer, of course.'

'Mac Ford,' I said. 'I've heard of him. Got a weird name or something, hasn't he? I've seen it in the papers.'

'Ford McKenna Ford is his real name, but everybody calls him Mac. He used to manage Slim and Rebecca both, but Slim left him after the divorce. Mac's taken care of Rebecca since he stole her away from her original manager back when she and Slim were just selling their first songs.'

'Stole her?' I asked. 'That happen often? Managers stealing each other's clients away, I mean.'

Ray smiled. 'You *don't* know this business, do you?'

'So let me in on it.'

Ray leaned back, glad to take back control of the conversation. He threw his big snakeskin shitkickers up on the desk and intertwined his fingers into a headrest. Suddenly he'd changed from a serious, scared middle-aged guy about to lose it all to the country-music-industry insider who was holding court for the uninitiated. His ego was back in gear.

'Harry, I once knew a guy who paid an artist's manager ten thousand cash under the table to talk him into a record deal that wound up ruining the singer's career. The first thing you learn in this business is that people will lie to you when it's goddamn easier to tell the truth, and would be a hell of a lot less to keep track of in the bargain. You got to watch out for yourself, 'cause the wounded are left behind or eaten.'

'But what about Rebecca?'

'Rebecca Gibson came to town in the late Seventies, with a little bit of talent as a singer, a lot of determination, and a whole lot of undiscovered talent as a songwriter. She had hair bouffed up to the ceiling, an ice-cream-cone bra, and dreams. That was about it. She got a job as a waitress and worked the open-mike nights for about two years before her first manager discovered her. He was a guy named Will Harmetz, and he was known then for hanging around the Trailways station like a child molester.'

'Was he? A child molester, I mean?'

'Let me put it this way. Rebecca spent most of her time with Will on her back with her legs in the air. But she was over twenty-one and he blew enough smoke up her ass that she was willing to put up with it. Besides, the world wasn't exactly beating a path to her door. Then she met Slim.'

'And started to blossom.'

'You bet your ass she did. Slim taught her a lot, and she taught him a lot. They were going places, and the first thing they had to do was find a real manager. Mac Ford was just starting out then, but he was taking in some of the hippest young country acts around. He wasn't getting very far with most of them, but he was in there punching. Rebecca had a long-term contract with this slimebag Harmetz. If I remember correctly, he was putting together a deal to have Rebecca start a tour singing in truck-stop restaurants. You believe that, man? Truck-stop restaurants ...'

'So how'd he get her out of it?'

'Rebecca was going to go to Harmetz and just tell him she wanted out. Mac knew better though. He knew Rebecca would eventually be worth something, and he figured Will Harmetz probably knew it, too. He also was savvy enough to know that if

Harmetz figured Rebecca was about to jump ship, he'd just get the wagons in a circle.'

Ray was the Charlie Daniels of the mixed metaphor. I struggled to keep a straight face.

'So what did they do?'

'By this time, Slim and Becca were living together and planning on getting married. Harmetz didn't mind so much that she wasn't doing the horizontal bop with him anymore. After all, there were other girls out there. Now that she was near her midtwenties, she was quickly becoming too old for him anyway. But she arranged to meet Will at his office for one last bout on the leather couch. She must have put it to him, because he fell asleep afterward. Rebecca lifted some of his letterhead, and Mac forged a letter releasing her from her contract. He forged Harmetz's name, then had a friend notarize it for him.'

'They forged a release?' I asked, surprise in my voice.

'Sure, happens all the time. Then they made a few crappy-looking copies of it and planted them in file folders. Rebecca stuck the original back in Harmetz's filing cabinet. And when he started raising hell about having her locked in on a long-term management contract, she just produced her copy and told him where to find his.'

'And he fell for it?'

'Wasn't nothing to fall for,' Ray said. 'Wasn't nothing Harmetz could do. They had him by the short ones. Besides, this kind of shit happens all the time. Harmetz knew how the game was played. He certainly wasn't surprised.'

'But you'd think he'd at least go to court and fight for it.'

'Oh, he tried. Threatened to, anyway. Said he owned twenty percent of everything she ever did for the rest of her career and a hundred percent of the name Rebecca Gibson. Becca just laughed and told him to get a life. An artist and a manager have almost a marriage. You can't sue somebody to make 'em love you when they don't anymore.'

'Given the way this society's going, I'm surprised somebody hasn't tried it,' I said. 'But okay, we'll add Will Harmetz to the list.'

'Well, you can add, but it won't do any good in his case. He got drunker'n Cootie Mae Brown about five years ago and fell off a houseboat out in Percy Priest Lake. He washed up on the beach at Hermitage Landing on the Fourth of July weekend.'

I drew a line through Will Harmetz's name. 'Okay, so much for that. What about Mac Ford?'

'Well, I could see Mac Ford killing somebody. He is, after all, a manager. But it don't make sense. He and Becca got along. They'd been working together for years. She was all set to make him some serious money. Mac's kind of a wild man, but why would he want to kill her?'

I couldn't answer that. 'Okay, no motive for him. Who else?'

'Well, there's Faye Morgan over at CCA.'

'All right, that's something I don't understand. What's the difference between a booking agent and a manager?'

'A booking agent actually arranges the dates. The personal manager handles an artist's business affairs, approves contracts, negotiates deals with record companies. Basically, anything an artist needs. You got to understand, Harry, some of these kids come up here out of these small towns where the most sophisticated thing they've ever seen is the VFW hall on Friday night. As a rule, they ain't too well educated, and most of them are a little light in the basic-brains and common-sense department.'

Ray smiled like a cat with a mouthful of warm mouse. 'Why there's one famous-as-hell country singer, and I ain't going to tell you who he is, who can't even read. Literally can't sign his own goddamn name.'

'But how do these people survive?' I protested. 'It's got to be a cut-throat business. Record deals have got to be complicated. How do they protect themselves?'

'Most of them can't,' Ray said. 'That's why it's so important to have a manager you can trust. And a booking agent who's working for you and not against you. It's real difficult, too, 'cause a lot of these yahoo hillbillies come up here and get lucky enough to cut one or two hit records, and all of a sudden theirs don't stink anymore.'

'Get the big head, huh?' I realized we were getting sidetracked, but on the other hand, if I was going to jump into this cesspool, it sure would be nice to know where the rocks were.

'They can get to be real assholes, some of them. And the ones who come across nicest on the interview shows and at Fan Fair and stuff like that are usually the biggest assholes of all.'

'Was Rebecca one of them? Did she have the big head?'

Ray hesitated, unsure, I thought, of what he really wanted to say. 'A woman with Rebecca Gibson's talent was entitled to be a prima donna,' he said. 'You don't realize the pressure that's on these people. Of course, you're going to be difficult when you go through what these people go through. Especially when it takes as long as it did for Rebecca.'

'Did it take a long time for her to get a break?'

'Rebecca Gibson worked her butt off for over ten years before she started to make even a little bit of money. Anybody who works in this business long enough gets hard, Harry. You got to be. Nice guys get served up on a plate. So you've got the natural, understandable artist's temperament combined with a residue of vinegar left over from the struggle and all the times she got screwed. The two albums she did early on that cratered. All the broken promises, the rip-offs. Hell, the heartbreak.'

'So she was difficult?'

Ray sighed. 'Man, you hit her on the wrong day, she'd rip your face off and stuff it down your throat before you could get your jaw shut back.'

'Funny,' I said, 'she seemed just sort of flaky on the stage. Cute and flighty.'

Ray snorted. 'That's the act, man.'

'Woman like that must have made a lot of enemies. Tell me about this Faye Morgan.'

'Faye Morgan,' he said. 'Best booking agent in the business. One of the few booking agents with a reputation for being straight with artists and promoters both. Usually an agent will lean toward lying to one more than the other. But not Faye. She lies equally to both.'

'I thought you said she was straight.'

'In this business, if you lie to everybody equally, you are straight.'

Christ, I thought. What am I getting myself into?

'Great, so how are they connected?'

'Faye and Mac worked out a deal about six months ago, giving Faye exclusive rights to schedule and arrange dates for Rebecca. See, Rebecca's got an album in the can. Supposed to be out next month. Everybody figures it's going to be her breakout album. Coming out on Sanctuary Records.'

'Never heard of them.'

'Hottest independent company in the business,' he said.

'Why an independent? Why not one of the big companies?'

'Sanctuary's independent, but they're distributed by Warner,' he explained. 'They've thrown a lot of money behind this album. It's all contracts, man. Numbers and contracts.'

'Which can be forged, torn up, changed . . .'

'At the drop of a hat,' he said.

'So the hottest booking agent, the hottest manager, and the hottest independent record company were all getting behind Rebecca Gibson.'

'You got it, big guy. Rebecca Gibson was going to be fire in the sky.'

'Only now she's the coldest thing going – a corpse in a casket.'

Ray gritted his teeth and forced a smile in my direction. 'Harry, you got a weird sense of humor.'

Ray continued on for another hour with his insider's account of the music biz. Funny, I'd gone through my phase of wanting to be a musician. The attention, the glamor, the babes. Great fantasy, only in my case I spent most of my daydreaming playing air clarinet to Benny Goodman records rather than air guitar to Dire Straits. I liked the stuff I heard back in the Sixties, but my father had a collection of old jazz 78s that really stole my heart. I'll take the Quartet's Palomar Ballroom recording of 'Vibraphone Blues' over 'Sympathy for the Devil' any day. Charlie Watts hasn't got a thing on Gene Krupa.

Fortunately for the music world, I gave up that fantasy early. And the more I learned about the music business, the more I realized how fortunate it was for me as well.

I sat down in my office, alone now, and reviewed my notes. Where should I start? There were so many people who might have wanted to take a shot at her. Jealousies, rivalries, old simmering hatreds that erupt in passion and violence and blood. Treacheries and betrayals, lies and counterlies and counter-counterlies.

I shook my head, trying to stay focused. Too much to think about lately, all this chaos. Maybe I should run downstairs and get the late edition of the afternoon paper, check up on the day's developments.

I threw my coat on, but the phone rang just as I was headed for the door. I reached for it instinctively, quickly, then stopped with my hand just above the handset. I fingered the tape in my pocket, the one where somebody had told me to enjoy these last few days of mine. What if . . .?

To hell with it. If it's the same caller again, damn him, let him hear my voice. He can't hide behind an answering machine forever, and neither can I.

I picked up the phone. 'Denton Agency,' I said, coldly, professionally, partially holding my breath.

'I need a private dick.'

I spewed out a breath and giggled like a teenager. 'Well, honey, you've come to the right place.'

'Good,' Marsha said. 'I'm beginning to miss you a lot.'

'Just beginning?'

'Okay, *already* missing you a lot.'

'Yeah, well, if it's any great comfort, the hormone levels are climbing into the stratosphere on this end, too. How are you? How long can you talk?'

'I'm fine. Who knows how long this blasted phone will hold out. They allowed food and supplies through today. We got Sterno, soap, batteries, and flashlights. But you know what they sent us to eat?'

'What?'

'MREs.'

'MR whats?'

'Meals Ready to Eat. Government supplies. Can you believe that?'

'Oh, no. You mean that freeze-dried shit?'

'Apt description,' she said, then sighed. 'Oh, they're not inedible. Filling, reasonably nutritious. But tasteless.'

'When you're a free woman, we'll hit the best restaurant in a four-state area. My treat.'

'Something with spices and sauces and bottles of wine, right?'

'You got it.'

'I think I'm becoming sensorially deprived,' she said. 'All I've thought about for the last day and a half is food and sex. Not necessarily in that order. What have you been up to today?'

'We went to court for Slim's preliminary hearing.'

'How bad is it?'

'As much as I hate to admit it, he could've killed her.'

'You think he did?'

'I don't know what to think.'

'You sound pretty preoccupied with it.'

'I was,' I answered, 'until you called. Now my preoccupations have changed. How's Kay holding up?'

Marsha's voice lowered. 'Frankly, she's becoming insufferable. For the first day or so, she was as terrified as a cornered rabbit. But now she's convinced we're safe in here and she's yacking away at ninety miles a minute all the time. And I can't get away from her. The politics in here are weird, too.'

'What do you mean?'

'Well, there are five of us in here. Me, Kay, and three morgue attendants.'

'Let me guess: the three morgue attendants are all male.'

'And all under about twenty-five.'

'You don't have to say it. I get the picture.'

Five people trapped together in tight quarters: two women, one in charge, and three young males. Yes, I thought, the dynamics could get a little touchy.

'So we're all doing our level best, but frankly, it's getting tough. I'm afraid we'll kill each other before the wackos can get to us.'

I rubbed my forehead and fought the cramp that had erupted in the crook of my neck from having the phone jammed in there.

'Jeez, Marsh, I don't know what to say.'

'Don't worry about it. Just hang in there. We'll be all right.'

'Wait a minute,' I said. '*You're* being held hostage and you're cheering *me* up. What's wrong with this picture?'

Her laugh was broken by the popping of the phone and about two seconds of static. When she spoke again, her voice was filtered through a layer of hiss. '—got to go. We've had to start rationing phone calls. We had a problem with a couple of the guys making long-distance calls, and we can't seem to get Kay to limit her calls to less than a decade. I'll—'

Another loud pop, then silence, and finally a dial tone. I placed the phone back on its handset, then turned and looked out my window in the other direction, toward the east, where Marsha was. Where I couldn't see her or feel her anymore, at least not in reality.

But that's okay. Reality sucks anyway.

Chapter 17

The afternoon traffic on Gallatin Road slowed first to a crawl, then to a dead stop. I looked down at my watch; too early for rush hour. What the hell was going on? I wondered. To my right, a guy on crutches passed us on the sidewalk.

We sat there for a while, then the traffic started moving again. As I approached a slight rise in the pavement and topped it, I realized what the holdup was. A tall, black-skirted, white-shirted woman with a badge and a feeble bleach job held up a stop sign about the size of a Ping-Pong paddle and guided another gaggle of rug rats across the intersection.

Okay, so I know I've got this thing about traffic, but I try not to get too iced about school zones. After all, we have to protect the flower of American youth, even the ones that carry nickel-plated .22s in their lunch boxes next to their bologna-and-cheese sandwiches. So I usually stick pretty close to the fifteen-mile-per-hour limit and smile at the crossing guards and behave myself. For some reason, though, it was making my skin crawl today.

Everything was making my skin crawl today.

I'd decided that since I could no longer stay focused on any one subject and was as restless as a six-year-old with ten more minutes left in time-out, I'd take advantage of my options as a self-employed person and blow off the rest of the day. I don't do that often. It's not so much that I'm self-disciplined; I'd just rather be doing something than not doing something. Most days, that is.

So I drove over to Marsha's department, where I watered plants and checked locks. Then I dug around in her desk until I found what looked like a mailbox key. I walked back down the corridor and opened her box to find several days' worth of mail stuffed in.

There was a stack of the usual bills and junk mail, and a couple of catalogs: L. L. Bean, Williams-Sonoma, and some adventure-wilderness catalog with a photo of a pair of well-sculpted rock climbers in their early twenties plastered across the front. The two were dangling off the side of a cliff, pausing in midrappel for a swig from some plastic bottle no doubt full of yuppie mineral water. Marsha loved this kind of stuff: hiking, rappelling, rock climbing – all the adventure fantasies that appeal to people with too much education, too much time spent in windowless offices, and usually, too much money. Marsha had even coerced me into springing for a two-hundred-dollar pair of hiking boots that I'd never used. We were both too busy, something that left me relieved and thankful. I'd never mentioned to her that the prospect of leaping off the side of a cliff with nothing but a designer rope between me and the consequences of violating the laws of physics made me very nervous. Like totally incontinent . . .

Besides, I have no great love for the outdoors. My idea of roughing it is when room service closes at ten.

I moped around for a while, then headed across the river. Once through the school zones, the traffic picked up and I soon found myself in the left-hand-turn lane near the old Inglewood Theatre, hoping for a break in the traffic. The light at Ben Allen Road changed over and I shot across two lanes while there was still time. Around the corner, past the steel-doored Death Rangers clubhouse, the chain-link gate across the entrance to Lonnie's junkyard – excuse me, auto-salvage and recycling lot – was shut tight. I pulled the smoking Mazda to a stop and set the parking brake.

The padlock on the gate was unhitched, so I figured he had to be there. Without thinking, I pulled the latch up on the gate and swung it wide. The hinges let loose with a long, high-pitched screeching sound.

Big mistake.

She registered in my peripheral vision as I stepped through the gate and started to close it behind me. It was a natural reaction, I guess; I hadn't seen her in days, didn't know she was back from the vet's. I smiled, started to say something in the usual baby talk she drove me to, then froze.

Shadow, Lonnie's ageing timber shepherd was charging me from across the yard. Ordinarily, that wouldn't have been bad. Except for the silence. No barking. No eager panting. No twitching back and forth of the long black-and-gray tail. She was low, close to the ground, coming straight at me like a runaway locomotive, except that she was in complete control. I could yell her name, but that's about all I'd have time to yell before she ripped my throat out.

I whipped around and threw all my weight into the gate, pushing it back wide-open again from where I'd nearly shut it. Thinking, lately, had been like trying to see through a fogged-up windshield. But I had sense enough to realize my only hope was to get that chain-link gate between me and her.

I caught a glimpse of her as I ducked behind the gate just as she became airborne. She was eye level with me by the time I got my head turned. I had my fingers intertwined in the chain link, scrambling like hell as I pulled it to, hoping she didn't have a taste for finger food. Shadow had to weigh seventy, maybe eighty pounds, and on her best days, she could outrun a Corvette from a dead stop for twenty yards.

She slammed into the chain link so hard that the fence shook. I felt her hot breath. Slobber splattered on me as I pulled the fence to and got it latched just in time to get my fingers out of the way.

She dropped to the ground after hitting the fence, but only for a moment. Then she was up on her hind legs, this time with a low guttural growl coming from somewhere deep inside of her that scared the slam-dunking hell out of me.

Behind her, the door to the rusty green trailer opened and Lonnie dashed out, zipping up a pair of tight Levi's.

'Shadow, cut!' he yelled. She jumped down, backed off two feet, and sat on her haunches. She was heaving like a marathoner at the Mile-24 marker, but she never took those black eyes off me for a second.

'You dumb son of a bitch,' Lonnie hissed as he came up behind her and laid a hand on her shoulder. 'You trying to get yourself killed?'

My heart pounded in my chest and an enormous pool had formed under each armpit. 'I didn't know she was back,' I wheezed. Lonnie squatted down and buried his face in the fur behind her ear, nuzzling her, whispering to calm her. 'You didn't tell me.'

He turned to me. 'You didn't ask.'

'She was so quiet,' I said, forcing my breath to slow to normal. 'You think she's going to warn you?'

I suddenly felt dizzy, clammy all over. 'If I hadn't see her coming . . .'

'Don't dwell on it,' he said. 'C'mon in now. And for God's sake, try to act like a sane person.'

I looked at her. Her eyes still had not warmed. Two rounded cubes of black ice stared out at me from gray-and-black fur. 'You sure it's okay?'

'It will be. C'mon.'

I unlatched that gate again. She seemed to stiffen for a second. Lonnie pressed his hand into her fur. I stepped through the gate, never taking my eyes off her. I'd gotten into nasty scrapes before, but never had I experienced anything like this. I never considered Shadow this way, as a killing machine that could be turned in my direction.

I closed the gate behind me. 'I'm sorry, man. I guess I just wasn't thinking.'

'It's not all your fault. She don't see so well anymore. Come closer and hold out your hand, slow. Don't make a fist.'

'Shadow,' I cooed. 'It's me, baby. Harry.'

The low growl from hell started up again. Lonnie rubbed her ears. My hand got within about two inches of her great black, shiny wet nose. I moved it closer, just a hair, then held it there.

She seemed to pause for a second, then sniffed the air expectantly. Behind Lonnie, I saw her tail wag. My heart backfired in my chest as she lunged, and I had this fragmented thought that this was what the jaws of death were going to look like.

Then her paws were on my shoulders, and her huge tongue was slapping across my face, wet and hot and sloppy. I relaxed and wrapped my arms around her in a bear hug. I lowered her to the ground, and she barked twice, loud and cheery. No big deal to her. All forgiven, all forgotten.

'No, baby, no chicken. I don't have any chicken today.'

She barked a couple more times, like *I could still eat you, bud*.

'What'd you do today, anyway?' Lonnie asked as he turned and headed back to the trailer. 'Crawl out of bed and eat a big bowl of stupid?'

'Sorry,' I answered, following him.

'I've seen you do some sorry shit before, but I'd have to rate that one about a nine-point-nine.'

'That low?' I asked, closing the door behind me as we stepped into the living room. I looked around. Every time I came here, he had some new piece of junk or equipment, exotic weapon, or electronic device. The place looked more like Frankenstein's laboratory than a dwelling – especially if Frankenstein drove a pickup truck and drank a lot of beer.

Speaking of beers, one came flying through the air toward me as Lonnie emerged from the kitchen. Two tops popped simultaneously as Lonnie pitched himself down on an overstuffed chair. I settled onto the couch, avoiding a large patch of thirty-weight for the sake of my good clothes.

'What's this?' I asked, eyeing a large carton on the coffee table.

'UPS man left it,' he said.

'Bet he didn't try to come through the gate.'

Lonnie laughed. 'He's got better sense.'

Curiosity got the better of me. 'What is it?'

'Let's see.' He whipped out a long pocketknife and thumbed a release on the side. The blade flicked open and glinted in the lamplight.

'What in the ever-loving hell are you doing with a switchblade?'

'This old thing?' he said affectionately as he slit the packing tape across the top of the carton. 'Hell, this's just a toy.'

I shook my head, then took a long pull off the can. My throat sparkled as the beer went down. I only had to wait a couple of seconds for the burn in my gut.

Lonnie ripped the top of the package open and dug through a pile of Styrofoam peanuts. He pulled out some packing slips and an invoice. 'Oh, yeah, I remember. Jeez, I ordered this stuff almost two months ago.'

'What is it?'

He dug deeper into the white, crunchy peanuts, then pulled out a small, green can. He handed it to me and I studied it. It weighed maybe a pound, maybe a little more, and except for the fact that it had a grenade pin and handle on the top, it looked fairly innocuous.

'I'm afraid to ask,' I admitted.

He sat back down in his chair. He held the sweating beer can in his left hand, and in his right, he casually tossed one of the canisters up and down.

'M-18 smoke grenade,' he said. 'Military issue. Pull the pin, wait a couple of seconds, and then over the next minute and a half, you've got a quarter-million cubic feet of dense colored smoke. I sent for the variety pack. What color'd you get?'

I looked down at the writing on the can. 'Red.'

'Great, I got violet.'

'Well, whoop-de-doo. Let's go outside and play.'

Lonnie scooted over and dropped his canister back into the pile of packing peanuts. 'What in the hell's going on with you, Harry? Lately, you been about as much fun as a bad rash.'

I put my head back on the couch and stared straight up toward the ceiling. The dirty-white and brown-stained acoustic tiles looked like someone had been spitting tobacco juice at them.

He stared at me until I became uncomfortable. 'What?' I finally asked, just to break the silence.

'I've known you for a long time, Harry, and you ain't never been this weird before. What the fuck's going on with you?'

'I wish I knew.'

I got up and walked into the kitchen. The sink was permanently discolored with grease stains and dirt. A huge, four-barreled Holley carburetor sat on the counter, the tops of its brass jets polished to a shine. I opened the refrigerator and grabbed another can of beer. It was the first time I'd ever done that without thinking.

Just make yourself at home, dude, I thought. 'Want another one?' I yelled.

'No,' he called. 'I like to savor mine. The delicate bouquet and the lingering aftertaste.'

'Yeah,' I said, walking back into the living room and pacing around with the can in my hand. 'It's the aftertaste I keep trying to wash away.'

'Who are you kidding, Harry? Don't pull that Sam Spade shit on me. You don't even drink that much.'

'Well, I may start.'

'Has it occurred to you that with all you're dealing with, you've got every right to be a little stressed-out?'

'Yes,' I said, 'I have the right to be a little stressed-out. I don't have the right to quit functioning, which is what I feel like I'm doing.'

Lonnie's heavy workboots hit the top of the coffee table with a bang as he stretched out. 'Look, guy, your girlfriend's a hostage, another friend's in jail for murder, and you're so fucking broke you can't afford to pay a lawyer to bankrupt your ass. And to top it off, my dog just missed chewing your nuts off by the thickness of a chain-link fence. You think there might be some situational triggers here?'

'Yeah, and as soon as I get this laundry list of situations taken care of, I'll be okay.'

'That's it,' he yelled, slapping the armrest of the worn red-velour chair he sat in. 'That's the problem. See? You keep saying *taken care of* and *fixed* and all that shit. You keep acting like you're going to solve some crime and be the big hero. And there ain't nothing for you to solve. It's not your business. You aren't a hostage negotiator and you aren't a homicide investigator and you're not, not a . . .'

He paused. 'Not a detective?' I asked. 'Or at least not much of one.'

'That's not what I meant. You still don't get it. What I'm trying to tell you is that you're going about it the wrong way. You can't be a detective here. So stop trying.'

'So what do I do?' I yelled. 'Sit here while the whole damn world swirls down the toilet?'

'If it does, you can't stop it, can you? But that's not even the point.'

'Then what *is* the point?'

He shifted up in the chair and dropped his boots on the floor with a thud that shook the floor of the trailer. 'Forget all this Mike Hammer shit. Go back to what you know best.'

I felt my forehead tighten involuntarily. 'What do you mean?'

'What did you do before you became a private investigator?'

'A reporter,' I said. 'You know that.'

'Right. And you were a much better reporter than you are a detective.'

'Gee, thanks,' I said.

'What the hell would you expect me to say? You were a reporter for, what, fifteen years? And you've been a detective maybe two years. Do the math.'

I set the beer can down on the coffee table, still unopened. Then I settled into the corner of the couch and found that I had unconsciously chewed a sore place on my lower lip.

'So stop thinking like a detective,' he said. 'And go back to thinking like a reporter.'

'You know,' I said, after a moment, 'I'd gotten out of that mind-set.'

'So get back into it. Forget about catching the bad guys. Go back to looking for the truth, just for its own sake. You do that, everything else will fall into place on its own.'

Then, for a moment, this incredible sense of calm came over me. Lonnie was right. I'd been trying to chase down and hog-tie something I couldn't even see. I began to see Marsha's situation in a different light, and Slim's as well. But there was one situation – the financial one – that had only one perspective, and that perspective was inescapable. In order to change that, I was going to have to do something I'd never done before, and I was real uncomfortable at the thought.

'Listen, pal. You don't happen to have an extra couple of hundred laying around somewhere you could loan me, do you? Just until the insurance company cuts my check?'

Chapter 18

Quit thinking like a detective; start thinking like a newspaperman. Fall back on what you know best. Go with what's worked before.

I drove home without remembering how I got there, ate dinner without tasting it, then stared at the tube without watching it. Marsha called about ten, exhausted, half-asleep. We made forced small talk for five minutes, then rang off.

Next morning, all I could think of was where to start. In my mind, I went back to my newspaper days, back to when I used to follow a trail to see where it was going, and not because I wanted it to go somewhere. That had been my problem the last few days; I was pursuing my own agenda, rather than reality.

I didn't know what good it would do, but the logical first step was to see Slim.

It had been years since I'd set foot in the Davidson County jail. Back in my younger days – the crime beat being a young man's game – I hung around the jail a lot. That was the old days. Everything was different now, I discovered as I crossed Second Avenue North and went into the ground floor of the Criminal Justice Center. The place was tighter, more efficient than it was in days past, when prisoners and staff would often mingle in a backslapping informality that was shocking to the outsider. Now the uniformed officers were crisp and almost military in bearing, while the plainclothes staffers wore pressed suits and wide polyester ties. The place was even quieter than I remembered, with little of the background chatter and metallic din that characterizes most jails.

I climbed the steep flight of stairs to the second floor, where I would be logged in and patted down before being allowed into the visiting gallery. A man in a gray suit with a plastic ID tag clipped to his shirt pocket that identified him as Officer Combs examined my driver's license and had me empty my pockets. Then I signed the log and was led down a narrow hallway, past closed doors and a few stray inmates in orange jumpsuits with DCSO –

Davidson County Sheriff's Office – stenciled on the back.

Everything was gray–painted cinder block and drywall, with slick linoleum floors, institutionally cold but clean and orderly. The first thing I noticed was the absence of that particular odor that's so indigenous to jails and prisons. It's impossible to describe unless you've taken in a lungful of it, but it's a strange mix of masculine sweat, cigarette smoke, disinfectant tinged with a faint trace of urine, and something else that's cold and sterile and unidentifiable, as if the concrete and steel had a smell of their own that was heightened and reinforced by the presence of so many incarcerated bodies. It's not an unpleasant odor; it's just more pervasive and omnipresent than anything else. I've never smelled it anywhere else but jails and prisons, but there wasn't any of it here.

Officer Combs led me into a rectangular room with a series of partitions on the long left and right sides of the rectangle. At the end of the room was a large plate-glass window that looked out onto a hallway, on the other side of which was the glass-enclosed room that was Central Control. Video monitors and electronically controlled doors oversaw access to every door, every elevator, every room in the facility.

A crowd of guys, a random mix of tall and short, thin and fat, black and white, lingered in the hallway.

'What're they doing?' I asked.

'Awaiting transit,' the officer said in a monotone. 'They've been sentenced and they're off to classification.'

Then I remembered what I'd been told years before; with the exception of the trustees and a few inmates with sentences short enough to serve locally, all the people in this jail were technically innocent.

Shows you just how far a technicality will get you, I thought.

Officer Combs motioned me toward one of the stalls on the left. 'Sit there,' he instructed. 'The prisoner will be here as soon as we can get him down from the fifth floor. You've got an hour.'

'Thanks,' I said, but he'd already turned and walked away.

I sat on a low circular gray stool bolted to the floor in front of a small ledge beneath a window. The glass window was about eight-by-twelve inches and looked out on a wall maybe two feet away. Slim would be led in by a guard, would squeeze onto the stool on his side of the metal wall, and we'd talk through a metal screen beneath the porthole.

There were so many layers of paint on the metal walls around me that I could see waves from the varying thickness. In front of me, someone had carved love graffiti in the paint with a ball-point pen.

JRF LOVES JIMMY, the message read, with a scratched heart around it. Not in this place, she doesn't.

There wasn't quite enough room in the tiny stall to spread my elbows out to the horizontal, which made me feel a bit claustrophobic. I wondered how I'd deal with being locked up, then hoped I'd never have the chance to find out. Voices echoed around me in hollow metallic ringing.

I heard the muffled sound of movement through the tiny screen, then a shadow moving against the wall opposite me. In a moment an orange jumpsuit followed by a uniform appeared in the window, then the orange jumpsuit settled down and Slim's face filled the small square of thick glass.

Slim looked tired, with deep-purplish-and-gray circles under his eyes. He was clean-shaven, though, and his hair looked freshly shampooed.

'Hey, Harry,' he said. The sound of his voice spoke of fatigue beyond help.

'Slim,' I said. 'How are you?'

'Holding on,' he answered. He settled down on the stool and folded his arms onto the metal ledge on his side of the window, as if he were trying to get his face as close to free air as possible. 'Can't sleep much, though.'

'Too noisy?'

'Naw, it ain't that. I just can't sleep. It ain't so bad, though. 'S not like it's the first time I've ever been in jail or anything.'

I must have unconsciously frowned at him. 'Don't look at me like that, Harry,' he said defensively. 'Coupla DUIs in my wilder days and one aggravated assault. I ain't fucking Jack the Ripper.'

I grinned at him. 'Okay, so you ain't Jack the Ripper. But you're in some deep effluent, Slim. I can't lie to you. I don't know what the hell to do to help you out. I've lost a little sleep myself the last couple of days.'

His eyes wandered down to the floor. 'Maybe nobody can help me.'

'No, I don't believe that. We just aren't there yet, that's all. You didn't kill her. We just got to find out who did, which is why I'm here.'

His eyes refocused on my face through the glass. 'You think that's possible?'

'Anything's possible, especially when it looks like it's your last hope. So let's get started. You knew her, maybe better than

127

anybody else. I've talked to Ray and he's filled me in on some of the background. I want to hear it from you. Who else could have killed Rebecca?'

Slim brought both hands up and massaged the tension out of his face. I started getting the jitters again, and almost reminded him we only had an hour. Then I decided to hold on and let Slim do this his own way.

'If I had to bet money on it,' he finally said, 'I'd lay it all on either Dwight Parmenter or Mike Pinkleton.'

'I know who Dwight Parmenter is, but who's Pinkleton?'

'Mike Pinkleton was her road manager, the head roadie.'

'Was?'

'Yeah, was. She fired him a week ago.'

'What for?'

'I don't know, although Mike was a pretty tough kind of guy. Biceps the size of half-gallon jugs and biker tattoos everywhere. Hair down to his shoulders, blue-jean jacket with the arms cut off. You know the type.'

'How long had he worked for her?'

'That's the weird part. Becca inherited him after our act broke up. That's how far back we all go. He'd worked for her maybe five, six years.'

'Then why would she fire him?'

'You find that out, you may be onto something,' Slim said.

'But you think he could beat somebody to death?'

Slim snickered. 'Wait'll you see him.'

Enough said. 'Okay, now why Dwight Parmenter? From what Ray said, he had a bad case of the hots for her.'

'Which is why he'd have done it,' Slim snapped. He jerked a finger at the window. 'You just don't understand, Harry. When it came to Becca Gibson, the only thing worse than wanting her was having her. She left a trail of bodies behind – used, abused, and excused.'

'I'm trying to understand that. I know she was a heartbreaker and a ballbreaker. But why Dwight Parmenter? If he had the hots for her and she turned him down, did he kill her just for that? Or did he wind up sleeping with her and then get thrown over? That's what I'm trying to figure out.'

Slim sank back on the stool, calmer now. 'I know they were doin' it,' he said. 'Both of them told me that. In fact, there were days lately where I'd get off the phone with one of them bitching to me about the affair, and then five minutes later the other one would call.'

'You were caught in the middle.'

'Yeah,' he said, his head drooping with the weight, 'just like I am now.'

'What about her manager?' I asked, shifting gears. 'What's-his-name . . .'

'Mac Ford. Yeah, he'll be able to help you. He knew more about the business dealings than anybody else. I'm pretty sure he'll talk to you.'

'Great, but what I meant was could he have killed her?'

Slim got this quizzical look on his face. 'Why? He'd worked with her all these years, trying to build her a career. Rebecca was going to take off. She was going to be really big, and Mac's cut was going to take care of the next three generations.'

'No.' He shook his head. 'Anybody in this mess comes out a loser, it's Mac Ford. Besides Rebecca, that is. Mac's lost a fortune. He'll still make money off her, though, off everything she's got in the can. He won't starve.'

'What about a will?' I asked. 'Becca have one?'

Slim looked thoughtful for a second, as if he were recalling some long-ago memory that made him feel warm inside. 'You know, back when we were married and it looked like we were going to go somewhere, I brought the subject up one time. Becca wouldn't even discuss it. I tried to tell her, "Honey, we could get in a car wreck or something." She busted my ass over it. Funny thing, Harry, she was scared as hell of death.'

His voice had become softer, lower, as if somewhere beneath the decade's worth of abuse and baggage and emotional garbage, he still loved her. Some people, I knew from hard experience, were just like that. They get under your skin, wrap themselves around your very nerve endings, and never turn you loose.

'Well, if it's any comfort,' I said, 'she doesn't have anything to be afraid of now.'

Slim's eyes glazed over, and I was sorry I'd said that. 'Nobody could ever understand it who hadn't been through it, Harry. That woman was the best thing that ever happened to me – and the worst. All at the same time.'

As I left the jail a half hour or so later, I thought of what Slim had said: *The only thing worse than wanting her was having her.* I couldn't help but think of Saint Teresa, and the price she quoted for inordinately strong desires.

Something about answered prayers and shed tears . . .

Chapter 19

The five hundred in cash Lonnie'd loaned me was going to be a pretty good cushion, but I still needed to stay on top of Phil Anderson at the insurance company to get my invoice paid. I got my car out of hock at the parking lot across the street from the jail, then navigated through the traffic back to my office so I could catch him before his usual round of afternoon meetings.

It was nearly ten-thirty by the time I hit the landing on the third floor and turned for my office. As I scrambled for my keys I heard the relays in my answering machine clattering away again, and a muffled voice leaving what sounded like the last of a message. I couldn't understand what the caller was saying, but the voice was Southern, almost hick.

'All right,' I said out loud, thinking it sounded like Phil Anderson, '*do that paperwork thing you do so well.*' For some unknown reason, I was in a good mood. Maybe it was just the apex of the bipolar roller-coaster ride. I hoped, maybe even assumed, that Phil was calling me with good news. I already had the money spent.

I pushed the door open just as the caller hung up. My ancient answering machine takes about thirty seconds to reset itself. I took off my coat and cracked a window to air the place out.

I opened my briefcase and took out the notebook where I'd made a page of notes after talking to Slim. The conversation with him had helped a little, but not much. I absentmindedly reached over and hit the play button. After the obligatory greeting from the computer chip, a voice dripping Dixie syrup began playing off the tape. It wasn't the voice I expected.

'Hey, you son of a bitch, this's me again. I just wanted you to know I ain't forgot the promise I made. You go ahead and have you a real good time, boy, because yo' good times is about to come to a end . . .'

Click and dial tone, fade the hell out.

'Jeezus H.,' I said, 'what is going on with this guy?'

I reached into my briefcase and recovered the tape with the first threatening message and slapped it in the machine. I hit the button again and listened to the first message.

Yeah, same voice. Same slurring of the words *son of a bitch*. Somehow, I'd managed to piss off somebody who sounded like they had a mouthful of cotton, or more likely, chewing tobacco.

I pulled the tape out of the machine and stuffed both tapes into my briefcase. If this kept up, I'd soon be heading to Wal-Mart for a case of answering machine tapes.

Who the hell could this be? The only thing I knew for sure was that I didn't know the person. Not only did I not recognize the voice, but the threatening messages had only been left on my *office* machine. After some nut I ran into made a couple of nasty phone calls to my apartment a few months ago, I'd had my home number changed and unlisted. So whoever was taking a turn at me now was beholden to the Yellow Pages. My only recourse was to save the tapes until I had enough of them to call South Central Bell and file a harassment claim.

I raked across my Rolodex cards until Phil Anderson's came up. Seven short number punches later, I was talking to his secretary.

'This is Harry Denton,' I explained. 'Is he in?'

'May I ask what this is concerning?' she asked.

It always irritates the pee out of me when somebody asks that. I've always wanted to say to some secretary: 'No, you may not ask what this is concerning, and if you do again, I'm going to come up to your office and rip your liver out through your nostrils.'

Boy, I thought, am I getting hostile these days or what? 'Certainly,' I said as politely as I could muster. 'I'm just following up on the case I completed for him.'

What I was trying *not* to say is that I'm calling about the damn money he owes me. That usually doesn't get you very far, I'd found.

'Please hold, Mr Denton. I'll see if he's available.'

I reread my page of notes twice before she came back. 'I'm sorry to keep you waiting, Mr Denton. Mr Anderson's unavailable right now. May I have a number where he can reach you?'

'Sure,' I said. What was I going to say? So I gave her my number and stared at the phone for a few seconds after hanging up.

In all the times I'd phoned Phil Anderson, he'd never not taken my calls. I began to recognize the foul stench of a telephone dodge.

Still fuming over the insurance company's shabby treatment of

me after I'd pulled their unaudited asses out of the fire, I dialed
Roger Vaden's office and took a chance on him being in. Lawyers,
I've found over the years, will rarely admit to being in their offices
when you need them, and on the few occasions when they are,
they are adamant in their unavailability for unsolicited phone
calls. Vaden was no exception.

'When do you expect him back?' I asked.

'I'm not sure,' the sweet feminine voice on the other end of the
line answered. 'Perhaps you could tell me what this is in regard
to.'

I suppressed the urge to bitch somebody out. 'I'm a friend of
Slim Gibson's. I'm a private investigator, and he's asked me to
help him out with this case. I thought I should at least let Mr
Vaden know what I was doing before I started doing it.'

'Oh,' she said abruptly. 'Please hold.'

I drummed a succession of fingers on the desk, waiting for
perhaps an hour or more during the next thirty seconds. Roger
Vaden's stiff, cool professional voice finally came on the line,
sounding much more in control than it did before Judge Alvin
Rosenthal.

'Yes, Mr Denton, what can I do for you?'

'I spoke with Slim,' I began.

'You saw him at the jail?'

'Yes, just this morning.'

'I wish you'd asked my permission.'

Something about his tone of voice made want to rear back on
my haunches and flash a fang at him. 'I didn't know I needed
your permission to visit the jail during public visiting hours.'

'You don't, but you do need it to question my client.'

'I didn't *question* your client. Your client wanted to talk to me.'

He backed off at that. 'Bickering like this will do us no good.
What do you want?'

'Slim asked me to do a little looking around. As a courtesy, I'm
making you aware of that. I don't know how deeply I'm going to
get involved in his case. As I'm sure you already know, the Slim
Gibson defense fund is a little on the meager side. Also, I'm not
exactly sure what I can do for him. He's in a lot of trouble.'

'I know,' Vaden said.

'You can do something for me – and for Slim. If I need the
leverage of working in an official capacity, I'd appreciate it if
you'd back me up.'

'Meaning?'

'If I get in a spot where I have to tell somebody I'm working
for you on Slim's behalf, that you just verify that.'

'I won't be responsible for you. I take no responsibility or liability for anything you do.'

'I'm not asking you to,' I said. 'But if somebody calls and says, "There's a guy here who says he's working for you," could you just say, "Yeah, he is"?'

'You *are* a licensed private investigator?' he asked.

'That's correct. I'm even bonded.'

'The problem is that I don't know how long I'm going to be on the case.'

'I understand. You're trying to get a criminal lawyer involved, right?'

'Yes, but I'm not having much luck. Mr Gibson is not being held in very high esteem within the local community. The press has pilloried him, practically convicted him. And with his limited resources, he can't afford the defense he needs. The only alternative, really, is the . . .' His voice faded away, as if he couldn't bring himself to say the two dreaded words.

'Public defender?' I asked.

'Yes. And that basically means he won't have a defense. More likely, he'll just have someone negotiate the length of his prison term.'

'Slim deserves better than that.'

'I agree. But what can we do? I'm not even sure what our opinions are. The judge will hear preliminary motions in about a month. It's going to take almost that long for defense to prepare. Which doesn't leave much time to find him an advocate.'

'And you're definitely not going to represent him?'

Vaden cleared his throat nervously. 'This is not my specialty. Even if I could afford to take the case on for what Mr Gibson can pay, I seriously doubt I'm equipped to give him the best representation possible.'

'How long have we got? Or rather, how long have you got before you're off the case?'

'A week. Perhaps a bit longer.'

I felt overwhelmed and frustrated by so much coming from so many different directions at once. 'Okay, listen,' I said. 'Let's try this. I've got a form that's just a simple boilerplate that says I've been retained by you. It's got some blanks to be filled in that describe what I'm supposed to be doing, and for how long. I'll fill in the blanks, sign the form, and mail it to you. If it meets with your approval, sign it and mail it back to me, along with a check for one dollar. I'll bill Slim for the rest when this is all over – that is, if he's in a position to make any more than the sixty cents an hour or so that inmates earn. Is that all right with you?'

'Yes,' he said, after a moment's silence. 'That will do. I can go that far, as long as there aren't any problems on the form.'

'Add whatever you need to in order to protect yourself,' I said. As if he wouldn't anyway . . .

'I'll turn it around as soon as I get it,' he said.

'Okay, Mr Vaden. It's a pleasure doing business with you.'

'I only hope this does Slim some good.' His voice relaxed now that the negotiations had ended. 'I'm extremely worried about him.'

'Yeah,' I said. 'Me, too.'

I filled in the blanks and typed up an envelope in about five minutes, then plopped a stamp on it and dropped it in the mailbox on the way out of the building. The sun was high above the Seventh Avenue buildings now; another beautiful spring day was in the making. We get about six or eight weeks every year in Nashville when this city is draped in the most glorious weather you'll see anywhere on the planet: temperatures in the low seventies, bright blue skies, little or no humidity. Sometimes I think this little balmy window between the frozen gray of winter and the sweltering red of summer is all that keeps most of us here.

The next step was to drop in on Mac Ford, Rebecca's manager, and get whatever I could out of him. I dodged a couple of cars and scampered across the street, then began the long climb up the ramps to the fourth floor of the parking garage. As usual, I'd come in late and lost my chance for a prime parking space. That didn't really bother me, though. The ramp wasn't steep and I needed the exercise.

There was a memorial service for Rebecca Gibson later that afternoon, down on Broadway at Christ Episcopal Church. I figured I'd take a chance on catching Ford, then head back downtown for the service. I wasn't sure what I'd get out of attending the service, but it seemed like it couldn't hurt anything.

I rounded the slick concrete ramp on the third level and headed, slightly winded and quickly moistening, up toward my car. Ahead of me, the faded; chipped paint on the wall gave the place a decayed look, and I fought not to think of how far my life had deteriorated in the past couple of years. Back at the newspaper, I had seniority in the parking lot as well as the office, with a prime spot in the employee lot down in the Gulch, the area that ran below the Church Street Viaduct down in back of the newspaper building.

What the hell, I thought, think of it as a built-in exercise machine.

Above me, there was a crash. Not a loud one, not the heavy metallic grind of cars slamming into each other, but more of a thud followed by . . .

Breaking glass.

I quickened my steps halfway up the ramp, then broke into a trot. A half-dozen steps later there was another crash, this time louder, followed by the distinct tinkling of shattered glass hitting concrete.

I accelerated from a trot to a run, but my street shoes were slick on the concrete and I missed a couple of steps, almost losing my footing. I reached out to regain my balance, then hit the top of the ramp. I whipped around a concrete pillar and saw, at the farthest end of the garage, a running hulk of a man maybe sixty yards away from me. All I saw was a blur of blue legs and a pair of arms in a checked shirt pumping away.

'Hey!' I yelled, without thinking. I put everything I had into it, figuring that somebody hauling ass like that in a direction away from me was certainly up to no good.

Whoever he was, he knew how to run. He outpaced me, getting to a large steel door with a push bar before I was even a quarter of the way down the building. He slammed the brass exit bar and was through in a half second, leaving only a puff of dust as the door closed behind him.

I ran like hell, hoping he's gotten stuck out there somehow. But the door exited out onto an exterior stairwell that ran straight down the side of the building to a driveway that led, in turn, to the alley behind the parking garage. I gave it all I had, but by the time I got to the door, I was puffing so hard I wouldn't have heard his footsteps even if he'd still been there. As I held on to the door to keep from being locked out of the garage, I caught a glimpse of him rounding the corner of the building and streaking into the alley.

There was no use following. He was long gone.

I sputtered, straining to get my breath back. Sweat had broken out everywhere, and I felt like ripping my suit coat off.

I pushed the door all the way open and stepped back into the garage. I wondered what the hell had gone on, when I noticed my shoes were crunching on the concrete. I bent my knee and examined the bottom of my right shoe.

Broken glass was embedded all over the sole.

Oh, boy, I thought. Somebody's in for a lousy surprise when

they get off work. I was debating getting involved with the police when I noticed a spray of broken glass on the concrete about a dozen cars ahead of me.

I worked myself up to a trot again, my fears growing as I approached the twinkling mess. Then I got to the car, which had been tucked in between two long sedans so that its nose was invisible unless you were right on top of it.

My car.

The windshield was smashed in, with a thousand bits of glittering safety glass all over the hood and a gaping hole right in front of the steering wheel. My heart sank as I walked over and surveyed the damage.

There was a large, ragged-edged chunk of brick lying beside the driver's side door, but no attempt had been made to break into the car. Mindless, idiotic vandalism, I thought. If I'd only been here a couple of minutes sooner, I thought, I could have stopped the guy.

Or maybe he'd have used the brick on my head.

The sweat I'd worked up turned into icicles as I realized what had happened. Was I getting paranoid? Somebody trashed my car, but didn't try to steal the stereo. I'm getting death threats on the phone and bricks through the windshield.

What the hell's going on?

Chapter 20

'What the hell do you mean?' I demanded. 'The police don't take these calls anymore? Lady, my car has been vandalized, for God's sake!'

'I'm sorry, sir,' the impersonal voice on the other end of the line said. Then she repeated her canned explanation of why the police are too busy to respond to routine car break-ins. There are just too many of them. She could, she offered, assign a report number that might satisfy my insurance company.

'I don't *have* any car insurance,' I protested. 'Since I'm an honest citizen, I can't afford it anymore.'

'Sir.' Her tone shifted to the stern one she used when her kids were out of control. 'It's against the law to drive without liability insurance.'

'Aw, assign it a number,' I said, giving her my best Bowery Boys go-to-hell attitude as I slammed the phone down.

I thumbed through the Yellow Pages and found the auto-glass companies. I called four of them and discovered, to my utter confounded amazement, that they all charged the same amount to replace my windshield.

'What a coincidence,' I said to Polite Young Receptionist Number Four. 'A hundred and fifty is what the other three companies said.'

'Oh, yessir,' she said, missing the massive dose of smart-ass I'd injected into my voice. I guess she wasn't too up on price-fixing laws, either. 'We all charge the same.'

She'd already told me that the windshield replacement would take a couple of hours, so I figured what the hell. Price fixing or no price fixing, I had them right where they wanted me.

'The only problem is,' I explained, 'I've got to be somewhere. I can't wait around.'

'That's okay, sir. We can bill your insurance company direct, then put your deductible on a credit card.'

I cleared my throat. 'I don't have any insurance.' I half expected her to hang up on me in disgust.

'Oh,' she said. Her voice dropped about fifty percent in volume. 'You seem like a nice guy. Noninsurance claims we'll let slide by for a hundred. That okay?'

I tried not to gasp. Ordinarily, I don't like benefiting from rip-offs, but in this case I'd make an exception. 'Sure, that'd be great. Can I put it on a card?'

'Sure, go ahead,' she said pleasantly. I opened my wallet and took out my VISA card, which the last time I'd checked still had just about enough left on the credit limit to cover the bill.

'We'll take care of it, Mr Denton. Thanks so much.'

I hoofed it out of the building and down Seventh Avenue to Broadway, pondering all the while the confusing array of moral choices that day-to-day living involves, not to mention the implications involved in a society that does everything it can to make being a crime victim as convenient as possible.

In a city where you can't throw a dead cat out a window without hitting a church, Christ Church stands out as one of the grandest. A nineteenth-century Anglican cathedral, its gray stone spires tower over Broadway just across the wide avenue from the federal courthouse.

In the end, I was glad I walked. The cars waiting to get into the inadequate parking lot adjacent to the church had traffic blocked all the way down the hill. Horns blared and tempers flared as even the usual crowd of winos that hung out on the steps of the church was driven away.

A crowd of people, dressed in everything from jeans and rhinestone-studded cowboy shirts to three-piece suits, gathered in front, milling about and making small talk. Women and men huddled together, their faces close, lips moving, with an occasional physical gesture of comfort or familiarity. On the fringes, television and print reporters scouted the crowd for celebrities. Off in another corner, one bright, young, fresh-scrubbed face was doing what looked like a live remote.

I hate funerals, but let this one slide with the rationale that it was a memorial service, not the full-blown pageant. As I crossed the sidewalk and stepped up to the entrance to the church, a few heads turned and checked me out. I didn't recognize anyone, and it was obvious from the casual dismissals that no one recognized me either.

I wove my way through the crowd and into the church. My eyes took a few moments to adjust to the subdued light. The narthex of the church was carpeted in a deep, thick red that felt soft and velourlike under my feet. Dark oak and mahogany trim surrounded the doorways and a dim light over a pedestal barely illuminated a registry for visitors.

I stood in line to sign the register, then wandered around and people-watched as inconspicuously as possible. I recognized several rising music stars, mostly ones I'd seen on the Country Music Television cable channel late at night. There were a few of the old guard around, but Rebecca Gibson's fans and friends were mostly young.

At the back of a group of five people huddled near one of the entrances into the church nave, I saw a face that seemed familiar. I couldn't remember where I'd seen him; he certainly wasn't any kind of big celebrity that everyone would know. But I'd seen him before, and it bugged me that I couldn't remember where.

He had hair down to his shoulders, although I saw in the subdued yellow light that he was thinning on top. He wore two big earrings in his left ear, gold hoops that were gaudier than what was usually considered fashionable for men.

Where had I seen this guy before?

He laughed at something the woman next to him said, then took a hit off a can of Coke.

That's when it struck me. I thought how odd it was that someone would be swilling Coke in church. Whoever this guy was, he had a habit of drinking sodas in inappropriate places, like in Judge Alvin Rosenthal's courtroom during Slim's preliminary hearing yesterday. He'd been lucky, I knew from my years spent in courtrooms as a reporter, to avoid a contempt citation. You just didn't behave that way in a courtroom.

Curious, I moved closer to the outer edges of the small group, catching glimpses of the conversation.

'I heard she had a development deal with CBS . . .' a feminine voice said.

'No,' another voice, this one male, said. 'It was for a series pilot on TNN.'

'Had she finished the other album?'

'Why did she fire . . .' That voice trailed off before I could hear the rest. I shuffled around, just listening and watching.

'There's a slew of people in this town that ain't sorry she's gone.' My ears perked up.

'Shh,' another voice said. 'Don't speak ill of the dead.'

'Why not?' the same voice shot back. 'It's the only time you've got a chance against 'em.'

'Mac, what do you reckon this is going to cost the record company?'

I turned. The long-haired Coke drinker took a last slug off the can, then turned around and pitched it into a wastebasket next to the stairwell. So that was Ford McKenna Ford.

'Beats me,' he said. 'They're speeding up the release of the new album, but who knows? Sometimes death makes an artist's career. You think Elvis'd be selling like he does now if he hadn't crapped out on a toilet seat?'

'Elvis dead?' a guy standing behind Mac said. 'Say it ain't so . . .'

Interesting perspective, I thought. From inside the cavernous church, the organist began a serene, somber dirge. A requiem, I thought, for a sweet, now silent voice. As the volume increased people slowly filed into the church. The group over near the stairwell that had been the subject of my eavesdropping splintered as well.

The Coke drinker lingered outside for a moment, talking to a young woman, early twenties tops, to his right. She had hair the color of blue coal, sharply drawn eye makeup, and candy-apple-red lipstick that was thick and bright enough to reflect what little light it could find. Even though he was fairly short, maybe five-six, five-seven, she was even shorter.

I stepped over to them quickly. 'Excuse me, but I couldn't help overhearing. Are you Mac Ford?'

He glared at me suspiciously. His eyes danced quickly and nervously about and there was something alive in his face that was almost a tic. He seemed wired, agitated.

'Yeah, I'm Mac Ford. What can I do for you?'

I held out my hand, but he didn't respond. 'I'm Harry Denton,' I said. 'I've been meaning to call your office and set an appointment. I'm a friend of Slim Gibson's, and—'

'If you're a friend of Slim Gibson's, we ain't got nothing to talk about.' He turned quickly and took his companion by the arm.

'Wait, just a moment of your time, please,' I said. I reached out and touched his arm. He stopped, stared down at where my fingers had brushed him just above the back of his left elbow.

'I don't think Slim had anything to do with Rebecca's death,' I said. 'I think he was just in the wrong place at the wrong time, and then made a series of terrible decisions after that.'

'That ain't what the police think,' he said. He spoke quickly, almost maniacally, with an intensity in his voice that made me glad I didn't have to negotiate a music deal with him. He had a trace of Southern accent in him, but spoke with the cadence and rhythm of a New Yorker.

'The police are wrong,' I said. 'I'm a private investigator, and I've agreed to help Slim out as much as I can, even though he can't pay me much, if at all. I'm sure it means more to you than most to find out who actually did this.'

The young woman turned her face up and stared into Ford's face. Ford looked back down at her and paused for a moment.

'Okay,' he said. 'This is my administrative assistant, Alvy Barnes.'

'Hi, Alvy,' I said, smiling at her. To hell with the executives; you want to get anywhere in this world, be nice to the people who work for the executives. 'Glad to meet you.'

She nodded and smiled as Ford continued. 'Call her this afternoon and set something up for tomorrow morning. I'm leaving town right before lunch. Becca's funeral is in Waverly tomorrow at one.'

Waverly, Tennessee, is a small town in west Tennessee, near Kentucky Lake and just north of I-40, maybe an hour and a half's drive away. I remembered from the newspaper articles that Rebecca Gibson had been born there to a mother who worked in the café on the square. Her father had been a truck driver, but he disappeared when she was six and neither she nor her mother had ever seen him again.

'Have you got a card on you?' I asked. 'I don't have your office number.'

He dug in the inside pocket of his jacket and retrieved a small gold case. Expensive, I thought, a little overstated but still classy. He handed me the card. MFA INC. it read, in a bold red script that whipped across the width of the black card with flair and style. Below that: MAC FORD ASSOCIATES, ARTIST MANAGEMENT.

'I'll call you as soon as I get back to my office,' I said.

'Right. We'd better get on in there.'

I let them go ahead of me, and then I took a seat near the back. Even though everyone was seated and a speaker had taken the podium, Ford McKenna Ford walked up the aisle with Alvy trailing him and took a seat right up front, dead center. In the pecking order of Rebecca Gibson's life, I figured I'd do well to remember who was in the first row.

The service lasted just over an hour, and by the time I got back to the parking garage across from my office, the shadows across Seventh Avenue had deepened. The temperature had dropped as well, like a spring cold front that moves in as one last insult from the past winter.

I climbed the ramp again to the top level to check out the car.

The windshield repairman had come and gone, and left behind what looked like a decent patch job. He'd even swept up most of the glass around the car, then vacuumed out the broken glass from inside. Not bad for a hundred bucks.

I figured I'd be in my office for a while longer, so decided to move the car down to one of the spots below. I sure as hell didn't want to run into the brick chucker again after dark. I fumbled with the door lock, then plopped in on the torn cloth seat without thinking.

For one brief, intense moment I danced around and did my vocal imitation of a Subic Bay sailor on shore leave as broken bits of safety glass embedded themselves in my backside. I jumped out of the car, swiping at my pants like I'd sat on hot coals. Then I realized I had ground glass stuck in my palms; long red scratches decorated the insides of my hands.

'Shit! Why do they call this stuff safety glass?'

I keep a box of tissues inside the car for emergencies, and this certainly qualified. I blotted the scratches on my palms until I determined they weren't going to bleed much anyway. Then I balled up a wad of tissues and dusted the car seat until I couldn't see anything else glittering. Gingerly, I slid back into the car, then hit the key. As the rotary engine whined to life I put the car in gear and headed down the ramp to a safer place.

This day had well and truly bitten the big one. As I crossed the street, with stray bits of glass still brushing my butt and the backs of my thighs, I wondered what else could go wrong. I jumped a couple of steps into the alcove and nearly mowed down the letter carrier as he stepped out the door.

'Hey, Kenny,' I said. 'Leave me much today?'

'Hi, Mr Denton.' Kenny had been delivering mail downtown since before Nixon resigned. Seeing him every day was like knowing the clocks were still running.

'Looked to me like a bunch of bills,' he said, dodging me on the steps and moving around me as slick as fish passing each other in a school.

'Great,' I said. 'Just wonderful . . .'

The red light on the answering machine was dark and unblinking, which meant no new threatening messages, but no calls from Marsha either. Not to mention no new clients. I realized that this day, lousy as it had been, had gone by so quickly I hadn't even had time to obsess on her.

Kenny was right: South Central Bell bill, two bills from magazine subscriptions, another warning letter from a hospital regarding a bill I'd had with them a few months ago and never quite gotten paid off.

Disgusted, I threw the letters down on my desk and kicked my coat off. The tie went next, then the shoes. I locked my office door behind me and didn't bother to pull the office window blinds as I stripped off my pants and held them over the wastebasket. I brushed them off as well as I could with a crunched-up wad of paper towel, then bent around in a decidedly kinky position to check out my own bottom. Like the inside of my palms, there were a couple of nasty scratches, but no profuse bleeding. I dabbed at what little there was with another tissue, then pulled my cheapie first-aid kit out of my desk. I painted the scratches with Mercurochrome, then stood around letting the stuff air-dry.

I pulled out Ford's business card and stapled it to a Rolodex card, then filed it away in the holder. I punched the number into the phone and waited through four rings.

'Mac Ford Associates,' a pleasant enough voice said.

'Mr Ford's office.'

'Please hold.'

Thirty seconds later Alvy Barnes answered. 'Hi, Alvy,' I said. 'This is Harry Denton.'

'Oh, hi, Mr Denton.'

I smiled. 'My father's Mr Denton. Call me Harry.'

A chuckle came through the phone. 'Okay, Harry. I guess you're looking for that appointment with Mac, aren't you?'

'Sure. What's he got?'

'How about nine tomorrow morning?'

'Works for me.'

'Done deal,' she said. 'See you then.'

I penciled the time in on my calendar while standing awkwardly waiting for the red stuff on my keister to dry. Just as I turned to stare out the window a while, the phone rang again.

'Denton Agency,' I said.

'Hello,' she said. She was tired, edgy. I could feel it through the phone.

'Hello, love. How are you?'

'Weary. It's been a long day. What are you doing?'

'Standing in the middle of my office with no pants on.'

'You *have* missed me, haven't you? Is there anyone else there?'

'Of course not. That's not why I have my pants off, anyway. Somebody trashed my car and I sat in broken glass.'

'What happened?'

'Well, my dear, there's some kind of weirdness going on here

145

that even I don't understand. Twice in the past two days, some kind soul has left a death threat on my answering machine. And this afternoon, somebody heaved a brick through the windshield of my car.'

'Jesus, Harry! Have you called the police?'

'They weren't interested.'

She sighed. 'The world's going to hell in a handbag.'

'Sure seems that way. What's the latest from the barricades?'

'They aren't giving an inch. They don't want Evangeline autopsied, period. And the state AG is waffling on the legality of turning the body over to them. He probably figures if he gives in, the public perceives him as a wuss. But if he comes right out and says no, some bloody fool may start shooting.'

'So as long as nobody does anything, everything's cool.'

'Hostage Negotiating one-oh-one in a nutshell. Keep everybody talking, but don't do anything to back yourself into a corner.'

The phone popped, followed by a short hiss. 'We don't have long,' she said. 'Are you checking my mail for me? Watering the plants?'

'Of course. What about your bills?'

'Anything pressing?'

'I'll have to check. Is it okay for me to open your mail?'

'Another level of intimacy. Sure, take care of it. I trust you. If you need cash to pay the bills, I've got an extra checkbook in my desk. If the bank won't let you write the checks, get the extra ATM card out of the same desk drawer. My access code is 4–2–9–7. Get the cash out of the machine and put it in your own account, then write the checks for me.'

Little by little, I realized, Marsha and I were rearranging her life – our life – to fit what was shaping up to be a long-term situation. For the first few days, we both assumed that whatever was going to happen would happen quickly and vanish before we had to deal with other options. But now, like a wartime siege or a rerun of the David Koresh Follies, it appeared we needed to learn to live with the day-to-day tensions of an illogical, unpredictable, and dangerous circumstance.

We were hunkering down for the long run.

Chapter 21

I'd just tucked my shirt in when the phone rang again. I dropped my necktie on the desk and leaned over to pick up the handset.

'Denton Agency, Harry Denton speaking.'

Nothing.

'Denton Agency. May I help you?'

Silence, then more of it.

'Hello . . .'

No heavy breathing, no moaning. No dial tone, either. Just the quiet. Then faintly, in the background, I heard the sound of a radio playing, real scratchy, like a cheap AM.

I felt a twirl in my gut, then suddenly a rush of anger. I fought to keep from screaming into the phone.

'Nice job you did on my car today,' I said, as casually as I could muster. 'Who are you?'

Nothing.

'We could get together, talk this out. No use in both our being—'

He/she/whoever hung up.

'You spineless rat bastard,' I growled as I slammed down the phone.

There had been only one time in my entire life when I'd resorted to carrying a gun, and I'd had to borrow that one from Lonnie. I despise guns, don't own one, and won't have one in my house or office. And as much as I dislike the government, it wouldn't bother me that much if the marines choppered in, did a house-to-house, and confiscated every last goddamn one of them.

On the other hand, I wish I had one right now.

That wouldn't do any good, though. What was I going to do, shoot the telephone? And if I'd had a gun, I might have put one into the guy that busted my windshield this afternoon. Then I could share a cell with Slim for a while.

I don't even have a carry permit, despite Tennessee's new Wild West law that allows anyone who's not drunk or crazy to carry a concealed weapon. Somewhere in my office desk, though, was a little souvenir of another case I'd worked on. Lonnie'd given it to me when I'd refused his offer to supply me with a guaranteed clean throwaway gun.

I opened my center desk drawer. In the middle of the pile of debris that passed for my organizing system, buried beneath a stack of old business cards with the wrong address on them, was a piece of hard, palm-sized black plastic with a black cloth strap hooked to the side. A white decal with a lightning bolt through it read z-force ii, and below that 80,000v. There were four metal prongs poking out of one end of the case, two pointed outward and two test prongs pointed inward.

There was a switch on the side of the case. I placed it in the palm of my hand, flicked the switch on, and pressed a button on the other side of the case from the switch.

A crackling sound filled my office and a bright blue spark danced across the test prongs. Real Frankenstein lab stuff. At the bottom of the case, another decal read WARNING: EXTREME DANGER. KEEP OUT OF REACH OF CHILDREN. USE ONLY AS DIRECTED.

I thumbed the safety switch down and pressed the button one more time to make sure it was off and quiet. Then I tucked the stun gun into the right pocket of my suit jacket and left the office.

Anybody who's hung around Music Row longer than your average tourist learns p.d.q. that there's a dark side to all the glitter and rhinestones. I was never an insider; even as a newspaperman, I was just another entity to be manipulated by the PR machine. Anybody who's lived here longer than a few months, though, picks up on it. It's not just the money and the drugs, the deals and the steals, the lives and careers made and ruined over a handshake that may or may not be as dependable as a signed contract, and God knows how dependable even a signed contract would be. It's something even darker than all that. I've always thought it was not only ironic, but poetically just, that Music Row after the sun sets is one of the most dangerous areas in the city to walk around unprotected. Muggings, rapes, robberies, even murder, are not all that uncommon on the Row. The sun sets, the vampires come out. Smart people carry wooden stakes and silver bullets.

I was glad I had the stun gun with me, even if the sun wasn't completely down yet. It was after five; the traffic on I-40 slowed to a walk in both directions as far as the eye could see. I turned left off Broadway and cut over to Demonbreum, then doglegged

left around the freeway entrance and wound my way on a side
street behind the Music Row Shoney's and onto Division.

Down Division, the Faron Young Building sat perched on a
bluff overlooking the traffic jam on the interstate. The two story
structure was brown brick and had a parking lot big enough to
accommodate a fleet of tour buses. I pulled into the lot and took
my choice of a couple hundred spaces.

The building was occupied mostly by independent record
companies, booking agencies, and freelance writers and photog-
raphers. Every office seemed to be related, in one way or another,
to the industry.

I scanned the directory, then moseyed down the hall to IBA,
the International Booking Agency. Most of the offices were still
open. I checked my watch again. Maybe I'd get lucky.

The decor was dark paneling, set off by worn carpet. The odors
of cigarettes and stale coffee permeated the hallways. I stopped
in front of a solid wooden door with a gold-and-brown plaque –
IBA – mounted on it.

Inside, an overweight woman with the last vestiges of teenage
acne and a terrible bleach job sat behind a gray metal desk. She
filed her nails with a scraggly emery board as I closed the door
behind me, and never missed a beat. To her left, a computer
monitor sat on the desk, its screen saver floating multicolored
balloons across the glass. Dozens of badly framed photographs
covered the wall, mostly head or group shots of country-music
acts. Three pictures over from the receptionist's desk, a photo-
graph of Rebecca Gibson strumming a huge twelve-string still
hung. It gave me a chill to look at it.

'Can I help you?' she asked.

I edged over to the desk and smiled down at her. There were
traces of tomato sauce on the front of her blouse, and her mismatched bright turquoise skirt threatened to disintegrate at the
seams if it didn't get some relief soon.

'I'd like to see Faye Morgan, please.'

The filing stopped as she focused on my face through smudged
wire-rim glasses.

'You got an appointment?'

'No, but it's about the murder of Rebecca Gibson.' I took out
my license case and flipped it open in front of her. 'My name's
Harry James Denton. I'm a private investigator.'

At that, she sat up and reached across the desk with her free
hand. She held the bottom of the license steady for a second as
she studied it.

'Dadgum,' she said. 'I never seen one of those.'

I smiled at her as sweetly as I was able, then brushed the bottom of her fingers with mine. 'It's real. I promise.'

She looked into my eyes and smiled, then settled back in the chair, hinges squealing in distress. 'I'll see if Ms Morgan has a moment to spare.'

I kept the smile pasted on. 'Thanks. I appreciate that.'

She picked up the phone and pressed the intercom button. 'Faye, there's a guy out here . . .' Then she spoke too softly for me to hear. I stepped away from her desk and studied the office. The waiting room was maybe twelve by fifteen, with a couple of doors leading off into what I assumed were private offices. Not much to look at, really, for an agency that billed itself as international.

Behind me, the receptionist hung up the phone. 'Ms Morgan will be right with you. Can I fix you a cup of coffee?'

'No, thank you. Say, you guys represent all these groups?'

'We have at one time or another,' she answered.

'Restless Heart, Willie Nelson, Asleep at the Wheel,' I read off the titles on the publicity photos. 'Carlene Carter! Wow, she's one of my favorites!'

I crossed the room over to Rebecca's picture. 'Too bad about Rebecca Gibson, huh? I only heard her sing live once, but she sure was something else.'

'Yeah,' the receptionist said. She was bored now, back to filing her nails. 'If you like that sort of thing.'

I leaned down toward her and lowered my voice to a conspirational whisper. 'What was she like? Really, I mean?'

The emery board stopped midstroke, and her voice lowered to match mine. 'Well, I don't like to speak ill of the dead, you know.'

Let me guess, I thought, in this case, you're going to make an exception.

'Yeah?' I said grinning.

'She was a b-i-t-c-h of the first degree. I mean, you know, you expect these hillbilly singers to be kind of temperamental. Know what I mean? But she was h-e-double-hockey-sticks on wheels . . .' She jabbed the emery board at me like a pointer, and as she did, an enormous slab of fat under her upper arm bobbed up and down in time to the shaking.

Behind me, a door opened and a throat cleared impatiently. I turned to meet a stern woman, medium height, small-boned, and very light, with curly auburn hair and light green eyes. She wore brown corduroy pants that fit tightly around her hips and narrow waist, with a silk blouse on top that matched the slacks perfectly. She was professional, subdued, and quite attractive.

'Gladys, hold my calls,' she said.

I turned and winked at Gladys, who retreated back into her desk chair like she'd been caught with her hand in the cookie jar, an experience she'd probably had many times before.

'This way, Mr Denton.' She turned and led me into her office. I followed as she held the door for me, then shut it behind us. Her office was cluttered with trade magazines, newspapers, and the obligatory autographed celebrity photos. A speakerphone sat on her desk amid the rubble across from a wall with a floor-to-ceiling bookcase jammed with books and mementos. I got the feeling she spent most of her life in here.

'Ms Morgan, thanks for taking the time to see me. I know you're busy.'

She sat down in a high-backed leather chair that could have been in a senior law partner's office. The chair seemed to engulf her. 'What can I do for you, Mr Denton? What's your involvement in this?'

'I'm doing some follow-up on the murder of Rebecca Gibson. Just trying to get some background.'

'Who hired you?'

I started to dodge that one, having hoped the subject wouldn't come up. Then I figured if she could be that direct, so could I.

'I'm working for Slim Gibson.'

Not a muscle in her face moved. I expected her to throw me out, but instead found myself being stared at. I stared back. The first hints of lines and furrows were just beginning to mark her face. She was in a high-pressure business and, I guessed, approaching her midthirties. She was at that point where stress and age would begin to wear at her natural beauty.

'Well,' she said finally. 'That puts us on opposite sides of the fence, doesn't it?'

'Not really. We're both after the same goal.'

'Which is?'

'That Rebecca Gibson's killer is brought to justice. That whoever killed her pays for it.'

'Rebecca Gibson's killer has been brought to justice,' she said flatly.

'That's still to be decided, isn't it? Innocent,' I said, though I wasn't sure even I believed it, 'until proven guilty.'

'My understanding from the police and from the newspaper accounts is that the physical evidence, the circumstantial evidence, and the testimony of eyewitnesses proves that Rebecca's ex-husband killed her. They'd fought off and on for years. He has a violent history.' She wove her fingers together into a tent. 'Seems pretty conclusive.'

'On the other hand, what was the motive? If it was just a passion murder, your typical domestic explosion, why didn't he kill her years ago when the fireworks were really flying? There's no evidence he wanted her back, so it's not a question of him being a spurned suitor. And while he inherits the song catalog – that is, if he's acquitted – the truth is he stood to benefit more in the long run if she lived. The bottom line is he had no reason to kill her. He doesn't really benefit from her death.'

'But no one benefits from her death!' Faye Morgan leaned forward and planted her elbows on the desk. It was the first hiccup of excitement I'd seen in her. 'If that's the deciding factor, then nobody murdered her!'

'And you can't hold Slim accountable for a revenge motive unless you consider everyone else who might have had the same motive.'

'What do you mean?'

'C'mon, Ms Morgan. Rebecca Gibson wasn't exactly the most beloved person in the cosmos. Even your secretary—'

'Gladys talks too much,' she interrupted.

'Don't be angry at her,' I said. 'She's not the only one who's said that to me.'

'Rebecca Gibson was just another Thoroughbred,' she said. 'Like many others.'

'Is that how agents think of their singers? Horseflesh?'

'The similarities are amazing, Mr Denton, especially toward the posterior end of the animal. If every difficult artist wound up being murdered, the entire industry would collapse.

'No,' she continued, 'you don't have much of a case here. It's straightforward. Slim Gibson beat his wife to death and now all of us will suffer for it.'

'Which leads me to another question. If you don't mind my asking, how much will *you* suffer?'

She relaxed in the chair and let her arms drop onto the armrests of the chair. 'For some reason or other, Mr Denton, I think I'll be candid with you.'

She returned my smile, which made me like her, even though I had no reason whatsoever to trust her. 'I appreciate that,' I said.

'IBA is a B-level booking agency. We handle all the big stars before they become big. We don't take on the new kids, unless there's something truly spectacular and promising about them, and by the time they start running around in the major leagues, they've gone on to somebody else. That's okay. My partners and I have made a good living in the last ten years or so booking Rebecca Gibsons into one-, two-, and three-night stands in places like Abilene and Tulsa. I know every honky-tonk operator from here to Bakersfield and back, and they all know me. Rebecca Gibson's death was a blow to all of us, yes. But we'll survive.'

'How long had you represented Rebecca?'

'I'd have to check my records for an exact date, but about eighteen months.'

'And it's been in those eighteen months that her career started to take off.'

'Yes,' Faye Morgan said. 'And she would have stayed with us through the release of her next album. If that turned out to be the breakout for her that everybody expected, then she would have left us shortly thereafter.'

'Isn't that frustrating?' I asked. 'To work so hard to build up an artist's career, only to have them dump you just when they could start to make you some real money?'

She smiled, but above the smile, her eyes darkened. 'Is the owner of a Triple-A ball club frustrated when George Steinbrenner calls his best players up to the Bronx? It's the nature of the business.' She shrugged her shoulders.

'Sounds more like the nature of the food chain,' I commented.

'That may be the most apt analogy I've ever heard.'

I learned forward and, without thinking, said: 'You seem like a nice lady. Why do you put up with it?'

She pursed her lips, then rolled her lower lip inward and bit it nervously.

'Sorry if that's too personal,' I said. 'Bad habit of mine.'

'That's okay. I'm just not sure I can answer it.'

I stood up and pulled a business card out of my shirt pocket. 'Look, I'm trying to help out a friend who's in trouble. All I want is to find the truth. If the truth is that Slim killed Rebecca, then that's where I'll be led, and that'll be the end of it. If you can recall anything that might help, I'd sure appreciate it.'

I laid the card on her desk. She picked it up and studied it for a moment. 'If I can help,' she said, 'I'll call you.'

'Then I won't take up any more of your time.' I turned for the door.

'Mr Denton,' she said.

'Please, call me Harry.'

153

'Harry—' She hesitated. 'There was a time when I loved this business. Loved being a player, loved the music. Loved hanging around with the celebrities, swimming with the sharks. But that wears off quickly. Now I just do it because it's all I've ever done. It makes me a comfortable living.'

'But the cost is high, isn't it?'

She grinned again, waving me off, all seriousness gone. 'Everything's expensive these days. Inflation . . .'

I opened the door to her office and stood there for just another moment. 'I hope you don't mind my saying this,' I said. 'I think you deserve better.'

'You're a gentleman, Harry,' she said sadly. 'I don't meet many of those in my business.'

'Yeah, well, nice guys finish last.'

She leaned her head back against the back of the chair. 'So I'm told.'

Chapter 22

I liked Faye Morgan. There was something subliminally attractive and appealing about her. For a woman who couldn't have weighed more then one ten, one fifteen tops, though, she sure carried a lot of weight around inside her.

I wondered what secrets she's got.

The light turned at Wedgewood Avenue and I started to ease out into the intersection, then realized the fool to my left had no intention of stopping simply because the traffic light facing him had turned. He roared through the intersection doing about fifty in a red Nissan pickup truck, ignoring the blaring horns and the raised middle fingers. In this town, green doesn't mean go; it means look both ways and, when all the idiots have finished running the light, proceed cautiously.

I cut over to Belmont Avenue, then out Belmont to one of the side streets. I managed to make my way over to Marsha's apartment in Green Hills without getting caught in the end-of-rush-hour traffic.

Her mailbox was jammed again, this time with a mixture of catalogs, junk mail, and windowed envelopes that looked like bills. I let myself into the apartment and was amazed how lifeless and cold it seemed. It felt good to be there, though, like it was my only connection to her. Sometimes it seemed like she'd gone away on a business trip or something, and soon I'd be picking her up at the airport.

I milled around aimlessly, then decided I needed focus. I opened the curtains and then the windows, letting the fresh air fill the place and drive out the stale. I pulled a beer out of the icebox – these things go bad, you know, if you let them sit around too long – and sat down at the dining-room table. I stacked the mail into separate piles: junk, this can wait, this can't. The pile that couldn't wait included her electric bill, the phone bill, the water bill, a couple of credit-card bills, and something that looked like a notice from the insurance company.

I opened up the bills and got them in order. There was a couple of hundred on her VISA card, another hundred or so on a Platinum American Express. The charges were all recent. I figured Marsha paid her cards off every month, unlike some of us who have to bloody well live off them.

I went into the den and dug through her desk until I found the extra checks she'd mentioned. There were a couple of payment books in there, one for the mortgage company and one for her car loan. I pulled them out and carried them back into the dining room. It was getting close to the end of the month. I thought I may as well write checks for those as well.

I opened the mortgage coupon book and gasped. *Twelve hundred a month in mortgage payment for a freaking condo!* Excuse me, but you can get a pretty damn nice house around here for that much. Who'd pay that much for a condominium, or as my father used to call them, condo-*minimums*?

That intake of breath was nothing, though, compared with the heart tremor I had when I opened the car payment book.

'*Four hundred seventy-two dollars and sixty-eight cents a month in car payment!*' I yelped. I knew you didn't get a Porsche 911 for the same price as a Ford Fiesta, but jeez, that much? Marsha paid almost as much a month for a car payment as I paid for apartment and office rent put together.

I was definitely dating above my station.

Figuring that forgery would make me less uncomfortable than putting Marsha's money in my checking account, I signed her name to all the checks and stuffed them into the appropriate envelopes. I'd seen her name signed before, and tried to halfway imitate it. Anybody who looked closely would never let it pass, but all the checks were routine monthly obligations, so who'd look that closely?

Doing her bookkeeping, sorting, and posting took me the better part of forty-five minutes. By then I was getting the beginnings of a blood-sugar-crash headache. I'd been so preoccupied since getting back to town last weekend that with the exception of dropping in at Mrs Lee's, I'd been living off whatever I could scrounge out of my own kitchen and fast-food joints.

Then I remembered Marsha wanted me to clean out her refrigerator. I was peckish, and a tad short of cash, so why not combine the two agendas into one? I went through the refriger-ator and found enough produce to make a big salad, as well as some eggs that were only a few days beyond their expiration date, and a couple of hunks of gourmet cheese that had the beginnings of a green sweater growing around the edges. A quart of milk was starting to turn, but being a bachelor, I was used to that. I pulled the salad together, then whipped up an omelette with spinach, feta cheese, and baby Swiss – minus the green fuzzy stuff.

An old Bogart film was on American Movie Classics, so I sat down to a solitary feast, a great flick, and a couple more of Marsha's beers. The evening went on and fatigue caught up with me. A little human activity had transformed Marsha's condo into a warm, safe, and comfortable place. I was in no hurry to get anywhere, and found myself slipping off toward the end of the movie. When I woke up, it was after ten. I changed channels quickly, but had already missed the local news. I thought about going home, but the drive was too long and I didn't feel like facing my place alone.

I washed the dishes and took a quick shower, then settled into bed with one last beer. I drifted in and out, tuned into the local ABC affiliate, until *Nightline* came on at eleven-thirty. I rarely get to watch Koppel because the local station delays the program to work in an hour's worth of syndicated oldies: *M*A*S*H* and *The Cosby Show*, the classics that win their respective time slots even though most people have the scripts memorized.

I was shallow enough into twilight sleep to recognize the opening theme music and claw my way to alertness. Live from Nashville, the Grand Ole Hostage Situation. Koppel did a quick recap, then introduced the filmed segment of the show.

A crisp, cool professional whose name I didn't recognize stood before the barricade at the foot of the hill on First Avenue. 'Ted, it would be almost comical, if it weren't for all the live ammo,' he began. 'A dozen armed Winnebagos manned by religious fanatics demanding the return of the corpse of their leader's wife have held off the Nashville Police Department for nearly a week now. And there appears to be no break in the situation expected anytime soon.'

The correspondent rattled on, summarizing the latest stuff everybody here already knew, then cut away to a remote beside the walled estate of Brother Woodrow Tyberious Hogg.

'The Pentecostal Enochians are an offshoot fundamentalist sect that bases its bizarre theology on a connection between the resurrection outlined in the New Testament with Enoch of the Old Testament, who was the seventh generation in line from Adam and only lived three hundred and sixty-five years, a relatively short life span in biblical days. The mystical conjunction of seven and three hundred and sixty-five has been used by the Enochians to predict the end of the world, which they believe will happen on October nineteenth, 1998. At the same time, the Pentecostal Enochians take an extreme view of the resurrection of the body, maintaining that cremation, dissection, and autopsy all deny everlasting life to the believer.

'The result,' the correspondent added, 'has produced chaos.'

Cut to the bad, homemade video of a polyester-suited, overweight Brother Tyberious Hogg standing red-faced at a podium, Bible in hand, spit flying from his mouth as he screamed:

'By faith Enoch was translated that he should *not* see death! Hebrews 11:5! And have hope toward God, which they themselves also allow, that there shall be a resurrection of the dead, both of the just and the unjust!'

The camera focused on the wide-eyed, enraptured audience, some with their heads rolled back, tongues exposed, spewing forth glossolalia as Brother Hogg took off in another direction with his own dramatic reading from what I thought I recognized as the Book of Revelations:

'And I saw an angel come down from heaven, having the key of the bottomless pit and a great chain in his hand. And he laid hold on the dragon, that old serpent, which is the Devil, and Satan, and bound him a thousand years, and cast him into the bottomless pit, and shut him up, and set a seal upon him, that he should deceive the nations no more, till the thousand years should be fulfilled. And after that he must be loosed a little season!'

Then we cut again to a shining fat face shrouded in the angelic wings of hair that sprouted down the side of a bouffant hairdo. It was Sister Evangeline, and she was near The Rapture herself as Brother Woody really cranked it up:

'And I saw thrones, and they sat upon them, and judgment was given unto them: and I saw the souls of them that were beheaded for the witness of Jesus . . .'

Weird stuff, I thought. Very bizarre. Cut back to the *Nightline* correspondent, who explained that ex-cult members had revealed that the group became polarized over Brother Woodrow Tyberious Hogg's recent disclosure that God came to him in a dream and told him to take another wife.

And wouldn't you know it, the wife God told him to take was Sister Jennifer, the sixteen-year-old daughter of one of the believers.

Now, I thought, we get down to it.

Sister Evangeline had gone along with it for a while, believing, of course, that her husband's dream was a divine revelation of the Lord. Pentecostal Enochians don't smoke, drink, dance, wear makeup, or play music during services, but if God tells them to bed a sixteen-year-old – hey, go for it. And gone for it they had, until Brother Woody tried to give Sister Evangeline's Cadillac to his new wife, Sister Jennifer. Sister Evangeline went ballistic, and apparently wound up overdoing what was supposed to be a simple dramatic suicide attempt.

As Ted Koppel introduced the guest for the discussion portion of the show, I laughed so hard I almost rolled off the side of the bed. I couldn't take it anymore, so polished off the beer, buried myself beneath Marsha's thick comforter, and pretended I could smell her hair on the pillow.

Maybe it's a measure of how frazzled I am these days, but I dropped off to sleep without setting an alarm clock. I'd completely forgotten my nine o'clock appointment with Mac Ford. I awoke in stages: first this dreamy, languorous, aroused state; then a dim awareness that there were other things that should have been on my mind; then a growing sense of panic; and finally, full-blown hysteria as I got my eyes open enough to hone in on the alarm clock, which read 8:25.

I shot out of bed and dashed for the bathroom, brushed my teeth, then scrambled around the bathroom until I found a package of pink disposable razors intended for legs rather than cheeks. I lathered my face with bar soap and raked the razor over stubble, hoping I wouldn't open up a spurter.

I could shave and wash my face, comb my hair, and get most of the sleep out of my eyes, but I couldn't disguise the fact that the same clothes I had on yesterday were going back on today. I took a wild guess that Mac Ford wouldn't care, even if he noticed. I was a little embarrassed about Alvy Barnes, though.

What the hell, I thought as I ran out the door with fifteen minutes to get from Green Hills to Music Row, you can carry this personal-grooming stuff too far if you're not careful.

Decades ago, the two parallel avenues that make up Music Row were just a couple of residential streets in Nashville. As the music business moved in, more and more of the older homes were taken over for commercial uses. Some of the most powerful independent record companies, agents, managers, accountants, and lawyers had set up offices in renovated old houses. Mac Ford owned one of them, and I was driving like hell to get there before nine o'clock.

All the craziness was for nothing. I pulled into a pea-gravel parking lot in front of a gray, nondescript two-story Cape Cod. I had about ninety seconds to spare before being late as I stepped through the oak-and-beveled-glass front door. Beige leather sofas sat in front of an open fireplace in what had once been someone's living room. Behind them, against the opposite wall, a receptionist sat at a desk manning a phone system that had eight lines all lit at once. I stood before her, trying to calm my breathing after the mad rush through town.

'May I help you?' she asked quickly between flashing lights.

'I had a nine o'clock with Mac Ford,' I said.

'I don't think he's in yet. Let me check with Alvy.'

I sat down while the receptionist juggled the phone lines and tried to reach Mac Ford's assistant. I settled into the soft, cool leather with an audible squish. The morning newspaper sat rolled up on a coffee table between the sofas. I picked it up and unfolded it. The news media having the attention span of a Chihuahua on methamphetamine-flavored Alpo, the hostage situation at the morgue had already faded into Section B importance. Today's lead story was on another shoot-out at a local public high school, this one ending when a Metro cop assigned to security duty had to blow away a sixteen-year-old who wouldn't drop his 9mm Glock because it would've dissed him in front of his homeys.

I shook my head and whispered: 'Fucking Looney Tunes . . .'

By the time I finished the story, with the requisite sidebar about how the anguished parents were going to file police-brutality charges and one motherthumper of a civil suit, Alvy Barnes had descended the wide oak staircase with an apologetic look.

'I'm sorry, Harry, Mac's not in yet. And I haven't heard from him.'

'Oh,' I said, trying to keep a smile on my face. 'Can I hang around for a bit? I'd like to see him before he leaves town this afternoon.'

'Sure,' she said, very sweetly. 'Why don't I get you a cup of coffee?'

'That'd be great. Cream and light sugar, if you've got it.'

'I'll bring it right in.'

Alvy walked down a hallway behind the receptionist and disappeared. She seemed intelligent, and was certainly young and attractive in a Generation-X sort of way. I never thought I'd be old enough to look at women that age and think: *She's too young for me* – but damn, here I am.

I wondered if Mac Ford was sleeping with her.

Alvy returned with a steaming Styrofoam cup of coffee that felt as good going down as CPR to a dying man.

'That's great,' I said after the first sip. 'Thanks. I'll just sit down here and catch Mac when he comes in.'

She smiled again and put her hand on my arm. 'I'll take care of that. He parks in the back and sneaks in through the rear stairway.'

'Hiding out, huh?'

She leaned toward me, her hand brushing against my forearm even harder. 'There's a few out there he needs to dodge.'

I watched her walk back up the stairs. I tried to avoid an avalanche of lascivious fantasies without much success. I sat down and picked up the paper with one hand, the coffee cup firmly glued in the other.

Section B was local news, with Day Six of the hostage story as the lead. A little clock in the upper right-hand corner of the page ticked off the hours that the crisis had gone on. A sidebar described the *Nightline* instalment from last night, not without some measure of civic pride. There was a brief mention in the main story of Marsha and the other people locked in the morgue, but since no one in the media knew about Marsha's private cellular-phone number, they hadn't been available for interviews.

On page four, buried beneath a two-column story on a zoning committee meeting, was a short piece about this afternoon's funeral for Rebecca Gibson.

I finished the paper and my coffee, then checked my watch: 9:40. Was Mac Ford doing a Phil Anderson-like dodge on me? Had I become a pariah? I shifted restlessly on the couch, impatiently flipping through the classifieds, growing more irritated by the moment.

Ten minutes later I stood up and stretched, about ready to blow the whole morning off. Alvy Barnes suddenly rounded the corner upstairs and scooted down the flight of stairs. She stopped on the landing.

'Good, you're still here,' she said. 'I'm so sorry. Mac just got in. I said something to him, but you know how—'

'Yeah, I understand. He still got time to see me?'

'Sure, c'mon.'

I followed her up the stairs and down a long, carpeted hallway on the second floor. While the first floor was a model of decorum and cool professionalism, the upstairs could have been decorated by a graphic designer in the middle of a psychotic break. Splashes of neon paint covered the walls, with movie and rock posters outnumbering country-music posters at least two to one. A stuffed groundhog perched in one corner, with a straw hat planted fashionably on its head and a corncob pipe stuck in its mouth. We passed open office doors with T-shirted agents in jeans and thousand-dollar snakeskin boots making deal after deal. I could hear shouts, arguments, pleas, manipulations. Inside one large office, a Xerox machine painted in desert camouflage clicked away.

'You guys are busy up here,' I commented to the back of Alvy Barnes's head.

'Oh, this is nothing,' she answered, outpacing me down the hall.

We entered an anteroom that had been converted into Alvy's office. It was a little more staid than the rest of the floor, but still revealed chaos as the operative mode.

'Wait just a moment,' she said. She walked over to a large heavy door painted bright chromium white and opened it. A cloud of blue smoke drifted out of the crack she'd stuck her head into, along with the booming rumble of a loud reggae beat. Ford's office, I surmised, must be heavily soundproofed.

'Mac, he's here,' I heard her say over the bass guitar and the steel drums.

'Yeah,' Ford yelled, 'get him in here!'

I swallowed hard, wondering what I was getting into. Alvy turned, waved me to the door, then held it open for me.

'Go on,' she said. 'You asked for it.'

I stepped into a thick cloud of cigar smoke illuminated by the kind of black light fixtures I hadn't seen since my days as an undergraduate. Alvy shut the door behind me. I squinted in the dim light, my ears aching from the thunderous reggae now confined to Ford's office. Across the large office, maybe fifteen feet away, Mac Ford sat sprawled out in an office chair beneath an enormous Tiffany lamp with about a ten-watt bulb in it. I squinted into focus. He was on the phone, shouting something into it I couldn't understand over the music. It was meat-locker cold, the air-conditioning turned up to goose-pimple levels.

Black light counterculture posters covered the wall: Jefferson Airplane, Jimi Hendrix, Avalon Ballroom stuff in that typeface that looked like melting letters and, I'm told although I never tried it, simulated reading under the influence of psychedelics.

Ford McKenna Ford, I realized, was a Neanderthal throwback to the Sixties.

And I was locked in his dream.

Chapter 23

From behind the haze of thick smoke, he motioned me toward a seat. My nose was closing up and the back of my throat felt scratchy. What was this guy smoking, old socks?

He continued the phone conversation as I shivered in a chair across from him. The Jamaican CD roared on, with the Bob Marley sound-alike wailing away unintelligibly.

I looked around. Clutter, chaos, piles of papers, magazines, framed gold records, photographs. A huge twelve-point buck with a pair of panty hose draped across the horns was mounted on the wall behind him. There were piles of empty Grolsch and Dos XX bottles everywhere, intermixed with discarded Coke cans encrusted with brown goo. A fisherman's net was suspended from the ceiling with dried Spanish moss hanging down like tendrils. The walls rattled with the energy and the sound. Another minute or so of this and I was going to break a window to escape.

Ford slammed the phone down and said something to me, but I not only couldn't hear him, I couldn't see his face through the smoke and the black light well enough to lip-read.

'Could we turn the music down?' I yelled.

He cupped a hand to his ear. Great, I thought, this interview is going just swell.

'Turn down the music!' I yelled again, this time motioning downward in a curve with my right index finger.

He said something like, 'Oh, yeah,' and reached for a remote control buried in a stack of junk on his desk. He fished it out, hit a button, and the huge speakers went quiet.

The silence was even weirder.

'You know,' I said, 'my landlady's hearing-impaired. You ought to talk to her about what you've got to look forward to.'

'Not a music lover, huh?'

'I'll let you know when I hear some.'

'Ooh,' he moaned, then laughed. 'That's not going to make you any friends around here.'

'I didn't come to make friends,' I said. 'I came to find out Rebecca Gibson's secrets.'

'If you do that, they won't be secrets anymore.'

'What's it matter to her?'

Mac Ford lodged the thick cigar in an ashtray, then found a bare spot on his desk and drummed it frenetically. He practically leaped out of the chair and circled around me. On a junk-cluttered bookcase, he found a neon hot-pink basketball and bounced it a couple of times on his hardwood floor, then let it fly toward the opposite wall. It bounced off the wall, then rolled around the rim of a basketball hoop he'd mounted above the door to his office. The ball circled the metal hoop three times and rolled off the wrong side.

'No points,' I said. 'If you don't mind my saying so, you're one of the most frenetic people I've ever met.'

That stopped him cold. He recovered the ball and dribbled it a few times, then palmed it and held it against his side.

'I prefer to think of it as dynamic.'

'Could you be a little less dynamic, then? I'm getting dizzy.'

'You know, I've already talked to the police. I don't have to talk to you.'

'I know you don't. I'll just repeat what I said yesterday. Surely you want the real killer to be caught as much as I do.'

'The real killer is caught.' He reached down and scratched his crotch through his jeans.

'Then humor me,' I said. 'How much money was Rebecca Gibson going to make over the next year?'

That seemed to catch him off guard. 'I don't know,' he said. He slapped the basketball and did an over-the-shoulder hook shot that missed the hoop by at least a foot.

'Take a guess.'

He grabbed the ball as it careened off his office door. He moved like a sixteen-year-old trying to impress the girl next door. 'Anybody's guess. The new album takes off, she picks up an award or two. Best estimate, maybe a million, million-three, maybe million and a half. Worst estimate, low six figures.'

'What's your cut of that?'

His nonstop motion ceased for just a moment, and he glared at me, insulted. 'My *cut* is whatever salary I take out of this place. MFA Incorporated gets a twenty-percent management fee from all its clients. And, by the way, we work our butts off for that commission.'

'I didn't say you didn't. I only ask because I'm trying to gauge how much everyone's lost.'

'A shitload,' he said. 'The world's lost a shitload.' He flung the ball in a wide arc toward the hoop again. This time, the ball sailed through the net without touching metal.

'Swish!' he called. 'She was a great talent.'

'Let's assume that Slim didn't kill his ex-wife. If you had a list of suspects that included everyone she knew, who would you pick out of the lineup?'

Mac Ford's face darkened, although in the dim light it was hard to tell, especially with the two-day growth of beard and the mop of scraggly black hair that draped down over his forehead after that last jump shot.

'That's a dangerous game, man,' he said. 'Unfounded accusations can get you in trouble.'

'Nobody's accusing anybody. But the way I see it, you're the second biggest loser in this whole affair. Rebecca Gibson lost her life.'

'Hey,' he said, letting another one fly to the hoop, this one swishing nylon as well. 'I've still got my health.'

'Minus a pretty good-sized fortune Rebecca Gibson was going to make for you over the next few years.'

'Okay, okay,' he said. He leaned against a wall and scratched at his chin. 'The way I see it, nobody benefited financially. We're all losers. So it had to be revenge or passion or something like that. An old lover. For that matter, a new lover.'

'Would that be Dwight Parmenter?'

'Maybe. If I was checking everybody out, I'd sure add him to the list.'

'Is he one of your clients?'

He snorted. 'Dwight? Hell, no. Dwight ain't got the fire in his belly.'

'But he might have enough fire in his belly to beat Rebecca Gibson to death with his bare hands.'

'Them's two different kinds of fires, bud.'

'What about this guy Pinkleton? The guy who was her road manager.'

'Yeah, she canned his ass a couple of weeks ago, wasn't it? She told me she was going to. Said he'd been hitting the nose candy kind of hard and equipment had been disappearing. She figured he was ripping it off and selling it to buy dope.'

'Isn't that something you would handle? Firing Pinkleton, I mean?'

'Becca was a control freak. I handled her contracts, money, billings, accounting, tour schedules, dealing with the battalion of idiots a major act has to deal with. But when it came down to the nitty-gritty of putting a show together, who played what and when and where and how loud, Becca did it all herself. Anybody who tried to tell her what to do got slapped down, hard.'

'So you thought she was hard to deal with too.'

Mac Ford crossed back in front of me and fell back into his chair so hard it rolled back and slammed into the wall behind him. He grabbed the now dead cigar out of the ashtray, then lifted his legs and let them fall with a thud onto the desk.

'You just had to know how to handle her, that's all. I never had any trouble with her.'

He reached into his shirt pocket and pulled out a disposable butane lighter, then fired it up and relit the cigar with the three-inch-long flame. He inhaled deeply, taking the smoke into his chest like it was a cigarette, then sighed as he exhaled a stream of blue toward the ceiling. Iron lungs, I guess.

I thought for a moment. 'So if you were drawing up a list, you'd put Dwight Parmenter and Mike Pinkleton at the top?'

'Yeah, that'd have to be it. You can take it to the bank, bud; if Slim Gibson didn't kill Rebecca, then one of them two others did.'

'Is there anything else you can tell me that might lead somewhere?'

He thought for a second. 'Nope, that's about it.'

'Okay,' I said. 'I guess that's all I need for now. Like I say, I'm just following a trail to see where it goes. Thanks for helping me out. Can I call you again if I need anything else?'

'Hey, bud, you call me anytime. Grab one of those cards off the desk. It's got my home phone number. And you be careful, you hear? Anybody that can beat the dogshit out of somebody as hard as he did Rebecca ain't going to be shy about doing it again.'

'That's already occurred to me,' I said.

He didn't look like he was going to make any attempt to crawl out of that chair, and I didn't feel like leaning across his desk through the smoke to beg for a handshake. I stood up and pocketed one of his cards, then turned for the door. As I opened it I caught a glimpse of him reaching for the remote control. He punched a button, and this time the room was filled with a raw, rocking beat that had the momentum of a runaway locomotive.

When I closed the door, the roar inside Mac Ford's office was muffled almost completely. Alvy Barnes sat at her desk, typing something into a computer. She turned and smiled at me.

'Get everything you need?'

'For the time being,' I said.

I reached into my pocket and pulled out a couple of business cards. 'I meant to give him one of these. Can I leave it with you?'

'Sure.'

'There's another one there. You keep it. Like I told Mac, I'm just trying to find out anything that will lead me to the truth. If you think of anything that might help, will you give me a call, too?'

She brushed the two cards into the center of her desk drawer. 'Glad to.'

'Thanks. It was good to see you again,' I said, turning to leave. 'By the way, how does he get any work done in there with all that noise?'

Alvy shook her head. 'Beats me. I've been working here two years, and he does that every day. He has a great mind, but it works in mysterious ways.'

I walked down the long hallway alone, then down the stairs. Next to the receptionist's desk, I stopped and listened. I was directly below Mac Ford's office. Amazing, I thought, these old buildings are really solid.

Outside, I settled into the Mazda and managed to get it cranked up. The traffic on Music Row was backed up so far I couldn't get out of the parking lot, so I turned and went down the driveway and into the alley, figuring I'd exit out onto a side street. Behind Mac Ford's building, like a lot of buildings on the Row, there was a private parking lot carved out of what had once been somebody's backyard. Signs warned strangers not to park and threatened towing to Siberia. Other signs marked off slots by name. The center parking space, the one closest to the back entrance of the building, had a sign that read RESERVED: MAC FORD.

A silver Rolls-Royce was parked in the slot. I don't know much about Rolls-Royces, only that they cost a hell of a lot and are real nice to look at. I don't know what year or model this one was, but I recognized the insignia.

On the back of the Rolls was a mounted vanity plate: TRUSNO 1. It took me a second to figure it out.

Trust no one.

My office building seemed especially dusty and seedy in the bright morning light, although damn little sunshine managed to filter in. Down the hall on the first floor, a door opened and a fat, balding man with thick glasses and khaki pants pulled up to his sternum looked out into the hallway. From under his right armpit, a shoulder holster with a Smith & Wesson .38 dangled loosely.

'Hi, Mr Porter,' I said as I passed.

'Hello,' he said, ducking back into his office and closing the door. Mr Porter was a gem dealer, had been in the building since the late Forties, and had seen life evolve from Ozzie and Harriet days until the time when he had to carry a pistol inside his own office. I'd seen him maybe three times since I'd rented my office. He never seemed to have any customers, never seemed to leave the place. I wondered if he lived there.

I trotted up the stairs to the second floor and turned the corner toward my office, then stopped. I reversed direction and went down to the end of the hallway and rapped on Slim and Ray's office door.

There was no answer, no sound from inside, so I went back to my office. Occupancy in the building had dropped off lately, with our two offices the only ones rented on the second floor. Maybe I should move, I thought. This old building wasn't exactly the most prestigious address in the city. On the other hand, it was one of the most affordable.

I unlocked my door and went in. The red light on my answering machine was blinking away. I pulled my coat off and hit the play back button, then grabbed a pencil to write down numbers.

Six messages; what a pain.

Lonnie was number one. 'Just checking in,' he said, followed by a message from Marsha saying she'd tried to reach me at home last night and was I okay? Ray was number three, asking me to call him at home. Number four was a hang-up. Five was Mrs Hawkins saying she hadn't seen me home in a couple of days and was I okay?

Blast, I thought, I could use a message from Phil Anderson about my check from the insurance company, not to mention a new client every now and then.

Message number six began with silence and I thought it was another hang-up, then an old familiar voice came on.

'Nice place you stayed at last night, you son of a bitch. Trying to hide from me? That it? Well, you keep right on trying, bubba, 'cause there ain't nowhere you gonna hide from me. You got that? Nowhere.'

I felt myself turning cold from the inside out, and like a knee-capped figure skater training for the Olympics, I found myself asking the age-old question.

Why me?

Chapter 24

I began working my way down the list, first with an answering-machine message to Mrs Hawkins to reassure her I was still around. I resisted the urge to think she was only keeping track of a tenant. She was a genuinely sweet old lady who seemed to consider me more of an adopted son than a paying customer. Then I tried Lonnie's number, with no luck there, either, and left a quick message telling him I'd drop by that night on my way home if he was around.

I tried once again to get Phil Anderson on the phone at the insurance company, but this time even the secretary got a little smart with me.

'I'm sorry, he's not available,' she said as soon as I identified myself. I felt the unspoken *at least not to you.*

'When will he be available?' I asked.

'I don't know,' she said, just the slightest little teaspoon of *screw you* in her voice.

'Would you mind checking?'

'I can't disturb him. He's in conference. If you'd like to leave a message . . .'

Yeah, I thought, I'd like to leave him a message. How about: *Fuck you, Phil. Strong letter to follow.*

'If you'd just tell him I called,' I said.

'I'll give him the message.' Click.

I growled out loud, then dialed Ray's number at home. It rang four times and an answering machine came on. Impatient and tired of having the phone glued to my ear, I started to hang up, then decided to at least leave a courtesy message.

'Ray,' I said after the tone, 'it's me, Harry. Just returning your—'

'Harry!' he burst in, yelling so loud it hurt my ears. 'Don't hang up!'

'Screening our calls, are we?' I said.

'Have to. It's these damn reporters. They're still calling two or three times an hour. Damn pain in the ass.'

I decided not to remind him that I used to be one of those pain-in-the-ass reporters. 'No problem. What's up?'

'Well, we think we might have found Slim a lawyer. You know a Herman Reid?'

I quickly ran through my mental database of lawyers. 'Yeah, saw him in court once. Top-notch fellow.'

'I talked to him this morning. He'll take the case, but he wants ten grand up front.'

I whistled. 'Justice ain't cheap, is it? Can you raise that kind of money.'

'I cleaned out my savings account and maxxed out the cash advances off my credit cards. I'm close. Few hundred more ought to do it.'

I marveled at the lengths Ray was willing to go to help out his partner. 'He's lucky to have you,' I said. 'I wish I had the cash to help you out, Ray. But I'm kind of strapped.'

'Don't worry about it. You're doing more to help this way. Slim's innocent and we've got work to do,' Ray said. 'Have you had any luck?'

'Not much,' I answered. 'I've been snooping around, just seeing where it leads. I need to get in touch with a couple of guys, if you've got addresses and phone numbers.'

'Let me get my black book,' he said, his voice fading as he pulled the phone away from his ear. I heard a rustling in the background, then: 'Okay, shoot.'

'That other singer in the roundtable Sunday night, Dwight Parmenter.'

'The current boyfriend . . .'

'You got it.'

'He lives in an old house with a couple of other guys down off Music Row.' I copied down the address and phone number as Ray read it off.

'The other guy, that fellow Rebecca fired a couple weeks ago. Pinkleton, Mike Pinkleton.'

'Oh, Jesus, Harry, be careful. That guy's rough as a corncob. Last I heard, he was living in a motel up on Dickerson Pike. You know where the Sam's Club is near I-65?'

'Yeah, great part of town.'

'Okay, it's down Dickerson Pike from there, toward town. On the right, the big motel with the neon American flag out front. I think it's called the College Inn or something like that.'

'Like one of those motels down on Murfreesboro Road? You know, the ones where the rooms rent by the week?'

'Exactly,' he said. 'Hookers, transients, outlaws on the run. Human garbage.'

'C'mon, Ray, human garbage has feelings, too.'

He snorted. 'Wait'll you see some of Pinkleton's feelings.'

'I got to run. You going to be in the office today?'

'Later this afternoon. I'm trying to scrape together the last of the lawyer money, then I'm going to go see Slim. You hear they impounded his bank accounts?'

'How can they do that?'

'The courts can do anything.'

'How's Slim going to pay his bills, keep his house note up?'

'I don't know,' Ray said, the weight in his voice heavy, stifling. 'He may lose it all. Maybe Herman Reid can get the court to unfreeze the assets before its too late.'

'We've got a little time,' I said. 'It takes, what, three months to foreclose on a house?'

'Something like that.'

'If I'm going to use the time we've got, I got to get moving, pal. Hang in there.'

I may hate guns, but I'm not exactly defenseless. If I'm going to hang around an outlaw strip searching for somebody who might just be a murderer, then I was going to use whatever I had to take care of myself.

I took the stun gun out of my pocket and fired it off a couple of times. Inside the right-hand bottom drawer of my desk, the deep, double-sized one, there was a pair of handcuffs, a pocket-sized can of Mace, and a fiberglass nightstick with a little extra weight in the end. I folded the handcuffs together and stuck them in my back hip pocket. They were cold and hard against my butt, but comforting in a strange sort of way. I slipped the Mace into my left pants pocket. Carrying a nightstick openly wasn't the coolest idea in the world, so I tucked it up under my coat as I left.

Heavily loaded and armed, I crossed Seventh Avenue and retrieved the car. I tucked the nightstick down between the console and the driver's seat, where I could yank it up in a flash. Then it was through the downtown traffic, past the construction on Second Avenue, up First Avenue, and across the river.

East Nashville slipped on like an old, comfortable sweater as I left the downtown congestion behind me. I headed out Main Street, past the empty grass lot that had once been the sprawling Genesco factory, then around the curve onto Gallatin Road. I left the main drag shortly after and made my way through the side streets to my apartment.

I needed a change of clothes, and if I was going to be out in the field for a while, I figured I'd better ditch the coat and tie. I transferred all my pocket clutter into the jeans, then pulled out the olive-drab field jacket I'd bought at Friendman's Army Surplus when I was on stakeout in Louisville. The stun gun and the Mace can went into the field jacket's large side pockets.

Outside, Mrs Hawkins was bent over a flower bed on the other side of the new garage with a towel in one hand and a huge clump of dirt in the other. I started calling to her as I went down the stairs so as not to scare her to death, and managed to get her attention as I hit the driveway.

'Harry,' she called. 'Where have you been?'

I stooped down next to her in the flower bed. 'I left you a message. Didn't you get it?'

'Oh, that darned machine. I forgot to check it. Pesky contraptions, telephones.'

I smiled at her. 'They ought to be outlawed.'

'Looks like you've been busy.'

'Very. As a matter of fact, I've got to be off now.'

'I'm glad things have improved,' she said. 'Sometimes I feel guilty taking rent from you when you're short of money.'

If she only knew.

'Don't be concerned about that,' I said. 'I'm delighted to pay you rent every month.' I stood up, hoping my nose hadn't grown to Pinocchio-like dimensions.

'I'll probably be home late again tonight. Don't you worry, okay?'

'All right, I won't,' she said, turning back to her flowers.

I headed for the Mazda, which was parked about halfway down the driveway.

'By the way,' she called. 'Did you see that strange man this morning?'

I turned. 'What strange man?'

-'Well,' she said absentmindedly, 'I guess you wouldn't have. You weren't here.'

'What strange man?'

'This morning. I slept late, until nearly seven. When I woke up and went into the kitchen to start my tea, there was a man walking down the driveway. He had a pickup truck out front.'

'What did he look like?' I asked, trying to keep my face somewhere in the same universe as casual.

'I didn't get a good look. By the time I got my glasses on, he was in the truck. He sat there for a few minutes. I didn't know what to do, so I got dressed and walked outside to get the paper. As soon as I stepped outside, he gunned the motor and took off. Made a lot of smoke.'

'Did you see what kind of pickup it was?'

'An old one was all I could tell. Faded gray, rust spots on the side. A Ford, maybe.'

I stepped back over and squatted down next to her. 'I'm sure it was nothing,' I said, feeling guilty for having lied to her twice in one conversation. 'But just to be safe, you be sure and lock up well tonight.'

She smiled at me slyly. 'Harry, this is the city. I lock up well every night. And there's a loaded shotgun in the closet.'

I smiled back. 'Good girl.'

I walked down the driveway to the Mazda, feeling about as low as a vagrant on Belle Meade Boulevard. Sometime back, a case of mine had inadvertently – and indirectly – placed Mrs Hawkins at risk. There was simply no way I was going to put her in that spot again. Something would have to be done.

If the bastard wanted to stalk me, let him. I can handle that. But if he starts scaring my sweet little old landlady, something's going to have to be done.

But what?

Chapter 25

I got this terrible taste in my mouth as I pulled out into the noontime traffic on Gallatin Road and headed toward Inglewood, like the coffee I'd had at Mac Ford's office wasn't going to stay down. I knew it wasn't the coffee, though; it was just another side effect of having the Ronco Stress-O-Matic going at full throttle. On the good side, the strain of the last few days had played hell with my appetite. It looked like I'd be saving lunch money today, at least for a while.

A few minutes later I passed under the railroad trestle on Gallatin Road and approached the old Inglewood Theatre. Just for shits and grins I turned left, drove behind the theatre, and coasted past Lonnie's place. His big truck wasn't there and I saw no sign of Shadow, so I continued on until the street intersected with Ben Allen Road, then made a left.

I'd gotten to know this end of Nashville pretty well over the past couple of years, and I knew exactly which motel Ray was talking about. Ben Allen Road dead-ended into Dickerson Pike near the motel, past the Ellington Parkway, and well into a part of Nashville known for its level of violent crime. There's not much street crime there, really, since no one would walk the streets anyway. But the string of small businesses – pawnshops, X-rated video outlets, used-car lots, mom-and-pop groceries – was prime pickings for holdup artists. An elderly couple who owned a small convenience market had been the lead item in the local news a few weeks back when three guys busted in to rob them and the two started shooting back. Seems they'd been hit before and had taken to packing .38s on their respective, arthritic hips. This time, for once, the justice system was saved the trouble. Even though they outnumbered the old folks, the bad guys lost. Two went down for good, the other paralyzed for life.

I was beginning to wish I didn't work alone so much. If Lonnie had been home, I might have asked him to go with me. In almost a flash of insight, I realized I was afraid, and I thought of my father's admonition to me as a young boy that the only way to fight fear was to face it.

Yeah, I remember him saying it, and I also remember it not helping very much.

I turned right onto Dickerson Pike, then immediately slid into the turning lane. I waited for a break in the traffic, then jetted across the oncoming two lanes and into the parking lot of the College Inn motel.

In the far past, back before the government built the interstate highway system and put half the small motels in America out of business, the College Inn had been a stopping place for tourists and a home away from home for politicians when the legislature was in session. But that was maybe four decades ago. Now the place was plain old run-down, a couple of steps above a flop-house, but not much. It was U-shaped, the three sides of the motel angling around the parking lot, with a closed swimming pool in the center of the asphalt baking in the sun. A coating of green slime thick enough to support several discarded beer cans covered the pool, and in the shallow end, the handlebars of a child's tricycle poked through the goo.

The asphalt parking lot was potholed, laced with cracks, and dotted with puddles of oil. I parked next to a Dodge van with a broken windshield and a faded coat of pale green paint. I stepped up on the curb, then over to a concrete sidewalk that led down to a wooden door with the word OFFICE nailed on in fake bronze letters. I twisted the doorknob; it wouldn't move.

I tapped a couple of times on the door. A moment later a dusty blue curtain was pulled back and a pair of dark eyes set against brown skin stared out, then ran up and down me like a scanner. The lock rattled and then the door opened a crack.

'Yes,' a warbling voice said. 'What can I do for you, please?' Strange accent, like a stand-up comedian's parody of an Indian accent.

'I'm looking for someone who's supposed to be staying here. I wonder if you could help me.'

The door cracked open a bit further. I could see an entire human head in front of me now, skin dark brown, eyes nearly black, the whites a catchy shade of yellow. The head was also at a level with my sternum, leading me with my superior deductive powers to assume I was speaking to a very short person.

'Are you the police, please?' he demanded.

'No, just a friend of a friend.' I smiled at him as benignly as I knew how and kept my hands where he could see them. I also wanted, if at all possible, to keep from having to produce my investigator's license. I don't know why, but I had a feeling nosy official-looking people weren't welcome here.

'Who do you want to see, please?'

'Mike Pinkleton. I understand he's staying here.'

'What is your name, please?'

'Harry Denton,' I said. 'If you'd tell him I'm a friend of Slim Gibson's, I'd appreciate it.'

'Stay right where you are, please,' he said, the *R*s rolling off his tongue as thick as curried eggplant. I nodded as the door shut and the locks clicked back into place. Thirty seconds later the door opened again, this time wider.

'Mr Pinkleton says you can go to see him, please,' the man said. 'He is in room number seventeen.'

'Thanks,' I said, 'Mr—'

'I am Mr V. S. Naipur and it is my pleasure to serve you,' he said, then slammed the door and set the locks again.

'Okay,' I said to the door. I turned and checked the room numbers. Seventeen was diagonally across the parking lot, past the concrete swamp, nestled in the ninety-degree angle the two converging sides of the motel created. A black motorcycle sat out in front chained to a support post for the awning that ran around the perimeter in front of the rooms. I crossed the lot and couldn't help but notice that I was being checked out – subtle signs like curtains being pulled back, doors cracking open a half inch for just a second, then closing again with a whoosh. I wondered how many tenants had outstanding arrest warrants.

I stepped over a broken concrete planter onto the walkway, stepped up to the door, and knocked. The door was painted a rust red, with the paint peeling in half-dollar-size chunks. I turned and looked at the bike, an old Harley. I don't know much about bikes, so didn't recognize the model or anything. But this one was stripped to the bones, just engine and frame, and chopped as well, its front end extended several feet, with high-rise handlebars and a single speedometer between the forks. Simple, basic, two-axled hell-on-wheels.

No answer from inside. I knocked again. 'Hello?' I called. 'Mike?'

'C'mon in,' I heard from inside. I opened the door. It made a swishing sound as it brushed across a stiff, thick shag carpet of red and green.

The room was a typically cheap motel room that had been too long without maid service: dingy sheets turning gray and a thin pastel-blue blanket thrown haphazardly across an institutional bed; scarred, mismatched furniture; an old color TV flickering away soundlessly in the corner. Dirty laundry lay in several mounds throughout the room, and there was a general air of mold and decay, all mixed with the scent of institutional cleaner. I hadn't smelled anything like it since my last visit to the men's room at a bus station.

'Hello?' I called.

'Yeah, gimme a minute,' came a gruff voice from the bathroom. Then there was the rattling gurgle of a toilet flushing, followed by running water. I stood there awkwardly, wondering whether or not to sit down.

In a few more seconds, all six and a half feet of Mike Pinkleton plodded out of the bathroom. His hair was either soaking wet or incredibly greasy, and hung down in a jet-black, shiny mop below his shoulders. He was shirtless and barefoot, his right arm laced from shoulder to wrist with tattoos. When he turned toward me, his enormous belly shook and I saw that tattoos covered his chest and other arm as well. He wore a long, straight, salt-and-pepper beard and his bulbous nose was huge. I sensed that he was biker to the core, and had lived every second of his life full throttle, front wheel off the ground.

I instinctively took a step backward at the sight of him, something not exactly calculated to give me the upper hand in the body-language department. Couldn't help it, though.

'Whaddid you say yer name was?' he asked. 'I can't understand that fucking Paki on the front desk.'

'Harry Denton,' I said. 'I'm a friend of Slim Gibson's.'

'Yeah, okay.' He stepped over to a round table in the corner, pulled a chair back, and shook it hard enough to scatter the dirty clothes on it all over the floor. He shoved it in my direction.

'Sit down.'

I moved around the piles of laundry and garbage, scooted the chair against the wall, and sat down. Pinkleton bent over, the seams on his greasy jeans straining, and opened a small refrigerator.

'Beer?' he asked, holding a can of Colt .45 malt liquor in my direction.

'No thanks.' Interesting definition of beer, I thought. He'd probably call a real Colt .45 a peashooter.

'Suit yourself.' He popped the top on the can, then strode past me to the bed. He settled down onto it with his head against the wall and the can balanced on his hairy gut.

'I don't want to take up too much of your time,' I said. 'I'll get right to the point. Slim's a friend of mine, but I'm also working for him. I'm a private investigator.'

He stared at me through a crack in his thick eyelids. I paused for a second, waiting for some reaction from him. All I got was an earthshaking belch.

'Slim's in jail now, and it's not likely we'll get him out anytime soon without some evidence that he didn't kill Rebecca Gibson. That's what I'm looking for.'

He drained the rest of the beer can in one long gulp, then crushed it and tossed it in the corner. Real casual, this guy. He sat up and plunked his feet to the floor.

'So you thought you'd drop in on me here and get a confession, then go tell the cops and they'd let Slim go.' His voice was barely audible.

'That'd make my job simpler, but that's not what I was expecting.'

He pulled open a drawer and fished around inside it, then pulled out a pack of smokes. He fumbled with the pack until a single cigarette extended outward. He grabbed it with his lips, then fired up a disposable butane and sucked in deeply.

'Goddamn cops grilled my ass for six hours,' he said. 'Reamed me inside out. I didn't have fucking nothing to do with killing Rebecca Gibson.'

'I understand she fired you a few weeks ago,' I said. Jeez, I hope this guy doesn't go ballistic on me or anything.

'People get fired all the time.'

'Why'd she do it?'

He turned to me and I saw something in his eyes that made me think if he didn't kill Rebecca Gibson, he could have. His lips were bared, revealing a set of yellow, rotten teeth with intermittent black gaps.

'She said I was stealing equipment.'

'Were you?'

Pinkleton got up and took two steps toward me, then stopped. His right hand clenched the cigarette so hard it twisted into a curve, then broke in two. The lit end fell on the floor and disappeared into the shag carpet. A surge of gunk came up into the back of my throat again, as bitter and vile as the last time.

'No,' he growled. I wasn't going to ask him that again.

A thin wisp of smoke rose from the carpet. I pointed nervously toward it.

'Ugh,' I stammered, 'that's going to—'

181

He looked down, then placed the heel of his bare foot over the smoke and mashed down. He ground the cigarette completely out.

'How long had you worked for her?' I had to ask him something, keep him talking. Otherwise, I was afraid I'd find myself sailing through the plate-glass window that looked out onto his Harley.

He walked past me to the refrigerator and pulled out another can of Colt .45. 'Too fucking long. Put up with her shit till I just couldn't take it anymore.'

'You managed her road show, right?'

He looked over at me, disgust on his face. 'I drove the semi and helped tote the heavy shit. Whipped the boys into line when they smoked too much reefer. Anybody messed with Becca, I took care of 'em.'

I leaned over, interested now. 'You were her bodyguard?'

'Nothing that fancy. I was just her big dumb fucking biker nobody wanted to mess with.'

He turned the tall can up and downed about half of it. 'Cut the crap. What do you want?'

'I'm just confused here, that's all. If you weren't stealing equipment and you were her bodyguard, why did she fire you after all these years? I'm just trying to understand this.'

Suddenly he slammed the Colt .45 can down on the washbasin counter next to the refrigerator hard enough to make dust come off the wall. I jumped, startled, and fought the urge to dive for the door.

'She fired me 'cause I wasn't fucking good enough for her anymore!' he bellowed. 'I started out working for her *for free*, goddamn it, back when she didn't have gas money to put in the truck. Now she's a big star, and Mike Pinkleton Biker Man ain't good enough for the high-and-mighty Rebecca Gibson!'

His head shook and his hair bounced off his shoulders.

'Why you?' I asked.

'I just told you why!'

'No, that's not what I mean. I mean, why you in particular? Why now? She'd known about the new album, the touring, for months. She knew things were about to take off. Why did she cut you loose when she did?'

His shoulders stooped and his jaw lowered to his chest, as if he were about to doze off on his feet. I could see when he turned back to me, though, that it wasn't fatigue or the effects of some drug kicking in that was causing this change. It was anger, anger to the point of hatred. I could see it in his eyes when he looked at me. Make that glared at me.

'I don't want to fucking talk to you no more,' he said, his voice low now, and mean.

'But wait, Mike, don't you see? Something about this stinks. I don't know what it means, but I've got this feeling—'

He was on me in a split second, his hands on my shoulders like clamps, jerking me up out of that chair like I was a rag doll that got in his way.

'Wait a min—' I tried to talk him down from wherever he'd gone, but it was too late. I felt the drywall crack as my back slammed into it, followed a heartbeat later by the back of my head. My ears rang for a second, and my skull felt like somebody whacked me with a nine iron. That was good, I thought. When you really get hammered, you don't feel it for a few seconds. I felt this from the get-go, so I was probably okay.

I slid my hand toward the pocket of my field jacket, fumbling for the Mace or the stun gun, whichever I got to first. It was too late, though. He had me pinned against the wall, the stench of unwashed body, partially digested Colt .45, and cigarette smoke in my face like garbage.

'I said I don't fucking want to talk to you anymore.'

I nodded. He doesn't want to talk, I'm not saying a word. It's that simple.

'Get the fuck out.'

I nodded again. His grip relaxed, and I slid back down to the carpet. The back of my head stung like hell and my shoulders ached from where he'd slammed me into the wall. I felt the lump in my right pocket that was the Mace can, and briefly considered spraying him down with it just to see the look on his face. But then I remembered what a security consultant had told me back when I was doing a story on self-protection, something that the Mace companies didn't particularly relish having everyone know. Mace, he said, is better than nothing. But for some guys, especially guys with a lot of bulk who aren't wired right, Mace didn't do anything but make them more pissed off than they were to begin with.

Mike Pinkleton looked like one of those guys. So when he backed off two steps and motioned toward the door, I took him up on the offer. I'd gotten nothing from Mike Pinkleton but a fierce headache, and the feeling that something still stank.

Nothing speeds up the onset of an impending bloodsugar crash like a rush of fear-induced adrenaline. By the time I got the Mazda started and peeled a little rubber out of the parking lot onto Dickerson Pike, I was shaking and sweating like Morris the

Cat in a room full of pit bulls. I'd met some mean people in my life, but never had I felt myself in the presence of such complete and unpredictable danger caused by a man who could still technically be called sane.

Mike Pinkleton killed Rebecca Gibson. As sure as I'm sitting here in traffic wondering if I need a change of Jockey shorts, he beat that woman to death. He's the only one who could have, the only one with that unique nexus of raw power and fury that could have resulted in that particular death. Over and over, it kept coming back to me, the fact that it's work to beat a human being to death. It's work to beat a human being to death.

It's work to beat a human being to death.

But then I calmed down and stopped rehashing my own anger, my own humiliation at being thrown around by the greasy hulk of a man with as much indifference as if he'd been kicking a stray dog. Mike Pinkleton could have killed her, yes, but he wasn't smart enough to cover it up. It wasn't his style. He's more the type that would have gotten in the cops' faces and said: *Yeah, I killed the bitch – want to make something out of it?* I wondered how Rebecca had reacted to him, how she'd found the spine to stand up and fire him.

She was one ballsy lady.

Chapter 26

Maybe it was dumb to go directly to the people whom I thought might have murdered Rebecca Gibson. On the other hand, when I covered political corruption stories as a reporter, I found the most useful technique was to ask the suspected politician a direct question, like: *Pardon me, Senator. Did you take that bribe?* Then watch the reaction. I call it the Shake the Tree and See What Falls Out theorem.

I dug through my notes, searching for Dwight Parmenter's address while sitting at a stoplight on Music Row. Parmenter lived a block or so before Wedgewood on a side street on the right. I stopped in front of his house and sat there for a moment trying to regroup. Parmenter lived in a Belmont-area house that had been a showplace fifty years ago, but had since been cut up into what had become run-down apartments. The house sat on a rise, with a half flight of concrete steps from the curb up to a buckled walk that led to the front porch.

An intercom with a series of white buttons hung barely mounted in the wall next to the door. Dwight Parmenter's name was third up from the bottom. I pressed the button and heard a buzzer somewhere above my head. A moment later a crackling voice answered through the cheap speaker.

'Yeah?'

I gave him my spiel, then stood waiting for a few moments. The voice came back: 'Second floor, apartment six. Up the stairs and on the right.'

An electronic buzzer went off. I pushed the door open and stepped into the entrance foyer. The place smelled of mold and cat urine. At least I think it was cat . . .

The bare bulb overhead was burned out, leaving the entryway about as dark as a closet. I pushed a second heavy door open and entered. What had once been beautiful oak-plank floors were scarred and pitted, with dark watermarks staining the honey-colored wood. A ratty carpet was nailed to the steps leading upstairs, which creaked and moaned as I stepped on them.

Blue paint flaked off the walls, with a thick coating of dust over everything. From an apartment below, country music of the Marty Robbins era filtered through a closed door. I climbed the flight of stairs as quickly as possible, turned, and found Parmenter's apartment. He answered on the second knock.

This time, I produced my license. He scanned it quickly, then compared my face with the picture on the ticket.

'Okay,' he said sullenly. 'C'mon in.'

I stepped into an apartment with twelve-foot ceilings, crumbling plaster walls, and old wooden windows that had to be held open with pieces of two-by-two. Dwight Parmenter wore a frayed white T-shirt, his skinny arms freckled and lightly haired. His face was thin, the kind of face that would sink in on itself when it got old. He hadn't shaved, and while that looked either sexy or artsy on some men, on Dwight Parmenter it just made him look like one of Walker Evans's Depression-era photographs. I guessed he was about thirty-five or so, and I concluded from his posture and his bearing that his years in the music business had been brutal.

'Thanks for your time,' I said.

'Sit down.' He motioned to an overstuffed green sofa with a rip on one end of the seat cushion. I sat, feeling myself sink into the padding as he sat in a matching lime-green easy chair across from me. He picked up a battered old acoustic guitar with nylon strings and slung it across his lap.

I looked around at the old furniture, the torn music posters on the wall, the ancient stereo system, and the stacks of LPs. 'Nice place you got here,' I said.

'Thanks. It's home,' he said.

We made a couple more passes at small talk. He offered me a beer. I declined. After a moment of awkward silence, I decided to jump in.

'I've been retained by Slim Gibson,' I said. 'He says he didn't kill his ex-wife.'

'You believe him?' Parmenter asked.

I rubbed my chin and thought for a moment. 'I believe him. And I'm looking for any information that will help clear his name.'

'I like Slim,' Parmenter said, his right fingers breaking into a little picking pattern on the strings as his left hand formed a chord on the neck. 'Even if he did kill her, I feel real bad for him.'

I studied him for a second. His right thumb hit alternating bass notes on the guitar as his index and second fingers picked the top strings in a catchy little melody. His left hand shifted from chord to chord flawlessly, but there was something curiously flat in the playing. It was as Mac Ford had said, there was no fire in his belly. He was an accomplished craftsman, a technician, but there was no passion in him anywhere that I could see. That struck me as odd for someone struggling in such a passion-filled, tumultuous business. And yet, word was he was in love with Rebecca Gibson. So there had to be some mettle hidden in him somewhere.

'You were there that last night,' I said. 'Anything happen that caught your eye? Anything a little weird?'

He stopped playing. 'Nothing that out of the ordinary. I'd done a few of these gigs with those guys before. Not a lot. This was just another one, that's all.'

'Did Rebecca seem, I don't know, like her normal self?'

He strummed another chord, as if buying himself a little time. 'Becca was always high-strung. Sometimes it was a little hard to tell when she was wired and when she was just being Becca.'

'Tell me what happened,' I said, softening my voice just a bit. 'After the performance was over.'

'Well,' he drawled, 'a bunch of us hung around, tossing back a few beers, trying to unwind.'

If Dwight Parmenter unwound any more, I thought to myself, we'd have to check his pulse. 'Did you talk to Rebecca?'

'Sure. I was always talking to Becca.' He hesitated, like he'd said too much then. I let it slip by unnoticed.

'I mean,' he continued, 'Becca and I talked a lot.'

I nodded. 'What'd you talk about that night?'

He shrugged, the skin on his unshaven jaw stretching around his chin. 'Same old stuff.'

I shifted on the sofa and brought a little iron into my voice. 'C'mon, Dwight. I feel like there's something here I'm not getting.'

'Like what?' His brow furrowed as he stopped midlick on the guitar.

'I've heard from several people that you and Rebecca Gibson had something going on. That you two were involved romantically.'

He leaned over the side of the chair and placed the guitar on the floor. He released it in such a way that it plonked onto the wooden floor. The *plonk* reverberated and hung there for a few moments.

'People say a lot that ain't true.'

'So you weren't involved with her?'

'Not like people think,' he said. 'I don't know why I'm even talking to you. I already told all this stuff to the police.'

'Maybe you're talking to me for the same reason I'm asking so many questions. Rebecca Gibson may have been difficult, but she was still one of the most attractive women I've ever seen in my life. She sure as hell didn't deserve to die that way.'

His jaw locked up and quivered a bit, the sallow skin on his cheeks pale almost to the point of blue.

'No,' he said, a hitch in his voice, 'she didn't.'

I let that hang there for a few seconds, then: 'You loved her, didn't you?'

He stared off into space, unfocused, silent. His eyes watered, and I saw for the first time evidence of what was hidden real deep inside of him. Mac Ford had been wrong. Dwight Parmenter had his passions; it was just that nobody else saw them.

'Yeah,' he said finally. 'I loved her. And I'd been watching out for her, taking care of her. She needed me. There's so goddamn many sharks out there. Nobody she could trust.'

'That's true,' I said. 'It's a lousy business.'

'That ain't the word for it.'

'Were you her lover?'

He brought his gaze back to my face. 'You don't pull no punches, do you?'

'Sorry, pal. I'm not in the punch-pulling business.'

He chuckled at that. 'No, we weren't sleeping together steady. It's not from a want of trying, though. Hell, I knew she'd been with a trooptrain full of men. Didn't make any difference to me. I loved her for what she was, not what she'd been. She used to tell me she loved me . . .'

His voice faded to silence. 'But not that way,' I said, filling in his blanks.

'She might have one day. I was the only man who ever stuck by her. I'd have never left her. The only way she'd ever gotten rid of me was by running me off.'

Or die by trying, I thought. But for once I had sense enough to engage my brain before putting my mouth in gear.

'Did you take her home that night?'

He shook his head. 'No. I wanted to. It was damn near the middle of the night, after all. But she said she'd be fine, that she had to tend to something – and I should quit worrying about her.'

He teared up again, and this time he lost control and covered his face with his hands. 'God,' he sobbed, his shoulders shaking, 'if I'd just gone with her. If I'd just made her let me take her home. You don't think she was afraid of me, do you? Was that it?'

He looked back up at me, his face wet. '*Was* she afraid to let me go home with her?'

I shook my head. 'I don't think that was it.'

'If I'd taken her home, none of this would've happened. Or maybe it would have happened to me. Yeah, maybe it would've been me. I'd have done that, you know. I would have, swear to God.'

I stood up. I'd done about as much damage here as I could, without learning much beyond the fact that I could bet the rent money on Dwight Parmenter being innocent of Rebecca Gibson's murder. If he killed her, he deserves a freaking Academy Award for Best Performance by an Actor Before They Attach the Electrodes.

'If it'd bring her back, I'd die for her right now,' he said. 'I'd have died for her in a heartbeat.'

'Yeah, Mr Parmenter, I believe you would have.'

No matter how much Rebecca Gibson had been the temperamental prima donna from hell, she had one decent man who loved her and mourned her death. Her memorial service had been nothing but a public display of envy, malice, greed, and networking. But here, in a solitary, run-down apartment, one man wept for her alone out of no other motive beyond simple human grief.

Maybe the thought of grieving for a lost woman pushed a few buttons of my own. Or maybe in this sea of lying, treacherous bastards, I found the thought of someone without ulterior motive touching. In any case, I spent the drive over to my office thinking about my short interview with Dwight Parmenter. I'd meant to ask him more details about that last night, about who he thought might have killed her. All that went out the window when I saw how deeply pained he was by talking about her at all. I felt like I hadn't learned much, outside of the comfort I could take from Thomas Edison's dictum: I've learned lots of things that don't work.

The downtown rush-hour traffic had thinned more than I expected, until I checked my watch and realized it was almost six o'clock. I made it back to my office without too much agony and found a parking space on one of the lower floors of the garage. I kept replaying my conversation with Parmenter in my head, and wanted to get upstairs to make my notes as quickly as I could. With my degree of mental fragmentation these days, I need to get everything down on paper.

One thing did bother me, though. Dwight Parmenter said

Rebecca didn't want him to take her home because she had something she had to take care of. What was it, I wondered, that someone could do at four a.m. on a Monday morning? Did she have to put the cat out? Wash her hair? Slap another coat of paint on the living-room wall?

What the hell was it?

The front door was still open, even though it was technically after business hours. I let it squish shut behind me and took the stairs two at a time. Behind me, I heard Mr Porter open his door a crack and check me out.

'Hi, Mr Porter,' I said behind me. He grunted and closed the door.

I hit the landing, turned, and headed up the last half flight to my office. Dwight Parmenter's voice was replaying itself in my head, his sobs echoing between my ears. I felt awful for the guy, I thought as I dug my hand into my jeans pocket to retrieve my keys.

That's when something shot out of the shadows and slammed into me like a cement sled. There were arms around me. I couldn't move. There was growling in my right ear and hard, fast breathing.

Then the pressure started, huge arms around my chest, pinning me, squeezing me. I fumbled, trying to fight, but my arms were jammed into my sides. I felt my feet coming up off the floor, and with that, little red-and-black sparkles formed in the corners of my eyes and worked their way toward the center of my vision.

Chapter 27

How odd to see my feet in the air in front of me, my knees cocked at right angles. I felt like the wimpy guy in a TV wrestling match you know was just thrown into the ring as fodder.

Whoever my attacker was, he was on me like Nately's whore. He growled loudly, his hot breath on my neck as he fought to force the last breath out of me. He was concentrating on squeezing my chest, and as he did so I felt my legs dropping back down toward the floor. We were jammed close to the wall. My shoes brushed against the plaster as they came down.

Suddenly I contracted my gut as hard as I could, crunching myself into a tight ball. I wedged my feet between the two of us and the wall, planted them on the plaster, and kicked as hard as I could.

He grunted loudly and fell back, losing his balance in the process, and momentarily easing his grip around my chest. As we fell backward I pulled my head in close to my sternum, then snapped up as hard as I could.

The back of my skull connected with his chin. He barked loudly in pain, then fell back against the opposite wall. My arms dropped free. I held my right hand out in front of me, balled it tightly, then ripped down hard to my right, as fast as I could in the meanest arc I could muster. I connected perfectly and felt the whoosh of air jet out of his lungs as my crumpled fist hit the collection of lumps between his legs.

He dropped. Match over.

I fell on top of him as he went down, my back on his chest. In a blur, I had the stun gun out of my field-jacket pocket and jammed it into his thigh behind me. I hit the button and a thin, watery scream escaped from his lips. He jerked so hard he almost threw me off him, but my weight held him down. His whole body gyrated and shook. I let him have about two seconds worth of Great White Light, then rolled over to face him.

My own breathing sounded like an air compressor gone wild.

My heart raced like it had never done before; there was a gang fight going on in my temples.

I stared into his face, trying to figure out who the hell he was. Slobber ran from his lips. His eyes were wide-open and wild, his color almost slate gray.

'*Who the hell are you?*' I screamed, inches from his face.

I heard thumping on the steps behind us. I jerked and turned, ready to fight again. Only it was Mr Porter, fat and breathless, with his .38 pointed in a two-handed police stance right at us.

'It's okay,' I gasped. 'It's over.'

Mr Porter stood two steps down the flight of stairs, his arms bent, covering the guy from behind the corner of the stairwell.

I grabbed the lapels of a dingy work shirt. 'Goddamn it, who are you?'

His eyes flicked back and forth like a Parkinson's disease tremor. For all I knew, after a couple of seconds' worth of stun gun he might not be able to figure out who the hell he was. But I'd been scared witless myself, and I was in no mood to feel sorry for anyone. I put the stun gun in his face, with my finger on the button.

'You want some more?'

An animal cry of fear jumped out of his throat, and his lips struggled to make the word *no.*

I got up on my knees, then reached down and ran my hands down his sides, around his pants pockets.

'Where is it?' I yelled.

He looked at me like I was from another planet. 'Where's what?' he croaked.

I recognized the voice. I'd heard it before, on a collection of tapes I'd pulled off my answering machine. The revelation that I had the death-threat guy made me even crazier. 'The piece! The knife! The slapjack! Where is it?'

I yanked on his collar, hard enough to make him grimace. 'I ain't got nothing,' he gasped.

I eased up on him, then backed off, leaned against the opposite wall, and squatted back on my heels. 'No gun? No knife?'

He pulled himself up on his haunches and leaned against the wall, sweat pouring off of him, color coming back to his face. He self-consciously put his hand in his crotch and rubbed gently.

'I didn't come up here to kill ya,' he said.

'Then what did you come up here for?'

'I just came up here to whip yer ass, that's all.'

I looked at Mr Porter, who had a quizzical look on his face as he stared down the pistol barrel.

I relaxed a little and lowered my hand holding the stun gun. 'You ignorant-assed redneck hillbilly, you came up here to whip my ass and you didn't even bring a *weapon*?'

Suddenly I felt insulted. 'What kind of wuss do you think I am?'

He looked up at me and gave me this look that was right out of an episode of *Gomer Pyle USMC.* 'I don't rightly know what kind of wuss you are.'

I couldn't help it; I broke out laughing, partly from relief, partly from the whole situation being so damned crazy. Mr Porter looked at me like I'd lost my mind. 'You want me to call the police?'

I stood up, trying to control myself. No use humiliating the poor sucker even further. 'No, I'd say we got things pretty well under control.'

Mr Porter lowered the pistol and inserted it gingerly into the small holster on his belt. Just to be sure, though, I kept my hand wrapped around the stun gun. I looked down at the guy as he gingerly massaged his groin. 'Just who are you?' I asked, this time more politely.

He cocked his jaw and looked at me as I stood above him. With that I saw his face as I'd seen it once before, from above and a distance, through the viewfinder of a videocamera.

'Holy shit,' I said. 'You're the bricklayer.'

He pulled his legs under him and started to rise. I backed off a step and pointed the stun gun at him. He stared at me like a puppy I'd just kicked the stew out of. 'Can I please stand up?'

'If you do it real slow.'

He slid against the wall as he stood. 'I'd be a retired bricklayer by now if you hadn't dogged me all the way to Louisville.'

I scratched the side of my head in the classic display of confusion. 'But how the – how did you find me? How did you know it was me? I was never any closer to you than a telephoto lens could get. We never talked, never met.'

'Rick Harvey and Steve White told me,' he said sheepishly.

I thought for a moment. 'Who the hell are—'

Then it hit me. 'The insurance investigators!'

The bricklayer grinned. 'Them two boys was awful pissed off at you. You made 'em look bad in front of their boss.'

I shook my head, exasperated. 'Well, I'll be dipped in . . .'

'You need me anymore?' Mr Porter asked.

I turned to him. 'No, thanks, Mr Porter. I really appreciate you helping me out. I owe you one.'

He turned, his massive belly shaking as he started down the

steps. 'I just hope you never have to repay the favor,' he said as he disappeared.

I turned back to the bricklayer. 'Them two boys is going to be even more pissed by the time I get through with them. C'mon, bud. This way.' I motioned toward my office door.

'Where we going?' he asked.

'My office. I'm going to dig out my tape recorder, and you and I are going to have a little talk.'

'Hey, no way,' he said, holding his hands palm out toward me. 'I ain't talking into no tape recorder.'

I pushed the button on the stun gun and sent a bright blue inch-and-a-half spark crackling across the test probes. 'You can talk to my tape recorder or you can talk to the police. Your choice.'

He shuffled his feet toward my office. 'Aw, hell,' he muttered, then groaned as he took his first painful steps.

I unlocked my office door and led him in. He took my visitor's chair while I dug the tape recorder out of a drawer and plugged it in. When the red light glowed, I pointed the microphone in his direction.

'All right, give me your name, the date, and the time.'

He cleared his throat and shifted in the chair uncomfortably. 'My name's Bubba Ray Evans,' he began. Then he studied for a second to remember the date and glanced down at his wristwatch.

I asked him a couple of questions to get him going, but once Bubba Ray got started, it was like a dam bursting. He told me the whole story, of how he'd been so careful to set everything up, how he'd been steered to a crooked doctor by a buddy of his, and how he'd done his wheelchair act so well the insurance company was about to roll over and settle before the lawsuit came to court. But he'd always been active, loved sports, missed his bass fishing, and the wheelchair was driving him crazy. He'd finally talked his wife into going on a short vacation, but even then they'd maintained the charade until they were sure they were safe and in seclusion.

Then two guys from the insurance company showed up at his house one night with a copy of the videotape. At first Bubba Ray thought they were there to nail his hide to the wall, but they kept being so danged friendly. Finally he figured out they were trying to warn him to drop his claim before he was brought up on fraud charges. And, he added, Rick Harvey and Steve White had been only too glad to give him the name of the guy who'd exposed him.

Bubba Ray'd gone nuts, but it was nothing compared to what the little lady did. She was tired of living off the proceeds of an itinerant, self-employed bricklayer's efforts. Because he was self-employed and acting as a contractor, the workmen's comp laws – which prohibit an employee from suing his employer for negligence – didn't apply. So Mrs Bubba Ray was counting on a couple of mil or so in a settlement. And when she figured out she wasn't going to get it, she went completely off the deep end. The deeper she got, the madder Bubba Ray got, until finally, what started out as phone harassment escalated into assault.

Only problem was, Bubba Ray couldn't fight any better than he could lay bricks.

I was furious at the treachery of it. Those two punk slimeball Clint Eastwood wannabes had ratted my wimpy butt out just to get even with me for making them look bad. The only reason I wasn't laid up in a hospital room right now was that they'd ratted my wimpy butt out to somebody who was even wimpier than me.

Bubba Ray talked for about forty minutes, and by the time he got through, I had enough sewage on these two fine, upstanding employees of the Tennessee Workman's Protective Association to have a shot at a Pulitzer Prize nomination if I was still in the newspaper biz. It was simply a matter of what I wanted to do with it. I sent Bubba Ray Evans on his way with a warning that I had his confession on tape, had saved all his death threats off the answering machine, and that if I ever saw his sorry ass again, he was going to be stamping out license plates for so long he'd wish he was back in that wheelchair.

I shut down my office and headed back across the river. In my apartment, I had a small bookshelf stereo system whose one bell-and-whistle was that it had a tape player with two decks. I copied off all the death threats onto one tape, then copied Bubba Ray's statement. I didn't figure it'd hold up in court, given the circumstances that it was taken under, but by God, it'd make a hell of a newspaper headline.

I pulled out my White Pages and thumbed through the *A*s until I found Phil Anderson's address. I scratched it down on a notepad, then changed back into a coat and tie. By seven-thirty, I was on my way to West Nashville with a pocket full of fun.

Phil Anderson's brown aggregate driveway probably cost more than my car. I glanced around at the neighborhood full of custom houses and wondered what it would do to Phil's spot in the homeowners' association to have my rustbucket Mazda parked behind his wife's Volvo.

I rang the doorbell and stood quietly, trying to keep my pulse down to a safe range. I heard soft footsteps, then a pretty but tired-looking woman with a toddler in her arms answered the door. A blue bandanna held her hair back from her forehead.

'Hello,' she said through the storm door.

'Hi,' I said, smiling as sweetly as I could pull together. 'My name's Harry James Denton and I'm looking for Phil Anderson. Is he available?'

'Sure,' she said. 'Let me get him.' Obviously, Phil hadn't trained his wife to protect him as well as his secretary. She held open the door for me as I stepped onto the parqueted foyer. The foyer faced up onto a great room, with maybe twenty-foot ceilings above. A crystal chandelier made up of about a thousand pieces of glass hung over my head. The steps leading down from the landing stopped at a carpeted hallway.

She went down those steps and stopped at the hallway. 'Phil,' she called, 'company!'

She turned and walked past me upstairs. 'If you'll excuse me now, I'm trying to get this one down.'

'I understand. Thanks.'

I heard steps from below, then Phil Anderson was at the foot of the stairs in a pair of worn jeans, a T-shirt, and an unfolded newspaper flapping from one hand. His smile disappeared when he saw me on the landing.

'Harry,' he said.

I plastered the biggest golly-glad-to-see-you grin on my face you've ever seen. 'Hey, Phil!' I said brightly. 'We have to talk.'

Phil Anderson sat forward in his BarcaLounger and rubbed his eyes, discouraged, as I punched the stop/eject button and retrieved the tape.

'Well, well, well,' he said. Then he let loose with a long sigh that faded to silence after a couple of seconds. I noticed that his thick Mississippi fieldhand brogue was nowhere to be found. The rhythm and cadence of his speech was now patrician, well educated.

'What are we going to do about this?' he asked.

I flipped the tape over to him and sat back down on the leather couch in front of a projection television that seemed about as big as a Volkswagen.

'That's a copy for your records,' I said. 'I've got the original stashed away.'

He looked up from his lap, where he'd been staring at the tape like it was going to bite him. 'Hell, Harry, you don't have to do that. What do you think we're going to do, break in and steal it?'

I shrugged my shoulders. 'You said it, not me.'

He picked the tape up and studied it. 'Well, turkey snot, I guess we had that one coming.'

'Listen, Phil, I—'

'Let's cut to the chase, Harry,' he interrupted. 'What's this going to cost me? If I'm going to be blackmailed, I'd like to get the bill up front.'

The hair on the back of my neck went on point. 'Damn it, Phil, you've been spending too much time around guys like Rick Harvey and Steve White! I don't blackmail people.'

'You don't?'

'No, all I want is what's coming to me. Pay my invoice, that's all. The bill was fair, you agreed to it before I ever started the job, and that's all I want.'

He stared at me in what could almost be described as amazement. 'That's all?' he asked.

'That's it in terms of money. I'd appreciate the chance to work with you again. You got any more work, send a little of it my way every now and then. You've seen what I can do when I set my mind to it.'

He laughed. 'Oh, hell, yes, I've seen that, all right.'

'And there's one other thing,' I said.

'Uh-oh,' he said. 'I figured there'd be a catch in there somewhere.'

'Fire those two assholes,' I said. 'Fire 'em cold. No termination. No notice. No unemployment. No recommendations. And if I were you, I'd have a security guard watch while they clean out their desks. That way, you won't turn up with any office supplies – or computer disks – missing.'

Phil Anderson settled back in the easy chair again. 'I'm insulted that you'd even think it was necessary to mention that part. Don't worry, those two are history. Say, Harry, why don't you come to work for me? I can make you a nice package. Salary and benefits – retirement, vacation, profit sharing. The insurance business'll treat you pretty well.'

A steady paycheck, paid vacation. Jeez, it had been a while since I'd had anything like that. On the other hand, with the exception of a few bad times, I relished what I was doing these days.

'Why don't I take a pass on that one for now, Phil. I've got another case I'm working pretty hard. Couple of other minor matters on my mind right now. But let's stay in touch.'

'Okay,' he said, pulling himself up out of the chair. 'Why don't I have a check messengered over to your office tomorrow morning?'

'That'll be great. I'll be in the office by eight-thirty,' I answered.

Phil's good-ol'-boy accent was coming back now. 'Hot damn,' he drawled. 'First thing in the morning. And Harry, I really appreciate you not going to the police or the newspapers or anything else on this.'

I smiled and stuck out my hand. 'My pleasure, Phil. Glad we could settle this between us, man-to-man.'

Phil led me to the front door and slapped me heartily on the back as we parted company.

'Hey, Harry,' he called as I walked down the driveway. 'What in the Sam Hill kinda car is that?'

'That's a Mazda Cosmo,' I said. 'Very rare . . .' I opened the driver's side door with a long, rusty squeak and got in. As I fired up the car and smoked my way out of his driveway, I could see him standing there, shaking his head.

'Well,' I said out loud as I pulled onto Sawyer Brown Road headed for Charlotte Pike, 'maybe I'm beginning to figure this *bidness* out.'

Chapter 28

The thought of five grand coming to me in about twelve hours made the drive back to East Nashville a whole lot easier. Most of the money would be gone before I even got to look at it, but at least I'd be caught up and back to ground zero.

Life was peaches and cream as I crossed the river and hit Gallatin Road toward Inglewood. I decided to celebrate. This time I'd go to Mrs Lee's and have one of the eight-dollar dinners rather than the usual four-dollars-and-change special. There are simply times in a man's life when he needs to get as crazy as an outhouse rat, and this was one of them. Steamed dumplings, sweet-and-sour soup, here I come.

It was nearly nine by the time I pushed the heavy plate-glass door open and entered the restaurant. There was a new red-and-green neon sign out front that blinked LEE'S SZECHUAN PALACE. I'd never known the restaurant had a name beyond Mrs Lee's. Business must be good, although you couldn't tell it from inside the restaurant right now. A couple sat alone over disposable plates in the corner, heads huddled so close together that they had to be either hard-of-hearing or in love.

There was no one at the counter, although that wouldn't have been that unusual this time of night. Mrs Lee was probably in the back helping her husband with the cleanup chores. I felt a pang of guilt as I pondered how hard these people worked: fourteen-hour days, six days a week, which used to be seven until Mrs Lee's health started to show the strain. Nowadays, at least, they took Sunday off.

Through an access window, I could see Mr Lee, his five-foot, one-hundred-and-ten-pound frame bent over an industrial stain-less-steel sink scrubbing out a shiny metal pan the size of a washtub. Sweat soaked through the back of his white T-shirt as his thin, sinewed arms wrestled with the metal.

I watched him through the window for a minute or so until the kitchen door swung open outward and Mary Lee walked through.

She was taller than her mother, nearly as tall as me, and athletically thin. Her skin was unblemished, just this side of honey-colored, and her dark almond eyes were almost perfectly symmetrical. Her long black hair hung straight and shiny to the middle of her back. To top it off, she's smart as a whip. Last year, she came damn close to bursting fifteen hundred on her SATs, and I was convinced she'd be off to college next year on a big fat scholarship.

Excuse me, I wax disgusting here. To my own very little credit, I had kept my torch for her properly concealed as well as carried and had never been anything but appropriately civil with her.

'Harry!' she squealed as she saw me. She took two quick steps toward the counter and bent over to wrap her arms around me.

'Hi, sweetie,' I said, when we'd separated. 'How ya doing?'

'Fine. I haven't seen you in here in over a week. Thought you got tired of us.'

'Never,' I said. 'I figured I'd give you a break, that's all.'

Her eyes were bright and danced in the harsh fluorescent light, although there were circles under them that I'd never seen before.

'Don't be crazy. I'm always glad to see you.'

I looked up at the clock. 'What're you doing working here so late? No school tomorrow?'

Mary leaned against the cash register. 'It's Mom's high blood pressure again. Doc put her to bed for a couple of days. I'm worried about her.'

'Yeah, me, too,' I said. 'She works too hard. You all do.'

'Hey,' she piped, 'somebody's gotta keep it going, right?' She picked up a green order pad. 'Besides, I'd rather be here than home. Mom raises hell when the doctor tells her to lie still. What can I get for you?'

'Aw, listen, Mary, if it's too late, you guys are already shutting down—'

'Don't be silly. That's what we're here for. Although I think there may not be any chicken left. I'll have to check.'

'That's okay. I'm going to try something different tonight. Got any sweet-and-sour soup left? Dumplings?'

'Yeah on both counts.'

'Let me have the Kung Bao beef dinner,' I said, reading off the menu, 'and some iced tea.'

Mary scribbled the order down. 'My, oh my, we *are* splurging tonight.'

'I'm celebrating cracking a big case,' I said.

She ripped the sheet off the notepad and slipped it under a clip on a rotating wheel in the top of the access door. Then she rolled the wheel around so my order was inside the kitchen and said something to her father through the hole.

'One of these days, you're going to have to teach me that,' I said. 'How long would it take me to learn Chinese?'

She turned and grinned. 'We speak a fairly simple Mandarin dialect,' she said. 'I'd say if you started right now and worked real hard, practised every day, I'd say maybe, I don't know, ten years or so. Yeah, ten years. You could make yourself sort of understood by then.'

'*Ten years?*' I said. 'Forget it, I'm too old.'

She giggled. 'Oh, yeah, right. Say, Harry. I'm going to need a summer job, and I'd sure like it to be something else besides this. How's about I come work for you? I'd like to be a private detective for a while.'

Something in my chest lurched. I didn't think my working with Mary Lee was a very good idea; the last thing in the world I needed was a gorgeous seventeen-year-old Amerasian girl sharing a one-room office with me.

But I wasn't going to tell her that. 'I probably can't afford you, Mary. Besides, it's not what it's cracked up to be in the movies. It's pretty tedious most of the time.'

She leaned in close to me. 'Oh, like this isn't?' she stage-whispered.

'Where you going to school next year?' I asked, grabbing at anything possible to change the subject.

'Well, let's see,' she said, counting off on her fingers, 'I've got applications in at Tufts, Brown, Columbia, Duke . . .'

I chuckled. 'Party schools, huh?'

'Yeah, why push myself?' She smiled back with a row of white teeth that lit up the room.

Behind Mary, a tray of food appeared in the window. I suddenly realized I was starving. Mary saw my eyes flick to the window and turned.

'Here we go,' she said. I pulled out the last ten-dollar bill from my wallet and handed it to her, then waited as she got my change.

'Can you come sit with me?' I asked.

She grimaced. 'God, Harry, I've got to help Daddy get everything cleaned up before we shut down at ten. Then I've got a couple of hours homework.'

'It's good to see you, dear,' I said. 'Don't work too hard.'

She disappeared into the kitchen as I took a seat at the table across from the couple. I dug into the soup, a thick, hot broth with a mélange of sweet, sour, and hot-as-hell tastes all mixed into one. Instantly, I felt this sense of well-being that I knew was probably biologically induced, since there really wasn't all that much reality to cause it. Things had gotten better, I had to admit.

The worst of my problems were still out there, though. Marsha was still hunkered down at the morgue and Slim was still in the county jail awaiting trial, both in their own way prisoners of circumstances beyond their control. And both innocent . . .

Of that point, I was sure. When I first read of how Slim had discovered the body, and how Rebecca Gibson had been battered so completely, I thought it probable that – despite my personal feelings for him – the police had the right man. The more I delved into Rebecca Gibson's world, though, the more I doubted that Slim was the only person out there with a motive to kill her. There had to be more, had to be something I wasn't seeing. I wasn't digging hard enough, wasn't pushing hard enough.

Wasn't asking the tough questions . . .

I ate my dinner in silence, and was mopping up the last few bites when I realized the couple across the room had left and I was alone in the dining room. From the kitchen I heard talking and the sound of water spraying, steam erupting. It was late, and I was beginning to feel the first bittersweet tinges of exhaustion creeping around the edge of my psyche. I've noticed that when I get this way, I become fuzzy-headed, loose thinking. Weird stuff starts to make sense, and perfectly sensible things become incomprehensible. It's a strange combination of fatigue and what I'd always imagined might be a kind of stress-induced dyslexia. All I knew was that I was going to sleep well tonight.

Well, not exactly. At least not yet. As I stuffed my throwaway dishes into a large waste bin near the front door of the restaurant, Mary stepped out with a brown paper sack with a grease spot on the bottom that was growing by the second.

'You going to see Shadow soon?' she asked.

It occurred to me that Lonnie might enjoy hearing about my adventure with Bubba Ray Evans and the insurance company. I could also write him a check for the money I owed him, as long as he'd hold it for a day or two before depositing it.

'Sure, I planned to stop by on the way home. This'll give me a good excuse.'

I gave Mary a hug like her uncle would give her, then waved goodbye to her father and stepped out the door into the parking lot. Gallatin Road this time of night is more than just a little creepy, with the eerie orange of the street lamps casting long, foreboding shadows. The Earl Scheib Body Shop across the street was empty and desolate, with shiny, jet-black windows and rust-red brick. I worried about Mary and her family being alone in the restaurant. Last year, the entire night shift of a Taco Bell in a little town just northeast of here was wiped out in a robbery that turned into a massacre. People are so damned crazy these days. I once interviewed an inmate at the Tennessee State Prison, a hard-core lifer, who told me *he* was afraid of the people coming up through the crime ranks these days.

I pulled onto Gallatin Road with the sack full of left-overs on the floorboard next to me. Traffic had thinned and I had one of my few rare times of hitting the lights correctly. I made it up to the Inglewood Theatre in a couple of minutes, then turned left, curved around, and pulled up to Lonnie's chain-link fence gate. I braked the car and tooted the horn a couple of times, then got out and stood by the fence. I'd learned my lesson the hard way about surprising Shadow, so stood politely back until I was sure she recognized me.

Her huge paws barely fit through the spaces in the chain link as she stood on her hind legs and nuzzled me through the wire. I held the bag up to the fence; she got a whiff of it and her long, bushy tail went into overdrive.

'Yes, baby,' I cooed at her. Damn dog always did that to me, makes me sound like an idiot. 'Look what I got . . .'

I opened the gate and eased through, then secured it back. Shadow was on my shoulders, her great wet snout rubbing streaks across my face. Usually, I'd have thought something like that was gross, but with her it never bothered me. I'm just glad she wasn't trying to rip my throat out.

From behind the trailer, maybe thirty feet away, Lonnie stepped out and cleared his throat.

'Well,' he called, 'you gonna give it to her or what?'

I motioned for her to sit. She settled back on her haunches, jaws already dripping at the thought. I pulled the greasy meat out of the bag, wadded it into a ball, and held it out in front of her.

'Speak,' I said. This low, throaty growl came out of her. I shook my head back and forth, needling her. 'Speak, Shadow.'

'You keep teasing her like that, she's liable to tear your arm off at the shoulder.'

'C'mon, baby, speak to me!'

She let loose with a rumbling that came from way down inside her, then erupted in a fearful bark that would've sent lesser men than me under the bed if I hadn't known her. I flicked my wrist, and this wad the size of a tennis ball sailed through the air in a slow arc. Shadow became airborne and I had to jump out of the way.

The meat disappeared before all four paws were back on the ground. I leaned down and rubbed my hands in her fur, smearing the juice all over her in what I hoped she'd think was an extra treat.

Lonnie wiped his hands on a pink shop rag. 'I'm about finished back here. Let's go get a beer.'

In the dim light, I could see grease streaks across his face and up his arms. 'What've you been working on?'

'I got an engine I'm rebuilding now, trying to make a few extra bucks. Six-cylinder out of a '68 Mustang. You remember Jack Stevens?'

We stepped onto the deck. Lonnie opened the front door of the trailer, sending a glaze of yellow light over the front of the junkyard.

'Stevens?' I asked as we walked inside. 'Can't say I do.'

'Used to work part-time for me skip-tracing, back when I was still doing a lot of that. Started working the same time you did, more or less.'

'Okay.'

'Anyway,' Lonnie said, opening the refrigerator door and pulling out a couple of cold brews, 'guy gets the hots for an old Mustang, so he finds a '68 coupe for sale down in the Spring Hill. Goes down, takes a look at it, gets crazy, writes a check. Doesn't take it to a mechanic or anything.'

He popped the tops on the cans, handed one to me, then chuckled. 'Dumb ass. Freaking car's burning a quart of oil every three days. Throw-out bearing squeals like a baby rolling around in a box of broken glass. Jesus . . .'

'What he'd do that for?' I asked.

'I don't know. Shit for brains, I guess. I made him a deal, said I'd do the rebuild for parts plus two hundred.'

'Some people got more money than brains,' I said, raising the can. The beer tingled all the way down. Delicious.

'Yeah, well, this dude ain't got much o' either.'

'Speaking of shit for brains,' I said, plopping down on the couch and spreading my feet out across the coffee table, 'have I got a story to tell you.'

By the time I finished the chronicle of Bubba Ray's assault and subsequent visit to Phil Anderson's house, we'd polished off most of the beer. Lonnie shook his head in amazement, sniggering at the thought of the incompetent attacker.

'Guy can't even sit in a wheelchair without screwing it up,' he said.

'Yeah. Says he's going to *whip my ass*. Like he's some kind of mean mother.'

'Well,' Lonnie said, popping up out of his torn, grease-covered easy chair, 'this guy must be a pussy if he couldn't whip your sorry ass.'

'What a minute!' I said to his back.

'Wait nothing,' he said from the kitchen. I heard the sound of a beer can being opened. 'Want another?'

'No, I got to go home. The upshot of this whole business with Bubba Ray is that Phil Anderson says he's messengering over a check tomorrow morning, which means I can pay you back.'

I reached into my coat pocket and pulled out my checkbook. I filled in $500.00 on the amount line, signed it, then handed it to him as he came back in with a fresh beer.

'Check with me tomorrow afternoon before you deposit it, okay? On the off chance that Phil Anderson doesn't come through.'

Lonnie grinned and shook his head. 'Why don't you just post-date the damn thing and mail it to me?'

'Just take the check. I gotta go. I need some shuteye.'

Lonnie sat up quickly. 'Hey, before you go.' He set his beer down on the coffee table, then disappeared down the dark hallway that led to the two bedrooms. Lonnie used one for an office, I knew, and one for the occasional times when he spent the night there.

He returned in a few seconds with a clipboard in his hand. 'Listen, I know you're temporarily flush. Or at least you will be if your check comes tomorrow. How'd you like to make a few extra bucks, anyway?'

'I don't know. What've you got?'

He held out the clipboard. 'You know I lost the bank and my repo work has gone down the toilet. Well, I got a new client today.'

I handed the clipboard back to him without looking at it. 'Aw, no, Lonnie. I'll have to take a pass on that one. I'm too frazzled to repo cars right now.'

'C'mon, Harry, it'll be fun! Take your mind off your other problems. Besides, these ain't just regular cars. Take a look.'

I took back the clipboard and tried to focus in the dim light. Several low-quality faxes were attached to the clipboard, with a logo and heading at the top of the first sheet that read LUXURY LEASING OF NASHVILLE.

'Whoa, what've we got here?' I asked.

'Yeah, cool, huh? These ain't no Ford Fiestas we gotta pick up here, bud. These are government-inspected, USDA prime.'

There were several pages of listings: Mercedes, Jags, Saabs, Alfas. 'C'mon,' I said. 'Who buys a car like this and then skips out on the payments?'

Lonnie grimaced. 'What planet are you from, bozo? Any fool can lease a car. It's making those five-hundred-a-month lease payments that's a bear.'

'I don't know, Lonnie. It sounds like fun, but I just—'

'I'll even save the best for you. Check the last page.'

I flipped through the pages until I came to the last one, which only had three cars listed. My jaw dropped, and I looked back up at him.

'Lonnie, I've never even driven a—'

Suddenly my heart jumped in my chest. I squinted hard and looked back down at the page.

'Rolls-Royce . . .' I whispered.

There, among the cars that Lonnie had contracted to repossess because their owners had failed to meet their just and legal obligations in terms of repaying a contractually binding financial agreement and instrument of debt, was a 1990 Rolls-Royce Corniche III, Tennessee vanity-license-plate number TRUSNO1.

And below that, the owner's name: F. M. Ford.

Chapter 29

'What's the matter?' Lonnie asked.

I stared up at him, trying to figure out just how much I should be shocked. 'You had a chance to look at these?'

He shook his head. 'Fax just came in this afternoon. I had time to glance over it, that's all.'

I held the clipboard up to him and pointed. 'That one. That guy's Rebecca Gibson's manager.'

He took it from me, then stared at the listing for a second. 'No shit?'

'He's a big-time music manager. Real hotshot.'

'I don't care how hot his shot is,' Lonnie said, letting the clipboard drop to his side. 'He's three months behind on his lease payments, and I got to repossess his car.'

I scratched the side of my head, a habit that I'd been indulging in a lot lately. 'How'd you get this gig?'

'Scotty Boles put in a good word for me. He knows I've got the equipment to snatch those kinds of cars without damaging them. You don't just set a hook on a damn Mercedes and tug it off.'

'Yeah, obviously,' I said, distracted. 'Of course.'

'What's eating you?' he asked.

I shook my head and sat back down on the couch. 'This is too weird. How does a guy who's one of the most powerful artist managers on the Row wind up having his Rolls picked up?'

'You'd be amazed at some of the cars I've repossessed,' Lonnie said. 'People live in mansions, then get their wheels yanked out from under 'em. Who knows?'

'It doesn't make any sense. Just doesn't make any sense.'

'I don't know what to tell you, Harry. You want me to call the office tomorrow and make sure they didn't make a mistake?'

I turned back to him. 'No,' I said with a little more force than I intended. 'Don't do that. But you can do one thing for me.'

'What?'

Steven Womack

'Hold off on this one, will you?'

He shrugged. 'Well, sure, I can do that. There's three other pages full I can grab first. But you know, I've got to get it eventually.'

'Just give me a couple of days, that's all. Something stinks here. I'd like to see if I can find out what it is without Ford knowing I'm out there digging in his garbage.'

'You know,' Lonnie said, 'if this guy Ford stuck to driving Fords instead of Rolls-Royces, he might not be in this shape now.'

I stood back up. 'Lonnie you're a good ol' boy. I don't care what anybody else says about you.'

'What's that supposed to mean?' he sputtered.

I opened the door of the trailer and stepped through. 'Nothing pal, I didn't pay any attention to those rumors about you and that goat.'

I shut the door just as his empty beer can sailed through the air and slammed metallically into the glass. Something told me that sleep tonight wasn't going to come as easily as I'd hoped.

The squeaking and swaying of the metal staircase up to my attic apartment almost woke me up enough to realize I was home. I unlocked my door, staggered in, and barely recognized the place. Not that anything had happened; it just felt like a year since I'd been there.

First things first: no messages on the answering machine, no interesting mail. I stripped off my clothes and got into the shower, letting the hot water rip over me so hard it left red streaks. I dried off, a little more alert now.

Why, I asked myself, hasn't Marsha called? Even though I didn't have any notion of what to say to her, I wanted to hear her voice. If it was just for five seconds, that was fine. I only wanted to know she was okay.

Then it occurred to me that the phone works both ways. I made a cup of Sleepytime tea, threw in a slug of brandy for good measure, and settled back into bed. It was almost eleven-thirty when I took a chance and punched in her number.

The number chirped six times before she came on the line.

'Yes,' she said abruptly. Her voice was sharp, tight.

'Hey,' I said. 'How are you?'

'Have you seen the news?' she demanded.

'No, I've been working all eve—'

'Turn on *Nightline*,' she snapped. Then the click of a cellular phone being disconnected.

I sat there dumbfounded for a second before panic set in. What in heaven's name could have happened that would— No matter, put the phone up and turn the damn television on.

The TV took a few seconds to warm up, but the sound came through quickly. A rerun of *The Cosby Show* was just ending, which meant there'd be at least three minutes of commercials before anything important happened.

As the color sharpened and the picture came into focus, a middle-aged white lady with a pained expression on her face began speaking earnestly into the camera.

'Painful bloating. Stomach upset. It got so bad I finally went to my doctor.' Then she smiled. 'Thank God, it was only gas. My doctor recommended Mylanta . . .'

'Christ Almighty, lady!' I yelled. 'You go to the doctor to find out you need to fart?'

I forced myself to shut up, then remembered that Mrs Hawkins couldn't hear me anyway. To hell with it; I hit the mute button.

Finally the pitches were over and the *Nightline* logo appeared. I hit the mute button just as the theme music started, then slugged down the last of the tea and brandy as they went through the preliminaries.

'Siege in Music City,' the narrator said. Then Ted Koppel's face appeared.

'What began as a bizarre, almost comical situation in Nashville, Tennessee, took a darker turn today as the founder of a fundamentalist religious sect that calls itself the Pentecostal Evangelical Enochians demanded that the body of his wife be turned over to cult members within forty-eight hours. If the corpse – which is now being held for a legally required autopsy in the Nashville morgue – is not released, cult founder Woodrow Tyberious Hogg has sworn that he will invoke what he calls the Enochian Apocalypse. Local officials interpret the Enochian Apocalypse this way: Heavily armed cult followers – who at present are surrounding the Nashville morgue – will begin their assault to retrieve the body of Evangeline Lee Hogg on Sunday morning, one full week after the siege began. In a moment we'll speak with the mayor and chief of police in Nashville and a Vanderbilt University professor who's an expert on cult behavior. But first, a little background from *Nightline* correspondent Dave Maresh.'

I pulled the covers up to my neck and settled into the pillow, my eyes wide-open, my neck muscles tensed. All I could think of was Marsha sitting with all those other people huddled in the darkness around Dr Henry's little battery-powered pocket TV.

'This is insane,' I muttered as Dave Maresh's rugged, jovial face filled the screen of my own television.

'The Pentecostal Evangelical Enochians are an eccentric bunch, Ted, even by today's standards. Members pride themselves on being the buckle of the Bible Belt. We've done some research into beliefs of the Pentecostal Evangelical Enochians, and what we're discovering is that this is a group so far afield they make David Koresh's Branch Davidians look like High-Church Episcopalians.'

Cut to a videotape of Reverend Woody in a white polyester suit, thumping his Bible on his knee, covered in sweat, with Maresh's voice-over continuing:

'The group draws a direct connection between Enoch of the Old Testament, who was the seventh generation from Adam, with the seven angels of the sixteenth chapter of Revelations, who pour out the wrath of God upon the earth.'

' "And the first angel went," ' Reverend Woody screamed, ' "and poured out his vial upon the earth; and there fell a noisome and grievous sore upon the men, which had the mark of the beast, and upon them which worshipped his image." '

Back to Maresh now: 'The Pentecostal Evangelical Enochians believe that the skin lesions associated with Kaposi's sarcoma are that 'grievous sore which had the mark of the beast.' AIDS, they say, is the biblically predicted precursor of Judgment Day. The Enochians also saw the 1994 bloody genicidal massacres in Rwanda, in which bodies floated down rivers so thick they became a cholera hazard, as further evidence of the seven angels and the impending apocalypse.'

' "And the third angel poured out his vial upon the rivers and fountains of waters: and they became blood!" ' Hogg was in a frenzy now.

'And in a videotaped sermon last year,' Maresh continued, 'which has only recently been made available to the press by a disgruntled ex-cult member, Hogg even drew an apocalyptic revelation from the career of Madonna.'

My jaw dropped as they cut to Hogg, an open Bible in his hand, at a podium inside a church that looked to me more like a bingo hall.

'My children, she is here! The Bible predicted her, and she has taken the name of the blessed mother of our blessed Savior! In Revelations 17, God tells us: "And there came one of the seven angels which had the seven vials and talked with me, saying unto me, Come hither; I will shew unto thee the judgment of the great whore that sitteth upon many waters, with whom the kings of the earth have committed fornication, and the inhabitants of the earth have been made drunk with the wine of her fornication. So he carried me away in the spirit into the wilderness: and I saw a woman sit upon a scarlet coloured beast, full of names of blasphemy!"

'She is here, my children! And her lies and fornication foretell of us the end of the world! The Great Whore who has stolen the blessed virgin's name is upon us now in these last days of the world!'

He seemed to be in a trance, possessed of the spirit, or something dangerously close to it.

'This is absolutely fucking insane,' I said out loud to a television that, once again, didn't bother to respond. Maresh continued his report, then wrapped it up with a quick summary of the week's events. Ted Koppel segued to a commercial, then came back and introduced his guests. I recognized the mayor and the chief of police, sitting nervously in front of two separate cameras as Koppel slipped them the tough questions in his own iron-fist-in-a-velvet-glove style.

'Chief Gleaves, you and the mayor both insist that you're not going to call in either the National Guard or federal agents. Yet isn't it true that if we are to believe the Enochians and their claims about weapons, they have you outgunned?'

Harold Gleaves shifted nervously in his chair, then gave his tie a Rodney Dangerfield tug. 'Well, Mr Koppel, I don't want to get into speculating what kinds of weapons they may or may not have down there, and I certainly don't want to disclose what we've got on our side of the fence. I'd like to emphasize that the important thing for us is keep the dialogue open. We've got a top-notch hostage negotiating team down there. We care very much about finding a peaceful resolution to all this. We're willing to talk. We want to talk. I only hope that the other side will remain open to that as well.'

'Good job, Harold,' I said.

'Mr Mayor,' Koppel asked, 'at what point would you be willing to request the governor to call out the National Guard?'

The mayor was a former entrepreneur who'd made a fortune in the car-parts business. Right now he looked like he wished he'd stayed in the private sector, where the only hostile takeovers he had to worry about were on paper.

'I've speaken – spoken – with the governor,' he said, stumbling over his words. 'I've kept him apprised of the situation. We feel like we're a long way away from having to call out the National Guard or seek federal intervention.'

'Good dodge, Mr Mayor,' I said.

Then Ted turned to Professor Barbara Hatfield, whom he had introduced as a Vanderbilt University sociologist who'd made a study of religious cults in the Deep South.

'Professor Hatfield, how serious are they? They must know that no matter how heavily armed they are, ultimately they'll suffer the same fate as Koresh's group did in Waco if they push the issue too far. Do you think they're willing to do that? Is this a suicidal group of martyrs at work here?'

Professor Hatfield, in her midthirties, a bespectacled, seriously academic lady, took her time and chose her words carefully: 'That's what causes me the most fear, Ted. Clearly, as our experience in Waco showed, there are levels of obsession at work here that make suicidal martyrdom a distinct possibility. The five innocent people trapped inside the morgue right now are the ones for whom I fear the most.'

My gut knotted up.

'At the very least,' she continued, 'we must take their threats of armed confrontation seriously. From Jim Jones to David Koresh, we've seen that these threats can be realized. The one depture here from recent events like this – and I'm not sure what the ultimate importance of this will be – is that their leader is not behind the barricades with them. If apocalypse comes to Nashville, Tennessee, we apparently won't see the Reverend Woodrow Tyberious Hogg go up in flames with his flock.'

'Good point, Professor Hatfield,' Ted said. 'Exactly how much control do you think Reverend Hogg is exerting over his followers? He claims to be only their inspirational and spiritual leader, and he insists that the criminal acts they've committed in the group's name were not ordered by him.'

'Well ...' She hesitated for a moment. 'I think I have to speak with some sensitivity here because we are still involved in active crisis management. But I am very dubious of Reverend Hogg's claims in this area. I think he has substantial control over his group. He may not be controlling their every action, but ...'

'You think if he ordered them to stand down, they'd do it,' Ted interjected.

Professor Hatfield nodded. 'Absolutely.'

Ted turned back to Chief Gleaves. 'With that in mind, Chief Gleaves, have you made attempts to speak with Reverend Hogg?'

'We've certainly made attempts,' Gleaves answered. 'But we

haven't had much success with opening a dialogue with him. As you said, he insists he's just their spiritual leader, and he claims that what they're doing is biblically sound and morally justified. We, of course, don't agree.'

'That's the understatement of the year,' I said.

'What about this business of giving the body of Reverend Hogg's wife back to the group? Is that in the realm of possibility? Can this be done without the government seeming to have caved in on the issue?'

Again, Chief Gleaves spoke up. 'What we're trying to do right now is reach an agreement with the group that will avoid bloodshed, and yet still allow us to fulfill our constitutional obligation to uphold the law. One avenue we're exploring is that while state law requires us to perform an autopsy in this case, it doesn't specify in medical terms what an autopsy actually consists of. So if we can reach an agreement whereby we perform the tests necessary to determine the cause of death, but do it in such a way that the religious strictures of the group aren't violated, then we may be able to settle this peaceably.'

Harold Gleaves was coming off very well. By tomorrow morning, the mayor would hate him.

'Even then,' Ted Koppel asked, 'the group would still face charges. Would they be serious charges?'

Gleaves hesitated a moment. 'My feeling is that we're probably looking at some weapons charges, trespassing, maybe a few others. Given the circumstances, nothing all that serious.'

'What about kidnapping?'

'Well, that would, of course, be up to a grand jury and the District Attorney's Office. My feeling at this point in time is the charges that are ultimately leveled will be in direct relation to the cooperation we receive from the group, and to the outcome of this situation.'

I whistled. 'Goddamn brilliant, Harold,' I said. If those people down there had any brains at all, they'd understand that Harold Gleaves had just given them an easy way out. Now if they'd only take it.

The conversation continued along those lines for another fifteen minutes or so, then Ted signed off with a teaser that tomorrow night's 20/20 would feature Baba Wawa interviewing a woman who claimed to be yet another bimbo who's claimed to have slept with Bill Clinton. Amazingly, he pulled it off with a straight face.

I punched in the cellular number and she answered on the second ring.

'Yes.'

'We have *got* to get you out of there,' I said.

She let loose a deep breath that had been locked inside her chest for too long. 'So you saw it.'

'Are you kidding? Of course I saw it.'

'Well, I don't know, Harry. I haven't heard from you all day. I thought you'd forgotten about me.'

I got the distinct feeling I'd been snapped at, and thought for a moment she was being funny. There was no characteristic tag laugh at the end, though, and I suddenly realized she was serious.

'You know better than that.'

'Do I?' she demanded, her voice as sharp as a hammer rap. 'I don't know, Harry. I really don't know anymore. I don't know anything.'

'Marsha, what's wrong?'

She laughed meanly. 'Oh, listen to you! What do you think's wrong? I've just been locked up in a looney bin for six days and nights! Other than that, I can't imagine what could be wrong!'

'Marsha listen to me. Something's changed. What's going on down there?'

There was a long pause, a strained and painful silence, punctuated by what sounded like a sob. Only I'd never heard her cry before; wasn't sure, in fact, if she even knew how.

'Oh, God,' she whimpered. 'I had to break up a fight today, Harry.'

I was stunned into momentary silence. 'You did what?' I gasped.

'Larry and Charlie got in a fight over a stupid, freeze-dried meal. They were beating the hell out of each other.'

Larry and Charlie were two of the morgue attendants, young guys who'd managed to make their way onto the civil-service list. Larry was white, Charlie black; both were high-school dropouts and virtually unemployable in the private sector. The low-level jobs at the morgue paid about as much as a career in fast food, only the benefits were better and you didn't have to work as hard. The thought of Marsha breaking up a real fight between these two gave me chest pains.

'So what happened?' I asked, horrified.

'I've got closure strips on Larry,' she sobbed again, then cleared her throat. Her voice became a little steadier, but still very soft. 'But I think he's going to take a couple of stitches if we ever get out of here. Charlie's okay. But there were nasty racial slurs – and threats. I mean, Charlie's the only black person in here with us. I think he's starting to get sensitive,'

'I can understand that. Are you okay?'

'I got shoved around a little when I jumped in a bit too close. But I'm okay. It's just we're all bored and dirty and tense and scared to death by all this. It's all too much to take, Harry. Kay's terrified. She locks herself alone in the back storeroom to sleep. There's this look in her eye all the time. She's starting to remind me of that girl whose brother gets killed by the ghouls at the beginning of *Night of the Living Dead*. She keeps talking about Jesus and God, which is really tough to handle given the circumstances surrounding this whole mess.'

'Where're you now?' I asked, trying to keep my own voice steady.

'In my office. Larry and Perry are in Dr Henry's office, and Charlie's back in the cooler, sleeping on a gurney. I've got them separated for now. I think they're all asleep.'

Perry Mascotti was third, and senior, attendant. He was older than the other two and had worked at the morgue several years.

'Last night, I caught Larry going through the file drawers in Dr Henry's office,' she said. 'I don't know what he was looking for, but the night before, somebody snapped the lock on the locked cabinet in the autopsy room.'

'Looking for what? You got any drugs or anything there?'

'No, of course not. But I don't think any of those three would necessarily know that. Kay's the only one who's certified to assist in autopsies and knows what's in that room.'

'This is terrible,' I said before I could censor myself. Probably not the smartest comment.

Her voice broke again. 'It's going to get worse.'

I tried to put a little iron back in my voice, hoping maybe that would help her. 'C'mon now, babe. You're in charge there. You're the authority. You've got to keep yourself together.'

'Stop the pep talk, Harry. I know what I have to do, and I'm going to do it. I just need somebody on the outside I can moan to right now.'

'I'm sorry. I never know what to do in situations like this.'

She almost broke a laugh. 'Well, the next time I'm a hostage, you'll know better.'

A long, deep sigh came out of me before I realized it. 'You're sounding more like you again.'

'I am me,' she answered. Then the damn phone popped again.

'I've got to go. I need to check in with Spellman before the phone dies, and then I've *got* to get some sleep.'

'Has he been out there the whole time?'

215

'Every minute,' she said. 'He's been a real trooper.'

'I owe him,' I said. 'Big time. Do me a favor, will you?'

'Sure.'

'Lock your office door. You got anything to protect yourself with?'

'I've got my thirty-eight.'

'Sleep with it next to you, okay?'

'I have, every night. Up until now, it was in case the wackos charged us and tried to get in. Now I'm not so sure.'

'No matter. Just watch yourself.'

'I will. Listen, this is a hell of a time to say this, but I love you.'

Something caught in my throat and I swallowed hard. I'm not sure either of us had ever come out and just said it quite like that. 'I love you, too. And one last question . . .'

'Yeah?'

'Is Charlie really back there sleeping with the stiffs?'

She giggled, sort of. 'It's the only air-conditioned room in the building.'

'Well, tell him I said to tell Evangeline hi.'

Chapter 30

The clock-radio alarm at seven sounded like an explosion. I jumped out of bed, instantly awake for that split second that it took me to turn the radio off, then back dead asleep as I sat on the edge of the bed. I felt myself falling over, until a voice on the edge of my consciousness told me that if I did, the whole day would be gone before I came to again.

I'd fallen asleep, finally, just as the sun began to shimmer greens and yellows off the tops of the trees outside my bedroom window. My eyes felt like somebody'd visited me in the middle of the night and stuffed a handful of BBs under each eyelid.

It had been days going on weeks since I'd felt anywhere near rested. It was hard for me to believe that barely a week ago, I was nestled in a field of tall grass, being eaten alive by chiggers, videotaping some buttwipe who's supposed to be paralyzed slam-dunking a basketball. If I hadn't been in Louisville, Marsha and I might have missed the call telling her to come in to work Saturday night, and now she might be out here with me wondering when the morgue siege was going to be over.

I headed toward the shower, remembering my encounter with the bricklayer. 'Shoulda hit him with that stun gun again . . .'

I wasn't used to the world at this time of the morning, especially after two hours' sleep the night before. At least I think it was two; hell, it could have been five minutes for all I knew. A warm front had moved in as I slept, and the cool spring weather had been swapped overnight for humidity and temperature in the high eighties. By the time I got to the office, it was past eight. I don't know why I was so worried about all this. Phil said he'd get the check here. It was in his own best interest to do so, and I've always counted on people acting in their own best interest. Lately, though, I'd begun to wonder. Maybe I was just feeling like the smallest guy in the feeding chain.

Once inside the office, I scanned the floor for envelopes that might have been slipped under the door. Nothing. No blinking light on the answering machine either. No calls, no check.

I slammed the door behind me, pulled off my jacket, then slid into my chair. Maybe I'd just slip off and take a little catnap for a while, try to make up for lost time. I closed my eyes, let myself drift, tried to let go of everything.

Only problem was, everything wouldn't let go of me. I kept thinking of Marsha and what might happen this weekend. Slim kept popping up in my mind as well. I imagined him sitting in jail, helpless, frustrated, with very few options left open to him.

Then there was Mac Ford's Rolls-Royce. The more I sat there, the more that kept coming back. Why? Why would a guy like that be in the position of having a car repossessed? I knew from my experience working for Lonnie as a part-time skip-tracer and repo man that there are certain symptoms that crop up in a deteriorating financial life, and these symptoms are as predictable as the stages of a terminal disease.

It starts out with there never quite being enough cash to cover the expenses, so you start loading up the credit cards. First the gas, then the restaurant and bar bills. But then at the end of the month, you can't pay off the credit cards, so you start paying the minimum balance due, but you keep charging those suckers up, anyway. Then you're getting cash advances to cover kited checks, or maybe you're borrowing off one credit card to pay another. Meanwhile the cash situation gets tighter and tighter; the lifestyle's out of control, like a cancer eating away at you. If you don't stop soon, it'll swamp you. But you can't, so you miss a car payment or a loan payment. The house payment's late and you drop your insurance. People start calling you around dinnertime, polite inquiries about late bills. You explain and mollify, placate and appease, for as long as you can. Then you dodge. You screen your calls, or you stop answering altogether.

Panic sets in and you feel like you'll do anything. By then, it's usually too late. Usually, the car goes first. The repo man comes in the middle of the night and rides off in your wheels. Then your house note's a couple of months overdue, and the mortgage company's sending you notices printed in red ink.

At that point, if you're still thinking fast enough on your feet to have a strategy, you start looking for a good bankruptcy lawyer and hope you can come up with the cash to pay his retainer.

So about two steps back from collapse was where I figured Mac Ford must be. The amount of cash it takes to keep an office like that operating on a day-to-day basis must be horrendous, but at the same time he had to have a ton of cash coming in. Where did the balance get upset? What went wrong?

What the hell happened? And what did it mean?

I didn't know if it meant anything. I'd been digging around for so long in the muck, I couldn't see clearly anymore. But for now, I had nothing else to go on. You pull a thread loose and you start unraveling and you see how long it takes you to get to the core.

I sat there thinking for over an hour, my mind running in circles, then drifting, then spiraling down into focus again, then losing the focus and floating off lazily, like in and out of the rapids down the Ocoee River.

Somewhere in the fog, I started to doze off. Just as I was about to cross over into the drooling-on-myself stage, there was a loud knock at the door.

'Huh?' I mumbled, my feet dropping to the floor with a painful clatter. My knees hurt from being hyperextended for so long.

'Messenger,' a voice outside called. I looked down at my watch, which read 10:15. Not quite two hours late.

I opened the door and a young kid with a knapsack in his hands and a bicycle helmet strapped on his head handed me a sealed envelope. I signed for it, tipped the kid my last two singles, then locked the door as he left.

Inside was a certified check for five thousand dollars. The way it made me feel, the messenger could've been straight from the Kentucky Lottery, which was where a lot of Tennessee gambling money goes since we can't have a lottery here.

I folded the check into my coat pocket, then reached for the phone. I tapped in seven numbers, then waited while an answering machine with no outgoing message clicked on. A few seconds later, a beep.

'Yo, Lonnie. Ed McMahon just dropped off my red Corvette outside. That was okay, wasn't it? Red, I mean. I know it's been done before, but I just didn't think the teal was me. Anyway, this means you can cash that check I gave you. Better get it quick while the getting's good.'

I started to hang up, then a thought struck me from somewhere in my still-asleep subconscious. 'Oh, hey, I got a favor to ask. That Rolls you've got to repo, the one belonging to Mac Ford? How about running a credit report for me? Let's see how much trouble the dude's in, okay? Get back to me. Thanks.'

I hung up the phone. The credit report would be a start, but just a start. I needed someplace else to dig, some resource. I needed someone who could show me the secret handshake. Then it hit me.

Agon Dumbler.

I slapped the side of my head with an appropriate self-directed critical epithet. Why the hell hadn't I thought of him before?

I don't like to cast aspersions on anyone's character, and I don't mean to get personal here, but Agon Dumbler was without a doubt the biggest asshole I've ever met in my entire life.

Agon's about five-seven, and the last time I saw him, he was pushing three hundred and fifty pounds. He wears cream-colored suits, silk ties, and sports a white Dick Tracy hat. He drives a mid-Seventies restored Cadillac Coupe de Ville, which happens to be one of the few land yachts large enough to carry him in comfort. In appearance, he's somewhere between Sydney Greenstreet and Rush Limbaugh, with a voice like Truman Capote on steroids. So it's putting it diplomatically to say that Agon doesn't exactly have a lot of dates. Luckily – because he's overbearing, arrogant, insensitive, totally lacking in tact or consideration. And those are his good points. He's the kind of fellow that when people speak his name, they usually follow it up with a good-sized hawker on the sidewalk.

But Agon Dumbler is also one of the half dozen or so best music-industry reporters in the country. His three-times-a-week column in the newspaper we both used to work for had gone into syndication a few years before I, euphemistically speaking, changed careers. This had the result of making him the richest employee on the paper within a year or so, not to mention the substantial extra income he made stringing under an assumed name for publications like the *National Enquirer*, which very few people knew about. Resentment at his growing reputation and wealth ballooned until Agon was forced to resign and open up his own office, which he did gladly. He repaid the newspaper's nurturance of his career by offering his column to the other Nashville daily at reduced rates.

I hadn't thought of him in years. Strangely enough, I never had much trouble getting along with him. He'd waddle over to my desk with a copy of one of my stories from the previous day's paper and proceed to rip it to shreds, ending with a supercilious, dictatorial lecture on how I could improve my work. I'd just smirk at him, nod, thank him for stopping by. The only explanation I have for my behavior toward him is that I just never felt that it was my place to interfere with another person's compulsive need to be an asshole.

The White Pages were buried in a stack of unanswered mail

and junk on my desk. I pulled them out without tipping the pile over, and thumbed through the business section. Under the *D*s, Agon had bought one of those new listings where they print your name in double-sized red type. His read: AGON DUMBLER, SYNDICATED COLUMNIST. There was a number, but no address.

I punched in the number. Two rings later a shrill voice with a harsh Brooklyn accent shouted into the phone: 'Agon Dumbler, Syndicated Columnist, may we help you?'

'Good morning,' I said. 'My name's Harry James Denton and I used to work with Mr Dumbler at the newspaper. I wonder if he has a moment to spare.'

'I'll see if he's in,' she screeched. Then, mercifully, I was put on hold.

Two minutes passed before a voice came on, and this time it was the phlegmy perpetually allergy-plagued voice of Agon Dumbler. 'Denton,' he drawled. 'Denton . . . Let me see, now, the name sounds familiar.'

'We used to work together at the paper. I was cityside, you were in the entertainment section.'

'I *was* the entertainment section,' he interrupted.

'Of course. And you kind of took me under your wing. You were my mentor.' I bit my lip to keep a straight face.

'Oh, yes, Denton. Young fellow, if I remember.'

'Yeah, that's me, Agon.'

Young fellow, my keister. Agon and I are the same age.

'So what can I do for you, Denton?'

'Well, you knew I left the paper a couple of years ago.'

'No, actually I didn't. I prefer not to have contact with' – he sniffed loudly – 'those people.'

'I know what you mean. I don't blame you. I've even left the field altogether. I'm a private investigator now.'

He made a sound like he'd just accidentally stepped into doggie surprise.

'Anyway, I'm working on a case and I've run into a dead end. I'm absolutely at my wit's end on something, and I remembered how whenever any of us at the paper got into this kind of situation, we always came to you.'

God forgive me, I thought, for lying to this poor man in such an unholy, brazen fashion.

'Yes, you all did, and if I remember, none of you ever appreciated it. Not one bit.'

'Well, I always did, Agon, and if I didn't let you know that, it was just because of the atmosphere down there.'

'Nevertheless . . .' he said, then let loose with a long sigh. 'What case are you working on?'

I gritted my teeth and steeled myself. 'I'm digging into the murder of Rebecca Gibson.'

'Oh, my heavens,' he blurted. 'Get thee behind me, Satan!'

'I know,' I said. 'It's a nasty one, all right.'

'Who are you working for?'

I hesitated. 'Well, I'll tell you, Agon, but you gotta promise not to hang up on me.'

'I never make promises.'

'Okay. I'm working for Slim Gibson, but before you say anything else, let me state that I believe he's innocent. Rebecca Gibson's killer is still out there.'

There was a long silence. I held the phone away from my ear, waiting for him to slam it down. Only he surprised me. 'What makes you think I can help you?' he asked softly.

'I need some information.'

'Ah, information is a valuable commodity. It's my stock-in-trade.'

'I realize that, but I'm afraid my financial resources are rather limited. My client expects to be impoverished by this process. Consequently, there's not much extra in the defense fund.'

'If it was *money* we were talking about,' he said, 'you'd definitely be out of the running. You certainly can't afford my consultation fee.'

I was confused. 'So what do . . .?'

'I'll tell you what,' he said. 'I have a one o'clock lunch appointment at the Sunset Grille. You meet me there at twelve, and I'll let you buy me lunch.'

Wait a minute, I thought. You have a lunch appointment at one, so meet you there at twelve, and I can buy you . . . I started to say something, then let it go.

'Sunset Grille at twelve,' I said.

'Twelve,' he answered, then hung up the phone without another word.

I pulled the cashier's check out of my pocket and stared at it. Sunset Grille, huh?

This check wasn't going to last long.

It's not that I have anything against the Sunset Grille, you understand. It's a damn nice place, very chichi, close to the Vanderbilt campus. It's more that I've left that life behind, for the time being anyway, and the thought of spending big bucks for lunch makes me blanch.

I stopped by the bank, deposited the check, took out a hundred in cash, and hoped for the best. The Sunset Grille was across the street from Faison's, another trendy restaurant, but one that I find much more laid-back and comfortable. I'd have rather been there anytime, but this was a command performance.

The kid handling the valet parking screwed up his face when I pulled the Mazda to a stop in front of him. When I got out, he inspected the car as if something inside might bite him.

'What kind of car is this?' he asked. He was early twenties, well built, genuine 1950s crew cut.

'Mazda Cosmo. Very rare. I'm restoring it, so be careful. Don't ding it.' I turned and walked into the restaurant as he snickered behind me.

'I have a lunch appointment with Mr Dumbler,' I told the young woman with the clipboard who looked like she knew what she was doing. 'Has he checked in yet?'

She looked over the top of the clipboard and curled her upper lip. 'Oh, yes, he's here. Try the bar.'

She pointed. I walked.

The bar was a darkened room, small, with booths lining two of the walls. Against the far wall, in the corner booth, Agon Dumbler sat taking up all but a couple of inches of the bench seat. He still wore the white suit, but he'd gotten even heavier since I last saw him. His skin stretched so far over the bones of his face I thought it would split. His eyes were swollen almost shut, and even in the lousy light, I could tell there was a pink splotchiness to him that I didn't remember seeing before. Age had not been kind to him. Frankly, he looked like hell.

'Agon, you haven't changed a bit,' I said, extending my hand toward him. Not only was it a lie, but it was the worst possible insult I could have dispensed. Only he didn't know that.

He stuck a fat hand out toward me and clasped mine. The hand felt hot, moist, yet somehow clammy at the same time. After we let go, I fought the urge to wipe my palm across my pants.

'How are things?' I asked as I sat down.

'Fine, Henry. Just fine.'

'That's Harry, Agon. Harry.'

'Whatever . . .' He stared away at the ceiling, forcing himself to appear bored.

The waitress came up and introduced herself, as all waitresses seem compelled to do these days. She handed us menus, then cocked her hand. 'Will this be one check or two, gentlemen?'

'Ugh, one,' I offered, pointing to myself.

'Can I get you something from the bar?'

'I'll have a glass of the Woodbridge merlot,' Agon said. I looked down at the wine list. Six bucks. I gulped.

'Unsweetened tea,' I said.

'We'll order now,' Agon announced. He then proceeded to order the most expensive item on the menu, some kind of steak doobie or something. I didn't read the description, only the price: $18.95.

I scanned the sandwich section of the lunch menu.

'I'll have the club sandwich,' I said.

After the waitress left, I lifted the glass of ice water and took a long slug, trying to steady myself.

'Well,' I said uncomfortably, 'shall we get right to business?'

'Splendid,' he said, 'Now, what are you attempting to do here?'

'I'm attempting,' I said, 'to prove that Slim Gibson is innocent of the murder of his ex-wife.'

'And what proof do you have?' he demanded. Why did I feel like I was talking to Professor Kingsfield in a remake of *The Paper Chase*?

I shrugged. 'I know Slim, and I just happen to believe that he didn't kill her.'

'Oh,' he said, then snorted, 'that ought to convince a jury.'

It was monumentally hard not to hate him.

I squirmed, trying to figure out some way to get what I needed out of him without letting him know what I knew in return. My prospects of pulling this off seemed dim.

'From all the people I've interviewed, I now have a composite portrait of Rebecca Gibson. That portrait is of someone who's spent years working to make it, is finally on the brink of major stardom, and who then, tragically, is brought down by the petty jealousies and angers of less-talented people. At first, it was just a matter of figuring out which little person she left behind was pissed off enough to kill her. Now I'm not so sure.'

The waitress brought our drinks and set them down. Agon picked up his six-dollar goblet of wine and snarfed down three dollars' worth in one gulp, then motioned to the waitress for another.

He glared at me, traces of wet red around his lips. 'Stop pulling my pud,' he said.

I fought a wave of nausea at the thought. 'What do you mean?'

'You've stumbled – and I think *stumbled* is the operative word since you were never a competent reporter – upon something that has made you suspect someone. Only you're not divulging who it is or what you stumbled upon. Let me tell you something, young man, you don't get anything in this world for free.'

I contemplated getting up and walking out. But he's right; everything had a price, and the price of getting what I needed from him was putting up with his crap.

'So what's it going to cost?'

'Information for information. If you know something, I want to know it. You find out who murdered Rebecca Gibson, it comes to me first.'

I sat back and breathed a sigh of resignation. I should have expected that.

'I have information that indicates Rebecca's manager may be in serious financial trouble.'

'What kind of information?'

'I know the guy who, within the next day or so, is going to repossess his Rolls . . .'

Agon whistled, then drained his goblet as the waitress brought him another. She set the glass in front of him; he wrapped one corpulent hand around the stem, then drummed a thick set of fingers on the table next to it.

'Well, well, well . . .' His eyes flicked from side to side. 'So Mr Ford has taken the high road to Needham . . .'

'Yeah, no kidding. What I'm trying to do is figure out what's going on with him. How could this happen?'

He looked from the wineglass to me, his eyes a glimmer of light through the slits of his fat eyelids.

'I don't know if this is going anywhere or not,' I said. 'The fact that he was hard up for dough is no reason to have murdered Rebecca Gibson. After all, she was going to make him a millionaire, right? That's why I don't think he killed her. Still, I want to find out where this leads.' I stared at him for a second as he polished off dollars seven through nine of the Woodbridge merlot. You know, these grape drinks last longer when you don't slug them down, I thought. Agon's liver must look like it has undergone an artillery barrage. 'So can you help me?'

He sighed. 'This is the very sleaziest form of gossip imaginable,' he said, lowering his voice well below the lunchtime din. I had to ease in closer to catch what he was saying. 'And I never pass on scurrilous gossip.'

'I know that, Agon,' I said. 'You've got too much journalistic integrity.'

God, I hope I wore my lightning-proof Jockey shorts this morning.

'Mac Ford is a man of many vices, and a man of great passions as well.'

'What kinds of vices?'

'For one thing, he smokes rather a large amount of marijuana. Always has. To him, it's nothing more serious than those foul cigars. I understand he grows his own, on some three hundred acres he owns in the Dominican Republic. He's paid off the local officials, goes down there several times a year to frequent prostitutes, party, and take care of his crop. He's also been known to roll a dollar bill up every now and then, if you get my drift. He drinks quite a bit of expensive brandy as well, although I'd hesitate to call that a real vice. Quite a lifestyle he has – traveling all over the world in pursuit of pleasure and his own screwy business deals. You know he's produced quite a number of albums?'

'Really?'

'Yes, all of them losers. The Bonne Nuit Haitian Smoke and Kettle Club Band, for example, a bunch of "Hey, mon" dope smokers and drum bangers. You know, those awful Caribbean metal instruments made out of oil drums?'

'Yeah, I don't know what those are called. And I never heard of the band.'

'Neither has anyone else,' he said. The waitress arrived with our food. Agon's steak was about the size of a small hubcap and covered in hollandaise sauce. It looked exquisite. My club sandwich looked feeble.

'Word on the Row is that Ford has made a string of imprudent decisions,' Agon said, sliding the first chunk of steak between his lips. His jowls vibrated as he chewed. 'You know he lost at least four major acts last year. Let's see, there was Cathy Fields, Alan Simpson, the Prospectors, Emerald Jade.'

I'd heard of all the above, since they'd each had more than one hit record in the past couple of seasons. Losing stroke like that had to knock hell out of Ford's cash flow.

'The conventional wisdom was that he'd lost his touch,' he said. 'While he was brilliant in his day, the magic is gone. Perhaps it's burnout. Maybe drugs, booze, age. Who knows? Some people have sense enough to see the end coming and prepare for it.'

He shook his head, cheeks packed with food. 'But most don't.'

'But there wasn't any evidence that Rebecca was going to desert him, was there? Had there been any talk of that on the street?'

'Nothing that I'd heard.' He polished off the glass of merlot and waved for yet a third. 'But that doesn't mean anything. It's not something that these rednecks usually plan out in advance. The managers often don't know until they get hit in the face with it. It's all done very secretly, with great treachery and a lot of behind-the-scenes manipulation.'

'Even if she was going to leave, why would it benefit him to kill her?'

His eyes narrowed until they disappeared and became thin dark lines across the pink of his face. 'That's what you have to find out, isn't it?'

'How can I do that?' I asked. 'That's what's got me confounded.'

'I can give you two pieces of information that might help.'

'Please do.'

He shifted his cud from one side to the other and looked impatiently in the direction of the waitress. I checked over my shoulder as she brought the glass and set it down.

'More tea?' she asked.

I let a thought slip into voice mode. 'Can I afford it?'

She laughed. 'Don't be silly. Tea refills are free.'

She topped off my glass and left. I took my first bite of the sandwich. Maybe it was the mood I was in, but it tasted like cardboard. Then again, how good can cold cuts on toasted white bread be?

'First of all,' Agon said when she'd left, 'it might help you to know that Ford has a steady lover. Someone who's been quietly with him for years . . .'

I waited while he chewed through two more chunks of steak the size of doughnuts. 'You going to tell me her name, Agon?' I asked impatiently. Careful, I thought, don't want to lose him now.

'Faye Morgan.'

I gave him a sideways look. 'C'mon, I don't believe it. She's in her thirties. I'd always pictured guys like Ford having *Beverly Hills 90210*-type babes.'

'That's who he's usually seen in public with. Faye's been in his life for years, though. They're both very closemouthed about it, but I've heard it's her choice that their affair remain discreet.'

'Given Ford's reputation, I can understand that. I hope she gets a blood test every few months.'

'That's tacky,' he said, 'but probably true.'

'Okay, what's the second thing?'

He swallowed hard and lowered his voice again. 'Well, this is something that only the very top people in the industry are aware of. The execs don't like to talk about it, and the acts themselves often don't know about it. But it's very common practise among record companies, management firms, and the like to take out the industry's own version of *key-man* insurance on their top acts.'

'Key-man insurance? You mean—' I was trying to figure out how this all fit together.

'Look, it's like this,' he said, using his greasy fork as a lecture pointer, 'you're a manager or a record company. You've taken some ignorant hillbilly with an eighth-grade education and a dynamite twang under your wing and you've nurtured him along for, say, two or three years with barely a return. If they up and decide to leave you or fire you, there's nothing you can do about it. That's the risk you run, and it's acceptable. But say your next Billy Ray Cyrus or Garth Brooks or Mary Chapin Carpenter goes out and gets sloshed one night to celebrate the first gold record and drives head-on into a tractor-trailer.'

'So the people behind the stars have insurance on them? I mean, they can do that?'

'If you're willing to pay the premiums, you can take out that kind of life insurance on just about anybody. Nobody wants to suffer through another Patsy Cline or Hank Williams. Can you imagine how much their booking agents lost?'

I stared at what was left of Agon's lunch for a second. He'd snarfed down the steak like a hungry mastiff. 'I guess I can dig around and try to find out. It's not exactly public record, but it can be done.'

'I can help you there, too, if you're willing to stick by our bargain.'

'If I dig up a story, you get it, right?'

He grinned and wiped his mouth with the cloth napkin.

'Okay,' I said. 'The deal stands.'

'I have a little network of people,' he said, lowering his voice yet once again to the cloak-and-dagger level, 'who keep me informed about things in the industry. They provide me with information, and in return, I supplement their largely meager paychecks. You'd be amazed how much secretaries know.'

'Okay,' I said. 'So you've got a mole in Ford's office.'

'And I'm willing to share her with you.'

I smiled. 'Great, who is she?'

He raised the glass of wine to his lips and downed a third of it in one gulp. Good, I thought, he's slowing down. Then he set the glass down a bit too dramatically.

'Alvy Barnes,' he said.

My jaw dropped and a little chunk of white bread fell out of the corner of my mouth onto the plate.

'Alvy Barnes? Ford's assistant?'

Agon Dumbler leaned back in the booth, stared at his empty plate, nodded his fat, pink head, and grinned.

Chapter 31

Agon Dumbler's second lunch appointment showed up a couple of minutes later, and I was left holding a check for $54.68, counting the tip. I stared in amazement as Agon waddled to a table inside the main dining room. His forty-five minutes with me had just been the appetizer.

I paid the check and left the Sunset Grille in shock. So Mac Ford's loyal assistant had been paid to funnel insider information to a syndicated columnist and *National Enquirer* stringer. Wonder how that would go over with the boss.

The sky was darkening outside, and the first few rumbles of a springtime thunderstorm were audible in the distance. The wind had picked up as well, with the poor suckers who'd waited an hour to eat outside in the courtyard now struggling to hold down their napkins and wishing they could get inside before the rain came.

I stood on the sidewalk while the valet parker retrieved my car. Just as the kid pulled up I glanced across the street as a white Rolls stopped in front of Faison's. I ducked down and got into my car quickly as Mac Ford parked on the street and got out of the car. His long hair was pulled back over an expensive sport coat. He wore a faded pair of jeans that probably set him back a hundred bucks. He was music-industry bullshit, all the way to his nonexistent bank account.

I jerked the car into gear and sped away, catching a convenient hole in the traffic on Twenty-first Avenue. I drove past the old Peabody campus, now part of Vanderbilt University, and all the way down to Division Street. My eyes still hurt from lack of sleep and lunch was sitting in my gut like a brick. The worst part, though, was that the thought processes were still fuzzy. I couldn't seem to get a clear picture of everything. Couldn't fit the pieces together . . .

Of course I couldn't fit them together; I didn't have them all. Somehow, I've got to nail down whether or not Mac Ford had key-man insurance on Rebecca Gibson. If he did, that didn't mean anything beyond the fact that I'd finally found someone who benefited from her murder.

But that was a hell of a lot more than I had now.

Would that be enough to take to the police? Would that be enough reasonable doubt to get Sergeant E. D. Fouch of the Metro Homicide Squad back on the case? Fouch would no doubt deny that he was even off the case, but I knew better. Once the police had someone in custody that they felt they could hang the crime on, they usually throttled back to a slow idle.

Which was the last thing I could do, no matter how tired I'd become. Fatigue at this level acts almost as a tranquilizer. Consequently, I didn't even care about the thickening Friday-afternoon traffic, which grew worse by the minute as the thunderstorms moved closer. I crossed the river and headed back into East Nashville.

And what about Faye Morgan? I'd liked her, felt something decent about her. How could she be involved with a sleazeball like Mac Ford?

'There's no accounting for taste,' I said out loud.

It was nearly two in the afternoon by the time I made it over to Lonnie's. I remembered to make sure Shadow recognized me before I entered the gate, then knocked loudly on the metal door. It took a few moments, then Lonnie slowly pushed it open, yawning and scratching his side.

'Sorry, I'd dropped off,' he explained, yawning again. 'Got to make a run up to Kentucky tonight. Trying to get a little sleep.'

'Stop yawning,' I said, walking past him into the trailer. 'You'll get me started and I won't be able to quit. You get my message?'

'Yeah, but I haven't had a chance to get to the bank yet.'

'That's not what I meant,' I said. 'The credit report.'

He nodded his head. 'Yeah, hold on.' I heard him yawn loudly as he walked down the narrow hallway to his office.

I paced the floor nervously, wishing he'd get a move on.

'Here you go,' he said, coming back with the shiny fax paper. 'But it ain't pretty.'

I sat down, then scanned the columns and the codes. My credit-report interpretation skills had become a little rusty since I'd largely given up skip-tracing the past six months or so, but I still recognized financial collapse when I saw it. There were two outstanding judgments against him, one for a default on a co-op mortgage in Manhattan; the other a signature loan to First American Bank in Nashville.

He was also months behind on credit-card payments, two other loans, and, of course, car payments. The Rolls was going this month; my guess is the year-old Ford Ranger pickup would be next. Even his house payment in Nashville was two months behind. And to top it all off, a check-clearing agency had reported a series of bounced checks, which in this state could land you in jail if there weren't so many of them being written that the jails couldn't hold us all.

Ford McKenna Ford was truly and genuinely in desperate straits. Everything he'd worked for, fought for, lied for, cheated for, and screwed anybody who got in his way for, was about to be lost. When word got out in the industry that everything had collapsed, Mac Ford would be history.

After all, nobody remembers a loser.

Alvy Barnes had an unlisted number, but a quick stop by the public library got me an address out of the city directory, which I verified through the Tennessee Department of Safety. If people ever find out how easy it is to track down people, and how much information is public and free, half the PIs in America will have to close up shop.

Alvy lived in a house off Belmont Avenue, near where Belmont crosses over I-440. I knew the neighborhood well, had once had an apartment over there myself before my ill-fated and ill-timed marriage. It's an area of older homes, some classic near-mansions, all mixed in with a variety of rental housing ranging from upscale, remodeled apartment buildings to tenement duplexes. It was a fun neighborhood, kind of funky. But I wouldn't want to walk the streets alone in the middle of the night.

By the time I'd tracked Alvy's home address down, it was nearly four. I gassed up the car and picked up an afternoon paper at the Shell station just across the river on Main Street. The headline read HOSTAGE SITUATION WORSENS and below the main story, a headline announced that the state attorney general had ruled Evangeline would have to have an autopsy. No way around it.

'Oh, hell,' I muttered, spewing a sigh of disgust. This wasn't going to cool anything off.

'Yeah, that be something, don't it?' I looked up from the paper to find an older black man with thinning, gray hair reading over my shoulder as we stood in line to pay.

'It's awful,' I agreed.

'You know, somebody oughta go in there and just get those people out of there.'

'Pump number six?' the cashier asked.

I nodded my head. 'Twelve sixty-four,' she said; 'plus thirty-five cents for the paper. Will that be all?'

'Yes, thanks.' I handed her a ten and a five, then stood waiting for change.

Back at the house, I waved at Mrs Hawkins through her kitchen window before she had a chance to come out and rope me into a conversation. Right now I didn't have the energy.

The answering machine in my apartment was empty, so I called my office. When I punched the remote code, the answering machine came back at me with two messages. The first was from Roger Vaden, Slim's first lawyer, who said he'd forwarded my agreement on to Herman Reid, who'd be taking over the criminal defense. That put a kink in my gut, since I was counting on being under some lawyer's aegis now. The second was a tight, frantic message from Ray basically asking where the hell I'd been. He hadn't seen me in the office in a couple of days and I hadn't called.

'That's right, Ray,' I said to the wall. 'I've been a little busy.'

I dialed his office number and got their machine. It was weird to hear Slim's voice on the recording, knowing where he was now. I found myself filled with a heaviness I hadn't expected; something about seeing an innocent man languish in jail gets to me. I had no sympathy for the guys who were in jail because that's where they belonged, but nobody can deny there are some there who shouldn't be.

I left Ray a quick message, then finished the rest of the newspaper. A few community leaders were beginning to question the wisdom of the mayor's decision to negotiate. There were also a few letters on the editorial page suggesting we just go in there and blow them all to hell, including one amusing epistle from a regular letter writer who suggested that since these people were so looking forward to being with Jesus, we should just go in there and help them along a little.

'Bloody hell,' I muttered. 'Idiots . . .'

Later, as I lay in bed and stared at the ceiling, I tried to will myself to fall asleep for a couple of hours. The brain would not disengage, however, and I kept running around in circles. I kept imagining Alvy Barnes and Agon Dumbler whispering on the phone to each other, telling secrets, giving away insider information, then meeting in a dark alley to pass an envelope stuffed with cash from his fat hand to her slender, pale one. Gradually, the visions began to run together until they became first a bit surreal, then fully-fledged dreams.

Without even being aware of it, I slipped off to sleep.

When I woke up, I was facing the wall. Only a faint glow of streetlights filtered through the shades. I rolled over. The luminous dial on the clock read ten-thirty.

I felt like I was slugging my way to the surface of a barrel full of fresh mud. My joints ached and my eyes burned, but it was a measure of how crappy I'd felt earlier that I perceived this as an improvement.

Painfully, I staggered to my feet and stumbled into the bathroom. A full sixty seconds of running warm water over my face followed by a serious tooth scrubbing got me to the half-alive point. I combed my hair back and pulled on a flannel shirt and jeans.

I thought about calling Marsha. Wondered, in fact, why she hadn't called me. I grabbed the phone, punched in her number, and got a busy signal. Maybe she was on the phone with Howard Spellman. Maybe they were negotiating an end to this mess.

When, I tried to remember, had I last eaten? I hadn't paid much attention at first, but hunger had caught up with me. Mrs Lee's was already closed, but I felt more like breakfast anyway. I jumped in the car and headed back across the river, to the all-night International House of Pancakes on Twenty-first Avenue. The IHOP had been a late-night mecca for decades. With this being a Friday night close to final exams at Vanderbilt, I was lucky to get a booth.

I snarfed down a plate of eggs and grits, toast and bacon, with two cups of decaf. Slowly, I was beginning to feel a little less fragmented. I walked outside into the brightly lit parking lot. Back in the cool night air, cars were rolling by in an endless stream from left to right. I remembered what Nashville had been like when I was growing up as a child. Back then, if you lived as far out as the airport, you were in the country, and the town went to bed so early you didn't need traffic lights after nine. That was a long time ago; that memory combined with all the perky, tight little undergraduates in the IHOP made me feel about a hundred years old.

I got back in the Mazda and joined the long parade. I cut left on some side street, then jogged my way over to Belmont Avenue. Down Belmont past the International Market, I turned right up a hill into a neighborhood of restored nineteenth-century homes. Inside my shirt pocket was a slip of paper with Alvy Barnes's address. I unfolded it and held it up to the window, reading it by the flickering silver and orange of the streetlights as I drove by.

A half block from Alvy's house, I pulled over to the curb and parked. I leaned down low in the seat and stared over the top of the dashboard, studying the brick-and-stucco two-story house. Sometimes it was hard to tell, but I think this one was rental property, a large, towering house that had been converted to apartments. The yard was neatly trimmed and bordered in sculptured shrubs. Whoever owned this place cared for it.

I left the Mazda behind and walked up the street. Alvy's house was on a hill, with a half flight of concrete steps leading up to a long walk that led to the front door. On either side of the double front doors, light filtered through drawn shades. I huffed up the stairs, then walked to the front porch. The front door was open, leading into a small foyer with four apartment doors, each with a brass number nailed to the front. Alvy's apartment was number one, the door to the immediate left. On the darkly varnished door, there was a white card in a holder: BARNES/HOYT.

I checked my watch. Midnight would be rolling around in a few minutes. I hoped I hadn't caught Alvy at a bad time, at least not too bad a time. I wanted to catch her off guard, but not in the throes of anything sweaty and embarrassing.

My knock echoed off the walls of the foyer, reverberating in the cramped space. Silence followed, so I rapped on the door again, this time loud enough to wake anyone sleeping. There was a rustle behind the door, then a female voice.

'Who is it?'

I cleared my throat. 'I'm sorry to bother you so late, but I'm looking for Alvy Barnes.'

A lock rattled, then turned. The door opened a crack. Blonde hair and clear blue eyes looked out at me from behind a cheap security chain. 'It's late. She's gone to bed.'

'I'm really sorry, but I've got to talk to her now. It's very important. You might even say it's an emergency.'

'Who are you?'

'My name's Denton. Harry James Denton.'

I heard an exasperated, impatient sigh, then she shut the door and relocked it. I stood there wondering if she'd gone to get Alvy or had just decided to close the door in my face. I looked down at my watch. I'd give her a couple of minutes before I knocked again.

I didn't have to wait that long. The lock rattled again, then the door opened without the security chain. Alvy Barnes stood in the doorway wearing a black satin bathrobe. Her jet-black hair splayed across her forehead. She looked tired and washed-out without all the makeup. Behind her, in a doorway inside, the blonde stood with her arms crossed.

'You have any idea how late it is?'

'Yeah, midnight.'

'What do you want?' she asked.

'We got to talk, Alvy. It's about Mac.'

Her face tightened. 'What about him?'

'I think he's in trouble.'

'What kind of trouble.'

'Money trouble, for one thing. Maybe more.'

She chuckled. 'Shoot, you're crazy. Mac Ford's got more money than Moses.'

'Then Moses went broke.'

She scowled at me. 'It's late and I'm sleepy. Call me Monday morning and we'll set something up.'

Alvy pushed the door to, only I stuck my foot inside and stopped it cold. I'd never done that before. Made me feel like a film noir star. She turned and glared.

'You can go now, Harry.'

'Alvy, we *really* need to talk.'

'Monday, Harry,' she said, her voice angry. 'Go.' She pushed again.

'I had lunch today with Agon Dumbler,' I whispered so only she could hear me.

What little color she had in her face faded away immediately. She looked behind to see if her roommate had heard me, then turned back.

'Oh, really?'

'Can we talk now?'

She rolled her lower lip out in a pout and bit it. 'Yeah, I guess so.'

Alvy held the door open and let me in. I got my first good look at the roommate; she was taller than Alvy, although about the same age. All she had on was a robe as well. I wondered how many bedrooms the apartment had, then decided that was none of my business.

'Alvy, you okay?' she asked, glaring at me. 'You need any help here?'

'No, Cheryl, I'm fine. He's a friend,' she said, resigned.

'I'll be in my bedroom,' she said. 'You need anything, just yell.'

I smiled at Cheryl as she turned and left the room, a smile that was decidedly unreturned.

'Sit down,' Alvy said. I stepped through a curved plaster archway into a small living room. A music video played low on a television that sat against the front wall across from a Mission-style sofa. A couple of wood and cushion chairs complemented the room, which was done in pastel blues and dusty roses. Art prints covered the walls: Georgia O'Keeffe's blossoming erotic petals, mostly, along with a stretched Navajo-print fabric in a box frame.

Alvy sat on the sofa; I sat in one of the chairs across from her and leaned forward.

'That fat bastard,' she said wearily as she settled into the couch. The bottom part of her robe shifted as she crossed her legs, exposing them most of the way to her waist. She was young, attractive. I tried not to notice. 'He always told me I could count on two things: his discretion and his checks being good.'

'It's not Agon's fault,' I said. 'We used to work together on the newspaper. I've known him for years and asked for a favor.'

'I hope I can count on your discretion. If Mac ever finds out I've been a source for Agon, he'll kill me.'

Her words made a shiver run up the back of my neck. I tensed and crossed my legs, grabbing my right ankle in both hands.

'You can count on my discretion, as long as you help me.'

'What do you mean?' Her eyes widened. She sat up straighter, the robe opening a little wider at the neck. If this went any further, I was going to have to ask her to retie the damn thing.

'Alvy, I've been doing some digging into Mac Ford's life. He's in a lot of trouble.'

'You keep saying that, but it's not true.'

'It is true. He's in hock up the ya-ya, and it's all about to fall in on him.'

'How do you know?' she said, her voice tense, strained.

'Because I do part-time work for the guy who just got hired to repossess his Rolls. I started digging, ran a credit report.'

Her jaw dropped. 'You can do that?'

'He's nearly bankrupt, Alvy. It's all caving in on him.'

'This is awful. I mean, the company, all the employees.'

I nodded my head. 'When he goes under, the company won't be far behind.'

She bit her lower lip again and her eyes became heavy with tears. 'We're nearly there now,' she whispered.

'Really?' I asked. She got my attention with that one.

She shook her head. 'Terrible cash-flow problems the last couple of months. But I thought it was normal business stuff. I

238

never thought it was because . . .' Her voice dropped. 'Mac's driven a lot of business away the last year or so.'

'He has?'

She leaned back against the couch, the robe nearly open now. If she was aware of what she was doing, she sure hid it well. 'Mac's pretty crazy sometimes, the way he goes off the handle and stuff. I've heard him rant and rave. . . . God, sometimes it's pretty scary. My roommate Cheryl's a part-time grad student in psychology. She says he's a rageaholic.' She smiled wanly. 'Oh, God, I hate this.'

'I need to know two things, Alvy. First, did Mac have key-man insurance on Rebecca Gibson?'

'What?'

'You know, did he have a life-insurance policy on her?'

'I think so,' she said. 'I mean, it's standard. But I don't know how much for. You have to understand, I'm Mac's assistant. I did all of his correspondence and scheduling, but there was a lot of business he kept private. Contracts, for example. The exact terms of the contracts with all the artists are something he alone knew. He kept them in his private files. There's a locked room off his office where they're kept.'

'Okay, fine. If there was key-man insurance, I want to know how much there was.'

'It's in those files. And I don't have a key to the room.'

'I can take care of that,' I said. 'The other thing I need to know is . . .' I hesitated, trying to figure out the best way to say it. 'Well, you said Mac had lost clients in the last couple of years. Was Rebecca Gibson one of them?'

'Oh, no,' she snapped. 'That's not possible.'

'Why not?'

'Because I'd have known. He'd have told me.'

'What if he didn't want you to know?'

'Why would he *not* want me to know? That doesn't make any sense.' She was almost angry now, but I didn't care. I was getting tired myself, and very impatient.

'Because maybe he didn't intend to tell *anybody*. Maybe he had a life-insurance policy naming him or the company as beneficiary as long as she was a client. Maybe he just figured something might happen to Rebecca Gibson, and he could collect the money rather than let her go. Then he'd not only have the insurance income, but a substantial income from being her artistic executor.'

She put her hand to her mouth. 'Oh, my God, you don't think—' Her eyes grew even bigger, and bright with tears.

'If it plays out like I've described, Alvy, then Mac Ford had the best reason in the world to want Rebecca Gibson dead. He's the only one who really benefits.'

'Oh no,' she cried, starting to weep. 'That's not possible.'

'And you've got to help me find out.'

She curled up in a ball, burying her head in her hands. 'No . . .'

I got up and walked over to the sofa, then plopped down next to her and planted a hand on her shoulder and squeezed hard. 'Maybe it didn't happen that way, but we've got to know. You get me into those files. If it's not like I said, nobody'll ever be the wiser.'

'I can't,' she sobbed.

I squeezed harder. 'You have to.'

She pulled away from me and jumped to her feet. 'No!' she yelled. The robe flew open all the way down to the loose knot at her waist. Her breasts were small, tight, with nipples so dark they were nearly black. I clenched my jaw, trying not to stare. Behind us, the roommate stepped back into the room.

'Alvy, you all right?'

Alvy turned, her hair flying. 'Not now, Cheryl! Leave us alone.'

Cheryl retreated.

'Alvy,' I said. 'You have to help me.'

'And what if I won't?'

'Then I'll drop back and punt. And in the meantime I'll make sure Mac finds out about your arrangement with Agon. You'll be done with Mac Ford Associates, and probably washed up in the industry as well. I hate to put it to you that way, but I don't have a lot of options.'

She glared at me, not bothering to pull the robe around her. 'You bastard!'

'Help me, Alvy. Damn it, you know how bad she was beat up? You know what it takes to beat a full-grown adult woman to death with your bare hands? Can you imagine what kind of death that is, to lie in your own blood so battered you can't breathe anymore, to be in that much agony and watching everything go dark around you, all alone?'

'Stop it,' she moaned. Her shoulders shook and she wrapped her arms tightly around herself.

I walked over to her and gently took a lapel in each hand and pulled her robe to. 'C'mon,' I said softly. 'I'm sorry. I don't mean to do this to you.'

Suddenly she fell into me and I had my arms around her. Her hair smelled warm and musty, her tears hot on my chest, her arms still crossed and cradled into me. I held her there for what felt like a long time, long enough for me to realize that I didn't need to be standing there like that too much longer.

She pulled back gently, her eyes moist and full, tears down her pale round cheeks. She looked up into my face, and I realized with more than a little bit of surprise that she intended to kiss me; either that or she was waiting for me to kiss her. Nice prospect, but unwise.

I pulled away, just an inch or so, but enough. 'That's not why I came here, Alvy. Besides, I'm old enough to be your . . . your older brother.'

She pulled away from me. 'Get out of here.' Her words were cold, but the edge had gone out of her voice.

'Tomorrow's Saturday. We can do it then.'

'Why do I have to be there?'

'Because if I break in, it's a felony. If you're there and let me in, then it's just treachery.'

She looked sharply at me. 'Not in the morning,' she said. 'People are usually there for half a day on Saturday. Best bet's later in the afternoon, say around two. Make sure you come in the back entrance.'

I left Alvy Barnes standing in the doorway in her black satin robe, the streetlights bleaching her out to the point where she became almost ghostlike. She was striking in a drawn, dissipated way. It had been a long time since I'd had a woman that young stare up at me with that look in her eyes. I walked back to my car thinking that I should have been proud for being so damned moral, but given that I'd just gotten her cooperation by blackmailing her, that was kind of hard.

Chapter 32

For the seventh time, I listened to the computerized operator tell me that she was sorry, but the cellular customer I'd dialed had either turned off the telephone or left the calling area. I appreciated her sentiments.

It was three o'clock in the morning; I had a headache the size of a Buick and sleep was a stranger. I dozed off when I first got back to the apartment, but that only lasted about twenty minutes. I woke up with a start, wondering where I was, where Marsha was, where the last few days had gone.

I rubbed my shoulders, which had about as much effect as the three aspirins I'd choked down an hour earlier. I craned my head backward, then both felt and heard the vertebrae in my neck pop like dried chicken bones. The aspirin had set my gut off, and a nasty bile taste crept into the back of my throat.

I'd seen crap come down before, but never in sheets like this.

I flipped off the light and stared up at the darkness. Outside, a car that badly needed a muffler repair roared by, megabass speakers thumping away in time to some urban rap ditty. In the distance, a police siren wailed away on Gallatin Road. Neighborhood dogs took up a chorus of barking in return.

Maybe the television. No, nothing on. Besides, I've got to get some sleep. If sleep won't come, at least lie here and rest. If I can't turn the brain off, at least try unplugging the body. Tomorrow was Saturday, but it wasn't going to be anything like a weekend. No decompression, no snooze, no rest. I needed to hear a human voice; I dialed Marsha's cellular number again and waited for the now familiar artificial voice of the computerized telephone attendant. I listened to her tell me how sorry she was three more times before I finally drifted off into a fitful and uneasy half sleep.

There was this old Three Stooges short where the boys played doctors and Moe turns to Larry and yells 'Anesthetic!' Larry turns to Curly and yells 'Anesthetic!' Curly yells 'Anesthetic!' and pulls out a hammer the size of a small beer keg and bops the poor patient on the head, sending him off to dreamland.

I woke up knowing exactly how that guy felt.

I stared into the mirror and realized that I had finally attained complete harmony in my life: I looked as bad as I felt. I started to step into the shower, then realized I'd had about a half-dozen showers in the last two days, and not one of them had made me feel any better. Was I filled with guilt about something and headed toward an all over hand-washing fetish? Is this what happens when frustration levels get out of control?

Coffee helped a little, and the morning newspaper brought me back to reality, although in a mixed-blessing kind of way. The siege of the Nashville morgue had taken up its rightful place as lead story once again, dwarfing even the latest genocidal massacre in some backwater third-world stinkhole.

The headline blared a warning of impending crisis. A full-color photo of Howard Spellman and the rest of the negotiating team huddled around a table wearing flak jackets dominated the middle of the page. Down below, a smaller aerial photo of a ring of Winnebagos, jammed together like covered wagons in a circle, spoke of the coming battle. I read the latest sidebar interview with the Reverend Woody T. Hogg, who claimed once again that he had no control over his followers but that God would speak when the time came right, and when Judgment Day came, it would rain hellfire and brimstone on all of us. All the wrongs of the world would be righted, all God's children brought home to redemption, and the purveyors of sin and those who denied the resurrection of the body would be called to task for their sin and disbelief.

The problem with this sort of blathering is that if you listen to it long enough, you actually start to be able to follow it. It starts to make sense. I put my head down on the kitchen table.

God, do I need a vacation.

I drove by Lonnie's trailer, but he wasn't there. Either he was still in Kentucky picking up cars, or he'd gone to ground somewhere to recover. I petted Shadow for a while, made sure her water and food bowls were full, then left Lonnie a note telling him where I'd be and what I was doing. I didn't expect anything particularly bad to happen today, but it never hurt to leave a paper trail with a buddy.

Alvy Barnes told me to come by the office around two, which meant I had just enough time to slide through the drive-in window, then stop by my office before showing up early enough to catch her off guard. There was some kind of riverfront festival going on downtown, so the traffic was as thick as sludge in a blizzard. I made my way around the fringes of the crowd and got to my office by avoiding Broadway. I parked the car near the front of the garage, then carried a sackful of Krystal cheeseburgers, fries, and a Coke upstairs. I don't know what self-destructive urge drove me to subject my stomach to a Belly Bomb assault during times of great stress. I ought to have more sense. If Marsha found out, I would undergo a severe corrective interview.

Maybe that's why I was doing it; right now I'd welcome even a chewing-out from her. If she were here, I'd give her a good listening to.

I ate at my desk while wading through the mail, which consisted of a medley of junk and bills. A quick tote of the accounts payable told me most of my check from the insurance company was already gone. No matter, I thought, if I could just maintain the next few days, I'd be ready to drum up biz again.

Right, like I could focus for shit on anything beyond the next five minutes. What if this was crazy? I thought. What if Mac Ford didn't have anything to do with Rebecca Gibson's death? Beyond the fact that I really didn't like the guy, there wasn't much to go on.

Finally the clock moved. I gathered up my trash and stuffed it into the wastebasket. Inside my desk drawer, a small zippered leather case held a set of lock picks that I'd bought from Lonnie. Ever since I saw him go through a couple of locked doors like they weren't there, I'd wanted to learn more about locks. Lonnie'd been glad to teach me, and in the past few months I'd gotten to where I could pick an ordinary cylinder without too much trouble.

I slipped the case into my shirt pocket, then almost as an afterthought tucked the stun gun into my other shirt pocket after first making sure the safety was on. I left the office and drove out Charlotte Avenue, under the interstate bridge, then turned left and crossed first Church Street, then Broadway, and on up to Demonbreun. Music Row was up the hill, past the loudspeakers booming country music on a warm Saturday afternoon and the tourists with white hairy legs, plaid shorts, and novelty T-shirts wandering in and out of traffic oblivious to the Nashville drivers.

I made my way through that maze, then down Music Row and parked in the block before Mac Ford's office. I nestled into the curb, between a Ford Ranger with a camper bed and a brand-new Saturn. I sat low in the seat, hugged the driver's side door, and by looking around the corner of the pickup, had a perfect view of the front door of Mac Ford's building.

There were two cars parked on the brown pea-gravel driveway, with two more on the curb directly in front. I sat there hidden for nearly twenty minutes before anyone came out the front door. A tall woman with a bundle of file folders got into one of the cars in the driveway, followed by a scruffy short guy with a briefcase in one hand and a portable phone in the other. He got into the car behind the woman, and the two backed out into the street and pulled away. The driveway was empty now. I checked my watch. It was almost one o'clock.

I sat there another fifteen minutes. There was no guarantee that the two cars parked in front of the building were owned by Mac Ford's employees. Alvy could be in there alone by now and there'd be no way for me to know it.

The sun was high now, and the inside of my car was turning into a greenhouse. I felt a sheet of sweat on my forehead, and suddenly wished I could strip off these clothes and dive into a swimming pool. I waited until I couldn't stand it anymore, then got out of the car and locked it behind me.

I walked quickly down the street, past the office building, then rounded the corner and walked down the side street. The alley that ran behind Mac Ford's building was empty. The parking slots were vacant as well. I decided to go for it.

I slipped across the grass and climbed the wooden stairs to the back door. The knob wouldn't turn; I thought for a second, then decided to try the doorbell. I pressed the small button and heard a muffled buzzer go off from somewhere inside the building.

Flies buzzed around me from the Dumpster out by the alley. There was no traffic. Silence everywhere. I didn't know the Row got so quiet on weekends. I was about to hit the buzzer again when I heard hard shoes on steps.

Alvy Barnes cracked the door open and glared at me.

'You're early,' she said.

I reached into the crack and yanked the door open, then stepped inside before she had a chance to do anything besides deepen her dirty look.

'You have a keen grasp of the obvious,' I said. I was in no mood for her bullshit. I wanted to get this over with as quickly as possible, then get the hell out. If this worked out as I fantasized, my next stop would be Sergeant E. D. Fouch's office at police headquarters.

'You can't just—'

'Move,' I interrupted. 'Let's do it.' I took her right arm just at the tricep and gently pushed her forward.

'Listen you,' she snapped. 'You can't come in here pushing me around like this!'

'Alvy, the sooner we get this done with, the sooner we can get out of here. Let's stop jerking each other around, okay?'

'I hate you,' she said. But she turned anyway and started up the flight of stairs behind her.

I followed her up the stairs, through a doorway into the second-floor hallway, then down to Mac Ford's office. Alvy's computer was on and there was a stack of papers on her desk. She pulled a key ring out of the center drawer, fumbled with the keys a moment, then selected one and opened the door. I followed her into Mac Ford's office as she switched on the overhead.

The only other time I'd seen it, it had been as cold as January and filled with the purplish glow of black lights. Now, without air-conditioning and lit by the harsh glow of a rack of fluorescent tubes in the ceiling, it looked dusty, cluttered, and full of junk that gave the place lots of class; all of it low.

'Ford's filing cabinets are in the closet, right?'

'Just one. He has one filing cabinet where he keeps his private correspondence and files. But I don't have a key to it. I don't even have a key to the door.'

I reached into my pocket. 'If we're lucky, we won't need one.'

Alvy looked over my shoulder as I unzipped the case and unfolded the side pockets. Each pick had its own little slot in the leather case. I took out a small black metal raker pick, a thin blade with a series of bends in the end that looked like a sine wave from the side. From the other side of the case, I took a tension wrench, an even thinner L-shaped blade that was flat at the end.

Down on one knee, I carefully put the tension wrench into the keyway like Lonnie'd shown me, then with my left index finger, I put just enough pressure on the cylinder to force the pins into contact with the cylinder body at the shear line. Then I gently stuck the raker pick in until I felt it hit the back of the lock. Lifting the pick just a hair, I pulled it smoothly out, feeling the raker hit the pins and push them up and down.

Nothing.

I tried it again. Sometimes it takes a few tries. Sometimes you have to pull the tension wrench out and start all over again. Sometimes it never works at all, at least when you're a beginner like me.

This time, I pulled a little harder and a little faster. I felt the cylinder slip just a bit, mainly by the change in pressure on the tension wrench. I tried it a third time, figuring maybe it was going to take a different pick. The only question was how much time we had.

I jerked the pick out; the tension wrench gave way, spinning the cylinder around and unlocking the door.

'Hot damn,' I whispered.

'Wow,' she said. 'That was cool.'

I looked up at her. 'Alvy, you've been watching too much MTV.'

I opened the door, half-afraid of what I'd find inside. The tiny closet was mostly empty, though, except for a couple of cases of Dos Equis and diet Coke in the corner, a small bookcase jammed with CDs, and a filing cabinet. There was a bare bulb in the ceiling with a piece of string hanging down. I yanked it, filling the closet with an unforgiving light.

The cabinet was a standard-issue, five-drawer filing cabinet, almond-colored, with the smiling skull of a Grateful Dead decal on the front of the top drawer. The tiny lock in the top right-hand corner was pushed in, locking all five drawers down.

'Okay, same scene, take two,' I said. I handed Alvy the pick case. 'Here, hold this for me.'

I'd never picked a filing-cabinet lock, but it looked like a smaller version of a standard cylinder lock. I used the same tension wrench, with a smaller diamond pick this time. After five minutes of fuming and cursing under my breath, I gave up on that and dug out an even smaller ball pick, which was a thin blade of metal with a round piece cut in the end.

That didn't work either, and I was just about to go outside and see if I couldn't find a big damn rock, when Alvy said: 'Here, use this one. It looks like the one that worked on the closet door.'

I took the pick from her. 'It may be too big, but I'll try.'

It took some boogering to get it all the way into the cylinder, but I managed to maneuver it past the tension wrench. It was hot as hell inside the closet, with a particular type of musty, earthy smell that made me speculate that somebody'd been burning something illegal.

'Damn it,' I muttered as the pick stuck. I pushed harder, and felt it bend a bit, then snap past the last pin.

I took a deep breath, then let it out slowly as I raked the pick through the cylinder. Just the way the Boy Scouts taught me to pull the trigger on a .22 rifle.

The tension wrench slipped and the lock popped.

'Awright!' Alvy yelled.

'Shhh!' I whispered.

'The building's empty,' she sad. 'Chill out.'

'Chill out, nothing,' I said, pulling the first drawer open. There were stacks of files jammed in tightly, in no apparent order. Chicken-scratch handwriting on the file-folder tabs was the only indication of each folder's contents.

'There must be hundreds of them,' I said, frustrated. I looked at my watch. It had taken nearly twenty minutes to get this far and the afternoon was slipping away fast.

'I don't know Mac's filing system,' she said. 'That is, if there is one.'

'Oh, I'm sure he's got one. It's just not from this planet.'

I pulled the top drawer all the way open. It was jammed with files, front to back. Then I checked the other four drawers. Same deal. It looked to me like Mac Ford never threw anything away.

'Okay, this is the only way this is going to work,' I said. 'You're going to have to help me. I'll pull the top drawer out and set it on the floor. Then you start at the bottom. You find anything with Rebecca Gibson's name on it, call out.'

She scowled at me. 'How did I get so involved in this?' she demanded.

'Alvy, every second we're in here, we run the risk of getting caught. The more you help, the faster you can get out of here.'

She ran her lip out again, but sat down cross-legged on the floor and pulled out the bottom drawer. I carefully pulled the top drawer off its track and took it out of the closet, then sat down on the thick Oriental rug in Mac's office right next to a large burned spot.

There wasn't time to examine the contents of each folder, but I flipped through the first few pieces of paper in each one. I wished I had more time; there were confidential contracts and pay schedules, notes of cash transactions that would probably have been received with great interest at the IRS, and stacks of paper that Mac Ford obviously didn't want anyone to see.

I heard Alvy sliding the bottom drawer shut just as I was halfway through the top drawer. I hoped she was being thorough, but decided not to piss her off any further by saying so.

Nothing in the first drawer. I groaned as I lifted the heavy drawer back onto its track and slid it in. My lower back twinged, and once again I had the privilege of experiencing the first few steps of middle age.

Alvy was into the fourth drawer as I painfully eased out the second and took it back into the office. This time, I thought I might have hit pay dirt. The first file had the name Dominic Wright penciled in on the tab. Dominic Wright had had his first hit song about two years earlier, a real tearjerker of a tune about a Kenwood driver losing the love of his life at the Zodiac Lounge when a Peterbilt driver steals her away.

That wasn't important, though. What was important was that I'd found the drawer with the artists' files. I thumbed through the stack, one after the other, reading off a list of the famous, near-famous, and never-gonna-be famous singers that Mac Ford had dealt with. Some of them surprised me; Mac had been in on the early careers of some of the hottest people in the business.

Been in, then been out, that is. I marveled at the levels of frustration, what it must have been like to build an artist up from nowhere, only to have them dump you when the money started to get good.

No wonder he was a rageaholic.

I flipped quickly through the folders and never found Rebecca Gibson's. I started at the front and went all the way to the back of the drawer again.

Nothing.

Maybe there were more in the next file drawer, I thought. I stood up, bent over, picked up the file drawer, then yelled as it slipped out of my right hand and fell like a hammer on my big toe.

'Damn!' I yelled through clenched teeth, trying not to drop the other end of the drawer. About half the folders had tumbled out onto the floor, leaving a chaotic pile of paper and cardboard. I eased the file drawer down onto the floor and sat down next to it.

'What's the matter?' Alvy said from inside the closet.

'Nothing that a week at the beach wouldn't fix,' I whispered, then louder: 'I need you out here.'

I heard her pull herself up off the floor. 'What happened?' she asked as I sat there on the floor holding my right foot and rubbing the toe through my shoe.

'I slipped.'

'I can see that.'

'Help me get this mess cleared up,' I said. 'We'll never get it back in order. Let's just get out of here.'

I got up on all fours and leaned over the drawer. I reached in and gathered up the files that were still in the drawer and mashed them forward to make room for the ones on the floor. As I did, one caught. It caught because it had been slipped into the bottom of the file drawer, flat rather than on its edge, with the rest of the folders covering it up. Scratched in ink on the tab was one word: GIBSON.

'Oh, shit,' I muttered. It was the best I could do under the circumstances.

'What?'

'Look.' I pulled the folder out. Alvy's face lit up like she'd just won the lottery.

'You found it!'

The folder was about an inch thick. I opened it. On top of the stack lay a boilerplate-printed contract with Rebecca Gibson's name typed in. On the last page, signatures and dates nailed down the deal. There were a few sheets of correspondence and copies of checks, minus commissions, paid to Rebecca. Another thick pile of stapled sheets proved to be Rebecca's recording contract, followed by a copy of an advance check for fifty thousand dollars. Eighty percent of fifty thousand dollars was probably more money than Rebecca, or anybody else in her family for generations back, had ever seen in one lump sum.

After a few more loose pages, there was another stapled stack of papers, this one headed ALLAMERICA SPECIALITY INSURANCE COMPANY, and below that: SERVING THE ENTERTAINMENT INDUSTRY SINCE 1969.

I whistled as I read through the first few paragraphs.

'What?' Alvy asked, looking over my shoulder.

'Here it is.' I flipped through the policy, doing my best to speed-read. Finally I got to the important parts, and when I did, it took my breath away. I turned to Alvy.

'Two million dollars,' I whispered, 'with Mac Ford named as beneficiary.'

Her eyes widened. 'Oh, my God,' she squealed. 'Two million dollars!'

I turned back quickly to the file. This still didn't prove anything beyond the fact that Mac Ford's financial problems would soon be over, and that wasn't enough to get Slim Gibson out of jail.

My eyes hurt. I picked up the file and limped over to Mac Ford's desk, set the file down on top of a pile of clutter, and flipped on his desk lamp. There were more loose pieces of paper, nothing beyond business stuff with lots of numbers, and Mac's private correspondence with promoters. One handwritten note outlined an agreement to slip Mac five grand on the side in cash in order to get Rebecca to agree to a series of dates in Texas, presumably at the insider's price.

'Crap,' I said, frustrated. I flipped quickly through the last few pieces of paper and was about to give it up when I got to the end of the file. An envelope, with its flap torn open, lay loose in the file. I picked it up. It was addressed to Mac Ford at an address that was not the office. I showed it to Alvy.

'That's his condo in Franklin,' she said.

I recognized the return address as Rebecca Gibson's. The envelope was postmarked two days before her death. My fingers shook as I opened the envelope and slipped the letter out. It was handwritten on plain white paper, the cheap kind you can buy at any drugstore.

'Dear Mac,' it began.

I've given it a lot of thought and decided that we've gone about as far as we can go together. I hate to do it like this, but I really couldn't handle telling you to your face. I also thought I'd send this to your home so you could handle telling the people in the office.

I've been negotiating with another manager who I feel can advance my career a lot farther, a lot faster. I'm sorry, but like our contract says, I'm giving you my thirty-day notice. Thirty days from your receipt of this letter, I will no longer be a client of Mac Ford Associates, Inc. If there's any papers to sign, please send them to me. I'm grateful to you and wish you the best of luck in the future.

Sincerely,
Rebecca

I eased back in Mac Ford's office chair, the springs squeaking as wearily as I felt.

'That's it,' I said.

Alvy'd been standing behind me, reading the letter over my shoulder.

'Yeah, that's it,' she said. Only there was an energetic edge to her voice, as if the thrill of discovery outweighed the terrible thing we'd discovered.

Ford McKenna Ford had murdered Rebecca Gibson. He'd done it quickly and, in terms of his purposes, neatly. Two million dollars was too much money to kiss goodbye because some goddamn ignorant west Tennessee cotton-field crooner got sucked in by a different snake-oil salesman. This might not be enough to convict Ford, but it would sure get Slim out of the crosshairs.

The only question was what to do with it. If the police came in

252

here and found this without a search warrant, the evidence would be tainted, inadmissible. But if an employee of MFA, Inc., blew the whistle and took it to them, would it hold up in a court of law?

I was willing to take my chances that it would.

'Let's get out of here,' I said. 'We've got one more stop to make.'

I stood up and dropped the letter back into the file, then tucked the file under my arm.

'Where are we going?' she asked.

'Just come on,' I said. 'This is some serious shit here, Alvy. We're going to the police.'

'Oh, no, we're not,' she said.

'Yes,' I said.

'No!'

I stepped to the door of the office and turned to her one last time. 'I'm not going to argue with you. Let's go.'

Then I turned and stepped through the door into Alvy's office.

'Oh, shit,' I said. Maybe it was the fatigue and stress, but this was becoming my favorite expression.

Alvy came up behind me. She grabbed my arm without saying a word and squeezed so hard it would have hurt like hell if I'd bothered to notice.

Mac Ford was standing in the middle of Alvy's office. In his right hand, he held what I can only describe as a very large, chrome-plated pistol.

Chapter 33

'Let me just ask one question,' I said. 'Why didn't you come in this morning and get rid of this file? You'd have saved us both a lot of trouble.'

Mac Ford stood there for a moment, his hand steady but his eyes clouded and thick, unfocused. It took me a few seconds to figure it out, but I think he was blasted out of his gourd. When he spoke, I knew it.

''Cause,' he said, his voice low, with just the edge of a slur in his words, 'she'd still know. Wouldn't have done any good . . .'

He motioned toward me, I thought, but then I realized he was indicating Alvy. She still had a grip on my arm. I felt a shove as she pushed me out of the way and walked past.

'Excuse me, *asshole*,' she said in passing.

She crossed the room, stood next to Ford, and crossed her arms with a nasty smile on her face. Smug little bitch, I thought. My headache, which had never really gone away, bounced back with a surge of pressure. I brought my hands up and massaged my temples.

'You told him I was here, Alvy?' I asked, shaking my head. 'I don't believe this.'

'Believe it,' she said. 'Actually, Harry, I knew about the insurance policy when it was taken out. And I found Rebecca's letter two days ago. I have my own copy. So you see, Mac and I are partners. I had to let my partner know you were onto him, and that you'd be here today.'

Mac held the gun on me and said nothing.

'What for? I mean, what's this going to get you?'

She took a step toward me, arms still crossed. She rolled her lower lip out again and did her best Winona Ryder. 'Half of two million dollars, smart-ass.'

Alvy stood to Mac Ford's left, facing me. She uncrossed her arms, then put her right arm across Mac's shoulders and laid her head on his shoulders. 'Right, partner?' she cooed.

I shook my head again. In my shirt pocket, the stun gun sat points down and useless. I could rush him, but there's nothing more dangerous and unpredictable than a man with a gun who happens to be in the middle of a good buzz.

No, I thought, I am well and truly pronged...

'You guys mind if I sit down?' I asked. 'I've had a lousy couple of days and my head's killing me.'

I didn't wait for an answer. I pulled out Alvy's desk chair, sat down, and plopped the file on her desk.

'Keep your hands in sight,' she ordered, then turned to Mac. 'I don't think he's carrying, but he has got a stun gun.'

'Get it,' Mac ordered, motioning with the pistol.

She stepped over and leaned across the desk, then reached inside my pocket and pulled the stun gun out.

'You don't really think this is going to work, do you?' I whispered.

'Oh, shut up,' she said. Then she slapped me, open-handed and hard. There was a snap inside my head, and I felt a burning on my cheeks. I fought the urge to jump up and choke her. She backed off quickly. I carefully rubbed the sting on my left cheek.

Goddamn Generation X-ers. Never trust anyone under thirty.

Alvy had my stun gun, and they both had me. It was so bloody crazy, I almost wanted to laugh. I was exhausted, at the absolute end of my tether, and I think on some level I wasn't really in touch with just how bad this really was.

I looked up at Mac. 'What are you going to do?'

'The first thing we're going to do is take a drive, say somewhere out in Rutherford County. Way out in the country. You ever drive a Rolls?'

'Oh,' I said, 'you mean it hasn't been repo'd yet?'

His hands tightened on the pistol, and he took a step toward me. 'You're a smart little son of a bitch, you know that?'

I held out my hand. 'I apologize,' I said wearily. 'You're right, I have a terrible attitude. It's hard to have a good one when—'

I stopped midsentence. Downstairs, there was the creak of a door being opened.

'Who's that?' Alvy said, her voice tightening.

'I don't know,' Mac said.

'Well, what are we gonna do?'

'Don't panic,' he said. 'Here, hand me his stun gun.'

She handed over the hunk of black plastic. Great, I thought. It's getting deeper by the nanosecond.

'Close that door,' he ordered.

Alvy stepped over and eased the door shut. 'What now?'

'Just stand here and be quiet.' Mac Ford's voice had lost its slur. Had adrenaline driven the other chemicals in his body into seclusion?

I sat at Alvy's desk as the two of them stood stock-still, the gun pointed directly at me. If I jumped him now, he might not shoot. Then again, if I'm wrong, it's not going to do me any good to get shot even if it does bring help. I'd never been shot before; I once interviewed a cop who said it doesn't usually hurt much at first. Just a stinging, burning sensation. It's later, after the shock's over, that you think the pain's going to kill you.

Great.

The footsteps grew louder in volume, up the stairs now, left at the head of the stairs, then down the hall toward us. I felt my heart pounding in my chest, and I was beginning to develop a touch of tinnitus.

The steps stopped in front of the door. Mac Ford lowered his right hand and tucked the pistol out of sight behind his leg. Alvy's hands were knotted into fists and held stiffly at her sides. The doorknob turned. I sucked in a deep breath and locked it in. I was trying to come up with a script, but all I could think of was *'Help!'*

The door moved. Alvy backed off a step.

Faye Morgan stepped in.

Oh, hell, I thought, so it ain't the cavalry.

'What are you doing here?' Mac asked, bringing the gun up.

Alvy shook her head from side to side, disgusted. 'Faye, you scare the pee out of us.'

'I told you not to come,' Mac said. 'I'll take care of this.'

Faye had on a pair of pleated khaki pants and a military-style shirt with epaulets. A large knitted bag hung from her right shoulder. Her permed red hair was full, bright. She was gorgeous, and what a hell of a thing for me to notice given the circumstances. I stared down at the floor, deflated.

'Mac, I had to,' she said. 'What are you going to do?'

His jaw tightened. 'I've got to take care of these two!'

My head snapped up. *These two?*

Alvy noticed it, too, and I saw a look on her face that was like a curtain dropping. Suddenly, what I had figured all along dawned on her.

'Maybe I'm naive,' I said to Alvy, 'but you aren't stupid enough to think he'd actually give you a million dollars, are you?'

The curtain-dropping look turned into terror.

'Okay,' I said offhandedly, 'so you are that stupid.'

She turned to Ford. 'Mac?' she said, pleading. 'We had a deal, an arrangement. Right?'

Mac Ford rolled his eyes. 'Get over there and stand against that wall, you little twit.'

She drew herself up straight. 'What about my copy of the letter?'

'I'm tired of fooling with you, Alvy. Screw your copy of the letter. It won't do you a bit of good after—'

Mac didn't need to finish the sentence.

'Oh, no,' she squealed.

'What's going on here?' Faye demanded. Alvy slowly backed up, her eyes open their widest, her hands crossed in front of her open mouth. Textbook terror, shock, disbelief, all interwoven on her face.

'Well,' I said brightly, 'let's review the day's events. First, I blackmailed Alvy into helping me get evidence that Mac Ford is a murderer. Alvy then sold me out in order to successfully complete her plan to blackmail Mac into giving her half of the two-million-dollar insurance settlement. Then Mac betrays her and is going to kill us both.

'Now tell me, Faye,' I said, turning to her. 'Just who did *you* fuck in this little drama?'

Mac Ford took a step toward me and pointed the pistol, as best I could tell, right at my forehead.

'For a guy that's about to take a record-breaking dirt nap, you sure are awful goddamn funny.'

'I'm sorry, Mac. It's that bad-attitude thing again. I'm so tired and stressed-out that my mouth is writing checks my ass can't cash. But I think you're making a big mistake here, buddy.'

'Fuck you.'

'Look, let's start with the fact that I'm sure you didn't mean to kill Rebecca Gibson. At least, that's what I'd say if I was your defense lawyer. You know, "That's my story and I'm sticking to it . . ." The bitch betrayed you, was going to cost you a fortune after you'd risked everything to put her name up in lights. So you went over to talk to her, to try to reason with her, to beg her to come back into the fold. She went to work on you just like she did everybody else. She got abusive, maybe even took a swing at you. You got in a fight, and in the heat and passion of the moment, she winds up dead. Worst-case scenario, you cop to involuntary manslaughter. You get five-to-ten, but let's face reality here. With prison overcrowding and the fact that despite your scruffy appearance, you're basically a middle-class professional with a lot of good contacts, you'll do maybe eighteen months in a minimum-security facility before you're paroled.'

'And lose everything,' he said. 'The agency, the career, the two million dollars.'

'Big deal,' I said. 'What are you, thirty-eight, forty? Another ten years, nobody'll remember this and you'll be back on top. On the other hand . . .'

All three of them stared at me. 'Yeah?' Mac said.

'On the other hand, you drive us out to Rutherford County and bury us in some farmer's field, it's premeditated murder. That's capital, pal. They've got Ol' Sparky working out at River-bend again. How'd you like to spend the next decade on death row, then get plugged in for your last ride?'

'That's if I get caught,' he said.

I waved my hand. 'C'mon, you'll get caught. Plus, you've got somebody here who knows you did it.' I pointed at Faye. 'You guys are tight as a duck's ass now, but who can say what's going to happen a few years down the road? She'll always know you committed three murders, and you'll always know she knows.'

Faye and Mac looked at each other. Behind me, Alvy slumped down against the wall and slid all the way to the floor. I wondered if she'd passed out and hurt herself, then realized I didn't give a damn.

'Don't listen to him, babe,' Mac said. 'He's full of shit.'

'Mac,' Faye said slowly, 'I think he's right.'

'No!' Mac screamed, the rage coming to the surface now. 'I won't give it up!'

'And to complicate matters even further, Mac, I left written instructions with friends telling them everything I intended to do today and telling them what to do if anything happened to me . . .'

That wasn't quite the truth, but it would do for now. I just hoped he bought it. I stood up slowly from behind the desk, my hands palm outward in front of me.

'You ask me, dude,' I said, 'it's all over.'

He moved the gun a little closer to me. 'Nobody asked you.'

'Mac, honey,' Faye said, 'he's right. It's not worth it.'

'It is worth it!'

'If they take you away forever, it's not! I'll wait for you. It's a chance for you to relax for a while, get out of this rat race. You're killing yourself. Look at you.'

'Shut up, Faye!' he screamed. His face was red now, his jaw shaking as he spoke.

I kept trying to come up with something clever to say to him, but the well had finally run dry. I'd said all I could, and unless I got the chance to jump him like in the movies, then it really was over. And although I'd never tried it, I had a feeling that movie shit wasn't going to work.

Behind me, Alvy groaned. I looked down at her. She was huddled in a ball, her head buried between her knees.

'Let's go,' Mac ordered, waving the pistol. 'Everybody out!'

'To the car, right?' I asked.

'That's right, smart guy. To the car.'

I crossed my arms and shook my head. 'No,' I said, with a voice inside my head wondering where the hell *that* came from.

He looked at me like I'd just spoken Farsi. 'What do you mean, "No"?'

'Tell me, Mac. What part of *no* don't you understand? I'm not going with you. I will not cooperate in my own death. If you want to kill me, do it right here in this room. But I promise you, I'm going to flop around like a largemouth bass and make an enormous mess for the forensics lab to go over.'

'You're crazy,' Mac Ford said.

'Nevertheless . . .' I leaned my hip against the top of Alvy's desk and tried to relax. I was too tired to deal with this anymore.

'Okay, we'll do it here. My office is soundproofed.'

'Has it been bloodstain-proofed?' There went that mouth of mine again.

'Move!' he screamed again, waving the pistol.

'Mac, please,' Faye Morgan said. 'Let's stop this.'

Alvy groaned again, loudly. 'Alvy, get up,' Ford said.

'Stop it,' Faye said, a little more sternly this time.

I closed my eyes, exhausted, lethargic, not giving a big rat's ass anymore.

'Get up!' he yelled.

'Mac,' Faye said, 'I can't let you do this.'

'You can't stop—' Then Mac Ford's voice cut off like the plug had been pulled. I opened my eyes.

Faye Morgan had a pistol of her own now, what looked to me like one of those small, lightweight 'ladies' guns' that are getting so popular with the paranoid cowgirl set.

'What the hell are you doing, Faye?' Ford said, like he'd just caught her driving with the parking brake on again.

'Put the gun down, Mac. It's over.'

'The hell it is. You put the gun down.'

'I'm doing this to protect you from yourself, honey. I love you.

'I won't watch you throw your whole life away.'

'Don't you see? I'm doing this for us. I'm closing the agency down. The two mil will get us off somewhere safe forever. We can retire, blow this shit off.'

'It won't work. It's too late for that.'

My eyes flicked back and forth between them like a tennis match. I decided that for once, I'd keep my mouth shut.

'Faye, you're starting to piss me off real bad.' Then he turned to me. 'Don't pay any attention to her,' he instructed. 'Get your ass down to that parking lot right now.'

I stared at him without speaking, and, more importantly, without moving.

'Damn you,' he growled. 'Move. This is the last time I'm gonna tell you.'

I set my jaw, wondering what it would feel like. Would I be able to stand it? Would it be over quick? I only hoped it wouldn't hurt too bad, then I thought of Marsha and the impending Enochian Apocalypse. I figured what the hell, maybe we're going to see each other sooner than I expected.

Mac Ford's eyes lit up. 'Damn you!' He raised the pistol. I closed my eyes.

It was only a *pop*, really, not like the explosion I'd always imagined.

Behind me, Alvy Barnes screamed, then started a continuous wailing. My gut clenched for a split second. My brain sent runners all over my body, collecting damage reports.

Nothing.

Then there was a clatter. I opened my eyes. Mac Ford had dropped the pistol and was staring down at his right hand in amazement, like he'd just seen dawn coming up at the exact peak of a cocaine rush. At the end of his shirtsleeve, a sloppy blob of red grew ever wider.

He looked up at me, then over at Faye. I looked at Faye. Her mouth hung open; her hand shook. There were tears in her eyes.

'Ow,' Mac Ford said weakly over the high-pitched siren coming from Alvy's throat. He brought his left hand up to cradle his right wrist. 'That hurt.'

I jumped straight at him.

Chapter 34

'So as it turned out,' I said, 'Faye Morgan was the only decent human being involved.'

'Present company excepted,' Lonnie said from inside the kitchen.

I put my feet up on his coffee table and stretched out. 'I'm not too proud of myself on this one,' I said. 'I blackmailed somebody into helping me, and then was stupid enough to trust her. I've lied, cheated, blackmailed not only Alvy Barnes, but basically blackmailed the insurance company into paying me the money they owed me. My karmic portfolio has taken a big hit this week.'

'My, oh my,' he said, settling into the chair across from me and parking a couple of tall glasses of Coke on the table. 'Aren't we into self-flagellation today?'

I raised my head. 'What, no beer?'

He pointed to the glass of Coke. 'Sun's not over the yardarm.'

'Excuse me,' I said. 'It's after eight o'clock. I've just spent the better part of five hours giving statements to a not-too-cordial group of police officers. The sun is definitely over *my* yardarm. I want a beer.'

'Well, hold off for a while. I want to hear how the rest of this played out.'

I sat up and took a long sip of the iced-down Coke. I had to admit it was probably better than a beer, given that a beer would have put me to sleep within five minutes.

'Faye Morgan knew that Mac had beaten Rebecca Gibson to death, but she genuinely believed that Rebecca had pushed him over the edge. She told me she never thought he intended to kill Rebecca. It was only when she saw that he was going to kill me and Alvy Barnes that she knew how far gone he was. She had to stop him. The whole thing was eating away at Faye so badly, I think she ultimately would have talked him into confessing anyway. Especially if she saw that somebody else was about to do hard time for it.'

'You think the district attorney'll let him plead down?'

I ran my hand around the condensation of the glass, the icy coldness of it soothing and pleasant.

'If he's willing to cop a plea, my guess is they will. Who knows, maybe they would have offered Slim a deal as well . . .'

'Speaking of Slim,' Lonnie said.

I let loose with a weary, lazy yawn that bent my jaws to the limit. I set the glass down on the coffee table and stretched.

'I phoned Ray from the police station, and he called Herman Reid, the attorney.' I said. 'Reid contacted E. D. Fouch at the Homicide Squad and verified that Mac Ford was going to be charged with Rebecca Gibson's murder. So they'll start the process to get Slim released.'

'Can they do that on a Saturday night?'

'Yeah. The next step will be to go before the nightcourt magistrate and get a release order. It'll probably take a few hours, but Slim should sleep in his own bed tonight.'

Lonnie cradled his hands behind his head and stretched. 'What about the tootsie?' he said, yawning himself.

'Alvy Barnes?'

'Yeah.'

'She's no tootsie,' I said. 'She's a pretty damn smart lady. The only mistake she made was trying to blackmail Ford without sufficiently covering her ass.'

'She'll know better next time,' Lonnie said.

'And you know what?' I added. 'I don't doubt there'll be a next time. This day would've scared some ethics into a normal person, but I don't think Alvy's normal.'

'She going to be charged with anything?'

'I doubt it. As long as she cooperates with the DA and testifies for the state, she'll probably walk.'

'So it's over,' he said.

'Yeah, I just wish it was the last crisis in my life I had to deal with.'

Lonnie grinned. 'Oh, yeah. That.'

'Oh yeah,' I mimicked. '*That.*'

'You know something, Harry. You're gettin' awful damn touchy these days.'

I stood up. 'I'm tired, Lon-man. I'm going home, try once again to call Marsha, then I'm going to sleep for about twenty hours.'

'Sit down,' he said.

'I don't want to sit down. I'm tired. I want to go home.'

'Sit down anyway.' Something in his voice made me do it.

'Listen, how long have we known each other?'

'A long time, I guess,' I said, caution in my voice. Where was this going?

'We've always been straight with each other, right?'

'Yes, we've always been straight with each other. Why do I get the feeling this is going to be a difficult conversation?'

He ignored my question. 'I've been listening to you bitch and moan for the past week about missing your main squeeze. Truth is, buddy, it's getting tiresome.'

Anger filled the inside of my chest to the point of bursting. I hammered it down, though, to keep from going off on him. 'Maybe you just don't understand,' I said through gritted teeth, 'what it's like to miss somebody that much.'

'Oh, I do understand, Harry. I do. More than you know. Twenty years ago, my first wife was missing for four days before they found her.'

'Found her?'

'Yeah. On the backside of a dump. Raped. Strangled. Buried in garbage. She was nineteen years old.' His voice remained steady, a numb monotone. I sat there for a few seconds, unable to speak.

'Well,' I said, staring down at the floor, 'don't I feel like a genuine asshole . . .'

'I sat in my apartment for four days, surrounded by my in-laws and my family and my friends, all of us crying and frustrated and helpless. We all sat there, waiting for the police to take care of it for us. And the only thing the cops took care of was notifying us she was dead. I always felt bad that I just sat there.'

'Lonnie, there was nothing you could have done.'

He raised his head and looked me straight in the eye. 'Yeah, but I'd have felt a fuck of a lot better if I'd tried.'

'So what are you saying?' I asked after a moment.

'Sit there,' he said. 'Let me show you something.'

He disappeared into the back room and emerged seconds later with a stack of papers and a manila envelope. He sat down on the couch next to me, then scooted the glasses aside and laid the stack of papers down.

'Look.' He opened the manila envelope and took out a stack of eight-by-ten black-and-white photographs. 'I've been doing a little surveillance of my own.'

He pulled the top shot off and set it in front of us.

'I stopped on the Silliman Evans Bridge over the Cumberland and took these.'

'You stopped in the middle of an interstate highway bridge over a river *to take pictures*?'

He shrugged his shoulders. 'Sure, why not? It was the only way I could get what I needed.'

He pointed to the middle of the photo. 'Here's the morgue, and if you look real closely, you can see – there, through the trees – the line of Winnebagos. The back of the morgue is actually open. There's no one back there.'

'Yeah, there's not enough room. That's a bluff that goes straight down to the river. Nobody could get out that way. They're trapped.'

'Ah.' He raised an index finger. 'Wait, Kemo Sabe.'

He shuffled the photographs and came up with another one. 'I had to blow this one up so much it's grainy as all hell, but you can see well enough if you try.'

I squinted. 'Looks like one of those spy-satellite photos.'

'Yeah, but look.' He pointed. 'Here's the back of the morgue. The back wall is actually fenced off by a high chain-link fence. That protects the air-conditioning units and the generator. There's probably concertina around the top.'

'Okay,' I said.

'And here are the two tiny slit windows in the back of the building. Those are the only two windows back there.'

'Yeah, I remember that. There's only a few windows in the whole building. They're just slits and they're bulletproof.'

'Now you see why, right? And here.' He pointed again. 'Look closely.'

I picked up the picture and held it close to my face. 'What is it?'

'What's it look like?'

I turned to Lonnie. 'A door?'

He grinned. 'An access door to the fenced-in area. So maintenance men can get to the units from inside the building. That door's probably in the basement.'

'Great,' I said. 'So Marsha and everybody else could get out if they had to. But to their immediate right and left, they're surrounded by the Looney Tunes Brigade.'

'Okay, fair enough. Now look at these.'

He pulled a few more photos out and spread them in front of me. 'I crossed the river on the Woodland Street Bridge into East Nashville, then drove around all over hell and back following the river. The metal scrapyards are down there, along with a couple of manufacturing plants, warehouses, and the bridge company. Not exactly Belle Meade.'

'Okay, so you got to tour scenic East Nashville.'

'Yeah, and I talked the security guard at the Leggett and Platt warehouse into letting me past the gates. If you go to the back of their parking lot, you're right on the riverbank, directly across the river from the morgue. On the East Nashville side, there aren't any bluffs. You're right on the water.'

I stared at the photos. Black-and-white shots of the river and the bank on the opposite side. The bluff coming out of the water was sheer mud for about twenty feet, then a tangle of undergrowth, trees sprouting at bizarre angles, and jungle that went straight up and appeared to be impenetrable.

'Great, you got shots of a bluff,' I said.

'The photos are misleading,' Lonnie said. 'Actually, that's a climb, but it's not straight up. Our biggest problem will be cutting through the undergrowth, but we can use the vines and trees to pull ourselves up.'

My mouth fell open. No, I was too tired. I couldn't have heard him right. 'Ourselves? Pull ourselves *what*?'

'Up,' he said. 'Pull ourselves up.'

'I thought this was some kid of academic exercise,' I said. 'You actually want to *go in there and get them*?'

He set his jaw and gazed at me stone-faced. 'You got it, big guy . . .'

I jumped up, agitated. 'You're – you're out of your fucking mind. For one thing, if that could be done, the police would have already done it.'

'No, they wouldn't,' he said. 'Their whole aim is to negotiate and avoid bloodshed. They're not into clandestine, deep-cover ops.'

'*Deep-cover ops?* You've been reading way too many Tom Clancy novels,' I said. 'We are *not* the freaking Green Berets.'

'Number one, I hate Tom Clancy. Bob Mayer's a much better writer. And number two, stop being such a wuss. A couple pair of bolt cutters, a machete apiece, some dark clothing, rope, a couple grappling hooks. We're in there, we're out of there, twenty minutes tops.'

'You're crazy,' I said, stupefied.

'Just call her on the cell phone and tell her to get everybody ready.'

'The cops are monitoring the cellular frequencies. I'm sure of it.'

'So what? It's a risk we've got to take. Besides, how they gonna stop us? It's no crime to take a midnight boat ride. It's your call. In or out? You want your girlfriend back or what?'

'You're crazy,' I said again.

He shrugged his shoulders. 'How 'bout it?'

I let out a long breath of tired air. 'One thing,' I said. 'No guns.'

His face screwed up. '*No guns?*'

'I'm serious,' I said. 'No shit here. I'm not going to get her or anybody else killed.'

Lonnie pursed his lips. 'Well, can I take some of my other toys?'

It may not be a crime to take a midnight boat ride, but it's sure as hell a crime to do it from the dock at Shelby Park. The park closes at eleven, and now here we were at one in the morning, coasting through the back of the park in a coal-black pickup truck with the lights turned off pulling a twenty-foot bass boat with a huge Mercury outboard mounted on the back.

We rounded the hill coming off the golf course from the Riverside Drive side of the park. Down the hill, on the other side of the small lake in the middle of the park, the green-and-white cruiser of a Metro park ranger pulled slowly away.

'Jesus, Lonnie!' I hissed.

'Be cool,' he said. 'He's headed away from us.'

'How can you see anything?'

'I can't. That's why we're going slow.'

There's a hairpin curve coming off the hill that doubles back on itself before splitting off in two directions near the ball fields. Lonnie managed to roll the truck through the turn without going off the side, then put the truck back in gear and cut to the left away from the lake and the park ranger. Above us, the spidery metal trusses of a railroad bridge over the river rose ghostlike and creepy. We drove through the parking lot under the bridge, then turned right.

'You see anybody up there?'

'There's a couple of parked cars,' I said. 'But I can't tell whether they're cops or not.'

'Probably kids committing terminal pleasure,' he said. He drove past the steep ramp down to the river, then turned the parking lights on and put it in reverse.

'I've got to be able to see what I'm doing,' he said, hanging his head out the window as we rolled backward.

The concrete ramp was steep, maybe a thirty-degree angle down a hundred and fifty feet or so to the river's edge. Lonnie backed most of the way down, then stopped.

'Hop out and direct me.'

I stepped out of the truck into the urban darkness of Shelby Park. There was an orange sodium light planted on a pole on the opposite bank, but beyond that, nothing. I could hear the swishing of the black water against the bank, and the smell of rot was everywhere; a dank, moldy smell that would have been unpleasant if I'd had time to think about it.

I stood next to the truck and motioned him down, watching carefully to see that the boat trailer was staying on track.

'When the wheels touch the water, let me know,' he said.

Another twenty feet or so and I stopped him. He put the truck in park and locked the brakes, then got out with the motor still running.

'Move, quick,' he said.

We pulled cases and bags out of the back of the pickup and stowed them on the boat. Then Lonnie went around to the stern and made sure the drain plug was secure and the gas lines squared away. I looked through one of the cartons and came up holding a canister.

'You sure we need smoke grenades?'

Through the darkness, I could see his teeth in a grin. 'Hey, c'mon. Let me play with my new toys.'

I shook my head. 'Okay. Let's do it.'

I got into the boat, then Lonnie backed the trailer the rest of the way into the water. He turned off the motor, set the brake, got out, and locked the doors. ·

'We just going to leave the truck here?' I said as he climbed in.

'Why not? When we get back here, I want to be able to drive right up on that trailer and haul ass out of here.'

'But what if we don't come back?'

Lonnie unhitched the towline on the trailer and pushed us out into the river. 'Then somebody'll find it in the morning, right?'

The Cumberland River looks to be a slow-moving, lazy ribbon of brown mud, but when you're out in the middle of it in a small boat, you realize there's every kind of mean current imaginable out there. The boat whipped around in the wrong direction, with the flow carrying us away from downtown almost immediately. Lonnie sat down in the driver's seat, or whatever the hell it's called on a bass boat, and hit the switch. The Merc coughed and spit and shook for a couple of seconds, then roared to life.

'Hold on,' Lonnie yelled. 'We're outta here!'

I huddled in the bow as he put the engine in gear. The river fought us for a second, but then the boat came out of the water with a howl and we were skimming across the surface of the Cumberland at fifty knots.

'Slow down!' I yelled. 'There's junk floating out here!'

Lonnie cut the engine back to half-speed. 'I just wanted to get us away from the park.'

He turned on the running lights, and we settled into a steady cruise upriver toward downtown Nashville. A low-lying fog enveloped us, throwing everything out of focus. Ahead, the bright lights of the city burned into the hazy night. I could barely see the ribbon of light that was the interstate highway bridge over the river, headlights bouncing like fireflies in the distance.

I fought off exhaustion. Up until now, adrenaline and fear had kept me alert, but now even that was wearing off. As we drew closer to downtown I wondered if I'd ever get enough sleep to make up for this past week. The bones in my neck were brittle; my skin seemed to crawl.

We broke through a patch of fog and into clear air. The bridge loomed over us; we were almost there. Lonnie yelled above the engine noise. I turned. He motioned me back. I scooted back across the crowded boat, dodging boxes and packs.

'When we get there, you tie us up. But don't get out of the boat yet.'

I shook my head. As we passed under the bridge Lonnie pulled a spotlight out of its holder on the side and flicked the halogen beam on. It crackled as it lit, the narrow tube of blinding bright light scanning the bank.

Then he stopped. Ahead of us, a mass of tangled driftwood and fallen trees looked to me to be the finest potential nesting place for water moccasins I'd ever seen.

He throttled the engine down to idle as we approached. I crawled out onto the farthest point of the bow, a line in my hand. I just hoped that whatever happened, I didn't screw up.

I snagged a branch with my bare hand and felt skin being stripped out of my palm. Lonnie cut the engine and immediately the current began pulling us away. I tightened my grip and pulled as hard as I could, and gradually, the boat nestled into the snarl of decayed wood. I tied the line onto a thick branch of a fallen tree and managed to secure us.

Lonnie came forward. 'Good job. We'll get squared away here, then walk that tree to the bank. Once there, we can pull the boat all the way in.'

'Okay,' I said, panting.

Lonnie handed me a pack, then passed me two fifty-foot coils of nylon rope, a Swiss army knife, a heavy-duty flashlight, a two-foot-long Khyber knife, four smoke grenades, and a pair of bolt cutters. We inventoried the packs a second time.

'What time is it?' he asked.

I hit the button on my watch. 'One forty-five,' I answered.

'When did you tell them to open the door?'

'Two. If we're not there yet, they'll check every couple of minutes. Marsha said she'd look for the key to the gate on the chain fence, so maybe we won't have to cut through it.'

'We'll each carry cutters anyway.'

I reached down and picked up a ten-inch-long black baton with a trigger and a safety ring on the side. 'What's this?'

'Jeez, be careful,' he hissed, then yanked it out of my hand. 'If we get in a jam and can't get to the top, this is a spring-loaded grappling hook. Attach the nylon rope here, pull this pin, point it up, keep your head down, and stand back. It'll shoot a grappling hook about a hundred feet straight up the bluff.'

'Why don't you carry that one?' I suggested.

'Good move. It's a mean mother.'

Lonnie stood up, pulled on his pack, attached the baton to a hook on his belt, and looked down at me.

'You ready?'

'No,' I said, standing up and throwing the pack on. 'But let's go anyway.'

I had on the hiking boots that Marsha'd talked me into buying, along with a pair of jeans and a checked black-and-white flannel shirt. I figured that was about as much commando as I could stand.

Lonnie, on the other hand, looked like something out of *Ninja Rambos from Hell*: shiny black nylon pants, black long-sleeved T-shirt, black leather gloves. And to top it all off, as he'd navigated us down the Cumberland, he'd smeared lampblack all over his face.

A wall of undergrowth, trees, vines, snakes, critters, and only God knew what else lay ahead of us. Lonnie pulled out his sealed beam and flicked it on as we made our way across the fallen tree and retied the boat. To random boat traffic, we'd look like a couple of night fishermen. And we were tucked in the bluff far enough forward to be unseen by anyone who might be wandering around above.

I still wasn't sure this was really happening, but then I gritted my teeth, pulled out the Khyber knife, and started climbing.

Chapter 35

Halfway up the slope, I thought my lungs would finally, and mercifully, give out.

I stopped for a moment, panting. 'If we even make it to the top, how the hell are we going to get them down?'

Lonnie was a half a body length ahead of me, his boots kicking mud and clumps of rotting gunk down on me. He turned, his face shiny, sweaty black in the dim light.

'This is the worst of it. It levels off near the top.'

'I'm not worried about Marsha,' I said, 'but Kay Delacorte's a middle-aged bureaucrat.'

'She's a middle-aged bureaucrat who wants to go home very badly.'

I dug my toes into the soft earth, grabbed another hunk of vines, and pulled myself up. Thornbushes had whipped scratches across my face that would be scarlet and on fire by morning. Maybe fifty yards lay behind us, and the boat was only a tiny speck bobbing in the water, hidden from view by the twisted debris of dead vegetation.

There was a rustle to our right; we'd disturbed something that I hoped would head away, rather than toward us. We climbed on, yanking and gashing our way through the undergrowth. Lonnie was right, though, and the last few yards were actually a gentle slope upward to a line of trees, the bases of which were buried in thick vines.

Lonnie stopped. 'We'll have a time hacking through that,' he said. 'But I don't see a way around it.'

Off to our right, a TVA high-tension tower jutted into the black sky. 'Are we even in the right place?' I asked.

'I think so,' he whispered. 'There's the brick smoke-stack at General Hospital. It looks to be in the right place.'

Once we stepped into the bed of vines, we sank in up to our waists. I wasn't meant for this sort of thing. Lonnie was loving it, though. He hacked away, ripping vines and working his way upward. I followed him as best I could, driven to stay close by fear as much as anything else.

We got to a little rise on the slope, just below the trees that marked the back of the morgue property. He dropped down, flicked off his flashlight, and motioned me to follow him. I turned my light off, and we crept forward.

'Damn,' he stage-whispered.

'What is it?' I came up behind him. His fingers were wrapped in the wire spiderweb of a chain-link fence.

'Okay,' I said, 'we cut through it.'

'Did you see the good news?'

I shook my head. He grabbed a fistful of vines and pulled them back. Beyond the fence, the brown brick of the Nashville morgue stared back at us, not twenty feet away. For the first time, I let loose with a grin.

'Nice shooting, cowboy,' I whispered.

I pulled the bolt cutters out of his knapsack, and he got mine.

'Be careful not to make any noise,' he said.

He started on the left; I took the right. We cut slowly, carefully, quietly upward, then curved toward each other and met in the middle. It took about five minutes, and when we finished, we pulled back a piece of fence in the shape of a four-foot mouse hole.

'What time is it?'

I checked my watch. 'Two-thirty.'

'Damn, we're really behind schedule. I hope they haven't given up on us.'

'They haven't,' I said. 'What's next?'

We were huddled just below the tree line. If we stepped forward two feet, we'd be potentially exposed. I stuck my head up slowly and looked; the front end of a tan Winnebago was visible around the corner of the building. A lone man stood in front of it, cradling a weapon. I couldn't see the other direction, but assumed they were still there as well.

'What if they've got foot patrols?'

'We'll have to take them out,' he said.

I glared at him. 'I've never taken anybody out before!' I whispered. 'They've got guns!' I wished I hadn't made him leave the guns at home.

His white teeth shown in the darkness. 'Nothing to it. Listen, dude, I'm going to crawl up to the tree line and cover the area. You're going to play hero.'

'I'm going to *what*?'

'You're going to crawl on your belly up to that gate and rattle it just a bit and hope somebody comes out.'

'Oh, shit,' I said.

'You up for it?'

'Oh, shit,' I said again, then gulped. 'Yeah. Let's do it.'

He moved forward and poked his head out of the underbrush. He leaned as far as he could to the left, then back to the right. Then he motioned with his arm.

I crawled up next to him. 'I think I have to go to the bathroom.'

'Stop joking.'

'Who's joking?'

He turned to me. 'You going or not?'

I moved up past him. He touched my arm. I looked back. 'I see anybody coming, I'll rustle the bushes, okay? Then you haul ass out of there.'

I nodded, then slid the pack off my back. I gently pulled a clump of vines out of the way and crawled forward. Every time a stick cracked, my heart stopped. Sweat ran down my sides. I crawled forward a few more steps, then past the tree.

I was out in the open, on a lawn that needed mowing and was wet with dew.

Thank God for high grass, I thought as I hugged the ground and moved slowly toward the chain-link fence. I figured there had to be a gate somewhere; it was just a matter of finding it. It was too dark to see, so I crawled along feeling a few feet at a time. For once in my life, I took the right direction the first time. I got to the gate and reached forward to rattle it, then looked up. The padlock was hanging there. Open.

God, what a woman.

I looked to my right, then left. The only person I could see was the lone sentry at the head of the last Winnebago in the circle. He had his back to me. I stood up slowly, lifted the padlock out of its hole, lifted the latch, and pulled.

The gate squealed. I stopped, hoping not to need a change of shorts before this was over. I pushed, putting pressure on the metal hinges, then pulled again.

The hum of the generator helped. Then the compressor on the air conditioner for the cooler cut in and I nearly jumped a foot. The fenced-in area was knee-high with uncut grass. I stepped quickly across, to the door, and turned the knob.

It moved in my hand. Please God, don't let them have any lights on.

I opened the door and stepped into the darkness. I pulled the door shut behind me.

'Marsha?' I whispered.

Then she was all over me, with flashlight beams held by four desperate people dancing behind her. She wrapped her arms around my neck, pulling me so hard I nearly broke. I wrapped my arms around her and lifted her off the floor. She wept silently, choking sobs caught in her throat, tears pouring down her face.

We rocked back and forth, locked together until our muscles gave out.

It was the finest moment of my life.

Somebody came up and put an arm on my shoulder. I turned. Kay Delacorte's tired, dirty, tear-streaked, gorgeous face stared at me, 'Hi,' she whispered.

I let go of Marsha for just a moment and wrapped my arms around Kay.

'We thought you'd given up,' Marsha said.

I looked back at her. 'Just late, as usual.'

The three men stepped over. Marsha held out her hand. 'Harry, this is—'

'No time for introductions,' I said. 'We'll have a party later. For now, we've got to get the hell out of here.'

'Okay,' she said. 'How?'

'Kill those flashlights,' I said. 'In fact, leave 'em behind. We've got plenty. Lonnie's waiting for us at the tree line. We cut a hole in the fence. We're going to scale down the bluff. There's a boat down there. When we step out of here, drop down on your bellies. Go through the gate and straight for the trees. There's one sentry, to our right by the last Winnebago. He's the only one I've seen. I'll lead. Kay, you follow, then Marsha. You three guys take up the rear and watch out for each other, okay?'

'Okay, man,' the oldest guy said. 'Let's go.'

The flashlights went out, submerging the room into complete blackness. 'We've only got about twenty feet of open ground,' I said, trying to keep my voice steady. 'Then we're in the bush. Once we get there, we're fine. Be careful, and good luck.'

Marsha touched my arm, and in the darkness I leaned over and kissed her quickly. There'd be more time for that later. I dropped to one knee, pulled the door open, and peered out.

Nothing.

I went out first, low, on my belly until I hit the gate. Vague black shapes followed me, their movements clumsy and slow. I crept across the slick grass, slithering side to side, hoping I'd get us back to the hole in the fence on the first try.

By the time I crossed the spread of open lawn, I realized I'd hit it wrong. We were on the wrong side of the big oak. Lonnie'd cut the hole on the left side, not the right. I hunkered down and followed the fence, hoping everyone was still behind me. Random night noises caught my ear: a siren in the distance, a tugboat's deep whistle upriver.

The breathing of people behind me.

My senses seemed on edge, on fire. I felt the ground beneath me as if it were moving itself, breathing in and out as we crawled across it like fleas on a dog.

Finally I came to the hole. I pulled off to the side. Lonnie poked his head out from behind the tree.

'Got 'em,' I whispered. He held an index finger to his lips.

Kay Delacorte came up behind me. I leaned in to her. 'Sit up on your butt, then slide legs first through the hole. Get out of the way and be quiet until we're all through.'

I pulled a piece of the fence aside, Kay sat up, pushed herself up on her haunches, then slipped in the wet grass and raked her leg across the cut chain-link wire, ripping her pants and gashing her leg bad enough for me to see it even in the darkness.

Her squeal of pain cut the night air like a thunderclap.

I looked up. The sentry had turned our way, holding his rifle out in front of him.

'Damn,' I grunted. 'Get on through.'

'Who is it?' the sentry called. Then, from inside the Winnebago, a spotlight came on, sweeping the area until it froze on the seven of us, lying there frozen on the grass.

'Move!' I shouted.

Kay tumbled through the fence just as the sentry fired. Marsha slithered forward on her belly. There was no time to do this gracefully; I jumped up, grabbed her by the waist, and threw her through the hole.

The sentry fired a second time, the round zinging off above my head. There was running, yelling from both our left and right. I lost sight of the sentry as I stared straight into the spotlight.

There was a clatter above me. Lonnie scrambled up the nine-foot fence with a mad rush. The chain link bent forward under his weight, which gave him something to hang on to. With one hand holding on to the fence, he managed to pull a pin on the smoke grenade and fling it straight at the Winnebago. Before that one landed, he'd cocked his arm and flung another.

There was a muffled *whomp* of an explosion, followed by another. Within a split second, we were engulfed in a choking purple-and-green cloud. My eyes burned, my throat ached. I coughed and spat, hard and disgustingly.

'This way!' I yelled. The last of the three men looked blinded.

Above me, Lonnie threw off two more smoke grenades to the right. There was a steady stream of gunfire now, all mixed in with screams and cries. The firing was coming from our left and right; with a little bit of luck, they were shooting each other.

The last man stood straight up. I ran over and grabbed him. He coughed and gagged, then threw up in front of me.

'C'mon, you can make it,' I yelled. Then I grabbed his shoulder and pulled him forward. When we got to the fence, I pushed down on his head and shoved him through. Then I dropped on my back and slid through the hole feet first.

I scrambled a few feet down into the undergrowth.

'Marsha!' I called. From the smoke and haze, I heard her call my name. Then Lonnie was next to me.

'We all here?' I asked.

'Yeah, five of them, two of us, right?'

I squinted my eyes and forced myself to focus on him through tears that were part chemically induced, part just from being plain damn overwhelmed.

'Yeah,' I gasped, breathless. 'That's it.'

He coughed and spit a wad himself. 'Let's get out of here.'

Getting down was a hell of a lot easier than getting up. The smoke drifted mostly upward, so by the time we'd gone halfway down the bluff, most of it had dissipated. A few minutes later we hit the mud bank. Marsha slipped and fell in the soft goo, but was laughing so hard she didn't care. I found myself giggling as well, my heart beating like a jackhammer.

Lonnie jumped in the boat and started barking instructions to everybody. Kay limped in, blood running down her leg, and sat at the end of the boat holding a life jacket like a teddy bear. Then Marsha got in, followed by the three guys. The whopping of helicopter blades grew louder from somewhere, but we couldn't see where. The gunfire lessened, and then seemed to stop. I untied the boat and pushed out hard, my two-hundred-dollar hiking boots sinking up to their laces. I jumped onboard; Lonnie fired the Merc up, and within a few moments we were out in the middle of the river, watching the heights above like dazed survivors of a great conflict reverently studying the battlefield as the smoke cleared.

Which I suppose wasn't too far from the truth.

Epilogue

Marsha reclined on a beach chair near the edge of the surf, an unread newspaper folded on her lap, a drink nestled in a depression she'd created in the sand. On the other side of her beach chair, a black plastic boom box sat baking in the Bahamian sun as well, Bela Fleck and the Flecktones softly pouring from the pair of speakers. Marsha looked relaxed for the first time in days, and she'd managed to gain back part of the ten pounds she'd lost, thanks largely to my insistence that we eat everything in sight. I came up behind her and rattled the sack I had in my hand as a warning; she'd been a little jumpy lately. This time, though, she didn't flinch. Maybe she was getting over it.

It had taken us a few days to quit buzzing. When the shooting started that Saturday night, the police assault team rushed in and took most of the Pentecostal Evangelical Enochians without a fight. Expecting a final confrontation at dawn on Sunday, the boys in MUST had gone on an all-out, edge-of-your-seat alert. At the first crack of gunfire, they did their own remake of *The Sands of Iwo Jima*. By the time Marsha managed to raise Howard Spellman on her cellular phone about halfway up the river, it was all over. The Enochians, with all their fundamentalist rantings and Second Amendment ravings, folded faster than a squad of Iraqi draftees. In the assault, a dozen were wounded, most just slightly. A couple of hours later, after the last of Lonnie's smoke drifted away and order was restored, three bodies were found in back of the morgue. In the wild, chaotic firing, they'd shot each other.

Police casualties: zip.

There was hell to pay for us, of course, mostly from the news media. How a penny-ante private investigator and a ragtag car repossessor managed to free five hostages when the police, the FBI, the National Guard, and the Boy Scouts were all held at bay was a subject of keen interest. The hardest ones to fend off were the tabloids. Marsha flat out refused to give interviews, but Kay Delacorte and the others were telling everybody to take a number, take a seat. Lonnie went to ground, as I expected. The last thing he wanted was anyone paying attention to him.

As for me, I thought about trying to parlay the whole situation into a few bucks. But then I decided money was too expensive to be made that way. I'd had my fifteen minutes of fame, and frankly, that was plenty. Maybe that was stupid, but I still had to look in the mirror every morning.

So Marsha and I ran and hid. At first, Dr Henry didn't want to give her comp and vacation time. Something about getting right back on a horse when you've fallen off. She threatened to quit, then sue the dog snot out of the city. He reconsidered. She told him we'd be out of the country for a few weeks – at least until the hubbub died down – and that she'd call him when she got back.

Maybe.

I sat down in the sand next to her and pulled a CD out of the sack. 'Look what I found in the hotel gift shop.'

She opened her eyes halfway. 'Wow,' she said, her voice almost sleepy. 'I didn't know country music was so popular down here.'

I yanked the plastic off and replaced Bela. I stared at the picture on the square CD case, with the word BECCA painted across the top in a bright yellow swash. I hit the play button and Rebecca Gibson's voice was there just like she was sitting next to us. I thought of that first night I'd seen her, her last night on earth, back home at the Bluebird Café. The first song was one that she and Slim had cowritten, a soft love ballad called 'When Your Heart Gets Lonely, Call Me.' It was a sweet, syrupy song that gave me a pain in the middle of my chest. Her voice was genuinely unique, pure, cutting, powerful. Now it was gone.

Well, maybe not, I thought.

The lead song finished, then the opening guitar licks of 'Way Past Dead' started.

'My love for you is way past dead,' I sang along flatly. I'm not quite tone-deaf, but I am harmonially impaired.

'It better not be,' Marsha said.

'Don't worry.'

'This is great,' she murmured sleepily.

'I think we're going to be okay,' I said after a few more measures.

'Yeaaahh,' she said, her voice drifting.

Then I settled down in the sand next to her, leaned back against the side of her beach chair, and rested my head against her arm.

She brought her other hand across and ran her fingers gently through my hair.

We sat there quietly as the Caribbean sun and Rebecca Gibson's voice warmed us and brought us slowly back to life.